I0730835

RAINE
OF
FIRE
SUSAN STRADIOTTO

Raine of Fire

Published by
Bronzewood Books
14920 Ironwood Ct.
Eden Prairie, MN 55346

Cover Design: MIBLART & Bronzewood Books

Interior Design: Bronzewood Books

Edited by: Sonnet Fitzgerald

Paperback ISBN-13: 978-1-949357-30-1

eBook ISBN-13: 978-1-949357-35-6

Printed in the USA

For Tyrone

CHAPTER 1

RAINE

APPLAUSE.

Flames licked a hot trail across his forearm as Raine caught the third baton, then the fourth. With two blazing torches in each hand, he held his arms wide and bowed to the congregating audience, soaking in the cheers as if they were sweeter than the air he breathed. At times, the ovation was indeed better than air. It sent a surge through his body and made stars twinkle at the edges of his vision, as such a thrill did with all his kind. If shelter and sustenance weren't necessary, a solid dose of human delight each day in reaction to his performance would be enough to sustain him eternally. Alas, survival in the mortal realm required him to behave . . . well, mortally. He had to eat, had to earn money to buy food. So, ever so careful not to allow his pinky finger, the one he created with glamour, to get in the way, he palmed the flaming torches in one hand and took off his top hat with a flourish. Rather than simply placing the hat for coin, he dipped his wrist to spin the batons again and elicit an encore of oohs and ahhs before he laid the hat near the crowd.

From his array of performances on the northeast corner of Wickney Square he made enough to pay rent on a tiny flat just down the street from the square and have a meal or two a day. On a good day, he'd be set for the week with his low-key lifestyle, but those days were limited to the weekends when shoppers gathered around the gag-worthy boutique shops in the city's center square. Why humans paid good money for the crap these shop owners sold—frilly clothes, smelly candles, and mutilated hunks of clay they called stoneware—was truly beyond his comprehension. But why in Ifrinn did he care, as long as they dumped their fair share of coin into his hat too.

Raine turned toward his equipment, smiling to hear several coins and the rustle of a few bills drop into the hat. He dropped the torches flame-first into a metal canister where the reservoir of fuel extinguished the fire, then he retrieved a set of staves. As he dipped both ends into the fuel, he scanned the crowd and pitched his voice in precisely the manner the humans thirsted for. "For the next sequence, I'll need a volunteer."

Eyes previously bright with amusement turned to the sidewalk. How utterly predictable. It was a rare mortal who embraced performing, one who likely had been touched by Raine's kind in one way or another, or a síobhra who'd yet to embrace his or her own power. Raine squinted, as much to hide the shifting sands in his eyes as to block out the rays of the sun. He used the sight—or what he called *faedar*—to interrogate the individuals who'd gathered, but none immediately popped out at him. Strangely, not one single person amid those gathered called to his nature, not a one emitted the telltale aura that signaled the need for levity or being worthy of a quaint little prank.

"No one?" he hawked to the onlookers. Then, playing their emotions like a finely tuned faelute, he added, "Is there not one sympathetic soul who will assist a poor performer in need?"

Raine turned before the crowd, slowly twirling the staves as they heated to the proper temperature so they wouldn't flicker out as they sailed through the air. Brilliance, it had to be. Garnering applause and money required brilliance in his performance, and he remained patient enough to ensure his audience would be dishing out a good deal of both. Finally, as he made his way to the far edge of the crowd, a silvery light above someone's head marched through the crowd. Raine strained to see the passerby, and when he caught a glimpse of the pinch on her face under her blonde hair and brows, he pointed a staff.

"You!" He paused as people gasped and looked around, all turning to where he pointed after they'd assured themselves he wasn't calling on them.

"Miss?" he said louder still.

The blonde woman stopped, her pinched expression opening in sheer surprise, and she hugged a khaki trenchcoat closer and locked eyes with Raine. She pushed the shoulder bag up higher and under her collar with the other hand. The woman's mouth formed a little O as she started to shake her head, but the silvery aura kindled. Yes, she was the right person for the job. He nodded and stepped through the parting crowd with a hand outstretched.

She tried to retreat, but her heels and the steps caught her up while Raine easily closed the distance.

"What is your name?" he asked.

"I–I'm sorry, but I . . ." Blonde curls swung around her head as she shook it *no*.

Never releasing his smile, Raine narrowed his eyes and reached for his ability to bend someone toward his will. With the *nudge*, the woman eased, her shoulders fell from her ears, and she placed a hand in his. But she still hesitated.

"Vanessa," she said, her voice hollow. She drew her brows together as if she didn't quite understand why she relented.

He turned to guide her to center stage, but through their touch, an overwhelming sense of shock and mourning accosted Raine. Something extraordinary and tragic stabbed into him so hard he couldn't make out the cause. He tasted metal, and a deep-seated need within him to transform her situation almost threw him off his game. He sighed. That was something he hadn't succumbed to in a very, very long time. Most of the time, he wouldn't get visions or feelings around the mortals unless he opened himself up to it. He blinked several times. The performance—he needed to focus on his show. He dropped her hand as soon as he had her situated and took another deep breath to center himself.

Their connection severed, Vanessa made a move to walk away, so he stepped into her path. He reached again for the gifts granted by the Goddess and allowed his irises to shift, easing the familiar contortions flashing across her face. "You don't wish to leave now, do you?" Over so many years, that sequence of brow bunching, eye widening, and lip pursing had become familiar when he *nudged* a human, swayed their will to match his own. And at last, her dismay no longer distracted him.

The audience murmured, oohed, and ahhed again.

Smiling, he turned back to the crowd and twirled the staves in several long arcs with the intent of soaking in cheers from the onlookers, fueling his performance toward the finale. He'd deal with whatever *that* was later—maybe. As the clapping and enthralled chants urged him on, Raine once again felt the surge . . . the high of praise and appreciation rushed back through him. Relieved for the moment of Vanessa's trauma and his unwanted urges, he turned back to her and asked her to remove her handbag and raincoat.

Vanessa stared at him with her brows drawn together and her head angled.

"Two minutes, love, and you'll be on your way and feeling a mite better," Raine whispered.

She removed her coat and purse and handed it over.

He thrust the staves toward her, handle first. "Hold these."

She staggered a bit under the weight, so he reached to help. "They're heavier than they look," he teased, a brow raised. "Got 'em?"

Vanessa nodded with a twitching smile, which Raine returned with more vigor. Good enough. He'd distracted her from whatever had been sapping her good humor. Small trick, but it also sated his urges a little. He draped her coat and purse over the small suitcase he used to transport his equipment. Before he stood, he sighted his gloves. Aye, those would insulate him from her trauma leakage. Needing no further distractions from his performance, he slowly donned the gloves. The motion was awkward with the extra numb digit on each hand. Standing, he joined Vanessa at center stage and positioned her to face the majority of the crowd.

"Relax now, follow my lead sure, and don't let go of the staff unless I tell you."

She was his tool now, and there wasn't need for her to know that he'd enhance her movements throughout the entirety of the performance. As was the case with most people he influenced, Vanessa would likely be impressed with her own abilities when it was all said and done. He smirked. Of course he'd allow that too.

Raine faced her and lifted his staff into a horizontal position over his head, then suggested with a look that she do the same. He twirled the staff in several arcs to one side then the other and flowed straight into the next flourish, which finished with the staff wrapped around the back of Vanessa's waist. The lit ends painted trails of light that would have been so much more satisfying had it been dark, but this would do. In natural response to Raine's pull, the staff Vanessa held above her head moved down and behind Raine's shoulders so that they stood in a semi-embrace completed by the staves. Then, Raine began to move, a dance. Her feet followed his as if they'd practiced together for long hours. Hoots and hollers from the crowd ensued as he twisted and twirled in the dance, all the time looking deeply into Vanessa's eyes to hold the connection and lead the choreography. He absorbed the levity from the crowd while he placed footwork carefully to ensure the trails of flame followed with exacting arcs and precision.

After several twists, turns, and reversals, Raine commanded, "Release your right hand."

Vanessa did, and she grew a bit breathless as Raine grasped the other end of the staff, sending her outward so that they stood apart with one hand holding on and the other outstretched. Then, at precisely the right momentum point, he barked, "Release," and pulled. When her hand freed, she elegantly twirled back toward him as if she'd practiced ballet since the day she'd taken her first steps. Meanwhile, Raine extended his arms and pivoted so that he'd end up directly behind the spot where she would stop. As he made the final swoops and planted both staves to one side, Vanessa fell toward his now-empty arm. He went to one knee and caught her in a dramatic dip with her blonde hair brushing the concrete, and bent his head to her chest. High on the mortal excitement, Raine breathed in the delight erupting from the crowd.

Afterward, he helped Vanessa to her feet and bent at the waist several times, devouring the ovation. He indicated his partner, because that was the performerly thing to do, or so the guild said. She offered a weak smile and patted her hair as if to ensure it was still coiffed. It wasn't. Raine returned to his bows. The crowd started to disperse, several of the watchers dropping money into the top hat as they went. When he turned back to Vanessa, all that remained where she'd stood was an empty space on the sidewalk. Her coat and purse were gone too. He looked over the heads, squinting until he found the silvery cloud moving away at a quick clip. Metal flooded his mouth again, and his stomach growled.

"Danu help me," he muttered, rolling his eyes. He dunked the ends of the staves to put out the flame, collapsed them, and dropped them into the suitcase. He looked back over the crowd to make sure Vanessa's aura was still in sight.

Following the cloud over the heads of the people in Wickney Square, Raine dumped the lighter fluid in a nearby garbage can. Yeah, that'd cause him trouble, but why not? He slid a match from his pocket, flicked a nail across the sulfur, and smirked as he tossed it inside.

BOOM!

Screeches. Chaos.

Perfection. He grabbed his case handle and hurried after the silvery cloud just as it took a right at the next corner.

"Shite." Raine dodged one group then the next until he passed the crowd and turned at the corner.

To his good fortune, he had a higher vantage point looking downhill toward the college at the low end of High Street. He caught the glimmer just as Vanessa, aura and all, ducked into a prominent pub in Wickney, the Local. That slowed his step back to normal and painted a smile across his lips. With a single nod, he took the first satisfied steps toward his normal after-performance routine: a whiskey with Dick, the afternoon bartender and a close friend.

Raine pushed into the pub through the ornately carved doors, dropped his suitcase at the coat check, and headed for the long, dark-wooded bar. Beyond, Vanessa's aura glinted but faded fast—a clear indication that she was coming to terms with whatever had her shaken so badly in the square.

As Raine approached the bar, Dick lifted a towel-covered hand. "Neat?"

"Is there another way?" Raine took his normal barstool at the end where he could see the door. Vanessa sat in the booth behind and to his right, close enough that he could eavesdrop if he felt so inclined—and, at the moment, he did.

Dick slid over an empty glass and poured the whiskey. "How was the show?"

"Good turnout. I haven't counted, but I think I made twice the normal Monday haul." Raine downed the dram.

"Another?" the bartender asked, then refilled the glass without waiting for confirmation.

Raine's attention piqued when the door opened again and a shadow stepped inside. Wearing a knee-length raincoat expensive enough to match Vanessa's, the man marched directly down the length of the bar. Raine kept his nose pointed toward the glass but glanced up and tried not to react as Vincent La Pointe—a prominent candidate in the current elections and someone who'd never, ever frequent the Local—made it into viewing range. Just then, everything clicked. Vanessa had looked familiar, and the reason behind that? She belonged to the most powerful family in the city, the La Pointes. So Raine had danced with the little sister of Wickney's future mayor.

Raine looked up at Dick, curling his fingers into fists and releasing them. The desire to move in on whatever was happening almost overwhelmed him. His tongue twinged with metal, his instincts begging to be set free. Puzzles, a new scheme, something twisted, manipulative . . . and fun. His mouth watered. But, no. He wouldn't give into that nature now or ever again. He'd sworn it off. He downed the second whiskey, needing to chase away the taste of metal along with the urge that'd certainly get him thrown into lockup down at WPD.

Just being who you are is illegal in this realm, wanker. Remember? But that didn't stop him from stretching his ear, trying to listen in on the La Pointe conversation in the booth.

Brother and sister exchanged hellos, and Vincent scolded her. "Do you know how poorly this could reflect on me and my campaign? Frequenting pubs isn't something that the *good* people of Wickney accept easily."

"I needed . . . " Vanessa started then lowered her voice to a point the remainder only came in unintelligible murmurs.

Vincent sighed audibly. "Very well." then his voice took on the same mumbling tone.

Raine rolled his eyes and tapped a finger on the glass. A third wasn't the norm, but the frustration and curiosity egged him on. As Dick reached for the bottle, a news bulletin interrupted the game on the TV. In front of the Wickney Court House, a group of reporters hoarded around a pair of police officers escorting in an older version of Vincent La Pointe into the building. Raine lifted his face to the television as his mouth gaped. The man wasn't in handcuffs, so not arrested—yet, but it seemed ominous. A headline in a red bar across the bottom of the screen read, "William La Pointe Named Suspect in Wife's Murder."

Well, well, well. The murder of her mother would certainly explain Vanessa's agitation in the square, as well as why the La Pointe siblings were having hushed conversations in a pub. Raine tried to listen to the conversation again but came up empty. Too bad being Fae didn't come with a heightened sense of hearing.

When the two officers and the senior La Pointe disappeared into the building on the TV, a woman stepped forward, and the headline switched to read, "Detective Kennedi Craine, Wickney Police Department" across the bottom. Raine listened, but Detective Craine answered very few of the questions shouted out from the cloud of reporters.

With a hand raised in a motion to silence the questions, she said, "We are merely questioning Mr. La Pointe at this time. When we have narrowed the suspect list and charges are filed, a formal statement will be issued. Thank you."

"Detective Craine!" one reporter shouted. "Can you tell us about the affair Mrs. La Pointe was having?"

The detective replied, "No further comment at this time," turned away from the cameras, and marched up the few remaining steps into the courthouse.

The camera switched to a young reporter, maybe fresh from journalism school, who adjusted his glasses before he realized the camera was focused on him. "Oh." He perked up and put on a mask that clearly showed his hunger to break the next big story in Wickney and make a name for himself. "Stay tuned to Channel Four for the latest updates."

The game resumed.

"Hell in a hand basket," Dick said, shaking his head as he poured the next shot of whiskey.

Raine turned on the stool and scanned over to the booth. He locked eyes briefly with Vanessa. She tilted her head, and he replied with a small smile, then pretended he was looking for the restroom. He asked Dick in a loud voice to further the rouse. Dick furrowed his brow, clearly confused as to why Raine—an afternoon regular—would ask such a thing, but he pointed to the front of the pub.

Raine downed the last dram and slapped a bill on the bar. "Thanks, mate."

As he walked to the door, he pulled out his phone. Careful to hold it only by the rubber case, he pressed a side button to wake it up, held it so the face-recognition would work, then tapped the voice icon and said, "Text Morgana" quietly into the speaker.

The electronic voice replied, "Did you mean M-Zero-R-Six-Four-N-Four?"

Raine said, "Yes." Because he couldn't touch the device for long, he'd done this enough times that the thing was learning, and he was grateful that he'd finally found a way to use the latest tech.

"What would you like to text?" the voice asked.

Continuing with the voice-to-text feature, he started the conversation.

Raine: Need a lookup

M0R64N4:   Not now. Busy.

Shite. She was the only person he knew who could get the info quickly.

Raine: Please? I'll make it worth your while.

No reply.

Raine: Name your price.

Nothing for a minute.

More seconds passed. He sank to begging.

Raine: I said please. Silence burns.

Three little dots scrolled across the bottom of the screen, and Raine pumped his fist and hissed, "Yesss!"

M0R64N4:   Fine. What?

Raine: Address for Vanessa La Pointe

M0R64N4:   100 Devereux Court #3

That reply came too quickly. Raine grabbed his suitcase from the coat check, pursed his lips, then texted back.

Raine: You know her?

M0R64N4:   Seriously, Bard, next time you need such common intel, ask that bartender you just passed.

Raine could feel the eye-roll in those words as he looked back down the bar at Dick. Shaking his head, he pushed through the door and lifted the phone again once he had both feet pounding the pavement.

Raine: OK what do I owe?

M0R64N4:   Some peace and effin quiet. OUT!

Raine shoved his phone into his pocket and marched up the hill, catty-corner across Wickney Square, navigating around the plethora of creepy statues and the fountain. He went two blocks up Main Street, then turned onto Aldgate. He ducked into the third doorway, typed in a door code, and climbed the stairs to his tiny flat above a cheap lawyer's office. At the sink beside the closet-like room that barely contained a three-by-three shower and toilet, he splashed a little water on his face. If he were mortal, that third shot probably would have done him in for a good afternoon nap. As it was, his Fae constitution was only a little fazed by the human distilled spirits. No, his conundrum was whether or not to fight the desperate need to interfere with the situation that'd presented itself to him when he'd made contact with Vanessa La Pointe. Unfortunately, he feared he'd already lost the battle with his nature.

Raine ran a towel over his face, opened his suitcase, and counted his proceeds from the performance. Indeed, it'd been a fantastic performance and overly profitable to boot. "Thanks, Vanessa!" he called to the empty room. Raine tucked half the cash into the puzzle box he stored under his nightstand, closed it back up, and glamoured it to look like just part of the furniture. Beyond the glamour, the intricate series of steps required to open the thing could only be discerned by another royal Fae. His wealth was safer there than in any of the mortal institutions that touted to hold someone's money but really invested it somewhere, charged the account holder tons of fees, and got richer and richer off the dividends the tiny print allowed them to collect on everyone else's money. Somewhere deep inside, Raine admired these bankers for pulling one of the better hoaxes ever on the unsuspecting public. Yeah, he had a bank account, but he only put enough cash in to be able to use those little pieces of plastic where cash just wouldn't do. If anyone was going to invest his money, it'd be him, so that he could manage his returns with better precision.

He paced for several moments, then gave in to desire and left his flat, bound for Devereux Court.

By the time Vanessa finally arrived back at her home, it was well past dark and likely past most normal mortals' bedtimes. Raine had wandered her entire townhouse—a British terrace-style home similar to the brownstone townhouses in New York City. The facade looked unoriginally identical to the other four homes in Devereux Court, and Raine double checked the number before letting himself into #3 with little ordeal. The standard steel lock was the cheapest puzzle in the book, and to any onlooker, it would have certainly appeared as if he just used a key and walked right inside—another resident of said home.

Raine sat on a stool at the uncharacteristic high-top table in Vanessa's breakfast nook, just on the other side of the modern kitchen. Mortals always went to the kitchen first when they came home, so he'd determined that was the best place to await her arrival. At the front of the townhome, the door closed and papers rustled, then everything fell still. Presumably she'd dropped the mail on the foyer table. Her heels clicked on the hardwood toward the kitchen for three, four, five steps, then she stepped onto the tile, dropped her purse on the counter, and flipped on the light. She didn't look up immediately, so Raine cleared his throat.

Vanessa gasped and stumbled backward into the door of her stainless-steel refrigerator.

Raine stood, holding up his hands. "*Nach tú*, Vanessa."

She scrambled for her purse, but she'd left it too close to Raine. He snatched it up before she could.

Jerking backward with jitters in her voice, she demanded, "Wh-what are you doing in my house?"

"Calm down," Raine said as a knee-jerk reaction, then slapped his forehead with the palm of his hand. *Shite—that's what all the crooks say, right?*

Vanessa went for the drawer beside the cook top.

Raine stepped closer. "Please. I'm sorry to scare you." That wasn't true. He didn't care if he scared her in the least, but it's what he wanted her to believe. Narrowing his eyes, he nudged her a little. "Just listen for a minute."

Her shoulders dropped "You've been following me since that spectacle in the square earlier. You were in the bar. Why are you here?" Her hands trembled as she reached slowly for the drawer.

"I-I . . ." He faltered on what came next. Strange. He never came up short of words. He looked around the room, over the whitewashed cabinets, and along the darker grout lines between the lighter floor tiles. What *did* he want? Why *was* he here? This Danu-damned Fae addiction was going to land him in more trouble than he'd been in since New Orleans. What words could he possibly use to explain? Suddenly, it struck. Truth, kind of. His eyes stretched to their fullest extent then narrowed again as his lips peeled back. "You believe your father is innocent, sure. I can help you prove it so."

CHAPTER 2

KENNEDI

The following day

HAVING GAINED ABSOLUTELY NOTHING FROM the interview with William La Pointe, Kennedi Craine left the interrogation room. She marched into the adjacent observation room, stopped between Vic and Harley to peer at the man through the one-way mirror, and planted her hands on her hips. The only suspect in his wife's shooting, William La Pointe sat calmly beyond the glass, elbows on the table, tapping the tips of his fingers together, waiting for the lawyer he'd finally requested. The crime scene had painted clearly that he'd killed Michelle La Pointe; for Christ's sake, he'd been holding the gun and standing over her dead body when the police answered the call from a concerned neighbor. There had been no other evidence. None. The neighbor hadn't seen anything either, only heard the gunshot. Yet during questioning, the retired Wisconsin senator had never once displayed a lick of behavior that suggested guilt. Shock, dismay, hurt, but nothing that screamed he had any animosity toward his wife.

Kennedi pressed her lips tightly and sighed through her nose. "Do we have prints back from forensics?"

"Yeah." Vic Clark, one of her junior officers, handed her a manila folder. "None but his."

"You called his lawyer, right?" she asked.

Vic nodded. "Yup."

"Was there anything else at all at the scene that leaves doubt that he's the guy?" Kennedi turned to the rookie at her other side.

Harley Gold folded corded arms across their chest, their navy uniform stretching to its limits with the motion. The officer lived at the gym when off duty. "Not a thing. Everything points to him."

Kennedi glanced over the forensics report in the folder, resigning herself to paper-pushing in yet another open-and-closed case. "Well, I guess we wait for the attorney. Vic, call the DA and see if he wants to press charges with what we have. Harley, go down and requisition new uniform shirts before you break the seams in that one."

She slapped the folder into a preening Harley's chest, rolled her eyes, then stomped toward her desk to type up the report.

With a jiggle of the mouse, the computer churned. Kennedi typed in her password and waited for the software to load. As she sipped her lukewarm dark-roast coffee, the infrequent elevator ding grabbed her attention. Out stepped a man, tall and slender at the waist but a bit broader through the shoulders, running a hand through sandy hair that that seemed to fall just perfectly to his high cheekbones when released. Kennedi stood, her chair rolling backward. No one had called to let them know a visitor had arrived. Certainly, this non-briefcase-bearing pretty-boy was not Senator La Pointe's lawyer. She lowered her paper coffee cup to the desk and leaned forward onto both hands as he swaggered in through the glass doors. "Who are you and how did you get past the front desk?"

The man strutted toward her with a smile growing on his lips and his black jacket flapping open like he was walking down a runway rather than into a police station. "Aye, well, Carl and I go way back now."

Kennedi peaked her brows. "There is no Carl on the desk downstairs. You need to leave. Now. Only authorized personnel are allowed on the fifth floor." She looked over at Vic with a *please-remove-him* glare and retrieved her chair.

The stranger stopped at her desk and reached for her cup of coffee. Just before he took a sip, he shrugged. "Maybe it was Carlo, was it?"

There was no Carlo either, but Kennedi couldn't pick up her jaw from the floor. The fact that this man had walked right up to her desk and taken her coffee without so much as asking had her in sheer speechless shock. She crossed her arms over her chest, took a deep breath, and breathed out slowly to keep from reaching across the table and yanking him by that pretty leather jacket.

The man's face squished, and he sputtered as he forcibly swallowed. "Ah." *Cough.* He blinked and grimaced. "Bitter . . . Why Starbucks if you're not drinking something tasty, or sweet?" He wiped his mouth on his sleeve and looked around until he found a bottle of water on Vic's desk, opened it, and gulped several long swallows. "Better," he breathed, replacing the cap.

"Excuse me." She eyed the stranger with a brow cocked, waiting.

He dropped the bottle and held out a hand. "Oh, I am terribly sorry. I'm Raine. Raine, uh"—his brows furrowed—"Abarta."

Lie? Definitely a lie. Lips pursed, Kennedi looked at the hand, certain that it had some rare and highly communicable disease. Or possibly the callous and dismissive demeanor would rub off if she touched him. "Well, 'Raine, uh, Abarta,' as I said before, this floor is for police staff only. If you wish to speak with someone here, make an appointment. Here's the number." She flipped her card at him and took her seat.

"Call me Raine, now," he said, and looked around all sides of her desk. "Where's your guest chair? You know, the ones every bobby has in the movies."

Kennedi ground her teeth. "You're not *in* the movies. Do I need to have you escorted to the exit?"

With no guest chairs to be found, Raine circled Harley's desk and pulled the empty chair over to Kennedi's desk. She leaned back, crossing a leg and her arms. Apparently, the man wasn't going to take the direct instruction to get out, and she really wasn't in the mood to remove him by force, so she stared at him with a look that she hoped foreshadowed her next move.

Unfortunately, he seemed undisturbed by her annoyance as he leaned toward her. Lowering his voice, he looked around as if he were in grade school about to spill the juiciest gossip. "This will seem, shall we say, unconventional, but I think I can help you with the La Pointe case."

Kennedi laughed. "This is a police investigator's office. We don't *do* unconventional here. I've asked you to—"

The elevator dinged again, and she rolled her eyes. How was she ever going to get her work done today if this revolving door action kept up? However, she recognized some of the members in this group. The four people entered the small office space, and Kennedi stood to greet them.

"You wait," she said to Raine, her eyes on the La Pointes while she held up a hand to silence any objection.

Kennedi crossed over to meet Vincent and Vanessa La Pointe and Senator La Pointe's two presumed lawyers. Only one of the two extras looked like a lawyer—a man in his late thirties, early forties at most, wearing a suit and carrying a leather case. The fourth person was a woman, older than the La Pointe siblings, possibly the father's age. The clothes she wore suggested she was on her way to an elegant dinner rather than making an unpleasant stop at the Wickney Courthouse and Police Department.

Keep it professional, Craine. Kennedi offered a hand to Vincent La Pointe, a man she would become very familiar with should he win the mayoral election. He had the potential to very well be her future boss.

Vincent La Pointe accepted her handshake with his characteristically charming and highly political smile, but he said nothing.

"We're very sorry about your loss," she said, then offered her hand to his sister in turn.

Vanessa, who'd been staring wearily beyond Kennedi, blinked several times until she came back to the introduction scene. Her eyes were red-rimmed, and her lips twitched in an attempt at a smile as she took

Kennedi's hand. "Thank you, detective."

Vincent introduced the lawyer, Andrew Gorman from Slagle, Bernard & Gorman. "And this is Doctor Elanna Bell, a dear family friend," he finished. Kennedi did the polite thing and greeted the woman, but she also quirked a brow at Vincent, hoping for a further explanation.

"Elanna is Mother's oldest friend," he answered her questioning look, then coughed. "*Was* Mother's friend."

Vanessa laid a hand on her brother's upper arm and sniffled, calling further attention to her post-crying eyes. "I asked her to come. Elanna is an aunt to us. She's been supportive since . . ." Vanessa raised a trembling tissue to her nose and sniffed again. "I'm sorry. It's just so fresh." Tears pooled in her eyes.

"I understand," said Kennedi, removing a hand from her plain-clothes pocket and offering it to the older woman. She was dressed in a near-formal, violet-colored dress, and further emphasizing her propriety, Elanna Bell wore her strawberry-blonde hair wrapped into a twist with a jeweled clip. As Dr. Bell accepted Kennedi's hand, her eyes glistened under false lashes, but there wasn't any sign of crying or streaks in her perfectly applied makeup.

Vanessa reached out and placed a hand on Kennedi's arm. Her voice pitched with urgency as she spoke. "You do believe my father is innocent, right? He couldn't have done such a thing. He's a good man. You have to believe me. He would never have shot Mom. Aside from the collection, he hates violence. He, he . . ."

Elanna turned and embraced Vanessa, shushing and rubbing her back.

Kennedi rolled her lips between her teeth and bit down. She relished the enigmas of her job, discovering what really happened, solving the crime, slamming the bars on the guilty, but dealing with the families was the part that sucked. Though she'd been trained in how to handle them with sensitivity, Kennedi felt awkward every single time. She lifted a hand to Vanessa's shoulder, patted a couple of times, and urged them toward the waiting area designated for this kind of situation. The young woman looked at Raine with heavy brows as they passed, but Elanna escorted her along with a motherly arm around her shoulders. Kennedi pulled up the tail, and as she passed her desk, she pointed at the obnoxious man still lurking. "You. Don't move. I'll deal with you in a minute." Then to Vic she added, "Watch him," and continued after the La Pointes.

Harley met the group of five on the way to the waiting area. "Heya, boss. Lawyer?"

Nodding, Kennedi lowered her voice and instructed her junior officer, "Make sure the family is comfortable. Coffee or whatever. I'll take the lawyer to his client."

She dropped off the lawyer and returned to her desk to handle the true annoyance of the morning. Unfortunately, Vic had turned his back to Raine and was working diligently on his computer. Raine, unsupervised, sat in her chair perusing the file she'd carelessly left open on the screen. *Damn!* She picked up her step, slapping Vic on the back of the head as she walked by.

He ducked. "Ow, wha—" then he blinked several times as if coming out of a fog.

"I told you to watch him." She gritted her teeth and faced Raine. "What the hell do you think you're doing?"

Raine stood, hands in the air, and his eyebrows shot up as if he had a right to be surprised by her outburst. "Uh. Ah. Just a little reading." He grinned and lifted one shoulder toward his ear.

Kennedi leaned over and pressed a couple of keys on the board; the screen went black. "I could arrest you just for that. Case tampering. Interfering with the police. Obstruction of justice. You need to go. Now." She looped a hand under his arm.

"But I think Vanessa is right," Raine protested.

Kennedi pushed him toward the door. "C'mon. Out."

Raine tugged away, performing a little pirouette. He came back toward her. Too close, nose-to-nose, and stared her down. "You're going to listen to her now, aren't you?"

Kennedi blinked and lowered her gaze. *Strange. What was that?* She pulled away, then looked back at him cautiously. "Vanessa La Pointe is an upset relative. Of course she's going to defend her father." Determined again, she grabbed onto his arm and pushed toward the door.

"But what if she's right?" he persisted. "Can I talk to William La Pointe? Maybe I can get something else out of him. I'm working wonders on you." He leaned into her, his crooning voice sliding over her skin like a desperate salesman's.

Kennedi shivered, recoiled, stopped at the glass doors, and faced Raine. Who the hell was this nobody? The flourish of hair and dance in his step. A Faerie? Maybe. Maybe not. Didn't matter. She bit down, feeling the muscle in her jaw tick, before she replied, "Listen, I've seen this a thousand and one times. The daughter is not looking at the evidence." Kennedi paused. Why the hell was she talking about this with some annoying civilian who walked in off the street? She blinked and shook her head to clear the insanity. Hardening herself, she said, "Again—obstruction of justice," and pointed toward the elevator.

Raine took a deep breath and placed a hand on the handle to leave.

Finally.

But relief was temporary. "What if I can help you with that other case? The one I was reading about on your computer. The Dragmaker. That's really a lame name, by the way. Who came up with that?" He threw a hand over his open mouth. "Oh, that wasn't you, was it?"

For what felt like the hundredth time that day, she rolled her eyes. For months on end, someone had been dressing up and artfully applying makeup to the statues in Wickney Square. Kennedi had to admit that she'd found every instance of one of the historical politicians dressed in drag, make-up, wig, and all, absolutely hilarious, but it'd offended several retired judges and cost the city thousands in cleanup. So yeah, they really needed to put a stop to it. Kennedi seethed, hating that she was about to let this oddity become her informant, but if there was the slightest possibility he could help, she could use the break. And then, what if he *was* right about the other?

Raine flashed his row of pearly whites and gave a knowing nod. "Yep, I know who it is *and* where you can find him."

RAINE

IN THE PASSENGER SEAT, RAINE leaned warily away from all the electronics. "So, you'll agree, will you, that if my tip turns out in your favor, I can chat with William La Pointe?" He kept his eye on the driver, the unexpectedly tall, strong, and spunky Kennedi Craine.

She tapped the steering wheel several times with her thumb. "You just help me find the guy, and we'll see." Her eyes never left the road as she sped around a corner.

Raine gripped the handle, but relaxed once they were on a straightaway once more. That wasn't the commitment he'd hoped for, but she'd give in eventually, like other mortals who dealt with the Fae.

Kennedi pulled the wheel to the left without warning.

Raine, unbraced and ill-prepared, careened into the passenger door. "Geez, where'd you learn to drive?" With one hand bracing himself against the dash, he latched onto the handle with the other and stared wide-eyed at the detective. She seemed to enjoy this little ride she controlled far too much, but didn't give off anything that his faerie nature could consume. *Odd. Has she been touched by the Goddess? That's quite a devious streak now, isn't it?*

It wasn't like he could drive better. He had learned long ago, but Ifrinn, he could compete with the oldest and blindest driver for an award in caution behind the wheel. He hated driving. Cars, like most other electronics, rebelled at his touch. But riding was worse, and his stomach clenched with every swerve.

Kennedi chuckled, clearly relishing the shock factor delivered with her assault on the road using tons of metal as her weapon. "Oh, let me think, I believe the name of the course was . . . *Police High-Speed Driving Training.*"

Point taken. Standard training for the bobbies. Raine pressed his gaping mouth closed. Her hands caressed the wheel and her shoulders remained at ease throughout the ordeal.

Cars. Of all the mortal inventions, Raine favored the unnatural machines the least. The metal contraptions burned fuels made by Earth from long-dead creatures, and that concept betrayed every principle of Danu's Order of Life. He longed for the simpler times when horses drew carriages around town. But then again, maybe he was only a recovering follower of the Goddess given that he regularly used other conveniences like electricity, which used the same fuels. So, fine, call him a hypocrite; the illogic didn't lessen his unease.

Kennedi took another breakneck turn, pulling him in the other direction.

"Whoaaa," he wailed. Maybe he should let go and tumble into the bombshell driving the car.

"What street did you say?" she demanded.

"Underwood Court."

When Kennedi took her eyes off the road and looked at the electronic map on the dash, Raine reached a shaky hand toward the steering wheel.

"What?" Her eyes glittered mischievously and threw Raine off his game. "A bit nerve-racking?" she asked with sheer delight in her voice.

"Oh, no. Just, uh, trying to help out." He failed to sound the least bit convincing. This had to be her trying to get back at him for the command he'd taken at WPD.

"There. Hang on," she said, wearing the grin of an imp as she slowed slightly to take the next left.

Raine breathed in through his nose and out through his mouth, rolling his eyes and bracing his midsection to control his gut. At least she'd slowed a little. She looked away, in the direction she was turning, and Raine said a little mental litany to Danu that they'd make it there alive. The tumult couldn't compare to traveling between the realms, but Raine would choose crossing the veil any second of the day over riding in a car.

"Number?" Kennedi barked.

"Eleven-oh-seven," he answered. Almost there, thank Danu.

When the machine finally came to a stop and silenced, several houses short of the destination, Raine reached for the handle and his insides settled as he stepped back onto solid earth. Most of the time, he could do without this era's technology malarkey in the mortal realm, but he couldn't go backward in time and just waltz back into Fae after what he'd done. So here he was—trying to fight his faerie nature so he didn't get arrested by the FVU, living with all this unnatural tech, and volunteering to figure out how William La Pointe wasn't guilty of his wife's murder. *Seriously, Raine, if Briar were here, she'd paint the street with your glittering blood.* The thought of his betrothed, wicked as it was, brought a short-lived smile to his face.

Kennedi circled the unmarked car, palming her gun at her side with one hand, the other pointing toward the ground. "You stay here."

He raised his hands and took a step backward. He'd follow at a distance.

She stepped onto the sidewalk but, before taking three steps, halted and looked back. "What did you say this joker's name was?"

"I didn't." Raine crossed his arms over his chest and lifted his chin. His stomach was settling, and the thought of Briar reaffirmed it was time to take back control of the situation.

Kennedi marched over, irritation twitching at her upper lip, and put her face mere inches from his—the second time she'd done that today. The smell of her was simply divine, like the fresh air when the sun shines after a storm. Her words, though, were anything but soft. "I understand you think this is some kind of game, but I need you to tell me now who my suspect is. In fact, I'm not certain why I came out here with you without knowing that information first. And without backup." Her brows pinched together then relaxed. "But so I can put an end to this prankster's distractions, I agreed to give you five minutes with Mr. La Pointe, and I'll stick to my word on that. So, ya wanna share?"

"*If* he talks, he only answers to 'King Ludwig'—but please be certain you pronounce it in the proper German."

She started walking; Raine followed until she whirled on him. "Where do you think you're going?"

He lifted a shoulder. It should have been obvious that he'd follow, but he'd let her put that together.

She shook her head slowly. "Uh-uh. No. You stay right there beside the car. Better yet, inside."

Raine held his ground for some time but eventually stepped back, not agreeing with her, but allowing her to think he relented. When she started walking again, he followed at a distance. Kennedi recited the address into a device attached to her wrist. Then, as she approached the sidewalk leading up to the townhouse at 1107 Underwood Court, she turned and climbed the steps. Just as Raine turned up the walk behind her, a black and white pulled up to the curb and the two junior officers he'd seen at the station hopped out and slammed the car doors.

"Craine," one yelled; Raine couldn't name which as he hadn't had proper introductions.

Kennedi spun to face them with her mouth opened, about to bark commands, but she plowed into Raine. They both toppled onto the ground. Thank Danu she threw him sideways, and his back landed on the soft grass. Raine's hands grasped the tight curves on either side of her hips, and their lips, noses, and foreheads collided clumsily upon impact. She sucked in a breath, then paused and looked him in the eye.

"If a quick tumble would have done the trick, all you had to do was ask." Raine cocked a brow and slid his hands up her sides.

Pressing her mouth tighter, she scurried off him, groaning. While he was still on the ground between her and the officers, Kennedi straightened her jacket, ire burning down her ever-shortening fuse as she pointed the gun away from everyone on scene and narrowed her eyes at him. "Wh-what the . . .," she hissed, tossing her ponytail back over her shoulder.

The officers nearby snickered, the more muscular one covering their mouth. The suggestion in their chuckles shifted her frustration from Raine.

"You two, shut it!" said Kennedi.

Raine sat up slowly. He surely hadn't seen *that* pleasant surprise coming, and suddenly, he wanted to follow her more. Although he was no longer certain his reasoning remained with the La Pointe case. Maybe more cases. *Puzzle after puzzle after puzzle? Oh how delightful.*

Giggling officers forgotten, Kennedi glared once again at Raine. "I thought I told you—"

He ignored whatever came next, stuck on the thought of helping her out more and more. It would be tons of fun, and it'd sate his Fae desires without putting him in harm's way. He pursed his lips. Maybe, just maybe, he'd gotten on to something.

Finished with her latest reprimand, Kennedi nodded the other bobbies toward the door. While she had her eyes on them, a slender man wearing a mime's get-up snuck out of the house and gingerly padded down the steps, white-gloved hands held high. Ludwig's lined eyes were wide, and his black-painted O-shaped lips mocked grave caution.

The smaller officer sniggered and pointed in a *you're-kidding-me,-right?* gesture. The other started mimicking Ludwig's motions.

Kennedi's brows peaked. "What is wrong with you two?"

Raine pointed over her shoulder at his fellow Wickney Square performer. "Um . . ."

"Shut up and get your ass back to the car!" Kennedi threw her non-gun hand toward her car, hitting Ludwig on the shoulder as he passed.

Ludwig bounced on the balls of his feet and started to run.

Amusement evaporating, the officer twins alerted. Their hands slid in unison to their gun belts, though confusion still ripened their faces.

Raine gained his feet, dusted off his pants, shrugged, and calmly uttered, "Yeah, that's your guy."

KENNEDI

THE MIME MADE IT HALFWAY to the corner before anyone made a move. Kennedi narrowed her eyes and glared at Raine; the man was certainly proving to be more of a distraction than a help. But she didn't have time to consider him much with a perp quickly getting away. A growl rumbled in her throat, but she put thoughts of Raine Abarta on hold, pushed between the three people blocking her way, and launched into a run after Ludwig.

The mime turned right at the corner.

"Clark, with me," she commanded over her shoulder to Vic, then to Harley, "Gold, circle around."

Adrenaline surged and the chase ensued. Kennedi sucked in a breath through her nose, gathering the oxygen her body needed to kick into gear, then pushed it out in measures between her lips. Clark's footsteps pounded in her wake. As she rounded the corner, Ludwig continued to run but glanced backward over his shoulder, a move that invariably slowed his progress. Kennedi pressed herself faster, closed the distance. Fire kindled in her muscles. Her mouth watered and she hungered for the catch.

At the next block, Ludwig turned right.

Kennedi smirked. "That's it. Gold's got you now," she purred under her breath, not that her prey could hear the satisfaction dripping from her voice.

As they rounded the next corner, so did Harley Gold, as expected. Kennedi trained with her two junior officers, so their paces had worked into sync over the last few years.

Ludwig stopped. Black and white paint outlined the surprise on his face as his attention swiveled between them and searched desperately for an out in the middle of the block. He cut across the street. A car's brakes squealed on the pavement to avoid hitting him; several horns blared. Just as the mime ducked into a small alley, Kennedi's unmarked police car crept to the corner, the cherry spinning. In the driver's seat, Raine Abarta put the blinker on and waited for every car at the corner to stop for a good two seconds before he poked the nose into the intersection toward the chase in progress.

"Ah, hell!" swore Kennedi, but she found a small gap

in the traffic on her end of the block and darted across the street at an angle, Clark at her heels. She was at the mouth of the alley well before Raine could pull the car to a stop. Her annoying informant could just wait wherever he halted. He couldn't run as fast as the officers, so she'd deal with him once they had Ludwig in custody.

Blocking the alley was an enormous wooden gate, ten feet at least. Ludwig tried to open it with several sharp jerks. Failing, he jumped to try to grasp the top and climb. Defeated in that effort too, he searched the trash-strewn alley and found a rickety wooden crate—something that produce had been delivered in probably ten years before. Kennedi slowed her run as she approached with her juniors in tow. The mime grasped the crate, his white gloves now dirty, and stepped up in a clear attempt to reach the top of the gate again. If the crate had been solid, he might have made his escape, but the wood splintered under his foot. He stumbled. Kennedi broke her jog within ten yards, aimed her gun, and narrowed the remainder of the distance with measured steps.

The perp didn't appear armed; in the form-fitting black suit he had little place to hide a weapon of any size. Instead, he turned and shifted his face into a dramatically sad expression that exaggerated the vertical black lines across each of his eyes. His dirty, white-gloved hands walked upward as if on glass to a surrender position, and he bowed as if he were a minion deferring to his evil lord.

Kennedi rolled her eyes. "Ludwig?"

The mime silently bowed.

She sighed, her elevated heart rate returning to a normal pace. "*King* Ludwig?" she tried again.

This time he looked up.

"State your full name," she commanded.

His entire demeanor puppy-dogged, his head tilting as if he heard, was intrigued, but couldn't understand.

She fought an urge to knock the drama off his face and huffed, "Vic, cuff him." She holstered her gun in the shoulder harness and recited Miranda, using *King Ludwig* as the man's full name. There were witnesses, and he'd responded to the name, so certainly it would hold. And if it didn't, maybe the arrest would scare enough flamboyance out of the man to keep him from decorating her city again in the near future. Kennedi turned to the mouth of the alley.

Raine Abarta strutted toward the scene just like he'd walked into her office earlier, as if he belonged there. She stopped and glared, her hands on her hips. The scowl must have worked, because he retreated without question.

To Vic and Harley, she said, "Get him to the station."

At the mouth of the alley, Raine stood next to her car with the back door held open. Vic pushed the mime into Kennedi's back seat, holding his head. Raine closed the door and turned to Kennedi, swiping his hands together in a *job-well-done* manner and wearing self-satisfaction all over his face. "See, we make a great team."

Kennedi glared and took a slow, deep breath. She owed her irritating informant five minutes with La Pointe. Then, done. Without looking away from Raine, she said, "Vic, Harley, take him back to WPD in the black and white."

She circled to the driver's side while her junior officers hooked both of Raine's arms. His eyes darted and he struggled against their apprehension. Kennedi smirked, ducked into her car, and left.

CHAPTER 3

RAINE

C AGED.

He leaned forward, as close as he could get to the bobbies on the other side of the wire grid. "I'm some animal now, am I?"

The burly driver, Harley Gold, cut a glance to the passenger, Vic Clark, who shrugged.

Throwing himself back against the seat, Raine peered through the windows at the passing city streets; the buildings grew taller and taller as they neared Wickney's center. He spat on the floorboard, but the uniforms in the front didn't acknowledge his defiance. Judging by the condition of the stained floor, he wasn't the first. Although he had to admit, aside from the mini-prison, the ride back to WPD was going far smoother than the ride out. Harley Gold turned out to be a much more cautious driver. Thank Danu for small miracles.

Raine appraised the duo in the front seat, pondering. They'd chortled at Ludwig's small performance, so perhaps . . . He clawed his fingers into the wire cage. "Officer Clark?"

Vic repositioned in his seat, looking openly at Raine.

Pouting, Raine asked, "You don't think they'll be too hard on King Ludwig now, do you?"

Confusion shadowed the man's face for an instant as he looked over at Harley, then he grinned, held his hands up, and performed the pane-of-glass imitation again. Both bobbies chuckled.

Vic sighed off the laugh. "Nah. He'll get a fine and maybe some community service in the form of cleaning up the mess. He likely can't be convicted of anything criminal, because anyone who looks at him will know it wasn't malicious."

"Good. I'd hate to wreck a fellow performer's gig so."

"Yeah," added Harley, "booking him'll just get one more small case off our desks. That chase, though . . ."

"And how you"—Vic nodded toward Raine—"got under Detective Craine's skin."

"Oh, totally!" Harley belly-laughed. "I've never seen her as uncomfortable as when you two took that tumble."

"Yup, I'd pay good money to see that again."

Raine sat back again, crossing his arms and smiling out the window. Aye, these two. He nodded. They were his *in* with Kennedi Craine.

Harley parked in line with the other identical panda cars. Behind the courthouse, the wiry bobby unfolded himself, opened the back, and leaned casually on the door while Raine stepped out. He offered a hand and a bit of advice. "Don't sweat Craine's temper. She's slow to warm up."

Harley Gold—a person who put Raine in mind of one of the courthouse's enormous cornerstones—slammed the driver's door with more oomph than necessary and lumbered around the trunk with their hand eagerly extended. Raine shook both officer's hands with no taste of metal and no assault on his emotion. His mouth flooded, however, and the muscles in his shoulders went languid over the camaraderie he'd coaxed into being during their ride back downtown. He pulled away and wiped his palm on his jeans, not wanting to drink in too much of their levity.

Good. His Fae abilities had returned to normal, only surfacing when he willed them. He couldn't be certain why they'd gone wonky when he'd made contact with Vanessa, but that'd landed him in this situation with the whodunit puzzle, and the Goddess might damn him to Ifrinn, but he couldn't walk away from a good conundrum. No, he was going to make the most of the situation.

Harley clapped a huge hand on his shoulder. "Let's go see how the boss lady's handling our clown."

Raine grinned. "Sure thing, mate, but don't call him a clown. Miming is art, storytelling through body and spirit. The talent takes study and practice, sure." He walked between Harley and Vic through the back door and up the service stairwell.

Both bobbies eyed him sideways, appearing thoughtful—as if they considered miming in a brand-new light. But they clearly didn't appreciate the skill, because they both botched another attempt at the invisible windowpane, then burst into laughter. Raine plastered on a performer's smile, jabbed them both on the shoulder in a playful gesture, turned, and climbed the stairs, stifling his groan.

The trio passed through the staff-only break area and into the long, open office where Raine had first met Kennedi Craine; also where she presently was handing off Ludwig to two other uniformed officers for processing.

"You should come to the gym after work," Harley clapped a heavy hand on Raine's back as they wound around the maze of desks toward Kennedi. They scanned Raine from head to toe and back again. "We'll get you in shape yet."

That grated. Raine didn't have an ounce of fat, and he certainly could outperform both officers. He considered their "boss lady," as they'd called her. Certain these two could help him win her over, he decided he needed their favor. "Tell ya what," Raine replied. "I will if you come perform with me in Wickney Square on Saturday."

"Deal." Harley beamed and held out a thick hand.

Raine raised one brow. "You want to know what kind of performance, don't you?"

Harley laughed, higher in pitch Raine had imagined. "Maybe I can learn to mime if it's such a talent."

Before they could shake on the deal, Kennedi marched over, scowling once again—this time at Harley.

The burly bobby pulled their hand back without the shake, seeming to shrink under the senior officer's ire. "I–I'll just get back to some . . . ah . . ." They ran a hand over their cropped haircut, then thumbed the air toward their desk. "Some, uh, paperwork. Yeah."

Raine shot Harley a finger gun. "Gym at six?"

Harley lifted one hand, thumb up, without looking back. Vic chuckled and skipped off to his desk too.

Turning to Kennedi, Raine pitched his voice so Harley could hear. "Don't you think you're a bit harsh on him?"

Harley spun the chair around, locked eyes with Raine, and corrected, "Them." Harley winked. "My pronouns are they/them, man, not he/him."

Kennedi issued a single chuckle with a smug little nod.

Raine twisted his mouth, considered, decided: *Definitely!* "They/them, is it? Got it now."

Then, he returned his full attention to Kennedi.

She motioned toward the front of the office and rolled her eyes. "Let's get this over with so you can get the hell out of my hair." She marched away, glancing toward the corner office. "Shit, Vincent's in with Captain Quaid."

Raine followed her gaze, slowing.

Kennedi pivoted, strode back to him, and grabbed him by the arm. "Bringing La Pointe back today wasn't a smooth move, so you need to get this done and get out of my work."

As they approached her desk, another plain-clothes officer, balding except for the stubble that horseshoed his head, strode over, hands resting on his belt. Kennedi's steps lightened as she neared him. "West, what are you doing on my floor?"

"Heard you nabbed the Dragmaker. Job well done!" West opened his arms, and to Raine's great surprise, Kennedi accepted the hug.

When they parted, she boasted, "Just returned from the chase. Get this"—she lowered her voice as if she spoke of some sort of taboo—"he's a clown."

"Ahem," interjected Raine. "A *mime.* There's a big

difference in talent and performance."

Both glared at him. Kennedi's expression said she'd grown tired of dealing with him, but West's looked more like a *who-the-hell-are-you?* glare. Raine forced his spine straight. As a member of the Wickney Performers Troupe, it was a matter of principle that he upheld the purity of a specific talent, and he wasn't about to back down.

"Well." West raised his brows, then turned so that his back faced Raine. He sat on Kennedi's desk, dangling a cowboy-booted foot; the toes polished to a gleam. "Chance the perp's Fae?"

Raine bit down to keep his jaw from gaping. That was the type of scandalous comment the man should have lowered his voice to utter, but Raine wasn't sure this guy actually *had* a lower tone of voice.

She huffed. "We've been through this before, West." Kennedi did lower her voice then. "Eccentricity doesn't equate to faerie." Her fingers idly flipped through a file on her desk. Not really looking at the content, she simply seemed to be stalling with this square-jawed, cowboy wannabe, full-of-himself man. Then a strange change came over her; she glanced past West at Raine and held out a welcoming hand.

Raine scowled.

"Raymond West," she said, her voice higher than it'd been before, "this gentleman helped with the apprehension. Raine Abarta, this is Detective Raymond West. He's with the FVU now, but he was my senior officer a few years back."

Diverting. She was definitely trying to change the topic. But why?

Raymond West didn't turn at the introduction.

"Well then, I should get back to work." He didn't stand immediately and said this as if he were trying to convince himself rather than really needing to go. "All right. Got a new case anyway. Someone OD'd on some sick faerie mojo last night at the Local U." He leaned in and pecked Kennedi's cheek.

Danu. Raine swore silently to the Goddess, but tried to hold his composure. He'd had his share of human-faerie interaction. In fact, he'd gained a bit of infamy among the Fae over the LaLaurie affair—a mutual addiction that'd torn apart his family and caused his mother to banish him from Faerie. Since then, he'd always taken care to keep the mortals from overdosing. That had become rule number one, and every Faerie in this realm knew the story. Who, no, which Faerie in their right mind would allow a mortal to OD after what he and Anemone had done?

Raine had to pack away those memories, keep up the mortal glamour, stay in the here and now. His upper lip twitched as he stared at the abrasive detective's back and I-own-this-place strut toward the elevators. That man and his ilk were the precise reason Fae thrived in the shadows and creative communities. Even though Raymond West didn't know he stood in the presence of a faerie—a once Fae prince—his prejudice made Raine feel dirty, lesser. It rankled, but he also thanked Danu for his fickle faerie temperament.

He easily shifted his attention back to his original reason for coming to WPD. He grinned at Detective Craine. "Okay, Ken, I held up my end of the bargain. I want to speak to La Pointe now."

She hesitated, twisted her lips sideways, then made her decision. "You get five *accompanied* minutes. Let's go." She pivoted and walked away. "And don't call me

Ken."

Raine grunted and followed.

Note to self: Always call her Ken.

KENNEDI

I TOTALLY SHOULD NOT BE SANCTIONING this. The former law student and detective in Kennedi Craine schooled herself during the short trip to the interrogation room. All his oddity said Raine was Fae, but she couldn't be certain unless he made a slip. Even if he was, she had to stick by her own advice to West. Fae did not equal bad. And, she quite possibly had another use for him. Maybe.

She glanced over her shoulder to ensure he still followed. Sure enough, he danced, strutted along behind her, and waved at everybody he passed. But why had he showed up *here*? Why did he help with the Dragmaker? And why did he want so badly to speak with William La Pointe?

Regardless of the conundrum that surrounded this street performer—a tidbit she'd learned after a quick database search—she had to admit that her Spidey-senses or sixth sense or whatever had her wanting to see how he interacted with her one and only suspect in the La Pointe case. She stopped at the door to the observation room, pointed to the empty patch of wall between that and the interrogation room, and ordered, "You. Wait there."

Raine Abarta held up both hands as if in surrender and leaned his back against the blah gray paint.

Inside the dimly lit observation room, Kennedi crossed to the equipment on the far wall and pressed the record buttons to record both audio and video. The signaling light flashed in the interrogation room, and the lawyer quickly silenced his client.

Kennedi rejoined Raine outside the interrogation room. "Ready?"

Raine held out a hand in an *after-you* gesture.

"This is against procedure, so the entire thing will be recorded. You don't mind, right?" She didn't wait for a reply before pushing the door open.

William La Pointe turned from his lawyer as they entered, his eyes red-rimmed with dark circles underneath and a muscle pulsing in his jaw. The man likely hadn't slept in two nights. The concrete beds in his jail cell wouldn't have made ideal sleeping arrangements for someone as well positioned as this man. And the night prior had been when the murder had taken place. Naturally, Mr. La Pointe would be beyond exhausted from first murdering his wife and then portraying the distraught husband. The SWAT team had literally apprehended him with a smoking gun in his hand. And, as suspected, his were the only prints on the weapon.

Business, Kennedi. She straightened her blazer. "Mr. La Pointe, Attorney Gorman, my regrets for bringing you back down here so soon." The officers had probably just gotten the ankle bracelet activated when she had dispatch retrieve him. Normally, she would never apologize to someone she so strongly suspected, but given his former position, she thought it'd be best to show as much respect as possible. After all, William La Pointe had been chief justice of the Wisconsin Supreme Court for two terms, and his son was now the favored candidate for Wickney mayor. If elected, Vincent La Pointe would be her superior. She sighed. "This shouldn't take more than five minutes. Then I'll have a squad car escort you back to Devereux Court."

"Thank you, Detective Craine," Raine grumbled and maneuvered past her. His demeanor had changed from that of a smooth talker, if a bit scattered. Now he appeared miffed.

But Kennedi couldn't care less if protocols interfered with his wishes. This *bard* was making a mockery of her investigation, and the sooner she was rid of him, the better.

Mr. Gorman stood, holding a hand toward Raine. "Excuse me, Detective, but who is this person?"

Kennedi opened her mouth and closed it, then huffed. "He's consulting on the case."

"Evaluating mental health?" Gorman tilted his head.

"Mmmm," was the only answer Kennedi could muster.

As Raine took the seat across the table, he cleared his throat and put on an overtly dramatic stage face. "Mr. La Pointe, I do hope you'll pardon this interruption."

Kennedi rolled her eyes.

William La Pointe's brows dropped to a salt-and-peppered V, and his stare lifted to Kennedi, questioning the intent of the newcomer.

"My name is Raine Abarta," Raine said with haughty inflection, moving slightly to regain La Pointe's attention. "As my partner said, I'm a consultant sometimes used by the WPD. Detective Craine here has so very kindly asked me to speak with you." He shot her a crooked smile. "Mind you, my fees are on the high side, so they are putting due importance on your case."

Kennedi sucked in a deep breath and eased it out. "Five minutes." She walked to the wall behind La Pointe and leaned backward, crossing one leg over the other at the ankle. So far, the theatrics were precisely on point.

La Pointe seemed to accept the false explanation at face value. Raine locked eyes with the man. He squinted, and Kennedi could no longer read much in his look.

"Tell me, Your Honor," Raine started, "how did you and your wife enjoy the opera last week?"

What the hell kind of question was that? Opera? Yeah, she'd known that they attended the opera, but it had nothing to do with the murder of Michelle La Pointe.

William La Pointe slumped back in his chair, easing a bit. "I, uh, we . . ." He turned his head to Mr. Gorman then back to Raine. He stiffened ever so slightly and whispered to his lawyer. After the brief exchange, he asked Raine, "What does this have to do with my wife's murder?"

Precisely! Absolutely the right question! Kennedi raised her brows as she watched Raine's absolute lack of reaction, as if he wasn't about to break character in this performance.

"*La Bohème* by Puccini, correct?" Raine ignored La Pointe's question. "I hear that Fluora Undici won an award for her portrayal of Mimì. How did you find her performance?"

"Frankly, Mr. Abarta," La Pointe snapped.

Good for him, Kennedi thought. Unleash your career's worth of training in truth-detection on this spectacle of a man.

La Pointe continued, still verging on irate, "I don't see how our date at the opera mat . . . matter . . . m-matters to this investigation."

From her viewpoint, she couldn't see La Pointe's face, but the sudden stutter was entirely out of character. Raine, on the other hand, appeared absolutely satisfied, like he'd just accomplished the very goal he'd tackled. What could he possibly be after?

Still, Raine kept his eyes in narrowed slits. "Very well, William. May I call you William?"

La Pointe nodded slowly.

Raine showed his teeth, appearing almost feral. "Have you ever had a pet, William?"

Kennedi poised her mouth in a *Wh . . .*, ready to burst into the conversation, when the answer came.

"Yes." La Pointe's voice took on a dreamy, distant tone. "When I was a boy, I had a bearded dragon."

"Aye, yes," commented Raine. "What was your wee dragon's name now?"

Kennedi huffed. "Seriously, Mister Abarta. Can you get back to the matter at hand?"

Raine closed his eyes, then looked up at her and nodded. "How long do I have remaining?"

The clock on the wall didn't seem to move fast enough. "Three minutes," she ground out. It didn't matter though. Once her end of this stupid bargain was done, she'd have him escorted out of the station and make it abundantly clear that he was never, ever to return unless it was in cuffs. His line of questioning was seriously incompetent. Silly. What the hell could he have hoped to gain from this? Curiosity be damned, she shouldn't have catered to his strange requests. Hoping the next 180 seconds would go much, much faster, she rolled her eyes and gave him a *wrap-it-up* sign.

CHAPTER 4

RAINE

IGNORING KEN, RAINE REACHED ACROSS the table, touched La Pointe's wrist, and prodded slowly, "No, I was correct at first about your bearded dragon. What was his name, William? Or Billy. That's what your mother would have called you now sure."

La Pointe's voice answered, but Raine discerned no words. Instead, the vision of the poised, steely-gray haired man clouded, and Raine slid into twelve-year-old Billy's skin. The young La Pointe's pride and joy over earning his first pet by doing all his chores and making the honor roll. In the pet store, he held a bearded dragon and whispered the name he'd decided on, "Nabu," thinking it sounded majestic and dragonly. The scales felt cool, metallic under his fingers, and Billy grinned up at his mother, her dark curls styled to perfection and a red polka-dot band tied around her hair. The joy blurred, smudged by more recent memories. Raine dismissed the happy memory he'd found, the one that allowed him inside, and pilfered through the few recent memories he could reach in La Pointe's mind. He could only dig so far in a couple of minutes, and he didn't want to surface further memories that would complicate the matter. Concentrating, his eyes shifted as images flew by like he was running through long, endless halls filled with both candid photos and portraits, until a splash of red crossed his vision. Raine stopped and dove into the pain associated with the darkening red. He rewound time from that moment and released his concentration to let the scene play out. His fingers curled arthritically as he stepped into an aged body and absorbed the memory—sights, sounds, smells, emotion, everything.

Despair exploded in his chest as his hand shakily reached out and picked up the familiar gun, the pool of blood spreading around his love . . . Michelle's . . . body. What happened? Why would anyone want to harm her? His lungs constricted, air thick and impossible to breathe. She'd never been anything but kind, recently spending every day at the hospice center. Words, a scream, a cry or plea for help, lodged in his churning gut. Maybe it wasn't her, he told himself irrationally. Crazed, confused thoughts screamed at him to reach down and shake her, to turn her face up and maybe see that it was a stranger. It had to be a hoax; Halloween was close. But his feet were glued and his knees were locked; he couldn't bend. He trembled in shock, staring at the vibrating gun and the blood turning Michelle's hair from a sun-kissed blonde to a blackening red. But then, there was the gun. The door closed. A gift box. Silken red lingerie half unfolded. The tissue paper folded over the side, soaking up more of her blood.

He reached for the note card; it shook in his hand too,

a blood smear on one corner. He didn't drop the gun. Why didn't he drop the gun? Note in one hand and iron in the other, he read:

Looking forward to seeing you in this. Soon.

All the love,

Mal

In this? In this lingerie? An affair? No . . . no . . . no-no-no! His eyes prickled; tears were on the edge about to spill—

Raine sucked in a breath, swallowing against La Pointe's shock and sorrow, now his too. So in the midst of finding his wife murdered, the poor man also learned she'd been unfaithful. What a gut punch. Raine studied him across the table. If he felt so low, why didn't this man glow with a desperate need for levity? Why had Vanessa, but not him? Seconds. Raine only had seconds remaining. He pressed his lips together and rewound the memory to just before William La Pointe arrived at the house. The scene worked in reverse until he stood outside in the night air, body ready to fold into a relaxing chair near the fire as he pushed it further, uphill toward his home. Devereux Court—the very court where Raine had been only the night before. Again, Raine dove fully into the experience.

La Pointe had spent longer than he wanted at Vincent's campaign headquarters and ignored the ache in his hip as he climbed the hill. He could already taste the whiskey and sweet tobacco from his pipe, and he yearned for Michelle's easy company. Every last detail depicted a normal autumn evening in the city. Cars lined the streets, the neighbors tucked quietly into their townhomes. A few lights still shone in the lower windows, but most of the first floors had already gone dark. As he passed

Mr. MacCaibe's home, a light went off and he made a mental note to check on the recluse across the way the following day, but he kept walking . . . one foot in front of the other . . . almost there. He scanned the cars, naming neighbors mentally as he took in each familiar vehicle, except two, a white sedan and—

"Okay. That's quite enough," Ken snapped.

Raine jumped. Yanked back to the present, he stood, the chair careening and falling against the wall as the pressure of the three people's suspicious glares scorched him. William La Pointe blinked and shook his head. Ken reached for Raine's arm, held him stable enough to stand as he breathed through the shock and eased his weight to the right, away from his own now-aching hip. He'd had stayed inside for too long; time moved differently when memory walking. It'd take some time to feel like himself again.

Ken eyed him suspiciously, as if she thought he might fall at any minute. After he nodded and shooed her away, she stuck her head out the door and called, "Gold and Clark!" and held the door open as they entered. "Mr. Gorman, Senator La Pointe, these officers will escort your client to the DA's office, then back to Devereux Court."

Vic Clark scratched the bridge of his nose and jumped in, "Yep, everything's ready. Just spoke with the DA; paperwork's waitin'."

"I'll grab the anklet and meet you out back," said Gold.

Mr. Gorman closed his briefcase, stood, buttoned his suit jacket, and motioned for his client to join him. William La Pointe stared at Raine as he moved, clearly unable to tear away his gaze until he'd stepped through the door and the barrier sealed between them. Raine sagged.

"What the hell was that?" Ken snapped.

Raine shifted his eyes, flitting glances around the room and searching for what might sound like a normal answer. His hands were trembling, now from more than just having held the gun. The urge to feed on someone's levity was becoming palpable inside, but uncertainty about what she'd witnessed while he'd been inside the memory set his nerves on fire. At length, he stammered. "Uh, ah, just trying to get a feel for the man." Yeah, that was truth enough. He picked up the fallen chair and tucked it back under the table, drummed his fingers on the aluminum back, then started for the door. Hand on the lever and viewing only speckled floor tiles and the brown, polished toes of Ken's boots, he added, "La Pointe didn't do it," then pulled the door open and limped away as fast as he could manage.

KENNEDI

THAT SPOT BETWEEN HER BROWS—THE focal point where all her concentration gathered if something didn't quite make sense—felt heavy as Raine pulled the door and breezed out. Crazy. The man was off his proverbial rocker. But something about those last words, *La Pointe didn't do it,* had been so incredibly assured. Could faeries read minds? She didn't have tons of experience with the Fae, but wouldn't it be common knowledge if they could? She'd ask West. Call it intuition, call it experience, call it insanity, but what the bard had said made her doubt La Pointe's guilt.

Kennedi popped her eyes wide, and she pushed off the wall toward the door. The junior officers, lawyer, and William La Pointe had gone down the back stairwell, and Raine stepped unevenly but determinedly toward the elevators as if he were a wounded animal trying to escape. His hands shook at his sides until one lifted and he dug his fingertips into his shoulder muscles. He surveyed the open office, twitching his gaze from one area to another, and casting glances backward over his shoulder. Outside the interrogation room, Kennedi leaned on the wall, watching while he limped away. He halted suddenly at the open waiting room door, his attention clearly drawn to something inside. He held a hand at the back of his neck and twisted to meet Vanessa La Pointe. Kennedi narrowed her eyes. *Interesting.* She'd gleaned that they knew each other before, but this confirmed the suspicion.

For the first time since he walked through the door that morning, Raine seemed paranoid. He looked pale in profile, darkness gathering under the eye she could see. *Had he been that way before? Or in the room? No,* she decided. Something had changed. He looked as though he were coming off a drug high, or possibly he was guilty of something. Too far to hear more than a murmur, Kennedi studied the pair. Raine's fidgeting calmed as he spoke in hushed voices to Vanessa, and the pinch on his face—

"You all right, Craine?" a gruff voice distracted her train of thought.

She spun, but seeing her old mentor, she sighed. "West. What are you doing back down here?"

"Can't seem to stay away. The OD case is going nowhere. No evidence, and the girl won't talk. Probably part of that faerie-loving—" West pressed his lips together, censoring himself for a change. "We just have too many of those sympathizers in this town."

Kennedi rolled her eyes. The old feud between humans and Fae never seemed to ease, and truly, she wanted nothing to do with it. As much as any officer of the law, she wanted to see justice served. However, she simply couldn't see hunting down one race for coupling with another. Everyone knew the addictive consequences of becoming emotionally attached. If they made that choice, well, who was she to object? She shook her head and went to her desk with a look back to the scene she'd been observing before.

Gone. They were both gone.

She moved toward her desk; West followed. She shouldn't say anything. It might cause a deeper conversation. But West knew her stance, so she ventured in a tone that she hoped dismissed the subject, "Can't prosecute a person for believing something different than you, West."

His boot heels clicked on the tile behind her. "I suppose. Anyway, I was heading out for a late lunch. Thought I'd see if you wanted to join?"

When she sat behind her desk, he sat on the corner of her desk and shot her that smooth grin of his—the one he used to win over so many of the ladies. As his former protégé, she'd seen all his tricks and charm on full display at one point or another, and it wouldn't work on her. She tried to ignore her growling stomach. "Maybe, though I should question this other woman who showed up with the La Pointes. Wanna sit in? Then we can grab a bite."

"Hell yeah." West slapped his black-denim-clad thigh and leaned forward, ready to launch into action.

"Hang on there, cowboy. I wanna take a spin through the data before running in cold." She looked over to the group of rookies congregating by the coffee machine. "Harris," she called to one, "can you prep Dr. Elanna Bell for questioning?"

"Sure thing," the boy—yeah, he looked that young

with his platinum-blond hair, round face, and dimples—put down the cup and skipped over.

"She's in visitor's waiting. The older woman who's"—Kennedi raised her brows—"dressed for a soiree."

Harris hopped to his task as Kennedi pulled up the case on her laptop. West popped a piece of gum in his mouth, crossed a booted foot over one knee, and bounced his toe impatiently.

"What's got you all riled up?" she asked as she perused the file, looking for the background on Dr. Bell.

"Pure boredom," he grumbled.

Kennedi held up a hand. "Okay, okay. Just give me two minutes."

West hopped up. "I'll meet you in observation."

She made a sound in her throat, half acknowledging him as she searched on the computer. Finally finding the name, she double-clicked and read:

Dr. Elanna Bell

Category: Friend of Deceased

Age: 58

Place of Birth: Hudson, Wisconsin

Interesting, she'd been raised in the same small town as the victim, so she wondered if they had known each other as children.

Marital Status: Single, never married

Harris's voice distracted her read, and Kennedi looked up to see Elanna Bell with her hand resting in the crook of the rookie's arm.

"Dark roast, medium, or light?" he offered, clearly

mesmerized.

Dr. Bell smiled at the boy and answered in her sweetest voice, "Medium, thank you."

"Cream? Sugar?" Harris beamed as he took her order.

Kennedi cleared her throat and eyed the rookie. The last thing she needed was a boy fawning over the family friend . . . not that Dr. Bell was discouraging the attention. Harris dropped her hand and moved into action, and Kennedi went back to the screen.

> *Occupation: Psychologist, Bell Family Therapy*
>
> *Parents: Samuel Bell, father—deceased. Jody Bell, mother—living at Willow Creek Senior Living*
>
> *Children: None*
>
> *Education: BS Applied Psychology, Brown University, MS Marriage and Family Therapy, Brown University; PhD Advanced studies in Human Behavior, Brown University*
>
> *Associations and Memberships: American Psychological Association (APA), membership current. Brown College Alumni Association, membership current. Alpha Chi Omega, alumni.*

Kennedi switched screens to double check. Both the victim, Michelle, and her husband, the prime suspect, William, had also attended Brown University. She lined up the windows on the screen. Both Michelle and Elanna had Alpha Chi Omega listed under associations and memberships. Michelle had received her MBA from Brown, then moved with her boyfriend William to Wickney. Elanna followed once she'd obtained her doctorate. It didn't seem like there was much else there except the life-long friendship between the victim and Elanna. Kennedi opened the image of the note card found at the crime scene and re-read the neatly penned script down to the signature—Mal. She clicked print. Maybe Elanna would be able to shed some light on that.

While she waited for the ancient printer to complete its work, she flipped back over to the virtual whiteboard and scanned the relationship diagram—images of the victim and her husband, their children Vincent and Vanessa, Vincent's pregnant wife Coralyn, and Elanna Bell along with every friend, neighbor, and acquaintance related of the La Pointes. A box with a blank space for the photo stared back at her labeled *Mal.* Their political opponents were also depicted in the diagram. Everyone whose name should be on that board was, pictures and all. But she couldn't shake Raine's presence for the better part of the morning.

The printer continued to churn. Images always took longer to print.

When she had scrolled all the way to the bottom, Kennedi added a new block to the screen. In the *Status* field, she selected *Suspect* from the list, tabbed the cursor to the *Name* field, and paused, tickling the keys with her fingers. Did she have justification for this? Her fingers worked, tapping but not really typing, and the screen blurred before her eyes as independent bits of information fluttered around in her mind's eye. At length, she returned to the *Status* field and changed it to *Person of Interest.* After all, she wasn't quite ready to read him his rights.

The printer finished, but before swiping the printout of Mal's note and attending to Dr. Bell's interrogation, she quickly typed: Raine Abarta.

CHAPTER 5

RAINE

RAINE LAY ON THE BED he never used for the mortal inconvenience of sleep, staring at the bumpy ceiling. After he had crawled through La Pointe's memory, as he limped toward the door, Vanessa had called his name and come to him from the waiting room. Despite the fact that her aura had shone with desperation for good news, he'd averted his eyes in an attempt to ignore how he thirsted for her levity, and he assured her that everything would be hunky-dory with a little time. Granted, he had no way to know if or when his reassurance would come to pass. She'd wrapped her arms around him, squeezing so tightly he'd gotten high right there in the Wickney Police Department and relished every moment of it. He needed that fix . . . to feed on her relief, to sate his withdrawals, and to help him ignore the pain he'd invited into his body. The surge of her energy eased his muscles, but his body still felt decrepit from melding with the senior La Pointe. The Danu-forsaken dangers of pilfering around in the mortal mind. Their bodies and minds were so strange to any Fae being, it always took him off guard when he felt the aftershocks.

While mortals slept to recover, such was uncommon among Fae. Even when they were as exhausted as Raine was then, they only dropped into an aware stillness. He'd limped all the way back to his flat on Aldgate Avenue, fallen into bed, and stared at the pockmarked ceiling for hours and hours on end, hoping his body would heal enough to move again without the constant aches.

Judging by the angle of the deep-orange light entering his flat, evening fell upon Wickney—a full day and then some had passed. He tested the leg and hip and said a long thanks to the Goddess that he'd finally recovered from the trip down William La Pointe's memory lane. In the unlikely event the two of them ever became closer, he'd have to tell him to get that pain checked out. Raine couldn't fathom how someone lived with it day in and day out.

He sat on the edge of the bed overlooking the street below. Horns blared. He ran a hand over his head, then stretched his arms and flexed his hands—glamour gone, his three fingers and thumb no longer throbbed. He certainly didn't look forward to sliding back into the four-fingered mortal glamour, but he wouldn't be able to leave his flat until he did. He couldn't sneak away without the widow O'Rourke next door asking how he was or if he'd found that special girl yet.

After all he'd seen in William La Pointe's mind, he had some loose ends he wanted to inquire about at the Local U that evening. Raine stood and stretched his legs, hips, and back, then sighed as he felt the thrum of the withdrawals returning. Vanessa La Pointe burned hot one way or the other; her emotional swings were extreme at best. In fact, Raine suspected her ups and downs might be what the human doctors meant by mood disorders. But, then again, who was he to say? All he knew was tonight, he needed to find someone else to make him a little happy so he didn't have to return to her right away. If he kept satiating his need with her energy, he'd never function without a regular fix. Yet the power of lifting her particular emotions was something he now yearned for. His mouth watered just thinking about it.

"No, Raine. You'll manage better with smaller doses," he scolded himself, and went to the shower—one mortal invention he absolutely adored. Thankfully, he hadn't returned to his home in Faerie for a long time, and that made walking away from the addiction a good deal easier.

Showered and dressed, he ventured out onto the nighttime streets of Wickney. Streetlamps flickered to life and cast an amber glow on the sidewalks as Raine wandered through the city square to the Local U, the lower level of the Local pub and better known to the Fae as the Underground. The upper bar catered to the college crowd in the evenings, which provided a nice cover for the Fae gathering in the lower levels. Maximus Linardi owned both. Maximus wasn't Fae, but he certainly was one of the mortals who'd been helped along in life by a faerie or two, and he'd joined the Alliance years before in homage to his Fae patrons. Raine recalled the love note that'd been at the scene of Michelle La Pointe's murder. He'd immediately wondered if Mal was short for Maximus Linardi. Now it was time to find out.

The temperature inside sweltered and bass thumped over the din of drunken college students crowding around the bar and leaking onto the dance floor. Tonight would be a crazy one, if the horde already present gave any indication. Raine hooked a right inside the door and stopped at the coat check. The young couple in front of him exchanged their coats for tickets and moved along.

When the attendant, Candi, turned, she immediately leaned closer to Raine and twirled one of her pink pigtails around a finger. "Haven't seen you in ages, love," she flirted.

Raine shelled his overcoat and handed it across the counter. "Nach tú, doll. Why've they got you working coats?"

"Oh, I'm giving the regular a break before it gets busy. I don't take the stage until eleven. You stayin' for the show?" Candi fluttered her dark lashes and flashed green eyes at him suggestively.

He reached over and laced his fingers with hers. "You bet sure."

Her immediate flood of joy trickled into him. Candi's emotions were simple and straightforward, and working in the Underground, she knew exactly who she was dealing with. He could drink just a little from her and remain even keeled. No withdrawals: she was safe.

She leaned closer. "Some girls are headed back to my place after. Wanna join?"

Siphoning the happiness she emitted, Raine had to shake himself clear to keep everything in order. The last thing he needed was any human getting attached, addicted, or worse, ending up at the local hospital in Fae detox. It'd send that West character into high gear. "Maybe another time then. Will Maximus be in tonight?" Raine asked.

"Rumors below say yes, but no one's seen the boss man yet." Candi released his hand, tightened one pigtail then the other, then jutted her chin. "Line's buildin'. See ya downstairs."

Around the coat check and down a dark hallway beyond the restrooms, Raine stopped at a door marked *Private* and pushed through. Ropes of dark pink, almost purple lights lined the stairway downward. The patrons of the Underground weren't teeming yet like the college crowd did upstairs, but a few lingered around a horseshoe-shaped bar. Black walls gave the illusion that the violet-lit center of the club faded off into a void. Serving drinks downstairs tonight, Dick silently lifted a bar-towel-covered hand in greeting; Raine returned the wave. Lights above the quiet stage where the show would take place later trended toward white, and clusters of empty tables crowded before it, awaiting viewers. Raine circled the bar and crossed the likewise vacant dance floor; his heels tapped on the hardwood as he moved to the back where Maximus kept an office. He hoped the owner might have slunk in through his private door in the alley, and if so, Raine might be able to slake his curiosity before the night devolved into the full party that loomed.

Raine knocked on an unlabeled door and stood aside to wait. Under the quieter music downstairs, the thumping from the bass filtered through the ceiling. That'd be drowned out as things kicked up in the Underground, but the evening was young yet. He turned when the door opened, and stood facing two un-glamoured Fae—both wider in stature than he, one with a Noble marque, but both lower in Fae rank. Raine raised a hand and dropped his glamour, allowing them to see everything Fae about him, the shifting of his eyes, his own marque, his four-digit hands, and the slight iridescent pallor to his skin. They both dipped their heads, deferring to Raine's royal position, and the marqued Fae opened the door and went inside. The common Fae held forward a three-fingered hand, ushering Raine inside.

Entering from the darker club, Raine squinted against the office-like lighting. A lounge lay between the door and Maximus Linardi's office, with black leather seating and cocktail tables between each pair of chairs.

Raine had never met either of the proprietor's Fae protectors, but the one's marque labeled him a child of the noble Fae, Saffron, with whom Raine was quite familiar. Positions of Fae royalty and nobility were only mildly observed in the mortal realm, typically with the bowed head of deference as the two guards had done. Any other courtesies were saved for Faerie. The common rule here was to behave as mortally as possible, and these Fae had the job of protecting the interests—probably both physical and practical—of Maximus Linardi.

The child of Noble Saffron asked pointedly, "Do you have an appointment with Mr. Linardi?"

"I do not, but there's an urgent ma—"

Saffron's child held up his marqued arm. "You may make an appointment, but Mr. Linardi has no availability in his schedule this evening."

Raine had been amid mortals for so long, his first instinct was to try to *nudge* the faeries before him, but he pressed his mouth into a tight line when he recalled that wouldn't work with his kind. Suddenly, the room felt more like the buffer zone it was rather than a lounge. After a moment of thought, he asked, "What is your name, child of Saffron?"

"Simmon." The black-haired Fae held out a hand to his partner. "This is Berry."

Berry dipped his head again but deferred all conversation to Simmon. Everything about their manners seemed curt and professional, showing the prescribed royal deference but also serving their duties to their boss. Raine couldn't see an opening and had to commend Maximus's wisdom in choosing faeries to protect his privacy and schedule.

Regardless, he tried a human tactic. "Does he have any *paid* appointments available? What would be the cost to see him this evening?"

Simmon shook his head gravely, his black hair not releasing from where he had it slicked back to a blunt line at the base of his skull. "Mr. Linardi isn't taking visitors tonight or for the next few days. Would you like me to check his schedule for next week?"

Raine huffed, then started pacing and rubbing a hand over his chin. As he walked, he glanced past the two guards at the door on the far side of the room—the one that supposedly led into Linardi's office.

Saffron's son clearly read his chain of thought. "Raine of Lady Amaryllis"—Simmon used the full and formal title, clearly emphasizing his knowledge of Raine's rank, but it meant very little in this situation, or to Raine in general—"any attempt to sneak past wouldn't be in your best interest."

"Truly, you'll protect the mortal's interest over that of your kindred, will you?" Raine tsked.

Simmon smirked. "The way I understand the matter, you've been banished. And maybe you can help me here, but I fail to see how anything with Mr. Linardi is a Fae matter."

Danu, he had a point there. It was only a Fae matter in that Raine—stupid as his addiction to her levity was—jonesed for the high he'd get from Vanessa once he'd cleared her father. He took a deep breath and pushed it through his nose. Maybe it'd be better this way. Make him wait a while, and perhaps his withdrawals would ease. Vanessa's rising spirits were the most addictive thing he'd experienced in a long time, since the Witch of Buchenwald. Raine pinched the bridge of his nose. That'd been a dark time. Ilse Koch got off in the extreme by collecting the numbered forearm tattoos of those who'd perished in the camps under her orders. Then there'd been that one other incident with his sister and Delphine LaLaurie, the one that'd resulted in his banishment from Fae. Raine shook his head, *No, no, not going there.* Vanessa was totally different. She was only in search of the truth about her mother's murderer. How could that have been dangerous?

Raine relented. "All right. Find me a time next week then," he said, recommitting to walking the straight and narrow, to only drinking enough emotional levity to keep his nature in check. Candi would be better for that.

Simmon donned gloves, then pulled out his smartphone and a stylus. After a couple of swipes, he said, "How's next Thursday at midnight?"

"Done," Raine answered without a second thought. "Give your father my greetings," he added as he reapplied his glamour and moved for the exit.

Back in the club, a few more patrons had turned out, but the atmosphere was still pretty chill. He leaned on the back of a stool and waved over the bartender. "Neat."

Dick looked at the stock in bar back and answered, "Gotta run upstairs."

"I'll take the first booth near the stage," said Raine and marched in that direction while Dick made for the stairs.

Seated at the dark, semi-private table with a good

view of the stage, Raine closed his eyes and pinched the bridge of his nose again. He'd enjoy the show tonight, but the conundrum of Michelle La Pointe's murder tickled the other part of his Fae nature—dìomhaireachdanseòlta. Faediom, he called it. The fact that Vanessa's problem fed both his levity addiction and relied on solving something: a mystery, a crime; Ifrinn, it was the best kind of puzzle! And the combination made for something he couldn't leave alone. It was like a scab that itched to be picked.

Now that he'd walked through William La Pointe's memories, they were his as well. But now, he no longer had the physical consequences of the memory walk, so he reviewed what he'd seen. The identity of Mal would obviously have to wait until next week unless Vanessa knew about her mother's affair. He made a note to swing back by her townhouse. Tomorrow, he added as an afterthought. Practicing moderation, right? Anything else, another clue or hint, should have been there in the murder scene or in what he'd relived. The street. He tried to focus on the scene just before La Pointe made it to Devereux Court. Nothing truly off-kilter presented itself inside the memory. He could now name whose car belonged to whom with the exception of the white sedan and the darker car. He strained within the memory to recall the license plate number or the form of the darker vehicle. It seemed larger than the sedan, but that didn't help at all. Too fuzzy. He'd been ejected from the memory walk at just the time where something might have become clear. Raine slammed his hand down on the table.

"Whoa!" Dick pulled back the lowball glass he'd been lowering to the table, the amber liquid sloshing as he did.

"Sorry," Raine said. "Just a frustrating night." He didn't think he'd be able to clarify that vision, so he'd need to make another pass at the memory walk, and the thought of going through that recovery again made him shiver. Or . . . The only other option available was . . .

He needed to visit Fae.

He knew of one and only one faerie who might disregard his mother's displeasure and help him inside.

"Should I leave the bottle?" asked Dick.

Raine nodded, eying the bartender speculatively. "You have waiters tonight?" he made small talk, wanting to make it seem like he was duly interested, and with the show tonight, it'd be one of the busiest nights for the Underground. Once he set the bartender at ease by getting him onto a topic he knew well, Raine would ask what he really needed to know.

"Yeah," Dick checked his watch, "but they're not on duty for another half hour." He leaned on the back of the bench opposite Raine. "That's about the time the crowd should build anyway. What brings you out tonight?"

Raine sipped the twelve-year old scotch. "Have you seen Trevon, by any chance?"

Dick thought for a few beats, pursed his lips, and finally answered, "Not for several weeks. You need anything else? Food?"

"Nah." Raine lifted his glass again.

"All right. You know where I'll be. Wave me over if you need something before Tina shows."

Alone again, Raine sipped the whiskey and kicked his legs up onto the bench, settling in and waiting for the show to begin. He didn't relish the thought, but he'd likely be staking out this place for the next several nights in search of his brother.

Two scotches in, a form blocked the light from the stage area, then slid into the other side of the booth.

Without the light from behind framing the figure, Raine recognized his intruder, straightened, and grinned as if he'd just found a pot of gold. "To what do I owe this extreme pleasure, Ken?"

KENNEDI

THAT GODFORSAKEN NICKNAME THIS STREET performer had decided was a perfect fit slithered under her skin. "I told you not to call me that. Detective Craine will suffice." She focused warning eyes on him, a man she really hadn't wanted to go in search of.

Raine Abarta turned and dropped his legs under the table, inching to the middle of the bench and leaning as close to her as possible. Kennedi fought the urge to back away as he wagged his brows. "You also told me never to come back to the station with a strong hint you never wanted to lay eyes on me again. You drink scotch?" He turned and waved to the bar.

"This isn't a social call."

The corners of Raine's eyes and mouth pulled down, his whole face stretching in an exaggerated frown as if she just told him his puppy had been hit by a truck. Kennedi trained her face, remaining absolutely composed, one-hundred percent professional, as a waitress in skin-tight jeans, a cropped sweatshirt drooping off one shoulder, hair tied in high twin buns, and a collar around her neck reading *PUDDIN* sashayed over. The only thing missing was the red and blue in the hair.

"Heya, Raine! Long time no see." Harley Quinn's twin plopped a hand on his shoulder.

"Tina, can you get my guest a glass?"

"Sure thing."

Do not roll your eyes, Kennedi! "You know, Mr. Abarta—"

"Raine," he snipped, reaching across the table in a far-too-intimate gesture. He seemed disappointed when Kennedi tucked her hands into her lap. After a tiny droop in his gaze, he refocused on her and flashed a more predatory smile. "Please, Ken. Call me Raine."

She pursed her lips. He really wasn't about to let go of that moniker. Fine. If he wanted to dance, she could play the game too. "You know, *Raine*, I could arrest you simply for being here. Maybe I should."

Regardless of the front Maximus Linardi put up as the Local U being an outlet for the Wickney Performers Guild, WPD had the underground club labeled as the place where faeries and humans congregated. West was constantly on a stakeout here, waiting for the next human to overdose on Fae juju, or whatever it was that caused the high. Kennedi wasn't about to try to find out.

Raine sipped his whiskey, sighing loudly as he swallowed. "On what charges? And exactly how would you explain *your* presence?"

The music crescendoed, and Tina returned with three lowball glasses—one empty, one with water and a stir-straw, and the other with ice. "Forgot to ask how you take it," she tilted her head and lifted a shoulder, "so I'm coverin' all the bases."

Kennedi didn't care to tell her that she *didn't* take it, and she was here on business, so she offered a professional and dismissive smile, and said, "Thanks." When the waitress moved along, she pushed the glasses aside, at the same time casually answering Raine's prior question, "Well naturally, I followed a suspect."

Ever the performer, Raine put a hand over his chest and feigned shock. "You cannot possibly mean to imply *moi*?"

Lights dimmed, and the audience that'd been filtering slowly in hooted and hollered as a jazz band moved into the pit next to the stage, the drummer pounding out a sequence on the set. When he finished, the tuxedoed announcer stepped to the microphone and started, "Gentlepeople and, ahem . . . Welcome to Wickney's Wild Wednesday at the Local U." Obviously, for their protection from any law enforcing lurkers, he wouldn't greet or name any Fae outright.

Kennedi forced out a quick breath through her nose. There went the hope that she'd be in and out before the spectacle began.

Raine winked at her and raised his voice to speak over the wail of the saxophone echoing the welcome. "Well, regardless of your purpose, I'm happy to have company for the burlesque tonight. Help yourself to the Bowmore." He waived a hand to the bottle.

Leaning toward him, she asked, "How are you so sure he didn't do it?"

The emcee interrupted, "Give a warm welcome to our first performer of the evening, Candi Crush!"

"He who?" asked Raine, looking at Kennedi over his glass. Before she could answer, his gaze flitted away. "Shhh, Ken. Candi's a doll. Watch." He lifted the glass toward the stage as a young woman took the spotlight.

White-blonde hair fading to pink ends and a sparkly dress to match grabbed and held the audience's attention. Wrapping her pink-gloved hands and the white fur boa around herself, Candi Crush posed with her back to the audience and peered over one shoulder with a *come-hither* smile painted on glossed pink lips. She dropped her false lashes as the band started a slow jazz number.

Frustration gurgled in Kennedi's chest, but she watched for a solid minute, maybe more, as Candi Crush performed a number of sultry hip sways, rotations, and thrusts, eventually turning to face the audience and revealing the slit in the front of the dress all the way to her waist and some strappy panty things beneath. At that point, Kennedi cut her attention over to Raine, who was clearly engrossed. One corner of his mouth tilted upward, and his eyes narrowed intently.

The beat quickened, the saxophone trilled toward the songs finale, the suggestive dance continued, the audience cheered, and Kennedi seethed.

As soon as Candi struck the final pose and the applause went up, Kennedi glared at a clapping Raine. "Okay," she began, taking advantage of the break. "How are you certain William La Pointe didn't do it?"

"Why are you so certain he did?" Raine asked without so much as a quirk of the brow.

Kennedi rubbed her hands together under the table. "I shouldn't be talking with a civilian about this."

Raine ignored her frustration, placed his now-empty glass on the table, and reached for the bottle. "All right. What evidence do you have against him?"

"The man was holding the gun," she blurted, and the rest just kept coming. "Lab confirmed the bullet removed from the body is from that gun. No other prints. Book closed. The end." She threw her hands in the air.

The bard twisted his lips to the side as if trying to decide what to say, but at the same time, he seemed to be getting keyed up on the conversation. The emcee tapped the mic, and it squealed. Kennedi plugged her ear closest to the stage just as Candi Crush appeared at the table, slid in next to Raine, and threaded her fingers through his hair. After he leaned over and gave her a quick peck, she swiped a pink-tipped finger across his lips to remove the glistening pink. "Enjoying the show, love?"

"Always." Raine hugged her tighter, then motioned across the table. "Candi, this is Ken."

Kennedi erased her scowl and forced a smile, reluctantly accepting Candi's hand to shake. "Detective Kennedi Craine," she corrected.

The dancer's pink-painted mouth and heavily lined eyes rounded. "Okay then." She pulled her hand back and gave her attention back to Raine, lowering her voice. "Thanks for the boost, babe. My next number's way better. Hope you stay."

Candi Crush left, thankfully, and Raine focused back on Kennedi with a series of utterings she couldn't understand. Mumbling. Grumbling. His eyes looking across the table as if he were reading a book. Then his face shifted. It felt as if he were tackling something head-first, a passion lighting his features with hyperfocus.

"Okay." He bounced a little on the booth bench. "Let's get back to it. Where'd the gun come from?"

So direct and insightful, unlike the questions he'd asked when talking with William La Pointe. She blinked at him several times. Of course they'd investigated the gun immediately with a background check on the serial number, but she hadn't expected him to think of it. "Purchased in the Burgh at Tofer's Armory."

"The Burgh?" Raine asked as he poured another dram.

"That's right. And licensed to William La Pointe,

along with one other at the same time."

"Any reason he wouldn't have gone somewhere closer to home?"

"Only place in the Wickney area that sells refurbished Webley Mark 3 .38 revolvers. La Pointe is a collector."

"Interesting." Raine tapped a finger across his lips. "And you know for certain William La Pointe purchased the gun in question?"

"Yeah." Kennedi nodded, but then thought about that a little. "I mean, he would have had to show ID, fill out the registration, and wait the three days before he could take possession."

"Ken, Ken, Ken," he chided and angled his head. "That wrinkle in your forehead says there's possible doubt. Of course, if you're planning to prosecute, there can be no reasonable doubt, true?" He took another drink. The bottle was a quarter gone, but he seemed stone-cold sober.

Odd. How the hell had this jokester turned into someone so shrewd?

The emcee took the stage again and introduced the next performer. Kennedi ignored the distraction and so did Raine as they both leaned across the table, his breath smelling of the peaty spirit.

Focus on the conversation, Kennedi. She was happy at last to have him intent on her topic of choice. "I'll get the receipts just to be certain, but there's no logic in someone else having purchased such specific guns disguised as a big-name collector."

Raine shrugged, a look of disbelief on his face. "Unless, of course, he's being framed now."

Kennedi had to take a deep breath to keep herself

centered. "And what evidence leads you to such a conclusion? That seems like a long shot." She maintained care not to speak about the note from Mal. That would be the only likely candidate if anyone was planning to frame Senator La Pointe. But who was this Mal person?

"Absolutely none," he answered with a shrug. "Just planting the seed of doubt, like any good lawyer will do. And that lawyer Mr. La Pointe had sure seemed worth every penny in the deep, deep pockets of the La Pointe family from Devereux Court, didn't he?"

"What? How do you know where he lives?"

"That's common intel." Raine dropped the empty glass back onto the table and gave her a look that asked if she took him for a fool. The fact that she did didn't sway him in the slightest. "I'll bet the bartender even knows that detail. Should we check?" he teased, and moved as if starting toward the bar.

How was he not showing any signs of intoxication? But his tolerance wasn't important, and holy hell, he was right about the doubt factor. Not only did she need the evidence that'd show his guilt, she needed to eradicate any possible evidence that he wasn't guilty. And she couldn't get it out of her mind how in tune Raine was with a family he had no real connection to. She toyed with a coaster the waitress had left, poured the water over the melting ice, and downed it.

"Scotch clears my mind," Raine said.

She twisted in the booth to watch the current trouper—a younger man, with small dreadlocks bouncing around his head as he poetry slammed something about lessons from math class. He was good, had the audience punctuating his stanzas with *Yeah!*, *Preach!*, or a whistle here and there, but she quickly tuned him out again.

Kennedi slid to the end of the booth.

"Leaving so soon, Ken?" Raine appeared sincerely distraught. "You'll miss the better part of the guild's performance."

She cocked a brow. "Poetry's not my thing. Info seems dried up too. Is there another reason to stay?"

"Truly? I thought we were making wonderful progress, Ken. Thinking we can become Raine and Craine, Wickney's Dynamic Detective Duo." He spread his hands in the air as if there would be a neon sign like he envisioned in his extreme fantasy.

She stared at him accusingly and stood, ready to leave the joker behind and put him out of her mind. She shouldn't have followed him here. Though he was challenging her assumptions, it wasn't serving any good purpose. She yawned.

Shifting his arms to a surrender position, he backpedaled. "Okay, all right, fine." He paused, then smirked. "Craine and Raine?"

"Not a chance," Kennedi snapped.

"Hrmph." Raine twisted his mouth. "Well, what about the lingerie and note?"

Her mouth betrayed her, gaping open for several seconds before she could form the question that demanded an answer. "How the ever-loving hell do you know about those?" With that little question, she'd admitted more than she should have and pressed her lips together. That case information hadn't been made public at all, had in fact been labeled top secret. So where had he come by it?

Really, Kennedi, you know the simplest answer to that. And it had little to do with the possibility he was a faerie. She slid her blazer to the side, exposing the tip of the holstered firearm and, more importantly, the cuffs at her belt.

He backed away, shaking his head and hands. "Whoa, no need for that. I'm only trying to help now."

She lowered herself back into the booth as the slam on stage wrapped and the audience roared.

Raine raised a single brow. "Ya see, Ken, some puzzles just can't be left alone."

CHAPTER 6

RAINE

TWO NIGHTS LATER, RAINE ROUNDED the corner from South High Street onto 10th and climbed the steep hill. Cool night air filled his lungs as he zipped his overcoat. He scanned the quiet city streets, the pointed tips of his dress shoes kicking rhythmically into his lower peripheral vision. Distant voices and a night train three blocks over provided a din of white noise absent of the crickets or frogs he'd hear in a less-urban setting. Amber streetlights cast a deep autumn hue on the sparse number of turning trees artfully placed in boxes along the street. Handfuls of fallen leaves blew past his feet. Two blocks up, Raine took inventory of the cars, naming owner after owner of the machines lining 10th and Pine. A horn blared, then a siren.

This was the third time in as many nights Raine had walked this path—the same steps he'd walked in William

La Pointe's memory. The first time he'd walked this way was after his meeting with Ken at the Local U. Then, his determination had set in, and now he couldn't let go of the mystery. Still, neither the white car nor the darker, larger one was present. Of the neighbors' windows along the street, the first and second floors were dark. Kitchens, home offices, and living rooms were no longer in use at the late hour, the inhabitants having retired to their third-floor bedrooms for the evening.

An interesting insight into human patterns, he thought. Having lived amid the mortals constantly for more seasons than he could count, of course he knew their sleep patterns. However, he rarely considered the small ways those patterns manifested. A wind whipped up the hill, and Raine's body was racked with shivers again. Not only did the cold wind bite, the thought of La Pointe's aching joints lingered. Thank Danu his body wouldn't go through such deterioration, but damn, the after-effects . . . It'd be a long, long time before he went on another memory walk, and in Fae terms, that could be a human decade or more.

After more than two blocks, he crossed the street at an angle, weaving between cars and approached Devereux Court. Numbers two and three were at the mouth of the court and both were dark from bottom to top. Knowing the hours kept by Vincent La Pointe's mayoral campaign, it was likely he and his sister were both at headquarters. In the townhouse that lined the back of the court, number one, the third-floor windows glowed. Raine stopped, watching the windows to see if any shadows would pass. For a good time, nothing.

Though he suspected it was about the hour when most people slept, Raine didn't know the time; he never wore a watch given the way most electronics fritzed when in contact with his skin for more than a few minutes. Bored, he turned toward number three—Vanessa's townhome—and William's light extinguished.

An electronic lock secured her home, and like he'd done before, he made easy work of it. After grasping the doorknob and simply holding it for a few minutes, the electronics inside went haywire. Then, he stepped from the shadows and walked right into Vanessa La Pointe's foyer. He checked the first-floor kitchen and sitting room before climbing the stairs, searching her office and spare bedroom, then going to the third-floor master bedroom to be certain she wasn't sleeping inside. The house presented itself in perfect, maid-prepared order, beds dressed beautifully and all daily-use items tucked away in their proper places.

Raine grinned.

Ideas sizzled.

In the bathroom, he pulled open the first drawer. A hairbrush and flat iron. *Seems like a good pair of kitchen utensils.* He tucked them under his arm. He stopped at the window, pulled back the curtain, and peered out over the sleepy courtyard. Still no sign of Vanessa, so he'd entertain himself for a bit while he waited. Before descending, he pilfered through the linen closet at the top of the stairs, considering the towels and paper products. *I'll come back for those.*

In the first level kitchen, he surveyed all the cabinet doors until he spied one so high it was certainly not used regularly. He climbed onto a stool and peered inside, ran a hand through the dust on a crock pot, chuckled to himself, and placed Vanessa's flat-iron next to the small appliance. Too bad he likely wouldn't see her confusion when she discovered it. *I suppose that's what imagination is for.*

Before leaving the kitchen, he grabbed all the forks from the silver drawer. On his way back upstairs, he spotted a small cabinet in the foyer and exchanged a pair of gloves inside the double doors for the hairbrush, then snagged a keyring from the decorative dish on the surface. Forks in hand, he made his way to Vanessa's office, shoving the gloves in his pocket as he climbed. Raine snickered as he lined the forks up perfectly in the small pen and pencil drawer of her desk, then he snagged all the pens from the cup on the surface and stopped to think, tapping a finger over his pursed lips. *Where would she have the least need to write, but still find these easily?* He skipped as the answer hit him, but first searched the entire townhouse for other pens or pencils she might have in more practical places.

He stored the writing utensils in the third-floor linen closet between the toilet paper and tissues, her keys in the refrigerator, a checkbook under the houseplants near the sliding doors in the back, and gloves between books on a shelf in her office. He exchanged the make-up remover with the hand-soap in the lower powder room, a basil plant with the flowers on the table in the sitting room, and a roll of toilet paper with the box of tissues on the entry table. Standing in the foyer, Raine looked around for the next little move he could make when he caught a glimpse of movement through the front window. He peered outside as the reason he'd come to Devereux Court climbed the steps—Vanessa La Pointe.

He scurried back to the dinette off the kitchen and waited.

The electronic lock beeped. Heels tapped on hardwood, the coat closet door opened then closed, and a pause lingered. Raine held his breath until . . .

"What the . . .?" Vanessa's voice started.

With a hand over his mouth, Raine stifled a chortle—she must have noticed the misplaced toilet paper. Vanessa La Pointe's heels signaled her approach to the kitchen. Lights on, she jumped back, gasping like she'd done the first time he came to visit with a free hand over her chest.

Raine, swallowing the urge to laugh out loud as she held a roll of toilet paper in her other hand, tried to harness his humor enough to level his voice. "Welcome home, Vanessa."

"Shit, Raine. What are you doing here? I hope you have good news," she said, recovering from her start and nonchalantly placing the toilet paper on the counter.

Darn, he thought. That didn't cause her enough confusion.

Vanessa opened a cupboard door, pulled out a wine glass, and held it up with both brows lifted in a *would-you-like-some-too?* question.

"Nah, I'm good. Unless you have scotch?" he suggested with a hopeful lilt.

"Sorry, but that tastes like dirty socks." She crossed the kitchen to the fridge. With a perfectly manicured hand, she pulled the handle and extracted a bottle of white wine from the door without the smallest glance inside.

Raine gritted his teeth. She hadn't seen the keys on the shelf next to the orange juice. Maybe that would be a breakfast surprise. But then again, if she had noticed them, he wasn't certain he could contain his laughter. Though he wouldn't get the chance to see her reactions, this way was better. She'd have lots of time to discover his little hidden gems.

She sidled up to the high-top dining table in the breakfast nook and poured a healthy glass of wine. "So, if you're here, that means you have news?"

Raine eyed her speculatively. A hint of hope flared around her, just whetting his appetite. He drank it in. "Well, I do believe your father didn't murder your mother, and I'm going to help get your father out of this. Just make sure you all keep your optimism high." Truth.

Her mood buoyed, hope burning a little hotter, then fizzled. "But that cop lady doesn't." Vanessa's brows dipped into a V as she gulped the wine, swallowed, and refilled her glass. Raine tasted metal when the silvery lights twinkled in a cloud around her as her need for a pick-up gathered. She spat, "Detective Craine is ready to throw the book at Dad, and everywhere we turn is crawling with reporters. It's horrible."

Raine took a slow, deep breath, his cravings building in the back of his mouth, enough to make it water. He had to sway her mood the other way. The combination of her distress and that little taste of her brief upswing in spirits had his hands trembling. He wrung them under the table. He had to think quick, or he was going to go into full-on withdrawals here in front of her. As Fae, he was unable to outright lie, so he stalled, "I, uh." Then with widening eyes, he recalled a truth: the two unknown cars. "There's evidence of someone else who may have been involved. Maybe a couple of possibilities." Vanessa's emotion bottomed out and started to climb, giddiness rushing back through her and pouring out. He drank, sating the need, with eyes closed in an attempt to hide the relief he felt and how he floated on the high as every hunger, thirst, and tremble inside eased away.

AFTER MEETING WITH VANESSA, HE stepped lightly, almost floated and maybe danced a little, on his way back to the Local. Downstairs in the Underground, he scanned the club in search of Trevon for a second night in a row. *Damn me to Ifrinn. If I don't find him soon, this routine is going to get too predictable.* Without the burlesque or any performances downstairs on a Friday night, the crowd was sparser than it'd been on Wednesday. Dick wasn't working, so Raine flagged over the no-name bartender and waited. He'd seen the guy before but had no desire to get to know him, so he made it short. "Bowmore, twelve, neat." He waited again. So much waiting over the last few days, he was about to go insane. That's what had driven him to creep into Vanessa's townhouse rather than just searching for the suspicious cars. His nerves had been on edge and he needed a bit of his own personal drug to calm them.

No-name placed the drink in front of him. "Anything else?"

Looking squarely at the dark woodgrain, Raine shook his head and pulled the glass closer.

Ken, while she'd pressed him pretty hard on how he knew about the lingerie and note from Mal, had in the end let him be for the last couple of days. He wondered about her as he tossed back the dram and circled his finger in the air for another. Before the unknown bartender could serve, a hand landed on his shoulder.

High enough on Vanessa's levity that his senses were dulled, he turned slowly to see a darker-complexioned version of himself.

Golden sands shifted in Trevon's irises as he flashed a grin. "Heard you were looking for me." The Fae held two of his three unglamoured fingers up to the bartender, seconding Raine's order. "What are we drinking?" His Noble marque shining in the black light gave him away as much as his Fae form.

"Bowmore," Raine focused on the empty lowball in front of him. "How's the faerie realm so, Trevon?" he asked dryly, dreading any answer his brother could give.

Trevon huffed and, ignoring Raine's small talk, said, "Maybe one day I'll convince you that Glengoyne's superior."

"Not likely."

Raine watched him in his peripheral vision. Trevon's gaze weighed on him with impending expectations. Raine braced himself for an interrogation. Clearly, Trevon attempted to sense more about why Raine had searched him out, but worse, he vibrated openly with Fae energy. It boasted of how the queen still welcomed her younger son with open arms, if Amaryllis could be considered the hugging type. Trevon didn't work to hide it in the least, a gloat that cut to Raine's very core.

After downing another shot of scotch, Raine took a deep breath and said on a sigh, "I need to get across the Veil." That was the only way he'd learn more about those two cars without delving into someone's memory again. He needed direction, a clue, something to set him on the trail. He held his breath while Trevon considered.

"That doesn't explain why you need me. Any Fae can help you across. And you're seasoned enough to sneak by the watch in the Wandering Wood."

"I don't know what other kind of wards Amaryllis has set up against my entry," Raine fudged. Truth, but not the entirety of his reasons.

"And?" Trevon prompted, seeing right through Raine's meager attempts.

Raine rolled his eyes. "And I stopped watching the time. I have no idea when the next window is." Still not the full reason.

Trevon sipped his scotch and breathed out at the first burn. "Manipulation is a keen part of our spirit, but you've definitely been away too long. You've gotta be the worst secret-keeper in our history, Raine. Any faerie in this bar could have told you when the next window is. You must do better than that, Brother."

Raine lowered his gaze to the minuscule drop of whiskey remaining in the glass. "Amaryllis forbade every Fae from helping me, and I can no longer open the Veil from this side. Our dear mother, in her wrath, made some deal with either Danu or Aodh to strip me of the ability to find the passage." Truth, but clearly not enough to satisfy the suspicion.

Trevon snorted his disbelief.

Raine turned on the barstool and fixed the Fae with a harsh stare. "Look, I don't know what I'm facing, and I have a shite-ton of questions. I called for you, because I'd like a little aid, and I—obviously in error—thought you might do the *brotherly* thing and help."

Trevon threw his head back and bellowed a laugh at the ceiling, then clapped Raine heavily on the shoulder. "Ah, so, if you were able to find someone to help and you went strutting back into the palace, you're worried about if our sister's still locked away in Danu's Hallowed Hills, about Mother's anger in regards to that whole Madame La Laurie situation. And"—he held his third finger in the air—"if I'm right, you're also worried about how heavy-handed our sweet mother will be about the ultimatum involving Briar?"

That about summed it up. Raine hung his head. "Don't let Amaryllis hear you call her Mother," he said. By Danu, Raine hoped all his brother's assumptions were enough to be believable. He didn't want Trevon or any other Fae involved in the La Pointe case. Selfishly, he wanted the faediom and its solution to himself—or maybe he'd share with Ken. Raine shook his head at that errant thought.

The other Fae chuckled a little more and returned to his drink. "Well, I might fry in Ifrinn for saying so, but some time back home will do you good." He held the glass up to Raine. "'Cuz you're definitely losing your Fae. *Brother.*"

KENNEDI

THE OVERHEAD LIGHTS FLICKERED AND went off, leaving Kennedi Craine cast in the blue-white light from the two monitors hooked up to her laptop in the WPD fifth-floor office. Every other desk in the long, open-air room remained quiet, the monitors black, having timed out after hours of non-use. Interrogation rooms, the guest waiting area, and the captain's office were all dark, but Kennedi had little to return to at her flat on the east side of town. That place was just as cold as this, and she had nothing to occupy her mind there, either, besides sleep. She was getting less and less of that these days, so she spent her time at the office when she needed something to pass the hours. Work never seemed to sleep.

She scanned through a twenty-year-old file, digitized images failing to meet the crisper lines and clarity of the present day's more advanced technology. She moved the mouse to the little encircled triangle, just about ready to watch the reel for maybe the hundred and twentieth time, or maybe five hundredth time. She'd seen it so frequently she could no longer keep track. That very video had haunted her since the first time she'd seen it at eight years old. Before she could click the mouse, a chill crawled from the base of her spine, up her back, and into her hair, tingling her scalp.

Something behind her bumped. The chair groaned as she spun around and scanned the office—blessedly still alone. Then she caught sight of a naked pink tail scurrying along the wall. Kennedi released a breath, reassured that no other late-working detectives or cleaning staff had wandered up behind her.

"Just a rat, Kennedi. Jumpy much, are we?" she mumbled to herself as she turned back to the screen and played the video.

The grainy scene appeared, and the only indication that the footage rolled was the slight jiggle of the camera in the wind and the digital timer in the lower right corner, marking the time of night changing as the seconds and minutes passed—11:07:29, 11:07:30. Another minute and a half of stillness, and there he was in fuzzy form: A man she'd searched high and low to find for so many of her adult years and had come up empty. Every. Single. Time. A face she thought she saw in the mirror from time to time but dismissed as hallucination. He walked across the screen and around the enormous hill at Wickney University Arboretum—the massive gardens protected by the same trust that'd established the college. The entire gardens were gated, but there'd been no footage of the intruder climbing a fence or venturing into any of the other areas. The gate locks hadn't shown any sign of tampering that night either, according to the unsolved case file.

There he was, her father, walking nonchalantly around the hill. More time clicked away on the clock—11:10:22, 11:10:23—and Kennedi watched both the scene and the time. Precisely when the numbers read 11:10:59, something flashed from his wrist, whiting out the camera, and when the image returned to focus at 11:11:01, the man was gone—vanished. He went down in the unsolved case files as a missing person. That second in time had been the very second when her father had disappeared from the Earth's face, and Kennedi had lost her mother to the all-consuming insanity. Caught on film by a rickety old security camera, the few seconds followed by a flash of light remained the only evidence.

She pressed the spacebar, stopping the video she knew went on for another five minutes of jerky, fuzzy footage of a landscape and absolutely no other movement. She reclined in the chair and rubbed her lower lip for a minute, then glanced up at the clock over the door. Almost ten minutes after eleven.

She quickly sat forward and typed in the web address she knew by heart. Yeah, she'd done this a time or two . . . or a hundred . . . before. Maybe obsessive. Maybe compulsive. But hey, everyone had their hobbies, right? The live footage of the arboretum appeared, the time 11:08:43, and her jaw dropped. Two men strode casually up to the hill having what appeared to be an easy conversation.

Kennedi squinted. The quality was far superior to the video she'd just watched, but it was still hard to make out faces in the dim light. She clicked the little square to stretch the image to full screen. Everything pixelated for a minute, then resolved, and Kennedi dropped a fist onto the desk when the face of one of the men rang a bell. It wasn't crystal clear like she'd hoped, but the way he walked, his stature, and his manner were the same.

One of those two men was Raine Abarta. She bit down, clenched both her fists and her teeth. That bard was involved in too much for any of this to be coincidence. This matter had nothing to do with the La Pointe case, but now he was popping up in other aspects of her life? Maybe he'd become her own personal ghost. Her cheeks suddenly flushed with heat and she stood, taking her coat from the back of her chair in a single motion. She was going to get to the bottom of this once and for all.

But glancing at the clock, she hesitated. Almost time. Before she darted through the double glass doors, down the stairs, and to her car for the short drive to the arboretum, she watched the screen. Would the same thing happen again? Would Raine Abarta and this other mystery person disappear into the ether just like her supposed father? How likely was that? She returned to her computer and focused on the screen one more time. The numbers in the corner read: 11:10:57, 58, 59 . . .

The screen flashed white.

"NO!" she yelled, dropping her coat and grabbing onto both sides of the monitor. It freaking figured.

She kept watching to be certain.

11:11:00.

11:11:01. The image of a lonely hill in an empty garden returned to the screen. They'd both evaporated into thin air. After giving the monitor a good shake, she threw both hands upward to the cosmos, then plunged them into her hair.

She tapped her foot and counted silently, *One. Two. Three.* Then she picked up her coat and darted for the door.

CHAPTER 7

BRIAR OF NOBLE SKYE

HER BETROTHED HAD VACATED THE bar stool an hour before, accompanied from the Underground club by his brother Trevon of Lady Amaryllis. Trevon had slowed at the foot of the stairs to glance over one last time at Briar before taking Raine to the Aos Sí, the faerie mound at Wickney University Arboretum.

Lurking within the shadowed recesses, Briar of Noble Skye lowered a fluted glass to the table and appraised her present companion, Simmon of Noble Saffron. "Do you enjoy my gift, Cousin?"

Simmon exhaled gratification after swallowing a greedy gulp of the precious Fae spirit. "How did you manage bring a bottle of fíon across the Veil?"

Briar narrowed her eyes. "A secret I shall hold forever close." She twirled the stem of her glass and cut her gaze back to the stairs, less than half invested in the conversation. "But I do it for only a few. There's no other ties quite as unique as ours, and I must honor that."

"Ah, family ties. How utterly human." Simmon kicked his feet up onto the booth bench. "How fares my aunt Skye?"

"Must we discuss how Saffron and Skye spend their time? Having a twin seems more of a bane than a blessing."

"Oh, but Briar," Simmon admonished, "their unusual status as twins earned them their Fae nobility."

Briar sipped again and swallowed, the liquid tingling and popping as it trailed over her tongue and down her throat. "Do you believe that Trevon will have success in restoring Raine's welcome within Amaryllis's halls?" She asked this question to maintain cordiality rather than because she was truly interested in her cousin's answer.

Regardless, he replied, "With my duties to Linardi here in the mortal realm and being estranged from Father, I fear that I haven't spent as much time at court as you. You would know the answer to that better than me, Cousin."

Briar barely heard his words; instead, she took note of how Simmon's marque glowed under the deep-purple lights. She ran her fingers over her own unglamoured marque. *Lady Amaryllis wears a flower too. Would it not make more sense to have someone who wore a semblance of the Faerie Star on the throne? There are some good things about this realm. How strangely beautifully the marques shimmer on this side of the Veil.* And they sparkled even more under the dark lights in the club. Breathing in deeply, she let out a sigh emphasized by an exacerbated moan. "I do pray to Danu that we are able to restore Raine's place in Fae, and that he'll remain willingly." Her vision blurred as she stared at the stool he'd vacated and the empty glasses still on the bar.

Time being relative between the realms left uncertainty regarding how much would pass here while she approached her fertile season in Fae. Though some number of mortal years away, she needed the child she and Raine were fated to have. *And the rites of courtship must happen before that time.* Trevon did the work of getting him into Fae, but Briar still needed to work through all the possible ways she could influence Raine to remain there.

"Given his circumstances and ill-favor with Amaryllis, would it be more prudent to choose another mate?" Simmon suggested as if reading her pearls of thought.

Yanked from her machinations, her eyes blazed at him. "I couldn't dream of such a demotion. Raine is second in line. That would put our child in the best position within the royal court. If I have a daughter, she would be first in line for succession to Lady Amaryllis's throne."

"I was merely stating that it'd be a shame to miss your season while holding out hope for one who's been exiled." He sipped. "And one who has shown you so little favor. You are a noble child yourself and could choose from any number of well-empowered Fae."

She pinched her lips and inhaled a long breath through her nose. "Don't be daft, Simmon. It's not that I crave motherhood. What Fae in her right mind would want to endure such a trial?" She laughed, a trill to a near cackle. "No, Cousin. I crave the power that comes with being the queen mother. As I am no blood relative, I have no hopes of securing the throne for myself. Queen mother would be the next best thing."

With a shrug, Simmon drained his glass and attempted

to pour another. "You're a creative Fae, Briar. You could find another path to the throne." Alas, only a few drops trickled into the bottom of the flute regardless of how hard he shook the bottle. He lifted the glass and let those drops tickle his tongue.

Briar watched him greedily lap up the last of the wine. It was good to have someone in the mortal realm who was so easily swayed by a small gift of fíon.

The sands in his irises swirled wistfully, languor apparent in the slack of his face. Dull of wits, and on a sigh, he said, "If only the human liquors offered the effects of our Fae spirits."

Briar's voiced her next objection more for herself than her cousin. "I have worked for an era or more to gain Lady Amaryllis's favor. I certainly do not dare ruin that by throwing her first son to the wind so capriciously. No matter his current station, she will have him back at her side one day. I only wish I could return before him, to be there with open arms when he arrives." While in Faerie, days or weeks might pass while only minutes passed in the mortal realm, but the Fae had no power to sway the order of events. Sequence was the only time-bound law. If Raine and Trevon passed through the portals before she, there was no way she could arrive in Fae before him. She lamented that she wouldn't be able to welcome him home upon his arrival in the Wandering Wood. "Waiting is tedium. Though perhaps," she mused, "I should visit Anemone upon my return before finding my love."

Simmon sighed, effectively dismissing her annoyance. "Tomorrow. Time matters so little between here and Fae." He pointed to her still half-full glass. "May I?"

Briar slid the flute across the table.

RAINE

RIPPED FROM A COOL OCTOBER night into bright light and humid warmth, Raine squinted and removed his overcoat. Instead of the early season snowflakes so likely in north central Wisconsin, flakes of light fluttered on the air around them in the Wandering Wood. There was no sun in Faerie, no central star that a planet encircled. In truth, the Fae realm wasn't a planet at all, but something altogether separate—a magically sustained dimension between other worlds. Points of gentle luminosity fluttered all around, casting enough ambient energy for the foliage to grow straight, in their desired direction, and never forced to bend toward a heavenly body. And though they seemed to fall, the light flakes evaporated before they gathered on the ground, again unlike the white blanket that loomed only weeks away in Wickney.

Trevon laughed and started walking. "Let's go before the watch comes."

Raine's hands began to tremble; his throat closed. His glamour slid away under Faerie's native power. Unable to hold it in place without long practice in his home realm, he released it like willing tension out of his shoulders. The gravity of being here pulled at him, weakened his knees. How right it felt to be home. He stumbled, took two steps, and braced himself against a tree. He wasn't allowed here, and the queen could sense those who were in her realm. Raine looked up at his brother. "I must be quick."

He took one step, recovering. The grass cushioned and embraced his heel, and Raine focused his intent on his memories of the Palace, the Great Hall, and the room filled with Fae glass. The once-solid trees of the Wandering Wood pulsated and hummed as he took the second step, and the ground beneath his heel softened to sponge. On the third, the Wandering Wood flickered as if the scene approached the end of an old human film reel. His fingers and toes tingled, a current of magic traveling through his body, listening to his intent. He trained his will on his reason for crossing the Veil. The Glass. The fear his mother would discover his presence had to wait. In three more steps, nothing but light engulfed him and Trevon. He floated, yet he still took step after step toward his envisioned destination. The Fae magic in action left no air for him to breathe as his intention became reality. After a full dozen paces, the Wandering Wood seemed a far-gone memory. Oh how he had missed the use of intent within the mortal realm, but it was owed to the fabric of Fae itself rather than a faerie's skill. He climbed the steps toward the Great Hall, soaking in its grandeur.

His breath returned, but it singed as it crossed his throat. *Ifrinn, the pleasure of intent is shite compared to returning home.* He tilted his head back to peer at the silver and golden spires topping the royal palace. His muscles coiled to dance into what had once been his home, but then . . . he hardened. Raine rooted his feet, balled his fists, and clenched his jaw to keep from running to the crystal column and hugging it like a long-lost friend. He glanced at the main entrance, holding his position. Could he toss intent and direction to the wind and run fast enough through the palace halls to avoid being noticed?

No. He could not. He had to avoid the alternative to his exile. He couldn't spend eternity in Aodh's Dark Dungeon. His nature surged back into his soul and through his limbs, but the Dark would devour him. No. He. Could. Not. *Search the mirrors for the memory, Raine. Glean the necessary information and make your way back to the Wandering Wood and cross that Veil to safety.*

He turned to his brother. "Trev—"

BRIAR

BACK IN FAE WITHIN THE Wandering Wood, she breathed easier. She always felt more herself upon her returns and couldn't fathom why Simmon chose to remain in the mortal realm with such regularity. When she visited her cousin at the Underground, that was easier. Yet moving through other places in the mortal realm left a sour taste on her tongue. She longed to wash it away, and she had the method in mind. As Briar stepped out of the Wandering Wood onto the crystalline fields before Amaryllis's palace, she ached at the possibility of being with Raine in Fae, unencumbered by that nasty mortal world's limitations, but she had to remain patient. Besides, she had someone else to see first.

She turned and walked along the tree line. Her intention centered and focused on Sanctuary, Danu's most sacred place in Fae, a place where her kind went to heal and connect more deeply to their Fae spirits. After a dozen or so steps, her feet landed on stone and she climbed into the rocky caverns, pushing aside greenery and the rainbow of flowers overhanging the ledges.

Crystal-clear and cool waters trickled, another ceaseless ambiance to set the backdrop for healing. If she had held the intention in her mind, Briar could have walked straight to her destination within Sanctuary, but despite herself, she surrendered to the sights, smells, and sounds and sense of pure replenishment she experienced when wandering through Danu's Hallowed Hills. Yet she had an agenda that wouldn't allow her to stay long.

Briar shifted her intention again, and she stood at the opening to her destination—Raine's sister, Anemone's, rooms. Inside, when Briar softly called her name, Anemone turned; the salt and iron scars puckered in a jagged line over one jaw and similar slashes marked her neck and chest where her tunic scooped toward her breasts. Fainter white lines striated the exposed skin beyond the lengths of her sleeves, and Anemone's eyes shifted nervously at every little sound. Briar's stomach heaved over the thought of how the mortals had forever marked one of the most beautiful of the noble Fae children.

Because of her scars, Amaryllis's daughter Anemone would never ascend to the Fae throne. The Fae, after all, valued beauty above many things. Yet, in the midst of every calamity lay a seed of hope, and it favored Briar. She might have considered Anemone kindred, but she relished the opportunity Anemone's misfortune opened up before her. That was *if* she could mate with Raine.

Briar held her arms open to her best friend. They'd been connivers in arms amidst the mortals at one time. That she saw opportunity in Anemone's situation didn't change that. Anemone moved into Briar's embrace. A hand shorter than Briar, she rested her marred cheek in the hollow at Briar's shoulder.

"How are you, dear friend?" Briar asked, shushing, cooing, and stroking Anemone's bronze hair while her eyes stared off into the distance. She didn't relish that she was here on such a mission, but she'd do it regardless or wait another age until her next fertile season.

Anemone pulled away and wrapped an arm around Briar's waist, pulling Briar further into her rooms. A smile grew crookedly on her lips due to the scar. At least Anemone seemed happy to see another Fae now.

When they entered her innermost room, a sionnach

hissed at Briar. Anemone picked up the pointy-eared vermin, stroked its back, made shushing noises, then sent it from the room. When she stood to answer Briar, her voice rang like clear bells on the wind. "I'm healing. It's been hard, but I'm happy to begin seeing others again. The Fae love beauty, and it's hard to have lost my own." A trembling hand drifted to her jawline. "And with it so much of my destiny. Time will heal, but I fear this will require me to learn to glamour within the Fae realm. What brings you to Danu's Hallowed Hills, Briar?"

Briar winced. Glamouring within Fae required more learning than almost any of their kind ever mastered. Regardless, she smiled casually at Anemone and clasped her hand between her own. "I have a favor to ask of you, dear friend."

RAINE

ALONE.

"Shite, Trevon," Raine uttered, the tiny hairs on the back of his neck prickling.

His brother hadn't joined him on the way to the Hall of Glass, which left the precise worry in his mind about getting detained. Or worse. Regardless, he pressed on. The columns shifted before him to open into a long corridor, mirrors decorating every wall between additional rows of evenly spaced white stone columns. After scanning the hall for another Fae, it seemed Raine was Danu-blessedly still alone. He trailed his fingers over a column. The grains within moved to where he touched, warmed, and backlit the shape of his slender palm and fingers. Harmonic words formed within his mind: *Welcome, child of Danu. What evil keeps my scion away? It sups from your croí and mine.*

Raine lifted his hands on a quick inhale. "I'm sorry, Goddess," he whispered, curling his fingers away from the stone. More than betraying Danu, he feared the Dark and Aodh, so onward. He approached the closest mirror and placed a hand against the cool glass, three fingers and a thumb splaying wide. Images whirred across the pane as fast as his Fae mind would work until the La Pointe memories he'd relived, the anchor he used to find that exact moment in history, appeared. He retracted his hand.

Along with the Fae intent, this was another thing Raine missed, the glass that held all memory. To search it, all he needed was an inkling of one memory to act as a compass, and the Fae Glass would find the fixed moment within all histories of all worlds and replay any scene requested. Unfortunately, he didn't have an anchor for the murderer's memories, or he'd be able to resolve the faediom without travail. But then again, where would the fun be in that? Raine smirked as the scene continued— the late-night limp up the hill on 10th Avenue toward Devereaux Court.

Before La Pointe glimpsed the vehicles Raine sought, the glass went light, the street disappearing in the white until only his face peered back at him with a moment of confusion. Raine lifted his hand again to reactivate the glass but stopped, interrupted before his fingers felt the smooth surface.

A voice akin to singing crystal froze his body. "My long-lost son." A singe crawled up his spine. His mother's words resonated happily on the surface, but they also intoned an ocean of birse and wroth.

Caught, he swiveled his attention away from the mirror. That she showed nothing upon her fine features worried him more than if her eyes had burned red with anger. "Mother," Raine lowered his gaze to the floor in prescribed deference. Yet he said no more. Amaryllis's mood would decide more of his fate than any words he could speak. He prayed to Danu that she'd find her benevolence as opposed to her fury, but her tone didn't offer much hope.

Before he'd lowered his eyes, he'd seen Trevon. His brother held an elbow out with Amaryllis's hand resting in its crook. The faerie wore a devious grin.

A small smile spread on Raine's downcast face. Unable to hold it inside, he lifted his head and hand, pointed to Trevon. "You played me like a faelute, my brother! Nice shavie, indeed."

Amaryllis, inserting herself between them, extended her hand to Raine, an undeniable expectation. But the motion permitted him a glimpse of his mother, the queen of Faerie. The demand for the respect due her position cocked her chin higher. She waited his response. Raine considered turning and stepping into the Wandering Wood, but she'd have the guard there before he could reach the portal. Instead, he responded in the way he'd learned and practiced early in his long life, taking her hand in one of his own and her wrist in the other, bending, and placing his lips over her Noble marque—a pure amaryllis flower in white with blood-red touches at the tips of each petal. The position put him in the most vulnerable state. Had she a sword in hand, his head might roll on the pristine floors. As he completed the show of obeisance, he glanced at his own marque. No longer muted and the spitting image of hers, it glowed almost as brightly.

Afterward, he stood.

Amaryllis's irises shifted, blue-gray sands melding and holding Raine under a proverbial microscope. "My son," she said finally on a sigh, as if she might, of all things, welcome him home.

No, that couldn't be true. Queen Amaryllis of the Fae would never forgive so easily.

She lifted her hand and tapped her middle finger against her thumb. Raine winced at the sound, like someone had struck a drum within the hall. Two Fae appeared behind Amaryllis and Trevon. Guards. One, the commander Aimery, was the only Fae guard in history to have earned and endured all ten of the guard's marques. He wore five knotted chevrons iron-branded into the skin on either side of his neck with subdued pride.

Raine took a step backward. Another. He closed his eyes and focused hard on the forest. When he opened his eyes again, he no longer stood with his mother and her guards in the Hall of Mirrors. He pivoted and ran. At a dozen paces, he ducked behind a tree, gripping the rough surface. Eyes closed, he held his breath and listened. Nothing. Then . . .

"Raine?" Another voice brushed over him like velvet.

Shite, would these ill-fated meetings ever end? His eyes flew open, dismissing the voice and searching behind him for the guards. He still hadn't been followed. Yet. Safety assured, he looked reluctantly in the direction from which he'd heard his betrothed.

Briar of Lady Skye stood, semi-sheer skirts falling around her bare legs, and her curves casting a shadow beneath the translucent fabric. Damn him, he felt the urge to both cover her up and ravish her at the same time. The revealing gown clearly stated that she was prepared to begin their courting rites. But he couldn't get his younger sister Anemone out of his mind. She and Briar had been two of a kind in their youth.

Now, Briar clearly had other motivation. She reached for him as she approached, her dark hair cascading over one shoulder. Deadly beauty. Raine had endured exile for both of them, another torment he couldn't escape. The painted smile Briar wore seemed as thin as the fabric of her gowns. What scheme had she cooked up this time?

"My love and future mate, how very lovely to see you again." Briar's hands seized Raine's, and she tugged him toward her. "I've missed you so. We have a lot to catch up on. Come. Visit with me in my home."

A small idea sparked. "Briar, by your welcome, I see you ready to join me in the mortal realm once again. How delightful!"

Briar tapped his arm playfully. "Oh, that much is silly and you know it. When it is my season, your mother will allow your return; we have already discussed as much. Our Lady Amaryllis craves an heir more than she loves vengeance." She moved closer, molding her body to his and leaning her mouth closer.

He groaned, grasped the sheer fabric, and pulled her tighter. Yes, this would be so satisfying. But how would it feel to be damned to the Dark because he couldn't tamp down his sexual cravings? *No, Raine, no time.* He tried to resist, but Briar ran her lips over his, teasing as her smile grew against his mouth. She smelled of flowers and a green field and tempted every basic sexual need in his being. Something rustled.

Eyes wide, he pushed her away. In a quiet voice, he hissed, "Briar, I can't. Exile, remember?" He lurched toward the portal.

But she held tightly to him, insisting, "Join me in my home. They will not enter uninvited. You came for the glass, true, my betrothed? I can help."

Raine jerked back to her. "Wha—" He looked past her to where Aimery approached at a leisurely pace, with Trevon at his side still wearing his self-satisfaction. Raine searched Briar's face. How had she known about the glass? Oh, Ifrinn, he didn't have the moments to care. He looked at Aimery and Trevon, then back to Briar, took a deep breath, clenched his jaw, and nodded. "Let's go."

BRIAR

SHE STIFLED THE GRATIFICATION OVER how her plan unfolded long enough to focus her intent on her rooms, thrilled to lie with Raine on the lush velveteen bed-dressing. The forest quavered, light beamed, then they stepped together onto the plush white rug at her bedside. Briar wished she was fertile now, that they could couple now, that she could conceive the throne's heir in the next moments. She turned to Raine, lacing her arms around his neck. They stood near the same height, and she leaned closer, wetting her lips for the kiss. A rumble echoed deep in Raine's chest. Perfect. He wanted her too. The more they could be together in this intimate way, the easier courting would be.

Their lips had barely touched when Raine pushed her away, his eyes widening. His face transformed, solidified into a scowl. "You said you'd help, Briar." He looked around the room. "Where is the Fae Glass?"

Briar moved closer, not ready to give into that just yet. "Raine, be at ease. You feel our connection; that much I can sense."

He swung his head back around to her, eyes swirling. "Aimery and Trevon may not deign trespass in your home, but Amaryllis will not hesitate."

Briar pouted, hoping it'd turn the light in her direction over his stupid need to use the glass. Why in all of the Hallowed Hills and Ifrinn would he want to be so deeply entrenched in mortal matters? She reached for him again, but he caught her hand before she could caress the back of his neck once more.

Raine jerked her close, hard. Strongly enough it pushed the air from her lungs as she crashed into him.

She ran a tongue along her lower lip. "You prefer harsh over sensual? That's not what I recall from our prior interludes."

He squeezed his eyes shut, and when he reopened them, flecks of red intermingled with the golden sands. "Briar, it is not the time." His eyes darted to the window, to the door, then back to her. Anger? Fear? What?

Briar sagged. "Very well." If allowing the use of her Fae Glass didn't win his favor, at least she'd have leverage over him by seeing what information he craved so desperately within the mirror. She rounded the foot of her canopied bed and walked to the armoire. Pulling both doors open, she held out her hand to the right side. "As you wish."

Raine darted over to the glass and splayed both hands onto the surface. Briar watched over his shoulder, committing every image that passed in the glass to memory.

When Raine came away, he scooped her into his arms and kissed her deeply enough that heat stirred between her thighs. She struggled to believe it was enough that he'd return the favor so readily, but he deepened the kiss and moaned into her mouth. She melded against him, her arms moving around his waist. Their mouths danced, but there was something off about the taste of the kiss.

She kissed him deeper, more urgently, trying to tease out his desire. Yet on her tongue she sampled gratitude and an undertone of betrayal. He pulled back, caressed her cheek. Then, as quickly as he'd swept her into his arms, he released her, took three steps away, and vanished.

CHAPTER 8

KENNEDI

"CRAINE, MY DECISION ON THIS matter is final." Captain Aleksander Quaid tossed a file folder onto his desk. "District Attorney Mitchell is on his way up from court, and we're going to begin the proceedings against William La Pointe."

From her reclined position in the captain's guest chair, Kennedi glared at her superior, who was well aware of her reluctance to finalize the case report that'd kick off La Pointe's trial. Beyond their disagreement over whether it was time to close the case, she hadn't slept much at all since she'd seen Raine Abarta vanish in the Arboretum a few nights before. With all that, she was in no mood to see her ex, Rhyse Mitchell. "But Captain—"

"Kennedi." He fixed her with a stare she'd learned well enough over the years, and his tone put her in a place of subservience, much like a father's would with an errant child.

She barely recalled being admonished by her own father, but Aleks's tone was exactly how she imagined a paternal scolding would sound, patient yet unmovable. He wasn't about to budge in the matter. All the notes were in the file on the computer. Aleks could and would remove her from the case and assign his brown-nosing lackey, Lon Urskuld, to the case if she refused. Kennedi huffed through her nose as defeat overtook her instincts to argue further.

Three knocks, a click of the doorknob, and a familiar face smiling through the door announced Rhyse Mitchell's arrival. As he stared at her, his eyes saddened though he maintained professionalism for the captain's benefit. Kennedi pushed out of the chair and crossed the corner office to the windows on the far side. Knowing she had to work with Rhyse, why had she ever dated him? She peered out and observed the midday crowd milling around Wickney Square. In her peripheral vision, she saw Aleks and Rhyse shake hands across the desk.

"Glad you called, Captain," Rhyse said. "I'd like to get this one wrapped up before the elections."

Naturally, they'd want it wrapped before Vincent La Pointe swept the race for mayor. Her mind spun. Could there be some underlying plan? Something Rhyse was pressing in favor of keeping the current regime in place? The incumbent, Joel Dixon, was doing nothing for the people of Wickney, and everyone loved Vincent. She doubted the result of his mother's murder case would sway his chances. Hell, in the footage she'd seen, there'd been an outpouring of renewed support and sympathy for La Pointe.

"Have a seat, Mr. Mitchell." Aleks smoothed his coat

in preparation to take his own chair, but meaningfully made eye contact with Kennedi before sitting. "Have you had time to read the case file? It seems that every last shred of evidence supports the theory William La Pointe murdered his wife."

Rhys answered, "Yes, I agree. There's plenty of evidence for the prosecution. Are you submitting it today?"

Kennedi clenched her fist inside her pocket. She wouldn't defy Aleks, but she had to make sure the prosecuting attorney understood there remained room for doubt. Her eyes remained on the square below as she said, "The evidence is strong enough to make a case. Sure."

She imagined the men exchanging glances behind her back as Rhys prompted, "But?"

Without turning, she continued, "But nothing. What difference does my opinion make? I'm only the one who's been leading this case."

"Yes, *Detective* Craine," Aleks interjected, "The evidence is solid. With the lingerie and note, we have motive. A jealous husband with a public reputation provides plenty of cause for the crime. We have a gun registered in his name, his prints are the only ones on the gun, and forensics confirmed the bullet that killed Michelle La Pointe was fired from that very gun." With every restated point the captain made, his voice grew louder, more punctuated. "Furthermore, La Pointe was holding the gun and standing over his wife's body. This case is open and shut, just like my detective here claimed when she booked him."

Kennedi sighed. "Yes, everything Captain Quaid says is true. We all know that. But there is room for doubt. The handwriting analysis on the gun registration isn't back yet. Credit card receipts from the gun shop to verify—" Out the window, Kennedi caught a flash of fire on the far corner of the square. "Verify that, uh . . . William La Pointe purchased the weapons and registered them," she finished slowly, squinting at the action in the distance.

Flames leaped into the air, then several balls of fire rotated in a circle. Juggling. She strained her eyes harder. "Ho-ly-hell." Her stomach clenched and her pulse pounded in her ears. Her trigger finger itched. Staying in that office was about the most pointless thing she could imagine in the moment. Aleks and Rhyse just wanted to prove their power and nail a highly visible, possibly corrupt politician. Kennedi had too many doubts.

"What is it?" Aleks asked, scraping the chair across the floor and joining her at the window.

She shook her head and took a step to the side, inserting more distance between them. "Nothing. Entirely unrelated," she answered, because it had absolutely nothing to do with the case—well, very little anyway. After what she'd seen on the Arboretum cameras several nights back, her mission with Raine Abarta had become far more personal. She whirled to face both men. "Can I have one week? Just one. If the evidence is that cut and dry, the trial shouldn't last more than a day or so, and you can wrap it up well before the election. Just one week?"

The men looked at one another. The DA seemed quiet, doubtful, and still pathetically sad while the captain pinched his lips together and turned to Rhyse.

Kennedi's knee bounced several times as she waited. Raine had nurtured the annoying seed of doubt in this case, and she couldn't let him vanish again. She'd pulled some strings and sent Vic and Harley to stake out his flat after he'd disappeared from the Arboretum. But he hadn't surfaced until now. She'd also gone to the Local U several times. Still, no signs of the bard for two days and nights. She glanced over her shoulder to be sure. Yes, there he was, playing with fire.

It seemed like five minutes passed while she waited for her superiors' permission, but it was probably only seconds. She finally ignored their speechless exchange and moved toward the door. "Think about it, talk about it, whatever. I'll check back later this afternoon. If you decide against me, I'll support the trial. No problem. There's someone I need to see." She blustered from the room, intent on getting to Raine.

Kennedi took the stairs to the back parking lot, then jogged up High Street and across the square to join the gathering people. Cheering swelled within the crowd, and slowly, Kennedi carved her way to the front just as Raine caught the end of a fourth juggling baton and bowed low, accepting the renewed applause. She reached into her blazer and released the snap securing her firearm, just in case. Then, with her hands on her belt, she watched and waited for him to find her in the crowd. When he finally made eye contact, his performer's face fell just a bit before he re-donned the mask and continued into the next act with a sly smile. As he performed, he allowed his gaze to drift back to her, smiling or winking each time. The infuriating man might just be happy to see her.

She stood taller and deliberately focused on the crowd rather than him. Yet her eyes gravitated toward the performance. It was much more entertaining than the burlesque and poetry slam, she thought, but banished that and looked beyond the flames. Nameless faces watched, unable to step away in the middle of one of his segments. Magically drawn? Maybe? She wished she knew more about the Fae.

When he paused, the people applauded and tossed bills upon bills into his bucket before making their ways along to their destinations. Kennedi had never paid a grand amount of attention to the street performers in Wickney Square adjacent to WPD and the courthouse, but she'd never seen civilians as rapt in any performance as they were now with Raine's fire juggling. That observation alone was enough to raise her hackles. Eventually, Raine bowed, signaling the end of the performance. The crowd dispersed, and Raine packed away his equipment into a rolling case.

When finished, he sauntered toward her with a licentious smile. "Ken," he drawled. "I thought you wanted me to disappear now. What brings you to my turf?" He spread an arm to indicate the street corner where he'd been performing.

For a beat, she simply glared at him. Had he intended the word *disappear*? Did he know that's why she sought him out? She'd rushed down here foolishly without thinking about how she'd approach him. Certainly, from his perspective, it had to look like she was in pursuit of him. And, in truth, she was.

"Yeah. No. I mean . . ." Kennedi started.

Raine cocked a brow. "If that routine leaves you speechless, you should experience some of my more satisfying performances."

Kennedi raised both brows. *The bard has balls.* "I'm not here for any of your performances. I have questions."

"Should we find a seat in the square so?" He nodded to the open-air garden with statues of the former Wickney city leaders watching over alcoves and benches along the sidewalks. Then in a blink, he pointed past her. "Or would you like to head back to the Local U? Maybe you could join me for a drink this time?"

Kennedi pushed her jacket to the side and slid her hand into her pocket, the motion revealing the badge and gun. "I'm on duty."

Dragging the case behind him, Raine started for the crosswalk. "That wasn't a no. I'll hold you to that drink then."

She closed her eyes on an inhale, tempering her response yet again, then reopened them and followed. Raine found an empty bench and sat, pulling out a newspaper that when unfolded encased birdseed. He tossed a handful. Pigeons swarmed in a frenzy, peck, peck, pecking at the seed like the questions pounding in her skull.

"So, questions?" Raine asked.

Considering, she stalled before asking about three nights ago. "I spoke with Tofer at the gun shop. He provided the receipts, and we've sent off images to a handwriting expert to forensically compare the signatures with La Pointe's. I still don't understand why you're so engaged in my case, but—"

"It's simple. Like I said before; some puzzles can't be left alone, now can they?" He focused his gaze forward where a large black-and-white pigeon chased off a few smaller ones. Afterward, he tossed another smattering of seeds in a different direction. "Watch." He pointed. "He'll chase the smaller ones off there, too, never mind that he didn't finish the others. It's dominance, a game to him. My interest in the case doesn't really matter though, now does it? There's something else on your mind." He sat back, and his eyes followed a runner in skin-tight clothes, full makeup, and a poodle on the end of a sparkling leash.

Kennedi cleared her throat. "The fact that you have

classified information is suspicious. It can at least be considered tampering with an official investigation. At the most—"

"That's not it, now is it?" he said.

She closed her mouth, reopened it, and closed it again—a damn guppy. "Fine!" Was she really going to ask this so bluntly? Yeah. She blurted, "I saw you the other night. You and someone I couldn't identify broke into Wickney University Arboretum, and then you both vanished. I ran down there, and there was no sign of either of you—at all. What gives?"

Raine remained silent, but a muscle jumped in his jaw.

"You realize trespassing is a crime? Reasons to arrest you keep stacking up."

Raine shifted, throwing an arm on the back of the bench and leaning toward her, close. "Ken, your threat is getting old now. You're stalling. Are you planning to arrest me on suspicion or charges of trespassing?" He paused and narrowed his eyes. "Or do you just want to get your cuffs on me?"

"Oh hell no. It's my job!" Kennedi could have sworn something moved in his eyes but shook her head and furrowed her brow. Something within changed, slipped sideways, for a lack of a better explanation. When she spoke again, it seemed the words were drawn from her and her voice sounded dazed. "No. I'm not."

Her ears rang. The Arboretum matter dulled, pushed aside in her mind. The La Pointe case took the spotlight again.

The irksome man beside her turned back to feed the pigeons as if she hadn't just threatened to arrest him . . .

as if he hadn't just propositioned her about the cuffs. He began, "Very well then, Ken. Do you wanna tell me why *I* keep running into *you*? I've lived in Wickney a lot of years, and I've performed at this corner at least three times a week for most of those years, and I'd never met you before. Yet since that one day at the station and that oh-so-exciting chase, you have come to find me twice."

Ah, hell, he had a point. "Tell me what else you know." She crossed her legs and settled in—seemed this conversation might last a while.

"You came running down here from your tower over there under that pretense, did you?"

Kennedi bit down, lowering her tone. "It's not a pretense."

Raine held up a hand. "Okay. Okay. Well, let me think now. Why is it you're putting trust in me again?"

Kennedi sighed and tightened her ponytail. "Because you—unlike all the *civilized* people involved in this case—raised doubts."

He tossed another handful of seeds, then ran a hand over his chin. "Nice. Happy you're admitting it so."

"But I am getting pressure to prosecute La Pointe." She rubbed her hands along her thighs. *Why would you admit that, Craine?*

"Ahh." Raine's face lit with understanding. "Fine so. Let's do things this way." He smiled, and she waited for him to continue. "As you seem to suspect I might be involved, I should tell you that I spent the night of Michelle La Pointe's murder with Candi Crush. You know, the dancer in pink?"

Raine waited for Kennedi to nod, then added, "Feel free to question her."

"What's her number?"

He flipped a hand in the air as if her number was too much to bother with. "I don't have that. She works five nights a week at the Local, so finding her shouldn't be a problem."

Kennedi pressed her lips together.

"Okay." Raine turned to her again, clearly deciding on something. "Let's look at three avenues. First"—he slid a slip of paper from between the newspaper folds—"here are two license plates that were present on 10th Avenue on the night of the murder." He held the paper out for a long time, waiting for her to take it from his hand.

She looked between Raine and the paper he offered as if it were poisoned.

"You are going to take it, now aren't you?"

She did. "If you weren't there, how do you know these were present the night of the murder?"

The man zipped up, shrugged, and said, "I already gave you my alibi for the night." Then, he moved forward, emphasizing his three-point approach. "Second, have you considered how much press Vincent La Pointe has gotten from this whole ordeal? I hear gossip in the square all the time. 'Did you see how down Vincent La Pointe looked on TV last night?' or 'Poor Vincent, can you imagine losing your mother just a month before the most important day in your career?' or . . . ." He stretched his eyes wide, threw a hand over his mouth, and pitched his voice higher, allowing it to crack a little at the same time. "'Oh my gosh, Martha, can you be—'"

Kennedi held up a hand. "I get the point. You're suggesting that he had potential motivation to cause this scandal." She considered. It wasn't entirely illogical.

Vincent's wife Coralyn had given him an alibi, but now that Kennedi thought about it a little more, William La Pointe *had* mentioned that he was helping his son down at campaign headquarters that night. Something there wasn't quite right.

Raine watched her while the information sank in, nodding. "You're seeing it now." He waved a hand in the air flippantly. "I haven't put together cause for any of the other family or friends, but please, do feel free to look at them too, Ken."

She gripped the park bench. Would the man never stop calling her that? Also, how dare he give her a task?

Failing to see, or maybe just ignoring her frustration, he took a breath and said, "My last point I'm not sharing unless you agree that I can come with you."

After the Dragmaker incident, she wasn't about to allow him on another ride-along. "Out of the question, Rayyy . . . ine." She wanted to throw back an equally annoying nickname, but Ray just reminded her of her ex-partner, Raymond West. The two couldn't be likened. They were, well, fire and water.

He folded the newspaper and placed it beside his thigh on the concrete bench. "Very well then, you have a couple of new avenues to research and should probably be on your way now. You *are* on duty, as you said. I'll see you the next time you come looking for me, Ken." He winked.

She tipped her head back, ready to growl her frustration. There wasn't any way she could just leave him if he had something else germane to her case. While she peered up at the clear blue sky where more pigeons gathered and circled overhead, suddenly, something came hurling toward her. She scooted quickly away from the white shit-bomb just in time. "Oh, ewww," she complained, then turned, losing her breath when she realized she now sat inside a grinning Raine Abarta's outstretched arm.

She stuttered then jumped up, checking her clothes for detritus and gathering herself. Finally, she huffed and stared down at the amused performer. "Okay, fine." She pointed at him. "But you follow instructions this time, or I will find a way to throw you in lock-up."

He chuckled, nodded once, and stood too. "Fair enough. Let's go question the shut-in who lives across the street from Devereux Court."

With a dramatic flare, Raine offered her his elbow. "Shall we, Ken?"

CHAPTER 9

RAINE

"**W**AIT, WILL YOU?" RAINE STOPPED Ken when she started for the southwest corner of Wickney Square. He motioned to his stage case. "I need to drop this off at my flat. It's only two blocks east from here."

"You can leave it at the station. That's on the way."

Raine stopped and considered. Leaving his stage case anywhere except his flat on Aldgate felt to him like leaving his right arm. It wasn't like there was any sacred Fae artifact inside, and the contents would seem rather mundane to the snooper, but it was his livelihood. And if someone did decide to pilfer through his things, he's pretty sure he had at least this month's worth of rent to be lost in cash. True, he hadn't counted yet, but the crowd today had been more generous than Danu herself.

Ken took a few steps, then, apparently registering that he hadn't followed, whirled around.

"Look, Ken," Raine said, "perhaps it's hard for an all-business woman like you to understand, but performing is well, everything to me now. I'd prefer to see it safely locked up at my place." He started toward the path on his left.

Her brow furrowed. "There's not a safer place in Wickney than WPD. We can put it in lock-up." Ken lifted and dropped both arms in a plaintive shrug and rolled her eyes. "Hell, I can post Harley as guard if you want."

The mention of Harley brought a smidgen of a smile to Raine's face. "But—"

"It'll be fine, I promise. And," Ken waved the paper he'd given her, "I'd like to get Vic and Harley on running these plates."

Raine twisted his lips right and left. Ken leaned toward the station, eyes widening, and waved an impatient *let's-go* gesture. His leg twitched with indecision, but eventually he figured it'd probably be best if he didn't bring her to his apartment right now. The mess would be truly embarrassing. He'd have to ask her to wait on the street or in the hallway, because his flat was littered with a veritable truckload of puzzles he'd collected recently. The thought reminded him that he needed to do a good purge, and maybe . . . He looked at the case beside him. Just maybe, it was time for a change-up in his street performance routine too.

Ken released a huff when he finally joined her, dragging his case.

At the station, he pocketed his proceeds from the show. After a little banter with Harley once they'd secured his stage case in a locker, Raine and Ken walked south along High Street, engines puttering by, brakes squealing from time to time, and a horn blaring. *Ah, the city. Never a shortage of loud machines, pollution perfumed air, and hard surfaces.*

Ken seemed wrapped up in thought, like she had something other than the case on her mind. For the moment, Raine kept quiet, but he moved a little closer to her shoulder as they walked. He scanned the tops of the buildings and the now-barren, human-placed, decorative trees; quite unnatural, if anyone would ask his opinion. A black swarm of birds flew south overhead in anticipation of the coming cold. Raine and Ken's breath clouded on every exhale. He didn't relish the coming cold either, but he also didn't have wings to join the birds in their southbound flight.

He had other matters on his mind he couldn't leave alone, like little scabs that needed picking. Raine contemplated what he'd finally learned in the Fae Glass's history and the questions they'd need to ask of the shut-in Sean MacCaibe. He'd give Ken a little nudge in the right direction when the time came. He simpered at the thought of the "right direction." *Well, I'll steer her right this time, sure. Maybe.*

When they reached 10th, they took a right toward the La Pointe residence and passed the familiar rows of town homes. They climbed the steps, and Ken knocked on the royal-blue door at 1021 West 10th Avenue while Raine glanced over at Devereux Court, number three to be specific. Though the little bit of misdirection around Vincent La Pointe had partially sated his appetite, he hadn't had a true joy-fix since he returned from Faerie, and his hand shook a little at the inkling of Vanessa. Memory of all the little misplaced household objects calmed his mild tremor as he wondered if she'd discovered them all yet. He'd have to come up with another excuse to visit soon.

The thought made his mouth water, but then again, his temptations were stronger after a visit to the Fae realm.

He looked away from Vanessa's front door and up the street. *Nah. I should probably see Candi instead. Safer now.*

"Raine?" Ken snapped her fingers in front of his nose.

"Yeah? What?" He jumped and twisted to look at her. The door hadn't opened yet, and he hadn't done anything to warrant her irritation this time.

"I asked you a question."

"Really?" Raine leaned against the brick wall on the tiny landing at the top of the steps, hands shoved deep into his trenchcoat pockets. "Sorry. Come again?"

"We already questioned Mr. MacCaibe. What else do you expect to learn?"

Hmm, how was he to answer that? Sure, the bobbies had probably questioned William MacCaibe about the hours leading up to the crime and if he'd seen anything out of the ordinary that night. They may have questioned him about the family, and certainly they would have gotten glowing commentary on William La Pointe and how sorry the shut-in was over William's loss. Raine couldn't tell Ken what he'd gleaned from La Pointe's memory: that William La Pointe had always taken time to visit with Sean MacCaibe, or that the former senator visited the hermit every week for a game of cards. So, when it came down to the line, if the questioning centered on La Pointe, naturally they would have learned little aside from the man's sorrow. No, they needed to press him in a different direction.

At last, Raine answered, or more accurately asked, "Did you learn anything from him about the weeks leading up to the murder? What about earlier in the day?"

Ken rolled her eyes and stage whispered, "You should have asked all this before we were standing at his front door. Hell, I should have anticipated it after your outlandish questioning of William La Pointe. You're not planning to ask him about the opera, are you? If so, this is a blatant waste of time."

The door remained still; no noises from the other side.

"No, no, no. Nothing like that." He flashed her a sideways glance. "But truly, Ken, don't you ever ask questions just to throw off your person or set him at ease?"

"Absolutely not." She straightened indignantly and stepped backward out of the patio alcove and peered at the window to the left of the door. "Maybe he's not home."

"He's home. Shut-in, remember now? His agoraphobia's too strong to step outside."

She refocused on Raine after scanning the other windows as well. "Really?" Ken propped a fist on her hip. "Is that so?"

"Mmhmm."

"And how, pray tell, do you know Sean MacCaibe is agoraphobic?"

Caught. Shite. Think quick. "We-elll . . . it's the only logical conclusion, sure. Since he's not physically unable to go outside, why else would he lock himself inside his home?"

Ken pursed her lips but hesitantly accepted his answer and knocked again. "Mr. MacCaibe? It's WPD. We have a few questions for you."

No answer.

"Give it a bit," said Raine. "He'll come."

Kennedi Craine leaned against the red brick on the other side of the landing, still watching Raine as if he might grow a second head. "It's farfetched for you to know so much about everyone connected to this murder, yet I can't seem to let you be." She pursed her lips, thoughts churning behind her narrowed eyes.

"So, that means"—he pointed to himself—"I am growing"—then to her—"on you?" He spread his hands to either side, his smile growing. "Didn't I tell you we'd make a dynamic duo?"

Ken closed her eyes and huffed through her nose.

Raine chuckled. "Tell me what you already know from your prior interrogation with Mr. MacCaibe, why don't you now?"

The info she dumped about their questioning was pretty much what Raine had expected. Then she added, "He didn't know Michelle La Pointe well, and there'd been nothing unusual in the hours leading up to the time of her death. He didn't hear a gunshot and never witnessed so much as an argument between William and Michelle. He's known Vincent and Vanessa since they were toddlers, and all the standard shit that goes with."

Raine stroked his chin as he listened, all very ho-dee-ho-hum. Expected. "Back up to the part about the gunshot. What kind of gun did you say it was now?" Raine recalled from La Pointe's memory that the gun had been a make and model from the late 1800s—the same variety La Pointe collected himself, but he hadn't recognized the grip when he held it in his hand.

"Webley Mark 3 .38 revolver," she answered. "And before you ask, it *is* possible that the particular gun could be fired indoors across the street and not be heard from inside MacCaibe's townhouse."

"Without a silencer?" Raine asked.

"There are no silencers for weapons that old." Ken snorted. "And silencer is such a misnomer. Regardless, the Mark 3 is a fairly quiet weapon . . . more of a popping sound than a boom."

Danu, Raine cursed to himself. Those details would have been nice to know. His memory walk limitations hadn't afforded him the knowledge of the gun's history or sounds. And when he'd searched the Fae Glass using the only anchoring memories he possessed, it was entirely possible that there had been a silencer, or whatever Ken wanted to call it, removed from the scene. Heck, it'd been possible that the murder happened outside the townhouse at Devereux Court and the body staged. But the basic logic didn't work out in favor of a different location either, as Michelle La Pointe had been lying in a rather large pool of her own blood.

The interesting thing—what Raine needed MacCaibe to focus on and hopefully reveal—was the driver of one or both strange vehicles parked in the area that night. License plates should do the trick, but eye-witnesses would boost the likelihood and prevent the *How-did-you-know-these-cars-were-there?* question. "Let's ask about what went on during the day. Have him look for something unrelated to the La Pointes. He may—"

The door swooshed open, and a thin, white-bearded, bald man stood as far back from the patio as possible, as if he might combust like a vampire in the sun. From the shadows, his head twitched left and right with his eyes held wide, as if the open air beyond his door might swallow him whole. A gray robe hung from his bones, and he rubbed his fingers quickly against his thumbs as he spat, "Quick. Hurry. Don't dally. Inside or go. Now." He jerkily waved his hands, motioning them inside and further emphasizing his desperate need to shut out the terrifying world beyond.

Ken stepped forward. "Thank you, Mr. MacCaibe, for seeing us again. We'll try to keep this brief." She crossed the threshold with a *now-or-never* glance back to Raine.

Following, he deferred to Ken to begin the questioning and looked around as they walked. Through a long and dark hall, MacCaibe shuffled along with them, trailing into the kitchen at the back of the townhouse. The home's layout seemed much like Vanessa's, but dingier, dustier, and less tasteful. The small dining area behind the kitchen had blackout curtains lining the windows rather than the plants Vanessa placed in hers, and Sean MacCaibe took a seat in a green-and-orange floral-upholstered folding chair at an olive-green folding table. The appliances and countertops were straight from the 1970s as well, and the apartment smelled like old food and unwashed feet. Raine thought La Pointe paid for MacCaibe's maid service. When had they last visited?

He hadn't obtained this image from William La Pointe's memories, and he was glad of that fact. Raine appraised Sean and quickly dismissed the idea of another memory walk, no matter how much information he'd gain. The man was bent in the back, and if as young as William, he wore his age far more severely.

Raine finally pushed away the heebie-jeebies and took the third and only remaining chair at the table.

Ken began, "Mr. MacCaibe—"

"Sean," the man barked, rocking forward and back in the chair.

"Sean," Ken echoed slowly.

"I-I've already told you everything I-I know about

what happened that day with the . . . er . . . thing." He pointed toward the front of the house, then clasped his trembling hands on top of the table. His eyes, yellow where they should be white, shifted between Ken and Raine, confused and paranoid.

"I know, Miste—, excuse me. Sean." Her gaze flickered downward.

Raine narrowed his eyes. *Is she uncomfortable? Ken? Interesting.*

She recovered. "We want to ask you more about what you noticed outside earlier in the day." She paused and looked at Raine.

"Oh, yeah. Uh, sure. Sean, can you just walk us through your day now?" Raine asked, narrowing his eyes and nudging the man toward calm and truth. "Anything you saw outside your window that day might be helpful."

The man's jaw worked wordlessly for several beats then his face went slack, the reels in his mind nearly visible as they spun backward in time.

KENNEDI

HOW'D HE DO THAT? A squint of his eyes, a stare-down, and Raine Abarta had the twitchy, irrational man tamed enough to appear as calm as any healthy adult. When they'd questioned Sean MacCaibe before, they'd trodden this path, asked him about his day, and learned absolutely nothing from his jittery discourse. People far more competent than Raine Abarta, fire juggler, had questioned this man and learned nothing that'd help in the case. They gleaned that he sat at his desk in the front window day-in and day-out, writing for the science fiction periodical *Worldview.* Interviews and far-fetched what-if type articles galore. If he'd been into politics, he'd be on the FBI watch list as one of the fanatic conspiracy theorists. Her eyes had crossed when she'd tried to read a few of his pieces, much like they did when she'd had any interaction with him before. That William La Pointe had been close to the man was something she couldn't wrap her brain around.

As she watched Raine patiently observing MacCaibe with narrowed eyes, she couldn't fathom why she was still allowing this investigatory, incompetent civilian into the case. Her skin itched with the wrongness of the situation, and to think, she'd been willing to defy her captain to hear him out. This behavior wasn't like her, wasn't anything she'd have ever done before meeting him. Sure, she'd used informants before in her course of work, but she'd never let someone else inside the case who didn't belong in a police investigation. Something, some feeling in the back of her mind or deep in her gut, urged her toward Raine Abarta.

Sean MacCaibe sat taller in his chair, his hands stilled on the table, and his face eased. Pushing his shoulders back from their perpetually rounded position, he seemed to be preparing for a performance. What. The. Hell? How?

Raine prompted, "Go ahead, Sean. Just recount your routine for that day sure." Raine's words sounded soft, coaxing, and it was clear that they had the same resonance to the man, allowing him to put aside his paranoid behavior and talk to the strangers in his home in an easier manner.

Kennedi turned sideways in her chair and crossed her legs, observing the conversation as MacCaibe began with mostly the boring routine she'd expected. A breakfast consisting of Nutella spread on toast and taken at his desk as the neighbors emerged from their homes, each making his or her way off to work. He cataloged every person on the street he could see from his front window.

Kennedi fought the urge to roll her eyes. "Seriously, Raine, this is a waste of time. Vic and Harley already collected all this information." She tried to hurry him along so she could get back to the station, follow up with the handwriting expert, and talk to Vic to see if they'd learned anything else from running the plates.

But MacCaibe kept talking, heedless of her interruption, as if the bard had him entranced. Raine also kept his focus on the man, but reached over and grasped Kennedi's arm. She started to speak but fell silent when she felt a current with his touch and her stomach leaped. The spot at the top of her spine snapped—a crack at the base of her skull relieving the long-held tension. But she hadn't twisted her head to elicit the pop. Raine's hand on her arm felt feverish, and she went utterly silent under the touch and foreign sensations.

Today, something about the interior of the townhome seemed more dingy than before, and she craved light and fresh air so hard that the stale smell made her stomach churn.

"There's a bakery," MacCaibe continued, "Moon Cake, at the corner that I can see from my window."

Raine licked his lips. "Hmm, that sounds good. Ken, maybe we can stop in when we're done here."

But caught up in her own confusion and the growing nausea, Kennedi barely registered the suggestion.

Still in his trance, MacCaibe appeared to ignore Raine's small talk as well. "The La Pointe twins go there every morning for coffee. Vincent usually before Vanessa. That morning was no different than any other. That friend of

Will's wife—the one who always dresses like it's time for some soiree—she came that morning, later, after everyone else had left for the day, and she and Michelle went for brunch at the bakery."

Kennedi blinked out of her daze, tearing her attention from Raine and the sudden illness that plagued her body. What had MacCaibe said? Oh, yes. Elanna Bell and Michelle had brunch that morning at Moon Cake. Another known tidbit. Her skin felt cold, but she started sweating. They needed to get out of that house before she threw up. She leaned in to say as much when—

MacCaibe continued, "While the women were at Moon Cake, a police car showed up. Seemed like he was just making the rounds. A black and white, standard issue, but a plain-clothed officer stepped out." His furrowed. "I remember his shoes. Cowboy boots to be specific, polished like you wouldn't expect from a real cowboy."

Across the card table, Raine leaned closer to the old man.

"Hey," Kennedi whispered, her pulse echoing in her ears and behind her eyes. Her breath quickened, grew shallower. She needed to escape the dark, dirty house.

Where his hand rested on her arm, Raine patted. Oh yeah, he still touched her. She pulled away, drying her palms on her jeans.

MacCaibe's ghostly voice went on, unmindful of anything around him, "Cop was bald. Strode up the street to the same corner as Moon Cake, back downhill to the car, then drove away. He seemed to have no purpose at all, just looking around. About a quarter hour later, the ladies left the bakery laughing and went back into William and Michelle's house."

A buzzing went off in Kennedi's pocket, and she

reached for her phone. *Vic Clark* flashed across the screen. "I have to take this." She squeezed her eyes tight and reopened them. "You wrapping?" she asked Raine as she stood, relishing the excuse to get fresh air.

Raine nodded; Kennedi swiped the screen and walked to the front door. As she stepped through the front door, it seemed the house vomited her outside. But her tight chest loosened, and her stomach settled a little. "Yeah," she answered, leaving the door open behind her.

"Hey. So I got the plates back you asked for," Vic said.

"And?"

"White sedan is a Lexus and belongs to a hairdresser Elizabeth Marie Carver who lives in a flat on 9th. The other one's an Escalade licensed to WPD."

"What?" Kennedi ran a hand over her forehead; the cold sweat had crusted there.

"Yeah, I did some digging around the station, and it appears it's used by the FVU for undercover jobs."

Kennedi looked back down the hallway toward where Raine still spoke with Sean MacCaibe. She could no longer see the duo sitting at the rickety table and turned away when the smell hit her again. She descended the steps. *Faeries thrive in counter cultures, so what's going on in this upscale neighborhood that would warrant an undercover FVU detective?*

"Craine? You still there?" Vic's voice interrupted her train of thought.

"Yeah, keep this info on the DL and play dumb if anyone asks you about that search. I'll be back within the hour." She hung up and marched back to the kitchen.

Raine was mid-sentence, thanking Sean MacCaibe. ". . . your time. Would it be possible to check out the view from your desk before we leave?"

"Of course," the man said, still under whatever influence Raine Abarta had mustered.

Raine blustered by. "Ken, c'mon. Can you snap a few photos of his view?"

"What about your phone?" she snipped back.

He hesitated. "It's old, and my camera sucks."

She took a deep breath, regretted it, and pulled her phone. At the desk, she slid the chair away and snapped a handful of photos while standing where the chair would be. "K. Let's go."

Raine grabbed the chair and pushed it up behind her. "Wait now. Sit and take a few more, will you?" He squinted again.

Kennedi glared at him. *Did something move in his eyes?* She sat gingerly on the edge of MacCaibe's chair and did as Raine asked, then jumped up. "Good?" She shoved her phone back in her blazer pocket and moved away from the bard, toward the door.

The performer gave a slow nod. "That should do it." Raine sat in the chair and studied the view.

She checked her watch.

Standing, he stared at her with his brows furrowed. "Why're you so jumpy, Ken? Not like you."

She took a deep breath and puffed her cheeks. "Just need to get back to the shop. If you're not ready, I'm leaving you here."

MacCaibe stood back in the shadows of the hallway. His hands fidgeted, rubbing his arms, scratching his beard, or tugging at the back of his neck. He'd also returned to his stooped posture.

"Thank you for your time," she said and stepped through the still-open door.

Raine followed and pulled the door closed with a click. Kennedi inhaled the city air, ripe with exhaust, but relished every second of it filling her lungs. Her eyes took a minute to adjust to the sunlight, and she pulled her coat around herself against the cool, but she wasn't about to complain. The crispness was the most refreshing thing she'd felt in a long time.

She descended the few steps to the sidewalk and waited for Raine to join her. "Learn anything?" she asked, genuinely curious because she couldn't understand for the life of her how the man gleaned his information.

He lifted his face to the sun, sucking in an audible breath through his nose. "Maybe." He held out a hand. "Shall we?"

Striding back toward High Street, a woman stepped out of her front door with a white, fluffy dog on the end of a leash.

"What the . . ." Kennedi huffed, then pressed her lips together. She could swear the air around the woman sparkled like glitter catching the sunlight. Kennedi blinked several times. Glowing halos around people were a sure indication she was about to get one of her debilitating headaches. She hadn't had those in a long, long time. "Ah, hell." She pressed her index fingers onto either side of the bridge of her nose, willing it away.

Raine placed a hand at the small of her back. "Everything okay?"

Kennedi started to shake her head but decided against it. She had about an hour before the splitting pain set in with full fury. Instead, she fished in her pocket for her aviators and put them on. In her bag, she kept the self-injection that'd ward off the majority of the pain if she could get to it in time. "I need to get back quick; I'm getting a migraine."

CHAPTER 10

KENNEDI

DAMNIT, IMITREX SHOTS GAVE HER the jitters. After returning from MacCaibe's, again feeling like the trip had been a farce, she'd stopped by her desk, administered the injection, and forwarded Raine the photos he'd had her take of the street. Why he wanted those, she couldn't fathom, but she sure as hell didn't have time to run the possibilities through her brain. Raine had taken his suitcase, pretended to be exhausted, and left rather urgently as soon as they'd returned. The man confused her thoroughly, and she was happy to have some work to follow up on that actually made some logical sense, so she had gladly waved him away.

Before heading upstairs to the FVU to find Ray, she stopped by Vic's desk. "You and Harley, go to the Local U tonight and speak with a girl named Candi Crush. Raine Abarta's alibi for the La Pointe murder. Verify that."

"Ah hell, Craine. I have a date with my girl," Vic whined. "It takes months to get reservations at Ciao Bella."

"Reschedule."

Vic had been talking about the high-class Italian restaurant for a few weeks now. She massaged her temples and turned her back, headed for the rear stairwell. Criminal investigations didn't allow time for a personal life; he should know that by now. Maybe her philosophy deterred relationships, but she had priorities. "I have exactly one week to hammer this out," Kennedi called over her shoulder.

Vic grumbled behind her.

Upstairs, she found her old mentor, Ray, sitting in his office with his feet kicked up on the desk and scrolling through his phone.

"Working hard, Ray?" She was the only person in the world who got away with calling the man Ray. Everyone else called him West.

His face lit as he looked up. "Hardly working." He dropped the boots, stood, and held his arms wide as he skirted from behind the desk. "How's my favorite detective?"

She moved into his embrace, hugging with a single arm. Raymond West had been a cop for almost as many years as she'd been alive, and she'd learned everything she knew about how to run a good investigation from him. He'd groomed her to take his position as lead detective on the fifth floor, standard investigations department, while he moved on to seven and the Faerie Victims Unit a couple of years back. And though she admired his career path, that move certainly would not be her next.

During the time she'd spent under his wing, he'd saved her life a few times over. He'd taken a bullet for her once. A solid man with a larger-than-life persona, he was the closest thing she had to a father. Hell, he'd been more of a parent than most of the fosters she'd experienced in the system after her mother's break.

"What brings you up to seven?" he asked.

"This La Pointe case." Kennedi's hands shook as she released the band tying back her hair and refastened it. Damn migraine medicine.

A shadow hovered over Ray's brow. "The one where the big-time politician murdered his wife?"

"That's the one."

"Thought it was pretty cut and dry . . . at least that's what Q said."

Kennedi pursed her lips and nodded, felt like smacking the heel of her hand square in the center of her forehead. Ray golfed with Captain Aleksander Quaid, Q to his best friends, every week. Of course they would have talked about work during their outings.

Ray's brows popped up. "But there's something else?" He took a chair at his little conference table to the side, holding out a hand for her to take the facing one.

Sitting, she said, "I can't explain it. I've got gut-rot. We're missing something big. This performer . . . the one you saw on five several days ago?"

Her mentor furrowed his brow again.

"Raine Abarta," she offered. When recognition dawned on his face, she nodded and continued. "He managed to plant what lawyers and judges call *reasonable doubt*."

Ray leaned onto the table and folded his hands between

them, waiting patiently like he always used to do when he wanted to press her into working out the logic in her own mind.

She'd pushed herself down this road already, but it wouldn't hurt to go over it with a colleague. "If I were on the jury, I wouldn't convict. And if I'm his lawyer, there are big inconsistencies. Or other possibilities."

"How so?" Ray asked.

"That's the deal, I don't have hard evidence in another direction, only theories."

He tilted his head toward the big-screen display in his office. "Wanna walk the board?"

She nodded. "Yeah, that'll probably help." Standing and talking through a case with him had always brought clarity. Maybe it was the motion, or something about saying her theories aloud that made things click when they wouldn't work themselves out. Or maybe it was just her old mentor.

Ray went to his computer. "Case number?"

Kennedi spouted off the ID by memory, and after a few of Ray's clicks, the touch-screen on the wall flickered to life with the images of everyone possibly involved displayed. She walked over and touched Vincent La Pointe's image. A window with his vital information opened below him. Kennedi touched the dropdown field labeled *Status* and changed it from *Family of Deceased* to *Person of Interest.*

Ray joined her at the board, his thinking pen in hand. A tick of his; Ray habitually twirled it while working a case board. "Really?" he pondered aloud. "You're interested in the mayoral candidate as a potential suspect?"

"Rumor mill has me thinking about it a little more."

Almost certain Raine was a faerie, she wouldn't nail him as her only source. She demurely continued, "Think about the motivation. He's looking for sympathy in the election, and this case has everyone in Wickney focused on his family."

"Doesn't make a lot of sense, Craine. Everyone here loved William La Pointe as senator. No reason for Vincent to off Mom and lock up dear old Dad just to gain favor." He looked skeptical with the pen stopped between his fingers.

Kennedi folded her arms across her chest. That'd been her initial reaction too, so why doubt it now. "What if he felt like he was under Daddy's thumb? Another question; I don't know their family dynamics. Haven't found a witness yet to attest to that. Strange, don't ya think?"

Ray touched the close button on Vincent's information screen and resumed the slight of hand. Twirl. Catch. Twirl. Catch. "Maayyy-be it's a possibility, but you're ahead of me. Let's circle back to the beginning." He touched the file with the CSI photos, then opened the photo viewer and took a small step back. "Walk me through the crime scene." Twirl. Catch.

Kennedi humored him, because he hadn't really been involved in the ins and outs more than that one interview with the family friend.

When she paused, Ray pointed to the photo of the lingerie box. "What about the Mal person? The best friend—what was her name again?" Ray moved the photo viewer aside and scanned the faces. "Ah, yes, Elanna Bell. Don't you think it's strange that she couldn't identify her best friend's secret lover? Don't girls talk about that shit?" He cocked a brow.

Kennedi backhanded him playfully. "Quit being

sexist.”

He chuckled. “I really thought the La Pointes were a happy couple—that kind of happily ever after bullshit that really only exists in fairy tales. Come to think of it . . . could the lover be Fae?”

Kennedi rolled her eyes and sighed, verging on a full-on groan. “There’s nothing otherworldly about this case, Ray. You’re far too wrapped up in this new FVU mindset. Given the Fae-related crime stats, not likely.”

“But that’s why we’re here.” He spread his arms. “It’s kind of like the X-Files.”

“Alien shit?” She grimaced.

“Hell yeah. Maybe they were chasing the wrong thing.”

Kennedi rolled her lips between her teeth and shook her head. “Since the Extirpation, faerie crime is like half of one percent, Ray. Seriously. Not. Likely.”

“Okay, okay,” he relented, searching the people boxes again. “I see you still don’t have a face tied to Mal’s profile. Have you learned anything else about him? Or her?”

“That’s another doubt. Nothing. Mal’s a ghost. Can’t find a name related that could be shortened to Mal. So, the only thing that note does do from a prosecution perspective is establish sufficient motive for William La Pointe. Or so says your friend, Q. Obviously, Mal’s a lover, but still a mystery.” Kennedi ran shaky hands over her head and paced; it’d be twelve hours before the Imitrex wore off and she crashed hard.

“So, you’re worried the lawyer will use it to cast doubt on the case?”

“Wouldn’t you?”

"All right. I can see it. What else?" Twirl. Catch. Twirl. Catch.

Kennedi reached over to the screen and tapped the photo of the handgun. The file expanded to fill a large forefront of the board, the title reading: *Murder Weapon.* Kennedi pointed to the make and model. "La Pointe has an extensive collection of this model of British military pistols. They're pretty rare."

"So, that also points to him as the perp." Ray shook his head, held the pen to his chin, and glanced at her sideways. "There may be questions, but this evidence is pretty solid."

Yes, he was right on the surface. "But this gun and one other were purchased recently from Tofer's down in the Burgh. Can't find any electronic record from La Pointe's bank accounts or credit cards showing that he actually bought the guns."

"They had to be registered."

"Checked that. Registered to William La Pointe."

"Kennedi, you know he could have come up with the funds outside of his normal means. Rich old dudes have safes behind some portrait in their houses, right? Did you check for a stash of cash?"

Hrm. Seemed too cliché. "No. Guess I can."

"And if he registered it, he had to show ID." Ray turned and stepped away, his bad knee locking and inflicting a limp for a few steps.

She glanced back at the gun. "Regardless, I've sent the receipt and registration off to a handwriting expert to verify his signatures." She closed the window. The more she talked about it, the more convinced she was that there wasn't any doubt that'd speak loud enough to *not* convict La Pointe. But there remained this feeling in the pit of her stomach.

Ray pointed nonchalantly toward the board, not really raising his eyes from the papers on his desk. "Who's the other person of interest? Abarta, you said?"

"Yeah, that's the street performer I mentioned earlier."

"How's he related to the La Pointes?"

Kennedi felt pressure between her brows. "He's not . . . Other than he is convinced William La Pointe didn't do it and seems to be doing everything in his power to convince me of that too."

Her mentor looked up with brows raised and eyes wide. "That sounds strange. And suspicious."

"You're right." She fidgeted, then reached up, closed the case file, and powered off the screen. "I should just let Aleks and Rhyse move forward with the case and be done with it." She moved toward the door.

"Wait, Craine. Let's circle back to your thought about Vincent La Pointe."

Kennedi flipped a hand. "Ah, that's nothing. The more I think about it, the more I'm convinced it's only the rumor mill."

Ray crashed down into his chair and clasped his hands on top of the desk, pressing her with the look he'd always given her after asking a question. Her mentor had rarely been wrong in his questioning in her experience.

She sighed. "Apparently, people on the streets are developing quite a bit of sympathy for him with the loss of his mother and his father being in the spotlight so much. It's emotion. Not fact."

"On the streets . . . " Ray drawled, one brow lifted in question or disbelief. "Rumors told to you by this street performer?"

Kennedi closed her eyes, trying to keep her anger and alarm at bay. She'd been taken, used for Raine Abarta's amusement. She bet he loved the secondary fact that being in MacCaibe's house had gotten the better of her. However, that didn't warrant the *behind-iron-bars* or *ring-of-salt* treatment Raymond West would bring down on Raine. She'd take care of Raine Abarta herself. She settled her gaze back onto Ray. "Thank you. You've been a huge help. I'll get out of your hair." She winked.

Ray ran a hand over his mostly bald head and cocked a half smile. "Good thing. It was getting all tangled and unwieldy."

She turned to go, but when she made it to the door, he called her name again. "You do realize that Fae M.O. is trickery."

"Thanks. But there's no proof Abarta is Fae. And he hasn't hurt anyone. I'll deal with him and make damned certain he doesn't interfere with any more official investigations."

Downstairs, Kennedi double-timed past Harley's desk, where Vic sat on one corner and the two chatted idly. Vic stood abruptly, straightening to attention, but Harley maintained the lounged position.

"Heya, boss," Harley said.

Kennedi breezed by with a passing, "Glad to see you haven't left to validate Abarta's alibi yet. Get your things." At her desk, she picked up the phone and dialed a number she wished she could forget.

"Hey there, Kennedi." the voice of her ex-lover

drawled.

She closed her eyes. "Rhyse."

Regretfully, she paused long enough for him to come back, "Here for you any time, tulip. Change your mind already?"

Kennedi placed a thumb and forefinger on the bridge of her nose. "Would you *not* call me that? And kind of, but not in the way you mean."

He hesitated, and when his voice came back, it sounded scorned but a good deal more professional and satisfied—maybe under the belief that she'd finally seen the logic in his and her captain's points of view. "What can I do for you then?"

Their relationship hadn't worked out for precisely this reason. He'd forever been trying to stop her free thinking, make her more compliant, get her to move in with him for *purely logical* reasons, get her to stop working so late at WPD, get her to dismiss the disappearance of her father. If and when she ever decided to really open up to another man, that man certainly wouldn't negate everything she stood for.

"I need a warrant."

RAINE

THUMP. THUMP. RAINE JUMPED UP from the chair, dropping the V-Cube. It clattered across the floor to the corner. He turned slowly around to take in his studio apartment, then went to the door, leaned over, and peered through the peephole. Ken, Vic, and Harley all stood in the hall outside.

"Shite," he hissed under his breath, ashamed over the piles upon piles of games and puzzles strewn around the place. He wished desperately he could glamour more than just himself. Instead, he scrambled over to several of the piles and at least straightened them, calling loudly, "Just a minute!" He kicked an open box under the bed and tossed the blankets up over the pillows, wondering why the embarrassment. Better yet, why did he desperately *not* want Ken to see his place this way now?

Knock. Knock. "Police. Open up."

That was Harley.

Raine stood straight and whipped his head toward the door. "What in Danu's—" he started, but stopped himself then wondered aloud, "Ifrinn, why? Why the official tone?"

He glamoured up, moved toward the door, and put on a smile. "What a lovely surprise now," he said, swinging the door wide.

"Raine Abarta," Vic started, dangling the cuffs, "you have the right to remain silent. Anything—" Vic kept talking, while Harley turned Raine around forcibly, but Raine merely narrowed his eyes at Ken with question and confusion. She looked back down the stairs, toward the door. She refused to look at him and fidgeted, her hands shaking.

When Vic finished his spiel, Raine asked, "What's this about?"

Ken's lip and one eye twitched as she turned to look beyond him. She scanned his small, mortal-like home with little more than objective interest. "Interfering with an official police investigation. Here's the warrant." She unfolded a paper and held it in front of his face. The letterhead of the Wickney City Courthouse and a raised seal in the lower corner proved it was official.

Raine read the words typed in the charges line. Outrage flooded his mouth. "I have not tampered with any bloody piece of evidence in this case." Yet he couldn't deny the second half. That had been exactly what he was doing, and he desperately wanted to continue doing. It was fun . . . a puzzle . . . faediom . . . and the thought of giving it up pierced his spirit.

Ken said nothing in reply as Harley and Vic urged him into the hallway, down the stairs, and once again into the back of their panda car. Once they had driven him the few blocks to WPD and escorted him to the sterile, windowless cell, Vic unlocked the cuffs.

Ken stayed on the other side of the bars, as far away as possible, with her arms crossed over her chest.

"Harley, c'mon," Raine pleaded.

Harley shook their head, turning away. "No can do. Letter of the law with this one. Sorry, Brah."

The two uniformed cops moved out of the cell and slid the bars closed, locking him inside. With held breath, Raine walked over and lifted his hands. He paused before grasping the bars to get a sense of the metal. When certain there was no iron, he wrapped his fingers around the cool bars. Thank Danu they hadn't locked him in the Fae cells. So, Raine concluded, at least Ken's conversation with the FVU hadn't revealed him as that kind of threat. He turned his begging to the woman he thought had been warming up to him. "Ken, why?"

Her eyes flickered in his direction, but she turned. "This case, *my* case, is pretty cut and dry, Raine. La Pointe is the obvious killer. I'm done playing games." She rubbed her forehead between her brows and pivoted to leave.

"But—"

"No, Raine. It's over." She kept walking.

"Did you find out why FVU was on the street that night?" Raine spouted. He hadn't truly wanted to talk about that, but it was the only idea he had at the moment that might get her to stay.

It did the trick. And with her stunned look, Raine didn't need magic to understand that the presence of the FVU vehicle on the street that night had absolutely slipped her mind.

Narrowing his eyes and nudging, he pouted. "It's all right, Ken. Like you said, you've had a long day. I can see exhaustion weighing down your shoulders. Go home. Get some rest but promise me you'll check out the SUV tomorrow before you throw the book at a distraught widower."

Ken turned back to him, her look downcast toward the concrete floor. Raine held his breath, gripped the bars tighter. Several heartbeats passed. When she lifted her gaze, just before they locked eyes, he saw it—a change in her. In her irises.

Sands shifted.

CHAPTER 11

RAINE

REAL, PURE, TOTAL, PERFECT, UNADULTERATED, complete, undiluted, gold-plated, genuine, wing-pluckin' boredom!

True, real faeries didn't have wings, but he had to entertain himself somehow, and the thought of Tinkerbell sitting around ripping out her wings because she had nothing better to do seemed apropos.

Tinkerbell, hrmph. Walt Disney's bastardization of every last tale that held something mouth-watering made him squirm.

"Pundiluted," he pontificated aloud. "No."

Raine scratched his jawline; his fourth finger moved with the action. He felt it scratching at his skin but no sensation in the extra digit.

"Hrm. Re . . . plete. Replete!" Momentarily, he was overly happy with his new word merge, but then he remembered it was a real human word, and cursed, "Danu!"

"Let's see, how about total-perfect. To . . . fect. Yeah. Tofect. Tofect boredom. Tofectly bored." He let that made-up word circle for a bit before he shook his head again. "Nah, sounds like a disease. Gah!"

Raine looked around at the barren walls and listened to snores echoing from the cell down the hall. He'd always credited himself with developing his human-functional skills to near perfection, but this aspect of human being, this sitting and waiting, he couldn't handle. His head resting on the painted cinderblock, he wished for Fae intention, but the ability to travel by thought was only available when inside the Faerie realm. Raine groaned and stretched out on the cement bench that doubled for a bed. It reminded him of the ledge in a tile shower. He couldn't muster enough exhaustion to sleep, so he stood up and paced.

Fortunately, he hadn't felt the need to visit Vanessa since his return from Fae. The visit to his mother's land had soothed the desperate need to drink from that mortal well of high spirits—for the immediate future. Once it started again, though, he might rip apart anyone in his way to see her again. And this ennui would certainly drive him there faster than anything. After his third lap around the tiny cell, he went to the bars, once again grateful for the absence of iron, and called out, "Guard?"

He waited.

The La Pointe case had been replaying in his mind since Ken had locked him inside and left for the night. What time was it now? He'd concluded he needed to provide his favorite detective with something more tangible.

Whatever had happened between the time he'd left her to follow up with the FVU and later yesterday when the three of them had shown up with an arrest warrant must have been enough to make his speculations seem like shots in the dark. After all, the white car being a hairdresser's certainly hadn't helped his case. No, it was time to spill something that'd certainly win Ken over.

Mal.

Still nothing from the police guard on duty. He called again, still running the case around in his head. The question was: How was he going to get Ken to listen? Or believe him? The exhaustion she'd worn before she'd left and that look she'd given him . . . He closed his eyes to view the image again. Vividly, she appeared in his mind's eye, and when she'd looked up . . . no, it couldn't have been true. Had it been a trick of the harsh, fluorescent lighting? There was no way he would have missed that! Right?

Raine gasped, scrubbed a hand over his face, then yelled again, "GUARD!"

Finally, he had a Danu-blessed idea, a little bit of sweet Fae trickery. He tapped his fingers on the bars and snickered as he finally heard the jingling of a keyring. This was going to be epic!

KENNEDI

THE LAST SHE RECALLED FROM the night before, Kennedi's room had been pitch black and she had the blanket in midair about to wrap herself tight for the night. But when she awoke, the bedroom glowed and she lay curled in a fetal position. Her body releasing, she stretched. Her feet dangled off the bed's end; her hands pressed against the headboard. After pushing a little blood back into sleepy muscles, she stood and stretched again. Reaching for the ceiling, she marveled over how long she'd rested. She never, ever slept until after the sun rose, but she definitely felt better for it.

Kennedi bent at the waist. She placed her hands flat on the floor beside her bare feet while the backs of her legs loosened. Blood rushed to her head. Folded over, her mind decided to join the waking world along with her body. Quick recall hit her; she straightened and hurried to the bathroom across the hall. No window there, she felt for the lights. A quick flip illuminated the small space. She leaned over the sink and stretched her eyes to make sure her imagination had been running wild the night before. With a heavy sigh, her shoulders fell. "Thank God!" Her eyes were back to their absolutely normal and boring mid-tone brown; no movement. No migraine either. She really hated taking time to visit Dr. Valley and enduring the battery of tests he'd surely order up.

After morning necessities, she grabbed her smartphone from the kitchen counter and put in an Imitrex refill with the pharmacy. The self-injection shots made her off kilter and jittery, but she couldn't afford to be caught without it if another headache struck.

Kennedi readied herself for work, prepped a bagel, and brewed a cup of go-juice. Coffee in hand, she was on her way. The final paperwork on the La Pointe case awaited her arrival at WPD. With any luck, she'd have it finished up by noon. Captain Quaid and District Attorney Rhyse Mitchell would be tickled that she'd decided not to make them wait any longer.

Feeling unusually refreshed, she decided to walk the two miles to the station that morning. She strode through the front door and greeted Callen Graham, the officer manning the front desk. The elevator at the back of the lobby dinged; the doors slid open. Kennedi double timed to catch it and pressed the number five. Alone in the car, she unlocked her phone and scrolled through her emails, deleting the regular notifications from IT and groaning as she accepted the invitation to the annual WPD holiday party. She'd hated parties ever since her first foster mom made her perform that stupid Irish stepdance in front of all her socialite friends. She'd tripped over her own feet, landed with her legs in the air, and that damn curly wig went flying across the room. Afterward, Kennedi had refused to take any more classes.

Email cleared, she flipped to her favorite news feed from Wickney Weekly. The bell chimed again as the feed loaded, and the elevator's steel doors slid open. Kennedi read the headlines crafted by Amy Jennings, the publication's founder, as she stepped onto the fifth floor. After a few more steps, she leaned her shoulder into the *Investigations Department* label on a glass door and pushed her way inside.

Amy, also Wickney Weekly's lead investigative reporter, had been a solid source for a number of case-breaks over the years, and if there was someone Kennedi might call a friend, it was Amy. Which reminded her, how long had it been since they did lunch? *Ah, heck, I'm a shit friend.* She marched toward her desk.

It was still early enough that the other officers who worked on the fifth floor hadn't showed up for work and the lights remained dim. Kennedi didn't look up from her phone as she navigated by memory and feel toward her desk. When she arrived, she jumped backward, her heartbeat galloping as her eyes landed on the man sitting behind her desk—in *her* chair—with his feet propped up like he owned the place, his hands clasped behind his head, and wearing a grin that said he'd just won a hefty lottery.

She looked around the office. There was no one else in sight, the lights in the waiting areas, interrogation chambers, and walled offices at the end of the room were still off. How had he gotten free from lock-up? Kennedi ran through the limited number of possible scenarios and made a mental note to ensure the guard on duty last night was written up and put on probation. Every question she could possibly ask seemed cliché, and she was certain he'd dance around the answers.

So she gritted her teeth and glared at Raine Abarta. "How the hell did you get out?" She threw the phone onto her desk, her hand moving for her sidearm. "What'd you do to the guards?"

"Oh now, they're fine down there." He shrugged. "Maybe a little sleepy now, but they'll be right as rain in a few hours then."

This infuriating man must possess the charisma to convince Diogenes the Cynic that wealth and politics were virtues. "Not likely." She set her coffee on the desk with a thud, flipped the snap on her holster and pulled the gun. With her free hand, she grabbed the desk phone and pressed a button, keeping an eye on the prisoner in front of her and cursing herself. Perhaps she should have let West have his fun.

Raine dropped his feet, spread one hand in surrender, and dropped the other to the button silencing the line. "What, Ken? No good morning?"

"It *was* a good morning," she scoffed; her brows raised. "Get out of my chair."

He deflated. "Don't you want to know how I got here?"

"Of course I do." But she was by no means convinced that he'd give her the truth about what he'd done to get out of that cell. "Are you planning to actually tell me?"

Raine threw a hand over his heart and gasped. "What, my dear, do you mean to imply?"

Disbelieving, she stared at him, trying to keep absolutely no expression on her face. Hell, what she should do is cuff him and march him right back down there. But he wasn't making any move for escape. She slowly lowered the phone to its cradle. Maybe that migraine did more to her yesterday than she wanted to admit. Perhaps she *should* make that appointment with Dr. Valley. Or with a shrink instead, because, damn her, her judgement seemed way off.

"Fine then." She waved him out of her chair and sat, placing the gun on the desk in easy reach.

He pulled over Harley's chair. "I merely reasoned with Heidi."

Who's Heidi? The overnight guard? Must be. Kennedi waited in silence for him to continue. Reasoning with a guard who'd been trained to resist prisoners' pleas was about as irrational as negotiating with a pig. He didn't explain any further, so she rolled her eyes and turned to the computer.

Raine reached for the wooden fidget puzzle on her desk—twelve interconnected colorful blocks. How odd that she felt they were exactly like the toy, disconnected pieces tied together by something unseen. What was the invisible string connecting her to this conundrum sitting beside her desk? She blinked several times to eradicate that thought.

After several iterations of reconfiguring the puzzle, Raine said, "I'll admit, some of the hints I've provided have been vague, but that's because I didn't think you'd believe everything I knew. And some of them, I can't explain how I know. I have new information, and I'm really no harm to your case, now am I?"

He didn't look at her as he spoke, and she registered a note of sadness in his voice. *Harden yourself, Ken.* She cursed. Damn him for getting that nickname to stick in her own brain.

He continued, "But I'm going to trust you enough to share the rest and hope that you'll trust me in return. You also shouldn't ask how I know this piece of information, because I still can't explain." His eyes remained downcast.

And damn her, because she was about to give in to whatever pull this man had. She was about to ignore everything she'd told herself and all her training. She was going to put off filling out the remainder of the La Pointe paperwork she'd been intent on this morning. Her ears were open again—so easily—but something felt different this time, as if he'd been trying to manipulate her before with his narrowed gaze each time he'd given her a new bit of information. But now that he didn't look at her, it seemed she was freer to hear what he actually said.

"I'm listening." She leaned back in the chair.

Raine's fingers worked the blocks with a proficiency she'd never seen, and he never seemed to think about the movements. Most people's brows dipped regularly into a deep V as they moved through dozens of configurations. Raine simply and systematically repeated the same steps forward and in reverse again and again, the expression on his face never changing.

Behind his closed lips, his mouth worked, then he swallowed before asking, "Have you figured out who Mal is?"

Kennedi closed her eyes tight then popped them wide. Her mouth took a minute to catch up with her brain, but then she recalled that he'd already known about the lingerie and the note. "No. I suppose you know?"

"I haven't verified my suspicion."

"But?" she prompted. If he had a lead, she was all over that one. Mal had been the one thing she felt might break the case . . . if indeed La Pointe was innocent.

"I think it's initials for Maximus Linardi." With this, his eyes flicked up to meet hers briefly then returned to the puzzle.

Ken's eyes popped open and her mouth worked like a guppy. She hadn't asked pointedly before, but she did now. "The owner of the Local?"

"The one and only," he said, still sounding a bit distant.

She thought for a beat and fired off a question she should have asked that night during the burlesque show. "How do you know about the lingerie and the note?"

Raine pressed his lips tight, fingers still working, but a scowl creeping across his forehead for the first time. So, that was the piece he couldn't, or wouldn't explain.

"If you won't tell me, then how am I supposed to believe a word you say? About this or anything else?"

He tossed the nails on the desk, coupled once again, and leaned closer. "Have you verified my alibi yet, Ken?"

"I—well, hang on." She hadn't personally, but had asked Vic and Harley to. Kennedi wiggled the mouse, pulled up the case file, and double-clicked on the photo of Raine on the virtual case board.

Raine scoffed. "Geez, Ken, I can get you a better picture than that now."

Kennedi tried to ignore him.

He chuckled, pressing on, "Person of interest, then am I? *Your* interest?"

She turned and squinted at him. "It's an official term, Raine. We flagged you that way when you showed up and wanted to speak with William La Pointe. That's—what do we call it? Oh yeah. Suspicious, Raine. It's. Suspicious." Focusing back on the screen, she scanned through the recent notes and highlighted the last line. "Looks like Candi Crush checked out."

"Great, then you have verifiable evidence that I'm not full of shite." He stood and took a couple of steps toward the elevator, calling over his shoulder, "Let's go check out Mal."

"Hold your horses," Kennedi called. She checked the clock above the door. "It's before eight in the morning. Linardi is certainly still in bed. And you're still in jail."

Raine hesitated, tapping his foot, then raised a finger in the air. "Then we"—Raine narrowed his eyes and lowered his voice along with his finger, pointing at her—"or you, should take care of that little problem first."

A groan built in the back of her throat and, given that they were the only two on the floor, she let it roll. Raine stood tall with his arms primly folded in front of his chest and lifted his chin at an angle.

Gawd that man had a dramatic streak! "Okay. Fine. Sit." She pointed to the chair, waiting for him to obey the order. Captain Quaid and Rhyse would probably have her head for this one, but she didn't care in the moment. She wanted this Mal person way more than she wanted Raine-the-annoyance behind bars.

As if to emphasize her inner thought, he skipped and double stepped—that over-the-top actor move where they kick backward before walking forward, his arms circling in a *gotta-get-going* gesture. Then with the back of his legs against the chair, he spread his hands, bowed, and fell backward into the seat.

Kennedi rolled her eyes, pulled up the second file on the computer, and grumbled, "And who the hell says shite anyway?"

CHAPTER 12

RAINE

LAUGHTER ROARED FROM THE DOUBLE glass doors barricading the office from the elevator, and Raine turned. Vic and Harley crashed in, coffee in hands and laughing so hard that Harley held their side.

"What's so funny?" Raine asked, standing.

They both froze. Smiles fell from their faces, and their gazes fluttered from him to Ken and back.

Raine lifted a hand nonchalantly and reached for Ken's coffee, answering their unspoken questions, "She's filing the paperwork to spring me. We came to an *agreement*."

"Uh, not so sure I'd put it in those words." Ken grabbed the cup from his hands before he could get it to his lips. When he pouted, she pointed to the pot on the wall, said, "Make your own," and returned to the work on the computer.

Standing, Raine bounced on the balls of his feet. "We're going to meet with Mal today. You guys in?"

Harley gave Raine a *right-on,-man* look while Vic rushed to the other side of Ken's desk, surprise widening his eyes. "What? You figured out who he is?"

Always a bit more aloof than Vic, Harley strolled over.

Raine eyed the paper cup in his hand, his mouth watering for the froo-froo drink. "That looks delicious. What I'd give for a mocha with tons of extra whipped cream and sugar right now."

Harley clapped a heavy hand on Raine's shoulder with a disapproving headshake. "That much damn sugar'll go straight to the love handles."

"What do you take in your coffee?" Raine asked.

"Black, man. Jolt of caffeine straight to the main line."

Raine stuck out his tongue. "Bleck. Disgusting."

But Harley only shrugged and turned when the glass doors swooshed again. Raine only recognized one of the two older men who strode in with golf bags slung over their shoulders. He turned to the coffee pot, whispering to Harley, "Strange that anyone would wear cowboy boots when golfing. How do you work this contraption?"

"Mornin' Captain Q, West," Vic, in Raine's peripheral vision, reached out a hand and shook both of the mens' as they passed.

Captain Q stopped at the desk. "Getting that La Pointe matter wrapped, Craine?"

Raine kept one eye on the scene at Ken's desk as Harley tried to explain how to work the machine. In the end, Raine didn't have to do any of the real work in producing the cup of coffee.

Ken's gaze lifted slowly from the computer. She first looked to West, who nodded, then she turned to her senior officer. "Soon, Aleks. I gave you my timeline yesterday."

Once again, blatantly ignoring Raine and Harley in favor of Ken, West cocked his head. Subtle, but not so much that Raine didn't catch the move. The look he flashed at Ken portrayed a note of confusion, but it was gone before anyone else seemed to take note. Raine remembered the officer from before and his dismissiveness toward anyone but Ken. It seemed that this Captain Q had his favor as well, but Raine felt certain there was more in his motivation with Ken, and that rankled. If he were a dog, he might piss to mark his territory. How utterly disgusting.

"How was the round?" asked Vic, clearly buttering up his ranking officers and at the same time, extracting Raine from his inner train of thought.

"Good, Vic," Captain Q, or Aleks as Ken called him, answered. "Maybe you should join us next time for a sunrise match."

Vic preened. "Certainly, sir. When's that?"

The two men moved along, toward the office in the far corner. The captain called back, "Every Tuesday and Thursday."

Raine accepted the cup of not-sweet coffee and crossed back to Ken's desk, Harley at his side. He cleared his throat and waited for Ken's attention. When her brown eyes landed on him, he asked, "We have some time before Linardi's likely at the club, right?

She nodded.

Raine couldn't keep bitterness from his tone. "Maybe

you should follow up with your friend there on that other matter . . . the SUV."

She read his disapproving tone and cocked one brow. "You wanna be back in that cell?"

"No, but—"

"Then I have to finish this paperwork." She resumed typing.

He might be treading on dangerous ground, but he quipped back as her fingers clacked over the keyboard. "But when you're done?"

"Fine," she breathed.

"Great." He leaned on her desk, earned another evil eye, and promptly ignored it. "Hey, Ken, can I run back to my place and grab some fresh clothes?"

Without a glance away from the screen, she told Harley to escort him.

"Sure thing, Craine," they answered readily. "Anything else going on this morning? Thinkin' maybe I can get in an early workout. I can drag this sucker along too and get him out of your space."

With a corner of her mouth lifted, Ken finally turned her attention to them. "You do that. And put him through the ringer, will ya?"

"Sure thing, boss. Let's go." They tilted a head toward the elevators.

Vic remained behind.

Harley and Raine bantered non-stop while they visited Raine's flat on Aldgate, while they strode back to the station, and while they changed into shorts and tanks for the workout. Simultaneously, Raine spent much of the short trip considering how he was going to convince

Harley that he was adept in the gym, when in truth, the thought of running on a revolving belt and picking up heavy metal over and over seemed like pure monotony. There was no way he'd be able to lift as much or run as fast, and certainly given the disparity in their statures, Harley wouldn't expect him to match ability. But Raine had other skills, and he'd use them well.

They tackled the treadmill first. Raine watched Harley press the pace up to 7.5 for the warm-up and reached for his own button. He narrowed his eyes at Harley and *nudged* as he pressed the button to 5.5.

Harley glanced over to check. "Dang. Nice work, man!" they complimented him, and cranked the speed up to what'd that work out to . . . *a six-minute mile?*

Raine trotted along at his easier pace, periodically pretending to up the speed as Harley actually did. "Dang . . . *pant* . . . the run's kicking . . . my ass today," they said between breaths. Pretty soon, sweat rolled down Harley's face.

Raine trotted along, and the next time Harley looked over, he grabbed his towel and wiped his own face. "No kidding, whew, my legs feel like jelly now."

Ten minutes passed, and Harley stopped his belt. Breathless, he said, "Wasn't expecting you to keep up. Nice work." They clapped a sweaty hand on Raine's bare shoulder. "Let's hit the weights."

Raine wiped Harley's sweat from his shoulder.

Feigning weightlifting would take a bit more finesse, but Raine was game. And when he had Harley believing he was lifting about half the nearly four-hundred pounds Harley did, Raine had to use all his acting skills to strain his face as if he struggled with the bar. He'd only put five-pound irons on either end, but the little *nudge* he continually gave Harley worked wonders. After the last set, he took a big drink of water, wiped his face, and shook his arms. "Dang, didn't think I'd squeeze in that last one then."

With the workout in the bag, they both showered, Harley washing away the sweat, but Raine only washing away the grime from sitting in that cell most of the night . . . and maybe Harley's flung sweat too. Gross. Whether or not he needed it, the feel of hot water on his skin refreshed him a little more. Before heading back upstairs, Raine suggested, "Should we get another coffee?"

"I'm game," Harley said.

A few hours after they left, with his sugar-laced mocha in-hand, Raine walked shoulder to shoulder with Harley back onto the fifth floor where Ken and Vic waited.

Harley strutted past Vic, teasing, "You missed one hell of a workout. Our boy here's a monster."

"I'm sure," said Vic.

Ken narrowed her eyes, clearly in disbelief, but Raine examined her closer to see if that glint he'd witnessed the night before would happen again. This time, nothing. Her eyes, while pretty and lined in some of the darkest and longest lashes he'd ever noticed on a human, were a flat brown.

Raine sat on the desk. "How goes it here, Ken? Learn anything about the SUV?"

Her brown eyes lowered to where he sat. "Would you not?"

"Not what?"

"Sit on my desk. There's a perfectly good chair right there."

Raine stood. "Oh. Uh, okay." He gave a flippant shrug but didn't take the seat she suggested. "The SUV?"

"Another dead end. It was an officer named Jory who works for West. He was following up on a case at that restaurant MacCaibe watches," Ken said dismissively. "Apparently they called in an incident the same night—someone going into withdrawals from a Fae relationship overdose." She waved a hand in the air as if the thought of that situation seemed more of an annoyance than the real and dangerous thing the anti-Fae zealots believed.

Raine bit his tongue, knowing exactly how dangerous it could be. Sexual release was the epitome of highs a mortal could experience. Drug highs didn't compare. When a human became emotionally attached to a faerie, it could and usually did result in lifetime insanity if they parted. But when a faerie connected emotionally with a mortal, they outlasted the human in both life and relationship. The combination of emotion and levity addiction was a harder bond than a human could know. Thank Danu that Candi had always insisted that no emotion was allowed on the occasions when they enjoyed one another's company. Easy, mutual high.

"And Detective West was there in a black and white earlier in the day?" Raine questioned.

"Same case," Ken continued, "He assigned Jory that night. Regardless, it's not unusual to have WPD unmarked vehicles out on the streets around town all the time. There's not a connection to the La Pointe case. Devereux Court is in downtown Wickney, and there could be any number of strange cars nearby on any given night for any number of reasons." She stood, shutting her laptop. "Should we head over to the Local and see if our friend Maximus Alan Linardi is in yet?"

Vic jumped to attention at Ken's prompt and moved

with her toward the back door. But Raine stood there with his teeth clenched, wondering about Ken's aloof explanation. What she said seemed perfectly logical on the surface, but the cars' presence hadn't felt usual to William La Pointe.

Harley started for the back, then turned. "You comin', Abarta?"

Raine forced his thoughts back to the here and now. "Yep." He followed the three detectives down the back stairs. He wasn't thrilled about having to walk into the Underground and try to meet with Maximus with three police officers in tow, but he'd make the sacrifice in return for his freedom. Maybe he was wrong about the SUV, but the strangeness in William's mind made him not want to let it go. Ifrinn! For that matter, why hadn't Ken followed up on the other car?

As he stepped into the crisp, bright, late morning and followed over to Ken's unmarked, he asked, "Did you talk to the driver of the white sedan?"

"The hairdresser?" Her brow raised in question for a second before she ducked into the driver's seat.

Raine pulled the handle, said a little prayer that she'd take it easier than when they'd gone after Ludwig, but before he closed the door, he considered the short distance to the Local. "Why don't we just walk?"

"Procedure," she answered and fired up the engine. The grin she wore as she watched him sent chills over his skin, but he closed the door and buckled up, pulling hard on the strap once the mechanism clicked into place. How bad could she scare him in a block and a half?

"The sedan?" he pressed, narrowing his eyes to *nudge* Ken. "The hairdresser. What's her name? Her, right?"

Ken sighed, apparently unaffected. "Raine, there's no way a young hairdresser is involved in the murder of an old man's wife. This is why I arrested you. You're grasping at straws and keeping me from closing this case."

Hm. Resistant to my nudge? She's close . . .

KENNEDI

SHE PARKED HER UNMARKED CAR on the street directly in front of the Local's double doors and leaned forward to peer up. The normally neon-lit vertical signage above the door was still legible, but harder to make out in the daytime hours. She didn't need to read it to know she was in the right location, but it gave her the view of the flats above the club too, all equally as quiet in the late morning. Harley and Vic pulled up and parked the panda car's front bumper close to Ken's back bumper, leaving barely enough room to slide in a broom handle. With the case of nerves Raine had shown at having to get into the car, she'd expected him to hop out as soon as she'd put the car in park. But he stayed seated with his belt secured.

He turned to glance backward up the street, then forward and downhill to Wickney University. "The front door won't be open yet. Dick, the bartender, doesn't arrive until one to open the place."

Of course he would know these details. "And I suppose you know of another entry?"

"Around back. Maximus's personal entry. He'll have to buzz us in. There's a small parking lot back there."

"Naturally," she muttered, starting the car.

The walkie went off, and she shared the information with her junior officers. Around back, they parked next to a black Escalade with blacked-out windows.

Raine released a relieved sigh. "Good, he's here."

At the door, he pressed a buzzer and stepped back, holding a hand forward for Kennedi to stand in front of the camera.

A voice on the intercom answered, and Kennedi held up her badge. "Police. We have a few questions for Mr. Linardi."

"One moment," said the filtered voice.

She turned questioningly to Raine, who leaned his back against the brick wall at some distance. He'd placed Vic and Harley between them, Vic fanning a folder with the necessary photos inside as he waited. Raine looked almost bored with his arms folded and legs crossed at the ankles as he waited. Everything about his posture said this was exactly the situation he'd expected. Instead of letting her suspicion drop this time, she asked, "Why are you so familiar with all this?"

Raine extended his arms. "These are my"—he lifted a pointed finger to his chin thoughtfully—"whaddaya call 'em now, stomping grounds?"

When the buzzer sounded, Kennedi jumped, pivoted, and opened the door. Holding it with one hand and sweeping her other toward the threshold in a *you-first* motion, she said, "Then why don't you feel free to lead the way, since these are your *stomping grounds* and all."

He gasped and a hand flew over his mouth. Then his eyes softened a bit as he teased, "Aw, Ken, where's that protect-and-serve mentality?"

She shrugged. "Don't see much here to protect you from." If he wanted to play games, she could too. She smiled.

But damn him, he outdid her. He circled his hands three times in front of him and bowed to her as if she were watching his fire juggling routine on the corner of Wickney Square. Harley chuckled and Vic covered his mouth to stifle his own laugh. Kennedi glared at the two officers until they thought better of the hilarity.

Raine stood, holding his head high, and stepped primly forward. "At your service, madam," he said in a very formal, British, butler-ish accent as he walked through the door.

The back stairs were more institutional than pub or club-like. They reminded Kennedi of the underbelly of WPD where they'd built the holding cells . . . the very place she had Raine Abarta locked up in the night before. She guessed the historic downtown buildings had all been crafted by the same handful of masons a couple hundred years prior. It showed. At the end of the long hallway, a man dressed in black from neck to toe waited with his gloved hands clasped in front of his body, his hair slicked back, and his head cocked to one side. The man was too young and his physique too wide at the shoulders yet lithe to be Maximus Linardi.

"Raine," he said as if they were the oldest of friends. "When did you start keeping company with bobbies?"

"Simmon," Raine answered as he arrived in front of the man and looked him up and down as if something about him had changed. "Nice to see you again too, and so formal now."

The man's expression didn't change when he asked, "How is Briar these days?"

Kennedi arrived at his side just in time to see Raine recover, pulling his dropped jaw upward. Shock danced across his eyes for a split second before he slid back into a stage mask. "I couldn't say," he said, the words clipped.

What's that look? Who is Briar?

Simmon added, "Your appointment with Mr. Linardi isn't until this evening."

Vic's and Harley's footsteps fell silent behind her, and Kennedi cleared her throat. "He doesn't really have a choice. Simmon?"

She waited for his last name, but no answer. The man turned from Raine to her, his hard expression softening very little. "I see. Well, Mr. Linardi has been expecting a visit from WPD. Right this way."

Inside, Kennedi felt like she'd finally entered a club, the lounge well-attired with leather, dark paisley carpet, and matching patterned wallpaper. Another man sat in one of the leather chairs with the Wickney Weekly journal held open before him. He didn't move the paper as they passed into the office where Maximus Linardi stood from his desk and extended a hand in greeting. Kennedi accepted the handshake from the mostly silver-haired man. It appeared as if he sported reverse highlights, the younger black intentionally woven in with the more-prominent, lighter strands. She'd seen photos of him, but never made his direct acquaintance. An inexplicable strength hung about him—his physique thick, but not fat. Still, it wasn't quite muscular either. Despite an odd remnant of sadness, a charm glimmered in his gray eyes. In truth, they matched the silver in his hair.

She could certainly see the allure. "Mr. Linardi, if you'll excuse the intrusion."

He waved a hand. "No, no. Please sit. As I'm certain Simmon mentioned, I have been expecting a visit from you since"—he swallowed—"Michelle's . . . uh . . ."

Taken off guard at his forthright manner and obvious distress over saying her name, Kennedi took the chair he offered.

When Linardi lifted his chin, Simmon exited, pulling the door closed behind him. Vic and Harley stood at parade rest in front of the door, and Raine skipped over to take the second leather chair in front of Linardi's massive cherry wood desk. Kennedi motioned to Vic, who came forward and spread the folder wide in front of Maximus Linardi. When he saw the image of the lingerie and note dipped in Michelle La Pointe's blood, the man got up and went to the bar behind his desk. "Can I offer you something?"

"We're fine, thank you," Kennedi answered.

With a gin and tonic in hand, Linardi returned to his seat. After draining about half the glass, he leaned forward and closed the folder, then peered up at Kennedi for several seconds, like he was reading her character.

She waited.

Finally, he pulled an envelope from his top desk drawer and slid it across the table. Grief striating his voice, he asked, "What is it you wish to know? I'm an open book. Here's a listing of my assets and accounts that you're free to research."

Kennedi stared him down, not touching the envelope.

Linardi pushed the folder with the photos back to her as well. "Yes, I sent those as a gift to Michelle. You'll find a copy of the receipt in here."

"Interesting, Mr. Linardi. It seems that you might have come forth earlier if you're innocent in the matter."

He turned sideways, reclined in the chair, propped an ankle over one knee, and folded his fingers in front of him. "You'll forgive me, but that forthcoming might have caused additional issues for the La Pointes."

She stared at him, unclear as to what precise issues that might cause, but she redirected. "Why don't you just tell me about the nature of your relationship with Mrs. La Pointe?"

"We were long-time lovers," he said as if it were the most commonplace thing in the world that a successful senator's wife would be having an ongoing affair with a man who ran a chain of nightclubs catering to both humans and faeries. "For many years. The three of us had a discrete arrangement. I loved Michelle and she loved me, intimately. Furthermore, I maintain great respect for William La Pointe."

"If that's the case, why would you have continued in secrecy?"

"Detective Craine, relationships aren't always as black and white as society would have us believe. I've never desired a wife. And Michelle relished her position at William's side."

Kennedi paused, and Raine took advantage of the gap in questions. With eyes narrowed, he asked, "Do you believe that William La Pointe could have murdered his wife? Maybe he was jealous over your affair."

"Fuck no. William La Pointe has a need for success, as did Michelle. I guess I do too, but in a different way." He smiled wanly then took another gulp from his gin. "William is greedy with his money and his career. He wasn't always around for her when she needed him. But I can assure you of this: he's always known about Michelle and me. In truth, our relationship provided him with a bit of relief from his husbandly duties, if you will."

"But that didn't change his hurt," Raine mused, his brow folding as if he were truly off put by these notions.

Kennedi examined the bard. The way he responded to Linardi sounded like *he* possessed the personal feelings and emotions that would be expected from the La Pointe patriarch. The possibility made absolutely no sense.

"Al contrario," Linardi retorted. "William La Pointe loved his wife just as Michelle loved him. They were partners in almost everything in life—except intimacy. The three of us had a solid arrangement."

Kennedi studied Raine. In a marked change from the time he'd questioned La Pointe, his current train of thought seemed on the up-and-up. She'd be damned if she could ever figure out this man who presently turned to her and switched again, grinning widely.

She caught herself and stammered, "Then why, if you don't believe him capable of murder, wouldn't you have come to William La Pointe's defense?"

He lowered his chin and simultaneously pointed those gray eyes at her. "Detective, you know my business?" He spread his hands to indicate the club.

Kennedi nodded as new logic about that coalesced. There were rumors that Maximus Linardi's business wasn't entirely on the side of their legal system.

"What kind of imbecile would I be to insert myself into such a public case?" he asked. "My involvement alone would cause more suspicion."

Then an idea struck. She scooted forward in the chair, resting an arm on the desk. "Any chance, Mr. Linardi, that whoever murdered Michelle La Pointe was actually after you?"

CHAPTER 13

RAINE

"Wow," RAINE SAID AS THEY exited the business entrance to the Local. He pushed Harley playfully with his elbow. "Ya think Vic'd be up for that with his girl?"

"Nah, man. He's got it bad for his girl. I just can't believe a high-profile politician would be in an open relationship," they answered.

Vic either didn't hear the conversation—unlikely—or more probably, he chose to ignore the off-hand banter. An open marriage wasn't anything Raine had considered, but why hadn't he sensed that when he'd seen the note and lingerie when he did the memory walk?

He also wondered if Ken's hunch about the murderer targeting Linardi was a better explanation. Maybe he should discuss it with Vanessa. That thought sent a thrill of anticipation up his spine. Danu, the high he got from that woman. No, who cared if he was denying his croí, that indulgence would put him down for the count for days while he wore off the high. The only problem with his choice to keep working this faediom with Ken was he had to deny his baser instincts and focus.

If Linardi had been in a long-term relationship with the La Pointes, someone had to have more information about it. Wrapped up in the possibilities, Raine walked absently toward the car and plowed into Ken's back.

She stumbled. He lurched forward to catch her, grasping at her waist. When his hands made purchase, they both fumbled and scrambled some more until he twisted her body in his grasp and stabled himself with his feet lunging forward. They didn't fall to the ground, but he held her quite intimately.

"Dayum," called Vic.

Harley moved to Vic's side, arms folded over their chest. "Might as well plant one on her now, man."

Ken placed her hands on Raine's shoulders, shock working at her speechless lips. Her cheeks flushed. He could kiss her. Ifrinn, he considered it. Instead, he held her protectively barely two feet from the ground and stared into her eyes.

"Awww, they're making love with their eyes," Vic said.

Harley chortled, "A romance novel in the making. Ya'll about done?"

Raine grinned. "I've got you."

"We should get back to the station," Vic said.

Harley snorted. "You two been takin' dance lessons behind our backs?"

Obviously flustered, Ken turned and shot a scathing look at Harley. She worked her feet beneath herself. Raine obliged and lifted her back to an upright position. He wanted to ask if it'd be such a tragedy. Instead, he stood, wrapped an arm around his own waist, and hinged forward as if he bore the purest intentions.

When she only glared at him, he tilted his head in question. "No curtsy, ma'am?"

Ken groaned, rolled her eyes, and pivoted toward the car.

Harley held out a fist which Raine bumped with a shrug.

"I tried," Raine said. "Listen." He lifted his arms and stretched toward the sky. Yawning, he made an exaggerated show of needing sleep after the long night he'd spent in the slammer. "You guys don't need me back at the station, true? After that stone bed and killer workout, I'm beat."

"Nah," muttered Harley, "but you're fun to have around while we work through the monotony."

"No," Ken shot back, harsh and decisive. "We definitely don't need you mucking around with this investigation any more than you already have."

Raine wagged his brow. "Aw, but you'll miss me? Right, Ken?"

By way of answer, she flung open the door, shot him a glare, ducked inside, and started the engine.

"Catch ya later, man," Harley opened their own door.

Raine walked toward the street at a slow roll, waiting for the cars to pass him and turn out of sight before he stopped and did an about-face, headed right back to the door they'd just exited. He hit the buzzer and waited.

This time, no voice sounded. But after five minutes, the door opened from the inside and Simmon stood there in full Fae, eyes questioning his return.

Raine weaseled between Simmon and the door jamb.

Simmon grumbled, "Mr. Linardi is busy now, Raine."

"No worries. I want to talk to you. Maybe Berry." He danced a turn as he walked down the sterile hall with Simmon at his back. "Can we do it over a scotch?"

"No bartender on duty yet."

"I think I can pour my own drink," Raine retorted. "Are you sure you're Fae, Simmon?" Raine schooled his face in a poor imitation of the man and dropped his voice. "You're so serious."

There wasn't any question that Simmon and Berry were both Fae, but they favored a more severe nature so heavily that Raine wondered if they could get high on human joy. Or maybe they were the dangerous ones and the reason the humans had formed forces against his kind. Well, that was insane. He'd been dangerous enough himself, but he didn't let it obscure his every-day jovial self. He couldn't deny that emotional Fae-human relations were dangerous to both their kinds, but Raine couldn't fathom living in this realm and brooding so. Between the abundance of ways to feed the dìomhaireachdanseòlta— police cases being his new favorite—and the plethora of people who tickled the Fae Sight when he opened his senses to their auras, Raine thought it must be a terribly boring existence to deny oneself.

Inside the bar, Raine moved behind the huge horseshoe-shaped counter, found a bottle of Bowmore 12-year and two glasses, and went to a booth near the office door. Raine filled the lowballs and took a healthy swig as Simmon lowered himself onto the black leather bench. He left his glass untouched.

Raine reached over and lifted the crystal. "I know, I know. You won't get drunk easily off the stuff, but if you drink enough . . ."

"Tastes like dirty socks. What do you want, Raine?"

"How is it we've never met? Here or in Fae, I mean." Raine let his glamour slide, easing into his natural form and dispensing with that worrisome extra finger.

The Fae shrugged a broad shoulder. "You've been wrapped up in your, uh, overground world, and I've been busy working for Linardi. I don't do the club scene and I don't do the street performer scene. I don't like putting on glamour." He glanced at the red-tipped amaryllis on Raine's forearm.

"But you're the child of a Noble Fae," Raine countered. "It's unlikely we would have never met in Fae."

"I didn't attend your mother's court. My people live apart from the Noble City."

That made no sense. His Noble marque labeled him the child of Saffron, who was Skye's twin, Briar's uncle. But he'd said apart from the Noble City.

"Truly? Where?" Raine widened his eyes. He hadn't had much opportunity to explore beyond the Noble City. Ifrinn! He wasn't certain who in Fae would even have the knowledge to guide him out of the Noble City.

Simmon pressed his lips into a tight line. "I don't understand what this has—"

Raine sighed and threw an arm on the back of the booth bench. "Would you just humor me? I'd love to visit wherever it is you're from. I didn't get much of a chance to explore Fae under the thumb of my mother." And maybe, just maybe, Amaryllis wouldn't sense his presence if he were somewhere else. He tucked that thought away.

A look flitted across Simmon's shifting eyes. Was that sympathy he showed as he relented? "We call it Nadarra."

Raine mulled over the meaning. *Natural* seemed an odd name for a city or town in Fae where everything was magical, but then again, if everything was magical, then magical was natural indeed. Like Simmon's marque. "So you never visited your father at court?"

Simmon hardened again. "No. Can we get on with this?" He waved a hand in the air in a *whatever-this-is* manner.

"What *do* you drink, Simmon of Noble Saffron?"

He winced, but quickly recovered himself. "Fíon," he answered shortly, indicating the Fae spirit.

"Ah, but that's rare. I haven't had that here since—"

"A few nights back," Simmon interrupted. "Your betrothed brought me a bottle."

"My . . ." Raine peered at him over the glass, holding every inch of himself perfectly still. "Briar was here?"

"Looking for you. When will you return to her, Raine?"

Danu, the tables had turned and it soured the whiskey on Raine's tongue. Something in him shifted. The thought of never returning crossed his mind. *Wha—why?* He shook his head. And while Briar held a wicked beauty and rocking curves, the thought of truly coupling with that thorn of a Fae made his upper lip twitch. Sex, sure. But having a faeling? Ifrinn, no!

"I'll ask again," Simmon started, a satisfied look settling over his face, one that said he'd won, if it was only through a tiny jab. "What do you want, Raine?"

Raine finished off his glass and reached across to grab

Simmon's. He didn't want the peaty spirit to go to waste. "Well, I'm not here to speak about your father or Briar or anything Fae."

Simmon cocked his head and narrowed his eyes. "That detective has you in thrall, doesn't she? Should my cousin be worried? Jealous, maybe? Dangerous, definitely."

"No," Raine snapped. "There's nothing between Ken and me." *At the moment.* "I'm here to ask you about Linardi's affair with Michelle La Pointe."

That zipped him up tight, and he made to stand.

"Wait, this is Fae-to-Fae, no worries about me spreading things to the mortals."

Simmon relaxed momentarily. "I'm not at leave to discuss their relationship with either human or Fae." He lowered his voice. "As much as I will say is that it endured for more than three human decades."

"Ah, Danu, that's longer than—"

Simmon nodded once and stood. "Do I need to show you the way out?"

Pieces and parts collided in Raine's brain. Maybe one of his little tricks he'd thrown in the mix wasn't so far-fetched after all. He hopped up from the booth and scurried toward the door, leaving the open bottle and glass on the table. "Nope, I know the way," he called back.

He had to get to Ken.

KENNEDI

"RAINE ABARTA IS NOTHING BUT a distraction," Kennedi commented for what seemed the hundredth time to her junior officers.

Harley quipped, "Maybe, but he's a good time, and we never would have known that Linardi was love-letter Mal if it weren't for him."

Without turning around, Ken could hear the shrug in their voice and the fact that they simply didn't care that Abarta threw a little chaos into their lives at work. Yet Harley Gold had a decent point, regardless of whether Kennedi wanted to admit it. "Anyway." She turned to face Vic. "Have you rescheduled your date night with Lauren yet?" She grabbed a stack of new mail that'd been dropped on her desk while they were out and rifled through while listening to more of the small talk.

"This weekend." Vic answered. "I had to beg the manager for a table at Ciao Bella within the next month, but the ring is burning a hole in my pocket. I'm ready to make that woman Missus Victor Clark." He took off his coat and slung it on the back of his chair.

Harley did the same just as Kimber, Quaid's administrative assistant, wandered over. "Detective Craine, a Miss Vanessa La Pointe is waiting for you in the guest area."

Kennedi looked up from the mail. "I wasn't expecting her. Did she say why she's here?"

"No," Kimber replied with a small head shake, and turned on her heel to head back to her desk outside Quaid's office.

Kennedi tossed the envelopes back onto the corner of her desk and went to see Vanessa. The blonde woman turned from the window as the door sounded. "It's about time. I've been waiting for almost an hour."

Kennedi crossed the small room to the window and

leaned on the sill with her arms folded. "I'm sorry to keep you waiting, Miss La Pointe. What can I do for you?"

"My father is distraught. I came to get an update on the case." She lifted her chin, an answer clearly expected.

"I'm afraid I don't have anything I can share with you at this time. If you—"

"That's unacceptable, Detective Craine. My father is innocent in this matter, and I need to know what you've been doing to find the real murderer." Vanessa placed a hand on her hip.

Kennedi fought the urge to cross her arms over her chest—*be nice to the families 101.* "Let me ask you this, Miss La Pointe. Were you aware of another man in your mother's life?"

The woman's bright blue eyes stretched wider than Kennedi thought possible. Those had to be contacts. Vanessa's jaw hung for several seconds before she passed over the shock and asked, "W-what are you saying?" She lowered her brows, then more adamantly demanded, "Do you dare accuse my mother, the victim of this horror, of having an affair?"

Kennedi shook her head. "I'm not accusing anyone of anything. I was merely asking a question."

"Well," Vanessa huffed. "I am quite offended by what the question insinuates. My mother and father were the happiest couple on the face of the Earth. That matter has been all over the local media, so you, Detective, are blind if you aren't able to see that with your own eyes. There's nothing, I repeat, *nothing* that would have caused my father to do such a thing to my mother and his beloved wife."

Kennedi dropped her hands to the windowsill beside

her. "Very well, Miss La Pointe. Given that I have nothing I am at liberty to share, what else may I do for you today?" *She's distraught.* The woman clearly just wanted to state her case, and the sooner Kennedi could be done with that, the better. Vic and Harley were likely already diving into Maximus Linardi's background, and she wanted to be there rather than talking to an upset member of the victim's family.

Vanessa took a faltering step forward on her breakneck heels and stopped. Her hands shook, contrary to the poise in her voice. "Detective Craine, when can I expect something to be resolved in this matter?"

Keep your words calm, Craine. "I assure you that we are researching every possible angle. I hope to have something hard by the end of next week, but I make no guarantees. Sometimes the truth is slow to emerge." But somehow, no—because of that damned bard's interference, Kennedi once again believed it wasn't William La Pointe at the other end of the gun. It frustrated her to no end that he'd been right about Mal.

Vanessa grabbed her white handbag from the table. "Very well. I'll follow up at the end of next week."

Kennedi dipped her head in what she hoped could be interpreted as agreement, yet she made a mental note to have Vic attend to Vanessa the next time. And if or when they settled back on William La Pointe as the key suspect, someone else could deal with her petulant demands. They wouldn't work anyway. "Vanessa," she called before the La Pointe daughter made it to the exit.

Not speaking, the blonde turned to face her.

"May I make a suggestion?"

Vanessa nodded once.

"Regardless of what I learn, I will not be able to share details of the case with a civilian or anyone in the family." Kennedi swallowed, bitterly biting back the fact that she'd already done as much with the bard. "I suggest you work through your lawyer, Mr. Gorman."

The woman jutted her chin. "Perhaps I'll just bring him with me next time." She clacked the rest of the way to the door on her white stilettos.

Kennedi let out the tense breath she'd been half-holding and glanced sideways out the window. Before Vanessa latched onto the knob, the door flew open, announced by a creak that needed attention. Raine bowled through the door and straight into the La Pointe daughter.

"Oh, I'm—" he started.

"Excu—" she said at the same time.

But then they both stopped, both looked down, both fidgeted, and both slowly backed away from the other.

Ah hell, Kennedi thought, rolling her eyes. *Here we go again with this calamity. I thought I was done with this for today. Clearly not.* After a deep-breathing attempt to maintain control, she asked, "What are you doing back here already, Raine?"

But it was Vanessa who spoke up. "I-I'll just . . ." She twitched toward the door.

Kennedi scowled. "And why are you two behaving like you were caught kissing under the playground slide?"

Raine perked, innocence washing his features as if he were indignant she'd suggest such impropriety. "I haven't a clue of what you speak." He turned back to Vanessa, and with a slight bow, said, "Miss La Pointe, I trust you are doing well today."

Vanessa, not quite the actor Raine was, tried to feign

the same formal nonchalance. She touched her hair gingerly as she spoke, "I–I'm well, Mr. A-Abarta." She glanced at Kennedi. "And y-you, sir?"

The bard beamed at her with a *grander-than-life* grin but didn't answer. Then, clear that she was out of her depth and losing her carefully crafted poise, she left.

Raine wandered toward Kennedi, arms open. "Oh love, you're the one I wanted to see."

She pushed a hand forward and eyed him with a *don't-you-dare* glare. Vanessa quickly forgotten, Kennedi turned her head a little, raised both brows, and waited for his explanation.

"Just hear me out, Ken," he started, begging alight in his eyes.

"I thought you were tired? Wanted to sleep?" She paused for an answer, but his imploring gaze persisted. They battled silently for several seconds before Kennedi decided she'd have to hear him out. Tamping down every fiber in her body that wanted to tell him to get out of her hair, her case, her life, she gave him a single, solemn nod.

He made his way to the window and stood next to her, peering outside toward the parking lot adjacent to WPD. "I circled back to the club and spoke with Simmon a bit more."

"Linardi's guard?"

"That's the one. He wouldn't say much, but I got the impression that the affair had been going on for a very, very long time. Say thirty or more years." He shot a suggestive glance toward the door where Vanessa had been, then back out the window.

"So you're suggesting . . ." No, he couldn't be suggesting that.

He tucked his chin and looked at her through the top of his eyes, waiting.

She crossed her arms. "Are you saying the La Pointe children might really be Linardi children?"

Raine flourished his hands. "See, Ken, we are of one mind." He nodded, satisfaction dripping from his smug look. He quickly became distracted and casually regarded whatever minutia stirred below. Then, some puzzle drew his brows together as he watched the street.

Kennedi pressed her lips tight. No matter the possibility, that suggestion seemed too far-fetched to be true, at least with the eldest. "So, you wanna explain how Vincent looks like a brown-haired, less wrinkled version of his old man?"

Raine held out his hands, clearly stating *I dunno* with a full-body shrug, before absently and slowly asking, "What about Vanessa?"

Still no eye contact, but he had her with that one.

"She looks like her mother. No way to tell without a DNA test, and what difference does that make to the case?"

"There is my theory about the election." He tilted his head.

"No, Raine. Just no."

Kennedi faced the window, following Raine's fixation. Vanessa and their family friend Elanna Bell stood beside a blue Escalade. Vanessa swiped a tissue under her nose, and Elanna held out her arms for a hug. As Vanessa moved inside, Elanna looked up to the window, darkness shadowing her eyes as if she could see them watching her and wanted to curse the whole of the police department.

CHAPTER 14

RAINE

A COUPLE OF DAYS LATER, RAINE rushed onto the WPD's fifth floor after his performance in Wickney square, dragging his gear by the handle.

Vic looked over Ken's shoulder, reading from the paper she held. Harley stood beside their desk, a gym bag in hand. All three looked at Raine simultaneously, but it was Harley who greeted him.

"You didn't have to hurry, man. If I knew you were comin' I'd've waited," the bigger bobby teased.

Raine pushed his shoulders down from his ears and painted a frown, but he quickly dismissed the feigned dismay. "Next time. Did you hear? The La Pointes are making an official statement about the case." He looked back to the clock over the double glass doors he'd just pushed through. "In three minutes—at one."

Moments before, he'd been thrilled to be rushing back into WPD, excited for more faedìom—more clues, more problem-solving, more tension-ridden interaction. And, if he'd admit it, he'd wanted to see Ken again. He'd missed their banter, and he certainly thought she'd been warming up to his subtle charm.

Her brows dropped.

He mimicked her expression.

She tossed the papers she'd been holding onto her desk and put her hands on her hips. Fascinating and hotter-than-Ifrinn in her exacerbation, she said, "How is it that you're always coming up with—Ah, hell, never mind." She led the way to the conference room.

Harley dropped the bag and jumped in line, Vic followed, and Raine fell in step beside him.

"How was the date last night?" Raine wagged his brows at Vic.

The man's face brightened, a smile tugging at the corners of his mouth and eyes. "She said yes."

Raine patted his shoulder, sipping a little of his happiness, though not enough to get a real buzz. He flashed a genuine smile, glad for the man. "'Grats!"

Inside the conference room, Ken had the remote in one hand, her other pushing her sports coat away and exposing her sidearm as she puckered her lips in concentration. The channels changed randomly, soap operas flickering by.

"Wait," Raine called.

Ken stopped pressing buttons and raised her brows at him in question.

"Is that *Days*? What's Marlena up to?" Raine asked.

"Gah, Dr. Evans is sexy, isn't she?"

Ken groaned, rolled her eyes, and kept flipping until she found the news coverage. She tossed the remote on the table and watched. Harley and Vic stood to one side, mismatched twins with their arms folded over their chests and their feet at a position only cops and the human military ever assumed.

Raine pulled out a chair and flopped down. "Got any popcorn?"

Ken scowled at him.

He shrugged.

A reporter's face appeared on the screen, the crowd milling in the background outside around what appeared to be a stage or dais. This was a family after Raine's own heart. What a performance they were planning. He wished he was there.

"Where are they?" asked Vic.

With the crowd gathered around a stage and the makeshift dais, it wasn't easy to discern the Brownstone townhouses in the background, but Raine had been there a number of times. "Devereux Court," he provided, stretching out to enjoy the upcoming show.

"We should go," Harley jumped in. "Maybe we can make it before they begin."

Eyes intent on the television, Ken said, "Crowd is too big. We'll get a better view here."

"Aw, bummer," Raine complained. "I'll bet the energy there's a real high."

A microphone wail grabbed everyone's attention, and Raine winced. He said a quick thanks to Danu herself for the insulation provided by the technology between them, but thought better of that. Danu wouldn't have a thing in any world to do with those purely mortal inventions.

The picture flickered but came back in a blink.

Ken said, "Damn TV. Isn't that one new?"

"Replaced last week," Harley answered.

Vic put in, "Must be the room."

Raine held his thoughts about the cursed tech.

A campaign manager stepped up first to introduce "Wickney's future mayor," Vincent La Pointe. The reporters crowded and the citizens cheered, and signs reading "La Pointe for Mayor" bounced amid the onlookers. Vincent La Pointe graciously thanked his manager and stepped to the microphoned podium. He raised one hand then the other, smiled, thanked all his supporters, and waited for silence to fall. Yes, he was the perfect picture of a politician, groomed to be on that stage and accepting all the energy the gathering would offer. Vincent La Pointe's pregnant wife stood beside him at his dais, poised, smiling, and clapping along. To the far side of the screen, Vincent's extended family gathered. His father looked on from behind him at an angle, with clear pride over the persona his son had assumed in the public eye. Vanessa stood to one side of their father, wearing an almost skin-colored dress and stilettos, her blonde hair waved perfectly around her features. Raine couldn't see her aura through the television and wondered if it showed in the moment.

The cameras panned over to the retired senator and his daughter, the topic of interest in this press conference, and as William La Pointe took the center of the screen, his murdered wife's best friend, Elanna Bell, stepped up to his side and placed an arm around the back of his waist, her eyes never once glancing away from his face to the cameras. At her father's other side, Vanessa focused solely on her brother.

"Well." Raine clapped his hands. "Seems there's another affair in the works with the La Pointes. Aren't they too old for that?" He scrunched his face at the memory of the hip pain he'd experienced.

The din from the onlookers died down, and Vincent started to talk about his campaign. He outlined plans for supporting the arts and increased funding for the FVU. At this, the camera panned over to a handful of officers wearing gracious smiles just off the stage. That cowboy jerk who Ken was so fond of stood front and center.

Vic poked fun, "Get a load of West. He looks a bit out of place in that suit."

Harley chimed in, "Still wearing those damn boots, though." They shook their head disapprovingly.

"I, uh," Raine stammered, "thought this was going to be an official statement about their mother."

The camera refocused on Vincent La Pointe, who frowned. "Only last night"—the candidate forced his face into stern sobriety with the pause for emphasis—"there was another faerie incident, and a student from Wickney University was admitted to the hospital with withdrawals from the malevolent influence."

Raine leapt up, tapping his fingers on the back of the chair. "Well, if it's not about the case"—he hooked a thumb toward the door—"I'll, uh, just be on my way." He faked a stretch and a yawn.

Before he pivoted to leave, Ken turned to look at him, a flash moving in her eyes. For a second, a very tiny instant, Raine lost all ability to breathe. It couldn't be, but her eyes (or more accurately, the Fae sands in her eyes) had definitely shifted. And in that flash, Ken looked *exactly* like Briar's mother—Skye.

Raine stood back and gaped at Ken. Feeling disconnected, far away, frozen, he couldn't believe what his eyes had just communicated to his brain. Was she truly? How? And how had he not known or been able to see?

"Raine?" Harley barked. "You okay there, man?"

Vic moved closer, holding his hands forward as if to catch him. "Yeah. You look like you're about to be sick."

Ah, shite! He closed his eyes, tucked his chin, and hid his hands behind his back while he refocused his energy into the glamour. "I'm good." When he reopened his eyes, he felt level again.

But now, Ken squinted at him. "What was that?"

Of course she'd be confused. He'd dropped his guard; his glamour had likely slipped; and obviously he'd allowed his own Fae features to surface. *Acting, yes.* He painted a slimy, wanna-be-seductive smile on his face and waggled his brows. *Get her back to not liking me much, quick.* "I haven't a clue what you mean, darling Ken," he drawled.

"Your eyes," she persisted, two lines forming the number eleven between her eyes.

Raine moved closer, sauntering. "What about my eyes, Ken?" He focused on hers. They'd settled now, but he wanted to put her off guard. "Are you enjoying looking into my eyes? I most certainly enjoy yours."

Vic coughed. Vincent La Pointe's voice from the television asked Detective West to come say a few words about the incident. Raine didn't want to be around for this kind of speech; he needed to get out of there. But he kept up his charade until Ken held her hands out to block his progression, then he took the forestalling hand and bowed over it. Tension moved between them, yet she didn't pull away. He pressed his lips to the delicate skin on the inside of her wrist, kissing then holding her hand as he backed away, only releasing her when the distance forced them to part. Before darting away, he made his voice a husky breath and said, "Until we meet again, my dearest Ken."

KENNEDI

FRUSTRATION THREADED THROUGH HER VEINS and Kennedi plunged both hands into her hair.

"Ya doin' all right there, Craine?" Harley asked.

She turned and paced to the far side of the room, then back to the table. "Get a tail on him. I wanna know everything he's up to."

Harley cocked a salacious grin. "It's against the book to tail someone you're interested in."

"I'm not interested in Raine Abarta!" Kennedi snapped, but under the scrutiny of both her junior officers, she stopped and took a deep breath. What was that she'd felt when he grabbed and kissed her hand? *Not allowed, that's what.* But then, it wasn't romantic interest. There'd been movement in his eyes, and it hadn't been the first time she'd seen that. It'd happened in her own eyes in the mirror that night after the migraine. But that didn't make any kind of sense.

Another deep breath, and she said, "He's still a person of interest in this case. He's too involved, and I want to know why. The tail, Harley. Now." She waited until they took the cue and left before she sank into the chair to finish watching the press conference. To Vic, she lowered her voice and asked, "Did you see something strange about his eyes?"

"Nah, but he did look a little green there for a split second. Something was off with him."

"Yeah." Kennedi grabbed the remote. *Focus. Work.* She measured her inhales and exhales until she felt somewhat normal again.

West finished his spiel, then Vincent La Pointe took the stage and recaptured the spotlight. The family and Elanna Bell closed in around him. "Thank you, Captain West," he said, and took hold of his sister's hand. "Now, to the matter of our mother."

Vic sat in the chair across the table from his boss. "Do you think Linardi's watching this?"

Kennedi shrugged, but focused harder on the image of the family on the screen. "Certainly possible. Have we started the background checks on him yet?" she asked absently.

Before her junior officer could answer, Vincent continued, "Our father has been wrongly accused of murdering our mother. While we fully support WPD, we do not believe enough has been done to clear his name."

William dropped his head, wiping an eye. Elanna moved closer and offered a handkerchief.

"We have opened up a hotline. A 1–800 number." His voice caught. "There must be someone out there who knows something about this, because my father, the former senator for this wonderful state of Wisconsin, is the best man I know. If anyone in my life has taught me what it means to be a man, to serve, and to just be a damn good person, it's William La Pointe. My family stands here before you, united in this belief and begging that someone come forward with any evidence that will clear my father's name. Every newspaper and broadcast station has this toll-free number and will post it on their websites and social media pages. They will run it in the papers and broadcast it at every newscast. Please." His voice cracked, and he stopped, sniffling and wiping away a tear. "Good people of Wickney, if there is anything, any shred of evidence that could help my father, we welcome it. Thank you."

Kennedi clicked the power button on the remote and flung it across the table. "That man is one hell of a politician."

Harley returned, dropping heavily into the chair next to Vic and damn near rolling their eyes. "Abarta's back at the Local. Sitting at the bar and chatting with the bartender. Daily routine."

EVENING USHERED MOST PEOPLE FROM the office toward home, their significant others, or out to dinner: anything to get them separation from their jobs. But Kennedi couldn't pull herself away from the desk. Work was the excuse, but this place felt more like home than her small, barren apartment. Aleks Quaid stopped by, rapping his knuckles on the desk.

"Captain?" Kennedi lifted her gaze from the computer.

"You should get home and relax, Craine," he offered, a scold veiled in concern. Despite Aleks Quaid's by-the-book manner, he was a good boss. He didn't want to see his detectives burning out. Truly, he probably was speaking from both places, captain and friend.

"Thanks, Aleks. I'm just wrapping up here, and I'll be on my way," she lied. Or maybe she didn't. She simply didn't know how long wrapping up would take.

When he'd left her there alone, she dropped her face into her hands and took several deep breaths. Thunder boomed outside, pulling her up from the re-focusing pause. From her desk away from the windows, the flash of lightning cut through the artificial light. Storms were nice—settling. Had she brought her tennis shoes and workout gear today, she'd change and head out for a run in the stormy night. Unfortunately, she'd left those behind. Maybe she'd walk instead.

She opened the side drawer of her desk, and the old, worn file folder glared back at her with a frayed tab and smudged label reading *Glenn Craine.* It dared her to open it, but she resisted. The video she'd watched so many times before also called to her, but she ignored that too. Instead, her mind drifted upstate. She lifted the phone and dialed.

"Minocqua Mental Health Center. This is Stacy. May I help you?"

Kennedi took a deep breath. "Yes, may I speak with Brenda Mason-Craine, please?"

"May I say who is calling?"

Closing her eyes, Kennedi pressed a finger and thumb on the bridge of her nose. "Her daughter."

"One moment."

One moment turned into five, but she waited. She had always waited on her mother, so why would this time be different? The time may have been because her wandering mother had to be found and escorted back to her room to take the call . . . or maybe just prepared by the nurse to understand the situation. But when Mom's voice came over the phone, something inside clenched at how weathered it sounded. "Kennedi, how are you, darling?"

Hot tears gathered in the back of Kennedi's sinuses as she answered with broken words, "I'm good, Mom."

"I've missed you, darling. I can't remember the last time you came to see me. How was prom?" her mother asked.

The tears sprang into Kennedi's eyes. "Good." She choked on the word then forced herself to recover, wiping away the tears that'd leaked down her face. "It was good." It didn't help for Kennedi to correct her. The psychiatrist said it was simply part of her mother's reality now, that her sense of time had become so warped that one day she would believe Kennedi was five and the next she'd recognize her daughter as a thirty-two-year-old. The doctors said that it was akin to Alzheimer's, but not a degrading condition, that her mother would be like this for the remainder of her life.

"When are you coming home, dear?" her mom asked.

Home? Kennedi rolled her eyes. This station with the crusty paint, heavy metal desks, and a resident rat was the closest thing to home she could fathom, but again, this was something she couldn't tell her mother. "I'll come and see you in the morning." As she said the words, she scribbled a note to Vic and Harley, stood, and dropped it on Vic's keyboard, knowing he'd be the more responsible of the duo.

"Oh, wonderful, dear! I'll see you then." The last words sounded like she'd moved away from the phone. Yet the line remained active.

"Mom?" Kennedi started.

But her mother had forgotten the call without hanging up. "Betty?" her distant voice sounded on the other end of the line, presumably calling a friend or a nurse in the home.

Kennedi dropped the phone in the cradle and crashed her head onto the desk just as another clap of thunder boomed outside. She counted her breaths for several minutes before sitting straight once again and looking back at the file in the drawer. She scrubbed the last tears from her face, refocusing her sadness. The man in that file bore the responsibility for her mother's condition, and she needed to find him. "One day, Glenn. One God-forsaken day," she vowed, and slammed the drawer shut.

With her black trenchcoat secured, she left the station under the cover of the stormy night. The thunder rumbled away as she stepped out the back door of WPD into the parking lot and started walking. The pouring rain had turned into a steady drizzle, the kind that would likely last all night and the entire day following. Kennedi walked. Aimlessly, she put one foot in front of the other and moved. Fog hung over the city, and the streetlights cast a burnt-yellowish hue through the haze and water. Red, yellow, and green auras hung around the traffic signals as they changed sequentially in the dark. The downtown streets were mostly empty, and a chill hung in the air.

Kennedi wasn't ready to go to her apartment. Energy still thrummed through her body, and she'd run if she had the shoes for that endurance. Her boots soaked through until her feet were so wet, she no longer avoided the standing water. She held her head forward as the rain continued to dampen and weigh down her hair. Memories of her so-called childhood drifted through her mind in flashes. One or another foster parent trying to connect with her to no avail before she moved on to another home. Happiness from when she had been a tiny girl in their suburban home haunted the edges of her memory, but those times were bright and evaporating, like when there's too much light in a photograph and it grows whiter and whiter over time. Everything else had simply been moving forward. She'd had a boyfriend here or there, but any kind of relationship also turned to vapor as soon as he wanted more from her than she could give.

Normalcy—a family with two-point-five children and a house with a little white fence—simply wasn't in her stars. Her life revolved around WPD and her need to one day find the person she believed was her father. Glenn Craine. Yet he could pass her now on the street and she wouldn't recognize him. That was how much time had erased from her.

Instead, she passed a couple giggling and kissing under a large black-and-white golf umbrella. She hugged her trenchcoat tighter and stretched out her step. She didn't look at the buildings, only walked, taking a left here and a right there, but just moving forward. Up one hill and down the next, left, right, left, she continued with water splashing at her feet and her hair now plastered to her head. Tears may have fallen, but they were hidden by the constant rain. This weather, odd for Wisconsin this late in the year, seemed to evoke this emotion. It was the one and only time she allowed herself to feel the pressure of her past. All other energy was focused angrily on Glenn.

A fence lined the road to her right, and she heard voices bickering in a language she didn't recognize. Kennedi looked around, placing herself in front of Wickney University, with the Arboretum just ahead. The couple stood near the gate, the woman gesticulating wildly and the man folded into himself. At that distance, they weren't clear. She could only make out their fuzzy forms, but the situation appeared on the verge of a domestic. Her senses tingled as she moved closer until she heard the man's voice clearly, calling the woman, "Briar!" as if it were a curse. Kennedi halted and moved deeper into the shadows of a nearby building. "This can wait. Let's go in first."

Raine Abarta. What in seven hells was he doing out here at this hour? Kennedi looked at her watch. Five minutes until eleven. Silence fell around the arguing couple, and they moved toward the electronic gate lock into the Arboretum. Sparks and lightning flew in the stormy night from the device. The gate slid open. Raine and this Briar person slid through the opening.

Kennedi's stomach hollowed as she looked at her watch again. Ice covered her skin. The precise time Glenn Craine had disappeared and the time she'd seen Raine disappear drew near. She darted after them, keeping her steps light and avoiding splashing into the puddles so as to not alert them to her presence. Inside, she moved to the grass to avoid the sidewalks and more standing water. She moved from shadow to shadow. The duo ahead of her lowered their voices as they walked toward the hill.

This was really happening. After so many years with absolutely no leads, this oddity had stumbled into her life and wouldn't disappear, and he seemed to be the key to figuring out where her father had disappeared to. Kennedi had never believed in higher powers or fate, but something obviously brought him into her life for a reason she wasn't going to analyze now. She followed them to the hill, and around it clockwise in slow motion. The thunder had stopped in favor of light, constant rain, but Kennedi could feel her heart thumping hard in her throat. It sounded in her ears like a drum line played within the Arboretum. Her feet moved to the rhythm. Two beats, step; two beats, step. Every few footfalls, she glanced at her watch again. Pretty soon—11:10—the digital readout started to blink. She kept circling behind Raine and the other woman, who both still appeared fuzzy up ahead. The next time Kennedi glanced down, her watch face was blank with a series of lines across the face. She tapped at it furiously. She wanted to know when it turned 11:11, but it wouldn't work. It then went entirely blank. She wanted to see the time, but she also wanted to see the couple at the same time, so looking up, she . . .

They were gone.

Then, everything started brightening. Kennedi felt her weight lifting, herself becoming as light as a feather, like she was floating on air. Or she was falling with a void above and below, nothing. The darkness and the rain vanished. Her clothes were still wet, her hair still glued to her head and face, her breath coming in bursts, gasps of confusion. Then the light grew so bright she reached up to shield her eyes from the whiteness stabbing through the opening into her brain. She felt the same pain that'd come with her migraines so many times before. Weight settled back into her body, gravity grabbing her and pulling her down faster and faster. No, that didn't help, only intensified a fear she didn't know was possible. She couldn't see anything at the bottom. Wait, what bottom? She flipped around in mid-fall, then back again. There was nothing below, above, anywhere. She sucked in a breath—warmer than the air had been in the Arboretum in the stormy Wickney night. She thought to scream as her heart pounded harder in her chest, a herd of stallions galloping through her body and trying to break free. She twisted in air trying to find an anchor—anything she could use as a focal point. But nothing. She blinked hard, trying to pull herself from whatever nightmare she'd literally fallen into, but nothing changed. Still cascading downward. It must be death—the white light people say they've seen. *I'm sorry Mom that I couldn't come before . . .* the thought trailed off as she opened her mouth and a sound ripped from her lungs so hard it seemed to come from every last cell in her body. Her strangled voice echoed all around her, lonely and terrified.

CHAPTER 15

RAINE

RAINE STEPPED FORWARD INTO THE bright Wandering Wood, light fluttering and falling around him like snow, softer than the pelting rain in Wickney before they'd traversed the portal. In two breaths, Faerie peeled away his glamour and Briar's beside him. Their clothes, hair, and skin also dried under his home realm's intent. Danu welcomed her children home, evaporating the water into the air. Briar reached under her dark thicket of hair and tossed it, the dry curls fluffing into perfection. She let out a long and vocal sigh as if she'd just sated her withdrawals. He had to admit, although it soothed his croí to be home, he didn't find it as elating as his impish betrothed. Strange. The last time he'd come, he'd wanted to relish his return. Now, for reasons he couldn't quite place, he only desired to discover Ken's true mam and sire.

A cold shiver shot through his spine at the word *betrothed*, and he stared at Briar.

She'd come to him at the U. "Lady Amaryllis has signaled our courtship should begin," she'd said. "She'll allow your return for a day. The plans for celebration have begun. As the rites prescribe, the nobles are collecting fruit from the sacred tree in Danu's garden as we speak."

In the darkness of the Local U, Raine had resisted until he'd polished off an entire bottle of Bowmore. Then, he had decided he would humor her. It had been a ticket into Fae, and he'd only discover Ken's parentage if he returned.

Facing her in the Wandering Wood now, Raine stifled a groan. A true seductress, Briar used her beauty as a weapon. He'd partaken before, long ago, satiating his sexual needs. But as he regarded her now, her physicality held little appeal. In fact, while he was permitted home, he felt a raw need to extricate himself from the betrothal.

Briar sauntered over and threaded her arm into Raine's. She moved close—too close. "It's so wonderful to be back here, and with my future mate to begin courtship."

Humans had a thing: fear of commitment. Maybe that's what poured through his croí now. He tried to free his arm from her grip, but she had him in a vice. He opened his mouth, ready to divert her intentions, when a shrill cry of utter terror cut through the Wood. He and Briar both searched the forest, spinning to find the noise. It bellowed again, shuddering through the trees and prickling his skin. Above. Raine stepped back from Briar and they both looked up to the shivering treetops. Someone or something in black had slipped through the portal and flailed into Fae. And whatever or whoever it was didn't have the ability to control the shift between worlds.

Shite. He quickly scanned the Wandering Wood for guards. Briar backed further away as the form plunged toward him. Raine lifted his arms to catch the body as it crashed wetly into him, plummeting them both the ground. Drenched hair slapped him in the face, and the impact ejected the air from his lungs with a grunt.

The follower lifted her wet head and started, "Ooohhhh, what the—"

"Ken?" Raine squinted up at her. His voice sounded uncertain, yet he felt something electric surge through his limbs. That she was here cut away his lingering doubts.

She looked into his eyes. His glamour lost to Faerie's will, Raine knew his skin glowed, his features grew more angular, and his irises moved. Ken studied him with a scowl, her obvious irritation twitching in one eyelid. Her irises shifted, too, but she couldn't be aware of that. Water dripped from her lashes, nose, and chin as she pushed the plastered hair away from her face. Danu hadn't welcomed her into Fae yet. Her jaw moved, her teeth chattered. Then, awareness or her police training taking her over, she pushed at his chest, scrambled to her feet, looked around the forest as if it were shrinking in on her.

Laughing deeply in her throat, Briar moved closer to Raine. "Ahh, my love, you've done it now."

"Shut up, Briar," Raine snapped, gaining his feet and reaching for Ken. His suspicion had been true. The wards cast on the portal wouldn't have let a mere mortal pass. The reason he'd relented when Briar invited him to Fae stared him in the face now. Kennedi Craine was indeed a síobhra—a Fae placed in the care of humans until she came of age. He moved closer, holding out his three-fingered hands. His voice guarded, he said, "Breathe, Ken. You're going to be fine now."

With her lips angrily pursed, her brows lowered, and her eyes wide, Ken's breath came in short bursts. She attempted to stare at his hands but kept scanning the scene for more danger. Each time she glanced at his fingers, her look said: *What evil is this? He's Fae. West was right.* But when she glanced away, there was a hint of wonder too.

Raine smirked a little to himself. What would Raymond West, leader of the Faerie Victims Unit, say or do if he knew his protégé, Ken, was Fae? The thought of the reveal to him made Raine's mouth water.

But to Kennedi, this concept, an otherness she clearly hadn't put stock into, appeared beyond her comprehension. She held her own hand up in front of her face. Three fingers trembled before her eyes. Her lips worked wordlessly. Ken's head jerked from side to side, panic taking over as her gaze darted to Raine, to Briar, to the falling lightflakes, and upward as if she could peer back into the mortal realm from where she'd fallen.

"Inhale, Ken now. Exhale." Raine mimicked the motion and started slowly toward her. "Deep breaths now." Why was he coddling her so when his faerie nature should have been taking over?

She backed away, looking back then stepping gingerly as if she might fall once again.

Briar cackled, paced. "I cannot believe this is what's had you so obsessed in Wickney," she sneered, waving a hand up and down toward Ken.

Raine took a minute, honed his ire, then glared at his selfish, affianced faerie, a minx who twirled a dark-brown curl between her fingers as she watched them with predatory eyes. Did Briar know who this síobhra was, through some unknown connection, her own kin?

Briar licked her lips. "Isn't she too old to be a síobhra?" Clearly she hadn't a clue.

"A what?" Ken snapped.

He moved closer to her, but Ken continued her retreat. Fear—something Raine wouldn't have imagined possible on this woman. *Not woman, this Fae.* By all that was sacred, why did she have to come into the change now? With his lips pressed tight, he focused, took one determined step forward in her direction, then with the second intentional foot placement, between one breath and the next, he stood behind her and caught her around the shoulders, bracing himself for her certain revolt and holding tight as she kicked into the air.

"Raine, get off me." There it was, the spunk so inherent to Ken—*his* Ken—but only a glimmer as she returned to her stammering. "How the . . . what the . . . where the . . ." She continued to wriggle in his arms.

"Would you hush," he hissed into her ear. Ifrinn, despite an urge to ease her into this, he wasn't good at this cosseting thing. "You've got this. Feel my breath. Breathe with me." He inhaled deeply, allowing his chest to expand and contract. When he sucked in again, she followed his movement. Two more times, they breathed together, and Raine felt the tension and fear fleeing her body in several more full-body convulsions. In his arms, she finally regained the careful armor she'd kept in place since they'd met.

"Well, well, well, Brother." Trevon's amused voice interrupted. "Mother will be so pleased that you've brought a toy into Fae. It should add some fun to the first mating ritual. And it *is* about time you returned to our ways." Trevon flourished a hand in the air, then his face drooped. "But of course you standing here, in this realm, is still a violation of your banishment."

Ken's gaze darted between all the Fae gathered. "What do you mean, banishment? How is that possible in this day and age? For that matter, how is—"

"The Lady permitted it," Briar snapped, moving toward Trevon. "I spoke with her."

Trevon glared at Briar, then flipped a hand toward Raine, the gesture a nonchalant and dismissive command. Two unknown Fae guards, low-ranking given their single chevron marques on the right sides of their neck, stepped to either side of Raine and seized his arms. The motion freed Ken from his grip.

Briar reached Trevon's side, and they both moved toward Raine and Ken in unison.

Raine glared and spoke through gritted teeth, "Do not do this, Trevon. I beg you."

The Fae lifted one brow and his chin to the guards, locking eyes with Raine one last time. "Don't worry about her, Brother. Your fiancé and I will take good care of your little pet." He lifted a hand to Ken's cheek.

Ken jerked away. "I don't know who you all are with your swirly eyes, missing fingers, and damn-near glowing skin, but I am no one's pet!" Her croí—her true heart, who she was at her core—had taken hold, and Raine felt pride swell in his chest.

Really? Pride?

He shrugged and went with it. If he was proud of someone else for something other than trickery or foolery, he'd have to toy with it later. For now, he could see strength coming back into Ken's posture, but his own croí split right down the middle. For all her training and all her poise in the mortal realm, it wouldn't hold up for a minute against a Fae of noble blood, let alone two.

Trevon's lecherous grin flashed. He ignored Ken's protest and moved closer. Raine thrashed against the guards holding his arms. Then, without his control, the lit forest shifted into dingy stone walls—the dark side of Fae where no lightflakes fell. His heart squeezed tight; his stomach rose sourly into his throat. The Dark. Raine bucked against his captors' hold, but they pulled him toward a prison he'd never leave without finding a way into his mother's good graces. Danu wouldn't even find him here in Aodh's domain.

KENNEDI

KENNEDI'S HEART PUMPED ICE WATER through her veins at lightning speed. Certain that cardiac arrest would take her to her grave any minute, she tried to calm herself against the battery assaulting her senses. Who the hell was this Trevon person, and why the hell was he moving toward her like she was lunch? She reached for her gun. Gone. So, hand-to-hand it had to be. She crouched, balling her shaking fingers—only three fingers now—into fists and holding them defensively in front of her. *Fae,* a voice whispered in her mind. She swiveled to get Raine into her field of vision but started when he wasn't behind her.

Her breath caught in her chest, and she pivoted back toward the other two.

The woman Raine had called Briar stood apart with a smug smile. She wrapped one arm across her chest under the other elbow and lifted a finger to her chin, watching with a wicked interest.

Trevon closed in and restricted Kennedi's air flow further. "Little síobhra, you really have no cause to worry. You are one of us, after all," he cooed. His eyes swirled, and for all the urgency she felt, he showed absolutely none.

"What does that mean?" She finally found enough words to ask one question.

"Why, dear, isn't it perfectly clear? You're a síobhra. You're coming into your Fae nature." He spread his arms as if speaking the only logical truth to be had, then looked up into the whiteness above. "It is a joyous event that happens far too infrequently these days." He settled his gaze back on her.

Kennedi's skin crawled. Other than the silly legends told by old Irish wives, that term had absolutely no meaning to her. She was no monster switched at birth for a sickly child. She'd been a normal child until she was nine and her father vanished.

The woman with the insidious laugh and the voluptuous brown hair didn't seem in a rush either. In truth, she seemed to be enjoying the theatrics. Kennedi almost expected her to sit back, pour a glass of blood-red wine, and watch whatever this show was becoming. That made her the butt of some evil joke. She seethed. Yet she couldn't find any more of her voice, so she just looked around and tried over and over to place where she'd landed. Light radiated from everything and burned her retinas. Hadn't it been night when she fell?

Again, short of breath, she asked, "What'd you do with Raine?"

Trevon tsked. "You just work with us, little síobhra, and we'll get him back soon. We promise now. Right, Briar?"

Briar bent her wrist backward, flourishing her hand. "Of course, Trevon. With this new faerie as a gift, Amaryllis will certainly grant Raine's freedom."

Kennedi suddenly flushed with heat. *Faerie?* "Why do you both keep insinuating I'm a síobhra or Fae? I was born on Earth, to a human mother and father."

The woman let out a long, trilling laugh. Then she sighed. "As Trevon said, 'tis what you are—a síobhra. A faerie coming into her powers. It's a fun and frightful time all at once. Forget what you thought you knew. You weren't born to one of those nasty creatures." She stretched her eyes wide, and they danced in the light.

"A . . . faerie?" Kennedi mused, then squinted against the light.

Trevon moved between her and Briar, hands held up in appeasement. "Hold tight there, little one. We'll not have you loosing any uncontrolled magic."

What the hell did he mean? *I'm not magical. I'm sure as hell not a fucking faerie!*

He stepped closer. "We'll just—"

Kennedi stepped back as he moved forward. But then, he vanished, just like Raine had, and arms gripped her around her upper arms and torso too strongly for her to fight. This time, the voice that whispered in her ear wasn't calming. At her back, Trevon's chest rumbled deeply before he said, "Let's take you to Mother. Briar, darling, lead the way?"

Kennedi writhed in his arms, but he squeezed tighter, and suddenly, the tension in her muscles ebbed. Strangely, she *wanted* to see whoever he'd just called Mother. The woman—no, *Briar*—bounced a couple of times in front of them and then walked. The air around her shivered, flakes of light dancing away from the epicenter, and Briar no longer stood in the forest, but in the midst of some kind of portal leading into a vast, open room. Kennedi gasped. This was the kind of shit that only happened on the SyFy channel. Trevon urged Kennedi forward, and no matter how hard she tried to dig her feet into the ground, she took one step, then another.

Confused at her own willingness to relent, Kennedi started, "Wh-why—"

"Relax, síobhra, it's just a little *nudge*," Trevon said. "You'll be able to do this one day too . . . once your powers have settled into place."

"Okay," Kennedi replied dreamily. They walked through shuttering trees, into whiteness, and into a marbled room. Briar stood in front of them, facing the most beautiful creature Kennedi had ever laid eyes on.

Of a height with the others in the room, yet seemingly larger than everyone else, the golden-haired woman stepped forward. Trevon released Kennedi, but she didn't think to back away. Something about the woman drew her closer. She wanted to be here, in her presence, in her light.

Trevon and Briar both knelt before the woman. Trevon leaned over her wrist and kissed an iridescent symbol on her forearm. The lady touched Trevon's head, then offered her arm to Briar. They repeated the same show of—what? Deference? Fealty?

What have I fallen into?

Kneel, Kennedi heard without seeing the source. It echoed all around her like when a woman had played crystal glasses in the church her mother made her attend. The demand hadn't come directly from the golden-haired woman, but Kennedi desired more than anything to please the voice and the woman. Not Kennedi's own will but the voice's brought her to both knees, her head bent in supplication. The woman in flowing robes of shifting colors approached. Kennedi couldn't find air, couldn't

216

find words, couldn't find her own will. She simply sat there and waited for the woman to reach her. More crystal goblets sounded on the air. Or was that her imagination? She couldn't see the source of the sound.

Somewhere far away, she heard another voice. Raine's . . . no, Trevon's, but they had a likeness in tone. Siblings. She didn't recognize the language spoken at first, but as she listened, the words came clearer. It wasn't a language she spoke, but Trevon told the woman—Mother, Kennedi guessed—that Raine had brought them a gift, a síobhra from the mortal realm.

Mother remained quiet.

Briar joined in the foreign language Kennedi could now, by some miracle of this lighted place, understand. "Lady Amaryllis, my queen, I beg of you. Because Raine has brought you this treat, allow him back into Fae and your grace." She bowed her head, but it seemed false as she continued, "I am so very close to my time, and wish to complete the ceremonies. I wish only to give you the heir you deserve."

The golden-haired woman, Amaryllis, raised her hands. "Perhaps I should consider your request, young Briar. Or perhaps you should mate with my younger son instead."

"But my lady," Briar said. Strange that her voice had no echo like the woman's. Instead, the tone of Briar's had a feeling like mist creeping across a dark landscape as she pleaded, "Your eldest son will produce one with better claim."

"Silence," Lady Amaryllis shouted, echoed by the unseen goblets. "Once I have dealt with our síobhra, I *may* consider your plea." Amaryllis approached, and the pulse under Kennedi's chin quickened, fluttered in her neck at the nearness of such astounding beauty.

Once again sounding distant, Trevon laughed. "You'll get accustomed to being in her presence, little one."

Somewhere deep in her soul, Kennedi thought to be angry, to rail against his condescending tone. How dare he call her *little one*? There were others in the room, but at the same time, there weren't, to Kennedi's focus. In the glowing shadow of Lady Amaryllis, she couldn't bring any recognition of the others' presence or any emotion to the surface aside from pure awe.

Lady Amaryllis leaned forward, placed a hand under Kennedi's chin, and lifted her eyes so that their gazes kissed. "Of whom are you descended, child?" Her skin aglow, she quizzically examined Kennedi. "To which Fae do you belong?"

Of course Kennedi had no answer, but she sensed the question wasn't directed to her. The woman's swirling eyes narrowed, and Kennedi could swear she felt pinpricks on her soul as Amaryllis rifled through her very being.

"Mine," A deep, husky voice ripped roughly through the fabric of magic woven around them, and Kennedi turned in unison with Amaryllis.

The Lady straightened, while Kennedi remained in her place on her knees. The voice had been clear, hauntingly familiar, but it couldn't be true. Kennedi couldn't make out the voice's owner. In her peripheral vision, Amaryllis's visage went deadly, and lower notes echoed on the goblets as she growled, "Noble Saffron? But you are not a mated Fae."

Then, seemingly through fog, a man stepped forward, his head lowered. Not just any man, but the man whom Kennedi had seen disappear on fuzzy film so many times before. Uncountable late nights she'd spent in her office watching the reel over and over again, counting the seconds. Her long-harbored fury seeped back into her, and she felt herself solidifying like candle wax as it cools and hardens. Perhaps her blood froze in her veins, because she felt colder still—an icy rage crackling around her heart. So close to her now stood the very person she'd longed to find and make pay for leaving her. For sending her into parentless adolescence. For all her toil. And for her mother's break.

Glenn Craine.

CHAPTER 16

RAINE

THERE IS NO FREEDOM, THE Dark answered to every machination Raine had considered for the immeasurable time he'd stumbled around in Aodh's Dungeon. He must have come up with two dozen ideas now, none of them easily devised.

The Dark leeched strength from Raine's body, mind, and croí. Guards weren't necessary, because no faerie who attempted escape from Aodh's Dungeon had ever found success. Raine shivered, unable to see his fingers even inches from his nose. The Dark had no need for structure either, as it extended to the unplumbed depths of Aodh's will. *The antithesis of Danu's Light.* Raine mused about how different Aodh's Dark Domain was from the Light. Where lightflakes fluttered through all Fae places touched by Her hand, Aodh's Dark smothered and slithered through the air in his Dungeon. Rather than nurturing a Fae's croí,

He saw to oppression, desolation, isolation, and despair within the endless Faerie prison—a mere step from Ifrinn's door. Somewhere in the utter blackness, another Fae wailed. Raine covered his ears, a meager attempt to block out the foreign pain so he could think.

He sagged and walked on—forever moving forward but traveling to no destination. Intention, in that place, had no meaning or magic. It enabled nothing. How long had he been in the Dark? Wandering? What had they done with Ken? How long had the distantly moaning Fae been here to send him into such keening? Raine fruitlessly sorted the possibilities.

And then, so small it could almost be overlooked, a tiny light shone in the recesses of blackness—almost swallowed by the Dark. Yet it held on and pierced through. Light fueled by Danu Herself. It steadied and grew. Raine's feet faltered, breath paused within his chest. Dare he hope?

"Raine of Lady Amaryllis?" a voice called from the prick of brightness, so distant it sounded hollow and echoed to reach him.

"Here!" He stumbled toward the small glow. "I'm here!" *Praise Danu for sending light.* "Who comes?" He quickened his pace to a trot, then jog.

"Speak more so that I might find you," the voice came again, still remote.

He waved his hands in the air—an absurd motion as there was no seeing in the depths of the dungeons. "Over here!" he called and ran onward toward the beacon. "Aimery? Is that you?"

"Yes, listen to my voice, make your way to me, and keep talking," the commander replied.

"I am." Raine's feet picked up speed. He ran now, heedless of any obstacles, as there were none in the prison. *Dungeon. What a backhanded name for this void.* There were no dank rooms with dripping water greasing the corners. No, it was vastly open, endless nothingness in every direction. Aodh's Dark Dungeon was a dungeon only of the mind, infinity being the boundary. Only one carrying Danu's Light could find a return, and Aimery bore that light. Raine scrambled for it with everything he had. More than his own croí on the line, he had to get to Ken.

One foot in front of the other, he moved. He adored getting the better of Ken in the mortal realm, but he'd be damned beyond the Dark and straight to Ifrinn if he'd let any other Fae have a go at her. Despite the heavy darkness, he still had her on his mind . . . not to mention Trevon's and Briar's deceit.

Stop it, Raine! Protect yourself in this. Get to Aimery. Get to the Light. To the Wood. Out of Faerie! Ken can handle herself. Although that'd be the last time he believed a word from Briar's mouth. Fae of the Light weren't supposed to have the capacity to lie explicitly, so her scheme this time must have been graced by Aodh. *Or...* He deconstructed Briar's words in the Underground:

"Lady Amaryllis has signaled our courtship should begin," she'd said. But that didn't mean she wanted the courting rites to begin.

"She'll allow your return for a day." But that didn't mean his return to Fae. Ifrinn, Raine, you didn't watch for the right specificity in her words.

"The plans for celebration have begun." She hadn't named the celebration.

"As the rites prescribe, the nobles are collecting fruit

from the sacred tree in Danu's garden as we speak." There are others that require fruit from Her gardens.

Whatever. He ground his teeth and ran. At this moment, Raine merely needed to escape the Dark.

His eyes stretched as wide as possible to let in Danu's light. Then he remembered Aimery couldn't see him. "Coming. Coming. Coming," he chanted as the light neared. By the time he reached the commander, his breaths came in bursts, and he latched onto a man he'd known for ages, searching for the green chevrons marking either side of his neck. "Oh, thank Danu," Raine breathed once he could feel another Fae with his own hands.

Danu's light stung his eyes, but he didn't care. It was the sweetest pain he'd ever felt. He opened his mouth to ask Aimery to get him back to the Wandering Wood, but those weren't the words that surfaced. "What did they do with Ken?"

Aimery held the light between their faces and shook his head. "She is in the Grand Hall with your mother and the Nobles. For you, my prince."

His trailing words said all Raine needed to know. His future in Fae at the moment was bleak. Raine could sense ire—not Aimery's, but belonging to the lady the commander loyally served; Amaryllis's anger—in the way Aimery tensed and looked away.

Raine pressed his lips together and took a deep breath. Heedless of his mother's bristling, he said, "Take me to the Great Hall."

Aimery moved. "Hold tight to my shoulder."

Raine latched on and held tightly as he followed the commanding guard. Aimery said no more, only walked. Would he take Raine to confront Amaryllis, or escort him to where the Veil parted the Wandering Wood and the other realms? The darkness faded into gray; the wailing Fae in the darkness behind receded into silence. Whiteness pressed away the remaining Dark tendrils and engulfed them. Still nothing but light appeared for several steps, then the Great Hall appeared, and Raine's feet were upon the silvery stone steps.

His mother stood before him, looking the picture of sweetness. But Raine knew the facade enclosed a viper. *Tread carefully.* "Mother." He fell to a knee and reached for her hand, for the marque, to show his respect.

She allowed him to take her arm and place his lips upon her marque, but her arm felt dead in his grip, heavy. And when he released her, she paced.

In the moments before Fae Queen Amaryllis addressed him, Raine's squinting eyes darted around the room. Trevon, behind their mother, smirked. To one side, Ken stood, dazed. Supported on either side by Nobles Skye and Saffron, her eyes looked into an unseen distance. At her mother's side, Briar sulked, her arms folded over her chest and her face drawn. Other nobles waited in the recesses, but only appeared like a faceless crowd to Raine.

"My son," Amaryllis started. "My hopefully-one-day-prodigal son." Raine's mother clasped her hands behind her back as she strode in front of her subjects. "When you visited before—though now that I consider, I am uncertain a *visit* is the appropriate term for your last entry into my realm." She turned to him, eyes as hard as the step beneath his feet. She lifted her voice, "What say you, noble Fae of my court?"

Theatrics. Raine kept his demeanor absolutely flat, refusing to show his nerves or resolve. Either could be used against him.

An anthem of *nay's* concussed the air, and after a moment, his mother held up her hands. The outcries died down. Raine kept his eyes on his mother, the queen and most powerful of the Fae of the Light. He focused on doing whatever necessary to see himself and Ken back to the mortal realm.

Raine had come here, a victim of Briar's manipulation, supposedly upon his mother's allowance. He'd once been close to his brother and Briar. Together, the threesome had played many a trick on unsuspecting humans in the mortal realm. But that'd been before the incident with Anemone. He hadn't fathomed how the events in New Orleans that scarred his sister had also changed Briar, but it seemed he could no longer put stock in anything she said or did. Then there was his brother, Trevon. How much of this had he helped Briar orchestrate? Perhaps these were lessons he should have learned during his last visit.

Amaryllis cleared her throat. "Well, there we have it. After your previous intrusion, I was in good spirits and on the precipice of lifting your banishment so that your betrothed might meet the demands of her fertility season and produce an heir to my throne." She turned to Briar. Sadness, perhaps feigned, pulled at her eyes as she tilted her head. "Dear, it does look like you'll be waiting another age before that time unless you wish to abandon the betrothal."

Briar curtsied. "No, my lady Amaryllis. I will wait." Though her words carried propriety, anger lurked behind her mask, unconcealed in the look she shot Raine.

The queen continued, "Or perhaps it is time I find a new mate for myself." She lifted her long and graceful fingers to her chin as if to remind herself of her own beauty. "Another heir may be the best answer."

A gasp went up in the crowd, reluctant claps turning to the applause and cheers expected of the Nobles when their queen made such an announcement. A few of the unmated Nobles puffed up at her declaration. But Raine's eyes—unconcerned with Briar's fury, not caring about his mother's relationship status, and only worried over one person—drifted over to the Noble Fae twins. *Thrall.* Who had Ken subdued so? If it was Saffron or Skye, that would be one thing, but if she was under the queen's thrall . . . Raine's chest constricted. Iron manacles would be easier to escape. The Dark *had* been easier to escape. He looked at Aimery, thankful.

Amaryllis—Mother—started again, "As for you, Raine. My son. It dismayed me that you so rudely disappeared before me in the Hall of Mirrors. Your betrothed was likewise distraught that she hadn't the opportunity to see you during your visit. What say you for your brash and disrespectful behavior?"

But he had seen Briar. Fighting the urge to peer over again, Raine lifted his chin. "Máthair," —he used the formal Fae for mother, hoping to appease her— "I journeyed into Fae last time for one purpose. I needed information from the Glas—"

"And did you find what you needed? Take it like the wretched thief you're acting?" Venom laced her words, and his mother's upper lip twitched as if she might snarl at any moment.

He sighed. "It was but a small matter. A clue in a dìomhaireachdanseòlta."

"You have not answered my question, mac," she spat, likewise calling him *son* in the formal tongue. A clear message that she sensed his attempt to soothe her nature.

"I thought I had found the necessary memory, but it

proved false."

Fire gyrated in his mother's vicious stare. "My mirrors do not lie." The double timbre of her position resonated in her voice. Then she breathed and slid into a place of calm so serene no one would know her infuriation. "You must have misread the information you saw."

"Maybe," he breathed.

Amaryllis walked, her skirts moving about her ankles. "I know not why you've returned now, but I must thank you for this little gift." She approached Ken, and Raine felt a jolt. He wanted to get up from his position on his knee and stand between his mother and Ken, protect her.

What? Why would I have such a desire? Confusion stayed him, and he bit down on the inside of his lip. Where had this urge to protect a human come from? *No, not human, she's a síobhra, remember, Raine?* How he'd get them out of this situation, he couldn't fathom. But he couldn't just let her fall victim to this.

"Ken," he called gently.

But she was catatonic at best, in between human and Fae, a moppet in stasis. She wasn't the person he knew, feisty and full of life, but his Ken had to be in there somewhere. Even if she was becoming Fae, it wouldn't change her croí.

Amaryllis closed the final distance between herself and Ken.

Raine could barely hold himself, and only did because he knew how precious a new Fae was to his mother. They weren't born often. Ken would be something worth protecting. "Mother, let her go, and we'll go back to the mortal realm. You won't see me again. That I can promise."

His mother ran a single finger down Ken's cheek, then rounded on Raine again. "Must you try me so, son of mine?"

Pins pricked his mind.

Amaryllis tilted her head as she regarded him. "Your . . . "

More pins and needles in his brain.

A smile drew itself on his mother's lips. "Your precious *Ken* will remain here, in Fae. She will learn our ways from her father, Noble Saffron." Looking up, then challengingly over to Saffron, Amaryllis tapped her fingers on her chin, musing. "Though I cannot piece together how he bore a síobhra without being mated, I shall worry over that another time. Yes. Nobles Saffron and Skye will see to your Ken's becoming.

"Meanwhile, you, my son, will serve out the remainder of your exile in the mortal realm or Aodh's Dungeon. Choose. Now." Behind those words, she clearly intoned her choice. After his second return, she wished him trapped in the Dark.

She studied him.

Of course I'm not going to choose Aodh's Dark Dungeon.

He'd no sooner had the thought than he was standing within the Wandering Wood on the threshold of the Veil between the realms—three tiny steps away from everything mortal. He sagged, then pivoted to return to the Great Hall, only to run headlong into Aimery.

"Shite, c'mon," he pleaded.

But Aimery stood firm, holding the light of Danu forward as a threat. The two one-chevron guards from before flanked either of his sides.

Raine slumped, sulked toward the Veil, and slipped between realms into the cold, dark, and damp of the Wickney November night. He fell to his knees and fisted both hands. With his head held back, face pointed toward the sky, he roared into the night while rain poured over him.

KENNEDI

EVERYTHING. ANY PHYSICAL ASPECT OF herself imaginable had slipped beyond her control. Kennedi wanted to clutch her chest with her strange four-digit hand, but for some reason, she couldn't move. This situation, whatever it was, proved how anxiety could easily be confused with heart attacks. What had just happened? Where was she? Why couldn't she react to what was going on? She just stood there, a frozen imbecile. And where had they—these Fae—sent the only person she could consider remotely dependable? Oh my God, she had cracked entirely. First, she changed physically, then she believed Raine was dependable? Of all people?

No, Kennedi, these aren't people; they're monsters. West had claimed as much, but had she listened? Nooo. Nothing, not one thing, about this place made sense. Even their words were off. A síobhra? Was that the same as a changeling? Irish folklore. A neophyte? A new faerie? And what the hell was *becoming*? The man beside her, Saffron, was her father—or at least the faerie who had disguised himself as Glenn Craine. The crystal-voiced woman had confirmed this fact. So, why in God's name didn't he look a day older than her? Kennedi wanted to scream at him, ask him questions, punch him, but she was frozen, in stasis. How?

Who uses this language? Raine had. He had used words like *shite* and *wee*, so of course he'd say other strange shit, too. But no one else used the language these beings spoke. And how did she understand when they slipped into that strange tongue?

Raine, her only lifeline, had vanished. Where had the golden-haired beauty—no, the queen, she suddenly understood—sent her own son?

BRIAR

BRIAR STOOD AT SKYE'S SIDE, mouth agape, staring at the spot Raine had been kneeling mere seconds before. Had Amaryllis sent Raine to Aodh's Domain or the Wandering Wood? She couldn't throw him into the mortal realm; the Veil wouldn't allow for that. The current turn of events had been the furthest thing from Briar's imagination. She understood the queen's fickle croí, but she hadn't expected such expedient eviction. She thought she'd made progress in swaying Amaryllis, but the contrary now seemed obvious. She'd worked so hard on Anemone and Amaryllis to win Raine's acceptance, but it seemed she'd have to find a new tactic. *Another age? Another mate? A mate for Amaryllis?* She had to make a new plan, and fast. Maybe she should visit her cousin again and discuss his suggestion of another path to the throne.

Queen Amaryllis flung a hand in the air and barked for someone to get her a chair. Trevon shifted away and back before another Fae could move, a plush, purple-cushioned chair poised to catch the queen's fall. Amaryllis sat, her face drooping with the movement, and tears suddenly poured from her eyes. Dramatic sobs wracked her shoulders, and she wailed, "My son, my son. So much loss . . .”

Every faerie in the Great Hall held utterly still, afraid to scour the queen's fragile state, until she dried her eyes and composed herself just as quickly as she'd broken down. Amaryllis stood, no wetness on her face. Her eyes shone crystal clear, sparkled even, as she turned to the Noble twins. "Take the síobhra. See to her becoming. Bring her to me when the change is complete."

Briar stepped forward, emboldened by the queen's interest in the síobhra. Raine had brought her to Faerie and she was a certain link back to him. "But my queen, do you not wish to oversee the new Fae's becoming?" She crossed and ran a finger down the side of Ken's slack face. "A síobhra is reason to rejoice, true, my queen?"

New ideas swirled in Briar's mind about how she might use Ken. When at last she swiveled to hear Amaryllis's answer, she saw her queen wore a terrifying look—a semblance of a fanged Merrow, the Fae's mortal enemy.

Amaryllis struck, sickly sweet. "My child, do you wish the same fate as your betrothed?"

Briar closed her mouth at this challenge. She shook at the possibility of being banished to either the mortal realm or Aodh's Dark Dungeon.

The queen pressed on, "Perhaps you can mate in the mortal realm, though I hold no faith that would produce an heir blessed by the Goddess. And therefore, any offspring would not possess a croí capable of ascending to my throne."

Despite the constant temperature in Fae, Briar's entire body went as cold as Earth's tundra. If she suffered banishment, her fertile season wouldn't come. No. If she was to use an heir to capture the throne, she had to mate in Faerie. But to wait another age? Impossible.

"No," continued Amaryllis, a single vociferation carrying every poisonous drop of a Merrow's venom. Then her voice settled. "Your transgression does not warrant banishment. But come to me, Briar of Skye."

Briar bowed to the queen, noting the omission of her mother's title. She glanced at Saffron. They'd both made grave missteps. He'd mated without rites. And she'd grown bold in her assertions, too comfortable with the relations she'd developed with the queen and her daughter. And that the queen had so subtly slighted Skye as well, Briar could only hope, only pray to Danu that they hadn't lost their stations entirely.

Amaryllis said, "I'll say this once. I want all evidence of my son out of my sight." She flipped a hand toward Ken. "Her, his toy." Then to Briar. "You, his betrothed." To Trevon. "You, his brother." Finally, she gestured at Saffron. "And you. A betrayer of what we hold sacred. I want you all away. Now. I wish time alone," She took three steps into the ether, to a final destination which was anyone's guess.

Trevon looked lost after the queen's departure. He looked to Briar with a questioning and searching gaze.

Briar wanted to laugh aloud at his crestfallen expression. Stiffly and ever-so-slowly, she turned to Saffron, Skye, and the síobhra. She inclined her head in the face of Skye's disapproval. "Shall we help Uncle with his daughter's becoming, Mother?"

KENNEDI

HANDS GRASPED HER ARMS AND urged her to walk.

"Walk," Saffron commanded, his voice like a

trombone, muffled, brassy, and sliding to lower registers.

Kennedi's feet obeyed the command and foreign urge. Though her mind railed against the notion, her body listened, still marionetted by Saffron. It had to be. She couldn't do much else. The three Fae, Saffron, Skye, and Briar, escorted her away from where the queen had been. As they walked, the surroundings changed, shifted. They were now in what these creatures might call a home. Yet it seemed too airy and sparsely furnished to be welcoming. Hell, she'd always kept her apartment to minimalist standards. Had that been a sign? They stepped past seating and eating areas, down a corridor too wide to be called a hall, and finally arrived at a door.

Saffron pushed it open. "Soon, Daughter," he said with lines pulling downward at the corners of his amber, swirling eyes. He tipped his head toward the other Fae who stood at Kennedi's back.

How strange, Kennedi thought. *Those drooping lines don't look like aging. Only expressing what? Sadness?*

Skye and Saffron moved down the corridor shoulder to shoulder with their heads tilted toward one another. Watching them, she noticed they carried the same height, hair color, and shape—twins. Kennedi opened her mouth to speak, but the bitter woman, Briar, pushed her in the center of the back. She stumbled inside, released from whatever spell she'd been under. The door slammed.

Kennedi spun, looking for someone, anyone else. Then, ignoring anything about the room, she pivoted, returned to, and pounded on the door. "No! Let me out!" She checked the handle, but it wouldn't budge. "Hello? Take me back to the forest! I'll go home and forget I was ever here. Help!" She kept screaming, pleading, and pounding for some time. How long, she couldn't say. Her fist ached when she finally gave up. She turned, putting her back on the door. Thrusting her hands into her hair, she slid down into a ball on the floor. *What the hell has happened?* She pulled her hands away, certain her hair had gotten thicker. "What the—" she started, looking at a strand she'd pulled forward. It shimmered.

How in God's name? That must be a trick of the strange light in this strange place.

'Tis not the doing of any mortal God, my child, came an ethereal, disembodied, and clearly feminine voice.

Kennedi scrambled to her feet, searching for the source. Nothing. She remained alone in the vast room decorated in white. Where had the voice come from? Foolishly, she looked up, asking, "Who are you?"

But the voice didn't reply, and the complete absence of a ceiling startled her into forgetting momentarily forgetting about the voice. She revolved slowly to examine more of her surroundings. A platform held a bed larger than any she had ever seen in the center of the room. *Ah, hell no. This better not be some human trafficking business.* Kennedi smacked her forehead at the flat-out stupid notion. Maybe she'd end up in the Minocqua Mental Health Center alongside her mother and whoever her mother's friend Betty had been. One mirror stared back at her from near the bed. Large paintings depicting trees, fields, lakes, and mountains hung on every wall, interspersed with white and gray marble-like pillars. The floor beneath her was cold, and only after taking in all of these surroundings did she truly register that she had control of herself once again, physically.

Kennedi ran to the window, white curtains billowing around her, but outside she saw nothing but more white. A void of light. She called into the cloud but all that echoed back to her was her own voice. The windowsill was low enough that she could step through, but what would she land on on the other side? Dare she risk it?

In the end she decided against leaping. She went to a table where food appeared before her eyes, a whole roasted bird and strange purplish vegetables. *How is that possible?* She pulled the roasted skin back on the bird. Steam lifted. She waited a second and dug her fingers into the white breast meat. She leaned down and smelled. It looked, felt, and smelled like a turkey, but she wasn't about to put it in her mouth. She picked up the purple bulb, turned it around, and tossed it back down with a huff. She looked up to where a ceiling should be. More white. When she looked back at the food, it looked as perfect as it had before she touched it. *No fucking way.* Kennedi paced. The chest pain returned, constricting tighter by the moment around her ribs. Thankfully the only thing she didn't have here so far was a damn migraine.

Eat, the ethereal feminine voice commanded. *Nourish your body for becoming.*

She spun again, but only faced the loneliness of the expansive room.

"Raine!" she bellowed. "Where are you? And what exactly have you gotten me into?" Kennedi looked around for another minute then went to the bed, pulled off the covers, and dragged them to the window.

CHAPTER 17

RAINE

SLOSHING THROUGH PUDDLES, RAINE CLIMBED the hill from Wickney University toward the main square. His hair plastered itself to his head, and rain droplets ran into his eyes. What was this heaviness sitting like a stone in his lower stomach? It slowed his walk and seemed as if it might eat him from the inside out. Danu, if one of his kind used the sight on him right now, he might very well glow with the need for a little human levity.

Head down so the water dripped forward, Raine slipped back into the human glamour. He marched up High Street on the opposite side of the street from the Local. One step. Another, then another, until the amber lights from the Tivoli Theatre's awning reflected in the drop-dappled puddles. Two more steps and he plowed into someone, only catching the woman a second before she toppled off the red stilettos and into his arms.

"What are you—" she shrieked.

Raine looked down at the woman he held in his arms, just inches from falling onto the wet ground. Vanessa La Pointe, her blonde hair hanging in waves toward the ground.

"I'm sorry, ma'am," he said, inflecting his words with a southern drawl and placed her back on her feet, then bowing in front of her. A smile tickled at the corner of his mouth as he inhaled her scent.

Vanessa brushed at her coat, striving for indignation, but her aura sparked with amusement. "Raine," she said on a sigh. "Why are you here? And without a coat or an umbrella at the very least?"

He didn't answer, didn't really want to indulge his cravings at the moment. No, he needed to wait until the Veil opened once more, cross between the realms, and find Ken. In the silent pause, Vanessa studied him a little harder, pushing her head forward as she squinted. "You have luggage under your eyes. What's wrong?"

Raine rubbed the skin as if he could get rid of the bags. "How's the campaign?" He fumbled with the words. "What about the house? Anything, uh, missing or out of place lately?" He quirked a brow.

Someone breezed past him. "Vanessa, what are you—?" Another woman's voice, deeper with age, sounded as Elanna Bell appeared at Vanessa's side.

Vanessa, still keeping a suspicious eye on Raine, answered the family friend, "All is well here. I'll join you in a moment." Then, quieter to Raine, she added, "Do you know the story on my father's case? You were there before. Are you able to soften that hard-nose Craine? It's been forever, and we're exhausted from playing these games."

"Shite!" Raine swiped a hand through his wet hair. Yeah, shite, he'd gotten a mite preoccupied, and with Ken's becoming, he'd had no time for any faediom. Though it twisted his stomach, the puzzle with William La Pointe could wait.

Yeah, while Ken's turning Fae, are you turning human? That was impossible, but he'd never felt the way he did over Ken. He couldn't explain why he wanted so badly to protect her. He narrowed his eyes and Vanessa's aura flared. On second thought . . . maybe just one more little taste.

Another woman, Vanessa's age but with dark-brown hair, stepped up. "Ness, what's up?" She scanned Raine from head to toe with a sour look on her face.

Raine flipped his wet hair from his forehead, spraying a light bulb above with a sizzle and hiss. "Don't worry, ladies, Ness here just likes things a little wet, if ya know what I mean." He wagged both brows, working hard to slide into his performer persona.

The brunette woman blushed, but she couldn't hide her amusement from him. Raine siphoned some levity from her, too, feeling the drug spread throughout his body and relieve some of the tension he'd been carrying over Ken. It helped, although she wasn't quite as enticing as her friend. That alone kept him from partaking too much.

Vanessa rolled her eyes. "I'll be just a minute, Sarah." She pulled Raine into a corner, and he went languidly.

"Seriously, Raine," she snapped, all levity gone, "it's been forever since we had any news from WPD. You're my in, and you promised to help clear my dad's name."

His was in a cloud mind –like state, making it hard to think. *Really? It can't have been that long. This little girl has no idea how long forever is.* It took him several beats to clear his mind, but finally, he started to think through timelines. Raine didn't know if he had returned on the same night they'd left for Fae. It was possible that months had passed here while he was in Fae with Ken. Raine looked up to read the marquee: *Wicked, October 5-November 12.*

Oh, good. He sucked in a deep breath, relieved that he'd returned at least close to the same night they'd slipped into Fae, given that the show hadn't started. *Forever* had definitely been an exaggeration. Silly human. "What's the date, Van—"

"Darling," Elanna called in her sing-song alto from behind Vanessa. "People are going to begin gossiping about you speaking with the homeless." She hovered, scanning to ensure no one could see the interaction. *This would be an embarrassment for people of our class,* her demeanor added.

"Raine?" Vanessa called and snapped her fingers in front of his eyes. Her curiosity turned to scorn. "You're drunk. Or high. Dammit, why in the world did I put any trust in a street performer?" She turned and joined Elanna and her friend, Sarah.

Raine skipped after her, feeling the high wear down to a gentle buzz. He couldn't resist. He put an arm around her waist and said, "Look, Vanessa, Love, gotta swim. See ya at your place later?" He dropped a kiss on her cheek, and inhaled deeply before wandering away with the high spreading into the space between his shoulders.

With each step, though, the numbing sensations ebbed. More and more practical shite popped into his mind and became poofy like popcorn. How was he supposed to get Ken back? What was he going to tell Vic, or—he shivered—worse, Harley. *How am I supposed to investigate this La Pointe case without an official detective?*

He stopped. *Wait. Why would I continue to investigate it?* He scratched his head, then said aloud, "Oh yeah, faediom," then continued walking.

But for some reason, the reminder of that puzzle tasted like heavy dark chocolate—the kind that tricked you into thinking it'd be sweet, but in the end, only made your lips pucker.

Raine smacked his tongue against the roof of his mouth just thinking about it.

At the square, he glanced at WPD, then turned left toward his apartment on Aldgate. Inside, he stripped and dried off with the towel hanging over the bar on the unused stove, leaving his clothes in a pile near the sink.

"Alexa," he called, and looked for the blue light swirling around the top. "TV on." He loved that these new human conveniences allowed him to partake like the normal mortals—almost.

The television flickered to life. "Alexa, play *Castle.*" He sat naked in the middle of his floor and watched. The female cop and the writer, Ryan and Esposito, it all reminded him of WPD. "That's us! And that contraption is just what I need." He grinned. "Alexa, call Morgana."

"Did you mean M.zero.R.sixty-four-N-four?"

"Yes." Raine rolled his eyes.

"Okay. Calling M.zero.R.sixty-four-N-four."

The phone rang.

"Yo," answered Morgana's clipped voice.

"Hey, I need one of those board thingies they have on the cop shows . . . *CSI, NCIS, Castle.*"

"What do you think I am, your butler?"

Raine stammered.

Morgana sighed loudly. "Get dressed. Get your faerie ass out of your flat. Run down to Office Depot. And get one for yourself."

"There's nothing techy about it?"

"Not a thing, Raine. Not a thing." Click.

THE SUN CAME UP—FINALLY. AFTER Raine had pilfered his stash of cash under the sink, he sat in the middle of his floor, still naked, absently piecing together puzzle after puzzle. He'd been trying to work out the details and devise a better plan. He needed to figure out the faediom once and for all, then bring Ken back from his home realm. For some reason he couldn't fathom, his desire to protect her wouldn't wane. And he liked her the way she was, didn't want her succumbing to her true Fae nature. She was too much fun, too easy to get riled up. No, he didn't want to change a thing.

As he organized the La Pointe problem over and over in his mind, he hoped—

Knock. Knock. Knock.

Raine jumped to his feet and ran to the door. He'd just cracked it when he remembered he was naked and unglamoured.

"Delivery, sir," the voice on the other side called.

"Just a minute." He shut the door, breathed deeply, and willed his body to change. He grabbed a t-shirt and sweats, then yanked the door ajar.

Two men carried in an eight-foot wide package. Raine led them to the far wall, kicking games and puzzles out of the way as he went. Once they'd placed his new toy, he rushed over to the counter, grabbed the cash, and shoved it, still wadded, into one of the men's hands.

Under his stocking cap, the man raised both brows. "You know this isn't the standard way business is done? It would have cost you half as much if you just let them deliver it."

Raine waved his hands in the air. "Banks, cards, blah-blah-blah. Don't you like making a little extra money?"

"Yeah." The man organized the bills, folding them around each other and slipping them into his pockets. "But . . ."

Raine ignored the remainder of whatever the nuisance said and scuttled them out the door. Returning to the package, he ripped away the padding, cardboard, and tape, then stared at the empty whiteboard.

What now?

Opening the second box they delivered with markers and post-it notes, he went to work. With a dry-erase marker in hand, he stepped to the board, closed his eyes, envisioned the murder scene, and started to draw. When he was done, the entire board was covered with art that could hang inside a museum somewhere. Maybe the Musée d'Orsay in Paris? But his attempt had done absolutely nothing in getting him closer to solving the case.

Holding the butt-end of the marker to his chin, he called, "Alexa, TV on."

Apparently, there was a *Castle* marathon running, because the same two characters as the night before bantered on the screen. Raine paced as their cheesy lines blared over the television. Pretty soon, the show cut to a commercial, but before it came back on, a broadcaster's face appeared.

"In local news, Dewey Thorne has been arrested by the FVU for seducing a sophomore at Wickney University."

Raine leapt up, threw on a jacket, and left. He'd head straight for Wickney PD after a short stop at the women's clothing store on the corner.

CHAPTER 18

KENNEDI

SHE'D CLIMBED OUT THE WINDOW on the bedding and into another window three times. Each time she arrived in a "new" place, it seemed she was in the same room. Same decorations, same white nonexistent ceilings, same bedding, same door, same always-hot food. With no exit apparent after uncountable hours, Kennedi flounced on the more-than-lush bed. She held her strange hands in front of her face. She curled her fingers inward to make a fist. She'd lost a finger and the three remaining had elongated. And her nails had hardened. They appeared lacquered, though she'd never painted them before. This must just be a part of whatever this "becoming" thing was. *Fae, you're becoming a faerie, Ken.* But people didn't just become faeries. They were entirely different races. *What the hell?* She flicked one of the nails, then scratched it against her skin. The nail felt as hard as an animal's claw and sharper than a razor's edge, yet it didn't cut her skin. And thinking of skin, that too had changed. She turned her hands palm down, examining the new tone. Not entirely a different color, but it'd taken on a bronze shimmer.

She took in a deep floral-scented breath and blew it out, wondering how long she'd be in this isolation before Saffron ("Soon, Daughter") would arrive. The magically appearing food remained on the table, and judging by the lighting inside the room and out, the time of day never seemed to change. She didn't feel an urge to eat or sleep or find any facilities for that matter. She'd certainly been here long enough to need a toilet, but there'd been no such urge. Did becoming mean she didn't have normal human urges anymore?

What. The. Actual. Fuck?

She hated that word, but it seemed like the only one fitting for her present situation.

The door swung open and Briar floated into the room. Once inside, the door closed behind her of its own accord. Kennedi's brows sagged. *More anomalies. Would they ever cease?* She couldn't tell if this woman's feet connected with the ground or if she moved by whatever weird faerie magic existed. Her dark hair also seemed to have a life of its own, the waves bouncing like one of those female lifeguards from Baywatch, although her body glided smoothly.

Kennedi didn't stand, but soon enough, Briar arrived at the bedside and took a seat. Anyone watching would have imagined they were high-school girlfriends. The smell of roses wafted over, and Kennedi almost gagged.

The dark-featured woman tilted her head but remained silent. So Kennedi spoke. "I don't presume you're here to take me back home?"

Resting a hand on the fluffiness beside her, Briar smiled. "Well, that would be quite dangerous for a síobhra, pet."

Kennedi bristled. "Don't call me that."

"Pet? Or síobhra?"

"Either."

Briar nodded, agreeing while not agreeing. "What connection do you have to my fiancé, Raine?" she asked.

"None," Kennedi snapped. "Well, none of my choosing. He barged into my—" She stopped herself short, drawing her brows together.

"Ah, pet. But there is a connection. I can see it upon you. How is it that you're so very close to my betrothed?"

Close? They weren't close. Were they? But Briar's word, "my," dripped with jealousy. Kennedi closed her eyes and reopened them slowly. "There is nothing *close* between Raine Abarta and me. He's been nothing more than an annoyance. Trust me, I am no danger to your engagement." She laughed, or attempted to. She'd never admit it, but saying those words put a nasty taste in her mouth.

Briar tilted her head in the other direction, intently examining Kennedi. "Then why did he behave so protectively over you? 'Tis not something within a faerie's nature until they are ready for a mate."

"What?! No." Kennedi waved both hands in the air, refuting such nonsense. "There is nothing of *that* nature going on."

Yet a little voice chirped, "Why?"

Kennedi looked around. "Did you hear that?"

Briar narrowed her eyes, and made a face as if Kennedi had just requested her firstborn child. *Or Fae? Síobhra?*

"Nevermind." Kennedi reached up to pinch her nose, but her longer-than-normal fingers landed higher on her face than she'd planned. She sighed. "Why are you here if not to take me back?" Damn, her voice felt thin.

"Do you feel any . . . different?" Briar examined her face, neck, and hands, and then she looked down toward Ken's feet. "You don't seem to be becoming as quickly as the síobhrí I've met before you."

"What on Earth do you mean? I'm entirely different!" She waved her hands in the air between them to demonstrate the oddity she'd become. "Yesterday, or whenever, I had four fingers on each hand, and my fingers were much shorter, and my nails were trimmed short, and—"

"Easy, pet."

Kennedi pressed her lips together and reigned in her outburst, breathing through her nose. Then *she* narrowed her eyes, her errant thought from before coming true. "So this 'becoming' everyone has been referring to . . . it's not some torture you're planning? It's more like something I go through? Like adolescence, or becoming an, uhm, vampire?"

Briar scoffed. "Vampirism is a disease, much like lycanthropy. Fae are natural creatures, pet."

"I have a name." Kennedi gritted her teeth. "Use it or leave me."

After another dismissal of her demands, Briar flipped over a hand and exposed her inner wrist. She rubbed a long, graceful finger over an iridescent sky-blue tattoo. "See this?"

Despite herself, Kennedi couldn't resist looking closer. 'Tis the sigil of Noble Skye. A Noble marque. I wear it because her blood flows through my veins, as Raine wears the red-tipped amaryllis flower."

Memories whirred through Kennedi's mind. She'd seen Raine's arms. "He bears no tattoo on his forearm."

"Ah, but he does. You've simply never seen it thanks to his glamour." Briar's irises swirled as if someone had blended a hint of molten gold with dark chocolate. She then narrowed them in much the same manner she'd seen Raine do on so many occasions. Extending her hand palm up for Kennedi, she asked, "May I?"

Kennedi felt a tug, and by the time she looked down, she'd already placed her wrist within Briar's grasp. "What on—"

"Please. Don't say Earth." The woman rolled her eyes, bending over Kennedi's wrist. "It's called a *nudge*, and you'll be able to do it soon enough." Briar rubbed a finger over Kennedi's forearm, the same place where she wore the Noble marque. Absently, she added, "As you're the child of Uncle Saffron, you should be marqued with the crocus."

Tension thrummed through every muscle in Kennedi's body. She considered pulling away, but had grown more curious than anxious throughout this conversation. Her stomach felt hollow with the wanting to know more about this place, about what this marque would signify, and about Raine's origin. She didn't breathe for long moments—longer than would have been possible before she'd lost her little finger on each hand. Odd.

Briar looked up, her swirling eyes attempting to puzzle out something.

"What?" Kennedi asked.

She moved closer, looking deeply into Kennedi's eyes. "Hmmm," Briar said thoughtfully.

Do not back away. Do not move, Ken. She smacked her forehead. *There I go again, using Raine's stupid moniker for myself.*

"You're . . . no." Briar backed away, graceful fingers stroking thoughtfully at her chin. "It's not possible." Abruptly, she stood. "Lady Amaryllis will be . . ." Her face shifted, hardened. She inhaled sharply, forced a smile, and turned for the exit, calling as she moved, "I must speak with Saffron." Briar jogged away, no longer seeming to float.

Kennedi stood and ran after her, but the door closed before she reached it. And when she tried the handle again—locked. She pounded the heel of her palm once and growled, "Damnit, no!"

She considered the exchange for a moment, then went to the ornately carved mirror hanging to the side of the bed. "Mirror, mirror on the wall, who's the fairest of them all?" she mused, chuckling. *Absurd!* Yet, at that point, it wouldn't surprise her much to have the mirror respond to any inquiries she might have. Or maybe not, because *she* wasn't the evil queen, right? Did that make her the princess? *Oh my, Kennedi, you've totally cracked!* "Mother, I'll see you soon in Minocqua," she said as she stepped up to the mirror.

The image in the mirror, turned at a slight angle, stared back at her. Her own image, no strange smoky faces or weird voice as she looked inside. Only her. She expelled a breath, her shoulders sagging with the release. The image appeared skeptical, though; naturally, as it reflected her own leeriness. She moved closer, reassured that it remained nothing more than a looking glass. She examined the woman—*Fae?*—who peered back, opening her eyes wider. Indeed, they swirled, but where Briar's had been chocolate and gold, hers were amber and bronze. The same she'd always seen in her bathroom mirror, but this time, no migraine accompanied the anomaly. She raised her hands to her face. Her cheeks seemed less full. Had her face elongated too, like her fingers and nails?

Eyes, slenderized face, elongated fingers, steel-like nails. What else. Skin not ready? Whatever that means. She rolled her eyes and thought about Raine. He'd brought on that headache. All of this was his doing. She recalled the first time he walked into the station. She shouldn't have been so lenient. Why had she been that way?

Briar's words echoed in her mind: *It's called a* nudge, *and you'll be able to do it soon enough.* The bard had been playing her from day one.

Kennedi clenched a fist then reached for the mirror. Maybe this, too, was an illusion? Aloud, aloof, and to no one, she recounted each of Raine's actions on that first day as she said, "Of all the pompous and arrogant—"

When her fingers touched the glass, her reflection vanished. Images flittered across the glass like it was a television screen rather than a mirror, and finally settled on the day Raine had entered her life, the moment he pushed his way into the investigations department on the fifth floor of Wickney Police Department. It was the precise moment she'd been reliving in her mind. "What the hell?" She watched as the exact scene played out before her, Raine flipping his slightly-longer-than-in-fashion hair. Every event that happened that morning replayed like a movie before her. She relived it, watching it through her own eyes. How was that possible? The cameras in her office were positioned in the corners. None could have seen Raine from the angle she looked at him now.

She considered William La Pointe and that absurd

interrogation Raine had executed. The scenes before her fast-forwarded, through the King Ludwig episode to her vantage point when they both stood in that room with La Pointe, Raine asking about the opera.

Kennedi jerked her hand away from the mirror. "What the ever-loving-fu—" She halted as the mirror returned to still, her reflection staring back at her once again. She sucked in a long breath. How long hadn't she been breathing?

Crazy, Ken, you're going bat-shit cray-cray!

Where had the vision gone? Was it real? She reached forward once more, pausing with her fingers millimeters from the glass. She forced her thoughts to something totally unrelated to Raine, choosing the lunch at Notting Hill Bistro on the corner of Aldgate and Main where she'd finally ended the on-again-off-again relationship with the district attorney, Rhyse Mitchell. With the thought fixed in her mind, she laid her hand on the glass.

Kennedi winced when she heard her own voice, an echo of what she'd said at the time. "Our jobs both require too much from us. We don't have time to be together."

Then the image in the mirror became crystal clear, again from Kennedi's perspective, looking into Rhyse's kind but tormented blue eyes.

"We can try harder. Schedule more time," Rhyse pleaded, reaching over to take her hand.

She'd allowed the touch at the time though she had wanted to pull away. There had never been real passion between them, only a commonality in their lines of work. The office flirting had been fun, but that too grew old. And the sex had never been anything to write home about— more mechanical than feeling, something to scratch an itch. All those feelings and memories came flooding back to her as she watched.

Her voice in the mirror said, "It's more than that, Rhyse. I don't want to have to schedule time with my significant oth—"

"Then I will." He leaned closer to her, closer to the screen—no, the mirror, but where she would have been in the reality of what'd transpired that sunny Wickney summer's day.

Hell, as she watched, she could sense the oppressive heat and humidity that'd gathered between the concrete buildings in the inner city. The invisible Kennedi in the mirror gave an audible sigh. "Rhyse," she said, "we need to be colleagues first. That will always be the case given our profession. It's in the best interest of the public. And the time we spend together away from our jobs feels more like friends than lovers. I want to be fair to us both. If there's someone out there for you who will love you like I cannot, I want that for you."

When Rhyse looked down, Kennedi lifted her hand from the mirror. She turned, stumbled, and caught herself on the wall, the gray-white marble cool under her touch.

All is well, child of Danu. You shall come to understand this artifact and many, many more intricacies of the Faerie Realm in due time. Be patient, my child.

Child of Danu? What?

The door opened.

Glenn Craine, Saffron, stood in the archway.

Kennedi's eyes prickled.

"Daddy?"

CHAPTER 19

RAINE

DANG, HOW DO WOMEN BREATHE in these? On top of being sucked into himself, the pantyhose itched. Why on Earth, or in any realm for that matter, would a human woman want to wear the absurd torture devices? The concept was as foreign to him as today's tech. The shoes he wore as he strode past one of the statues in the square toward WPD made it hard to walk, so he shuffled. They pinched his toes and the bottoms glided over concrete as if they were on ice. The teen girl in the shoe shop had called them "little-old-lady shoes." That explained why human women might hunch as they aged.

Outside WPD, Raine climbed the steps. The discomfort of the nylons sliding between his thighs gave Raine pause . . . and ideas galore. *Note to self, stock up on these.*

His shoes and the Danu-awful dress weren't better,

but he had more ideas on how to use the pantyhose than he did the rest of the old-lady getup. With his little, black, mailbox-shaped bag on his forearm, he held a handkerchief in one white-gloved hand. The gloves protectively covered his skin so he wouldn't have to touch iron while visiting Dewey Thorne, assuming they allowed him into the cells. With his middle finger, he pushed up round glasses before they slid from the tip of his glamoured nose. A woolly gray wig tickled his ears, but it didn't budge in the wind that signaled the arrival of a wicked Wisconsin winter. Ten steps, twenty, twenty-five, then he crossed the upper walk to the doors and reached for the handle to let himself inside.

"Hey there, ma'am, let me get that for you," called a gruff but familiar and lilting voice from behind.

Raine crouched lower, emphasizing the elderly stoop as Harley jogged over and opened the door. They pulled the door wide for the perceived little old lady, and at the same time, Harley scratched at the seam of their uniform pants, readjusting the hidden prize. Raine tucked his chin tighter to hide a slight grin. Though he certainly couldn't be recognized in the costume and glamour, he didn't want to tip his hand. Strange, he mused, how when he played someone so inconspicuous, humans simply assumed he wouldn't notice such crude mannerisms. Or perhaps Harley Gold simply didn't care. It might have been the latter.

"Can I help you find something, ma'am?" Harley asked, extending a hand for the elderly woman's elbow, assuredly with the kindest of intentions.

Raine moved achingly and let them oblige. Before speaking, he cleared his throat and pinched the muscles around his vocal cords, pitching his voice higher and forcing in a rasp of age. "Oh, yes, dearie. I'm afraid I need to find the FVU. They have my son locked up for some nonsense." Raine patted his face with the hankie. "I'm just sick over the matter, you see. Can you believe they'd accuse him of being a filthy faerie and taking advantage of that poor girl from Wickney University? He's such a sweet boy; there's just got to be some sort of misunderstanding."

Harley eyed the little old lady—Rosie, Raine would name her—suspiciously, but then shrugged and walked over to the elevator. "That'll be on the seventh floor. I'll introduce you to the FVU captain, and we'll get this all straightened out."

Raine followed Harley off the elevator—slowly and decrepitly as he'd seen old women do in the past. Ifrinn, all he really had to do was channel the pain he'd felt when he memory walked with William La Pointe. That ache in his hip had been sheer torture. Harley took meandering steps in a clear effort to not out-pace the "civilian" they helped. Being Fae made Raine a master of cosplay, and how people reacted to that simple trick didn't often satisfy his trickster nature. But for Harley to believe the vision so wholly, Raine had to stifle a bit of mirth. Raine would expect Vic to show deference to the aged, but Harley, a forthright and sometimes brash cop, surprised him with the amount of respect they offered. Raine would have a good laugh over it later, and maybe one day, he'd be able to share the little stunt with the cop that had become a pretty good friend. *Yes, that'll be better!* His mouth watered.

After ambling all the way to the end of the long room, Harley stopped at the door and waited. Inside the office, West stood.

Harley held out a hand. "This is Captain Raymond West. West, this is . . ." Their bushy brows furrowed as they realized they hadn't asked for the old woman's name.

West circled the desk with a hand outstretched, his pointed toes kicking into Raine's stooped line of vision. Raine slid his hand out of the glove—the perfect opportunity for a little memory walk. West seemed in perfect health, and Raine had been preparing himself for this one since the idea struck. Fortunately, he didn't worry about the same physical ailments he'd experienced with William La Pointe. Raine stretched his bare, age-spotted, and thin-skinned hand slowly, shakily toward West's. When their hands met, Raine flattered, "Oh, you're quite the large detective. My name is Rosie, Rosie Thorne," then he gripped onto the hand, tucked his head as if to cough, and pried into the man's recent thoughts.

West tried to pull away gently, but Raine held tight. Vaguely he heard a little chuckle—West's awkward voice—but then his full attention shifted into memory.

He felt a phone at his ear and frustration building in his chest. A woman's voice sounded sweetly through the phone, "Just keep it all quiet. As it stands, there's not enough evidence. And if they find something, we have the best lawyers, and they'll cast the necessary shadow of doubt."

Something about that voice wriggled under Raine's skin familiarly, but he couldn't place it.

Then, suddenly, the connection broke. West retrieved his hand and shoved it into the front pocket of his jeans. As Raine's head cleared, West backed away and leaned on the side of his desk, kicking one booted ankle over the other. "What can I do for you, Ms. Thorne?" His voice hardened. "I presume you have something to do with our perpetrator? Same last name and all."

"Sorry to interrupt, but you good here?" Harley asked.

"I've got work."

West flipped a hand and nodded, a ranking officer dismissing Harley Gold from his office.

Raine pinched his voice again. "I'd like to speak with my son, if you don't mind."

West bellowed with laughter. "That's a good one. You want me to believe that faerie slime-ball in there has a mother?" His chuckling rumbled again as he looked between the door and the stooped woman.

Careful not to fully unslouch, Raine stood a little taller and blended a bit of mother's fury with his thinning falsetto. He modeled the manner after his own mother's. "I don't know who you think you've got in there, sonny, but my boy is not a faerie. And as his mother, I have every right to see my son. And I believe the law says he has every right to have a certain number of visitors." Raine narrowed his eyes and *nudged* the officer.

West backed off his laughter and eyed Rosie skeptically as if deciding how much truth she could really be spouting. Or maybe he was sizing up how much of a danger the little old woman could possibly be. *Ha! If he could only see through the glamour.*

At last, he relented, pressing a button on the phone behind him on the desk. "Jericho." He released the button, and a crackle emanated from the speaker.

"Yeah, boss?" sounded an electronically muffled voice.

"Thorne's got a visitor. Come in here and show his mother to visitation."

"Sure thing."

West pressed another button, squelching the crackle, then circled back to behind his desk and sat behind his computer. He didn't look up when he said, "You'll only get fifteen."

Good. Enough.

The door opened, and a broad-shouldered woman filled the space, blonde hair pulled back and plastered to her head. "Heya, Cap. She ready?" The woman, Jericho, stood with her hands clasped at her back and feet wide, waiting for her superior's word.

Raine replaced his glove, still puzzling over the female voice he'd heard in West's memory.

"She's ready. Make sure you keep to high-security protocol," West said, still without glancing away from the screen.

Why had that voice been so familiar? *No time for that now. You've gotta get Ken back first.* He eyed West one more time and went through the door ahead of the officer.

Frisked and shown into a tiny cubicle with a chair, small desk, and hole-ridden pane of glass separating visitor from inmate, Raine sat and waited for the Fae to appear on the other side. While on standby, he scanned every nook and cranny of the tiny space to ensure there weren't any microphones or cameras. If there were, he planned to fiddle with them a bit and send them on the fritz. Fortunately, the bobbies didn't seem to be eavesdropping.

This visit hadn't anything to do with the Fae he came to see, but he needed information and a little assistance. True, he could have waited for another Fae to turn up at the Underground. And yes, he could have gone to see Simmon, but he worried over Simmon's relation to Saffron and Skye. The last thing he needed was to tip off anyone inside, like his betrothed, who might be waiting to accost him when he walked through the Veil and into

Fae. Likewise, he could have waited and attended the Performers Guild meetup next week in hopes of finding Floura Undici, the opera singer, or another Fae, but in the end, the timely lock-up of Dewey Thorne proved terribly convenient and gave him the opportunity to toy with both Harley and West a little. That'd been exquisitely fun!

The door opened, and an apparently human young man appeared on the other side of the glass, his sandy hair mussed. The officer removed the cuffs. "Fifteen," he snarled before ducking out and slamming the door shut in his wake.

Dewey Thorne took the seat facing Raine, who still wore the Rosie glamour, with a puzzled look drawing his eyes into narrow slits. Raine breathed deeply and as he exhaled, he dropped the *glamour*, stretching to his full Fae height, but still wearing the obnoxious wig and old-lady attire. He let his eyes swirl and his full Fae nature show, and he twisted his wrist around to put his marque—the emblem of Fae Queen Amaryllis—on full display.

Dewey gaped, wordless awe dripping from his visage, and he dipped his head forward in deference.

Raine clenched his will and pulled the glamour back into place, but he no longer pinched his voice as he spoke. "I need you to help me cross the Veil," he said.

The faerie's mouth worked wordlessly.

Raine narrowed his eyes and poured his noble magic into *nudging* Dewey Thorne.

"But—" Dewey started. Then his face twisted, shifted between the more slender and elongated Fae form and his human glamour. "I-I . . ."

Raine focused harder, pushed for Ken's sake. "There will be no backlash from Amaryllis. If there is, I vow to you it will rest on my shoulders alone."

Dewey's eyes widened and his glamour settled. A Fae vow, especially one from a Noble, held more value than all the gold in the mortal realm. It bound Raine to his word. It signaled that Raine would sacrifice his immortal being to keep his promise.

KENNEDI

SHE TURNED AWAY, SCRUBBED HER eyes, and swallowed several times to dislodge the lump. Why had she said that? This person or faerie or whatever he claimed to be hadn't been a father to her since she was nine years old. So why had she called him Daddy?

Focus, Ken. Focus on all the times you had to visit your mother in the upstate mental health hospital in Minocqua and how she forgot the smallest things. How does a mother forget the age of her own daughter? Don't forget, Kennedi, that this person—whether in Fae or on Earth—is responsible for her condition. That must be some kind of wicked juju he has to put someone in that condition. Plus, you cannot forget that he is responsible for your absence of any true parent throughout your teenage years. Remember those foster homes and how hard it was to talk to a complete stranger about some of the most personal and embarrassing things in your life. Just remember.

In the system, she'd been one of the lucky ones. All of her foster homes had been more than kind and accepting, but as an adolescent girl, she had enough to be uncomfortable about without having to adapt to a new home every few years. That said, Kennedi now considered some of her foster parents dear friends. She'd planned to spend Thanksgiving dinner with the Oxley family after she'd visited her mother. But that was neither here nor *here,* wherever here really was. It was most definitely *there.*

Coming out of the reflection, Kennedi blinked at the faerie standing near the door. Too many things about his features were similar to her own. They shared the same hair and eye color. And now, she shared that swirly thing he had going in his irises. *How can I deny him when we look so much alike?* Kennedi's face had always been closer to a plump, upside-down heart in shape, like her mother's, but in the image she'd examined in the mirror—before it'd turned into a TV or memory bank or, hell she couldn't say—her face had elongated. She didn't quite look like a horse, and neither did Saffron, but her face seemed more oval like his rather than like her Mother's. in that image. Perhaps that had been a trick. She considered looking back, but thought better of it.

Ken looked down at her clothes, still the ones she'd worn to work and in the rain. And while they had dried, they didn't feel crispy like they had been through a rainstorm. No, they felt soft against her skin. Softer than when she'd put them on in the morning. Saffron's attire appeared something entirely of another world. Somewhere between a Jedi's and that sparkly elf from the Fellowship of the Rings—a movie another one of her exes had taken her to on a date. That ex, Charles or Charlie . . . or maybe Chuck . . . really hadn't know her very well.

"What do you want?" she asked her father.

"I want you to walk with me, daughter of mine." His voice sounded gentle and remorseful, though that may have only been her desires made real. Who knew in this crazy, skyless, roofless, shimmering world? No one else here seemed that kind.

"And if I refuse?"

Saffron opened his mouth to speak then coughed, like the words didn't want to squeak past his vocal cords. "I will sit here and talk with you. But there is so much more to the Fae realm that I would show you. There is so much more I should explain, so many differences from the mortal realm. I believed I would never see you again when I left Brenda in Wickney. I-ah, well, er . . . ." He laughed, a hollow sound, only filled with *Why can't I find more words?* or *Why is this so hard?* Clearly speaking so plainly or emotionally didn't fit him. "I loved your mother." He paused again, barked another single laugh. "For a faerie to say that is something not quite natural, you should know. We do not normally harbor such mortal emotions, but I did with Brenda. And I did, no . . . I do with you. I waited for many human years, but you never showed any signs of the Fae. When your mother began to age, and I did not, well . . . ." He shrugged.

At some point in his speech—Kennedi was so constantly distracted she couldn't say when—Saffron had stepped inside the room. And when he'd finished, as if it listened to his words too and waited for a pause, the self-animated door closed gently behind him. He clasped his hands low before him, crossing and recrossing his thumbs. It piqued her interest that beneath the slit in the long robe, he wore simple, tan pants and a loose ivory tunic. His feet, also having only four digits, were bare. Kennedi fought an urge to reach down and pull off her boots to check her own, but she wriggled her toes inside. They pushed against the rounded toe of her boots. Had they grown longer too? She could only count four in the wriggling movement. She moved her own thumb idly. *At least I still have opposable thumbs.*

Her father swallowed as if this kindness and understanding, or maybe simply having her back here, pained him, then continued, "I didn't wish to leave, but there are good reasons. Please, Kennedi-bee." He held out a hand, palm up, an offering.

The knife of the childhood name he'd called her twisted in her chest, removed a scab over a wound she believed had healed and turned vengeful. She regarded his outstretched three-fingered hand. *Don't,* her inner self warned. *Do not let him get to you, Ken. He left you. Does it matter why?* Though she commanded herself, she felt the pull toward him. *Nudge* or her own curiosity, she couldn't be sure. Yet she latched onto the marble column and questioned herself. *Does whatever he has to say change the past?*

You may be surprised, my child, the ethereal voice from earlier answered. *Saffron is one of the eldest of my Fae children. If nothing else, he can answer many of your questions.*

Kennedi lifted her hand from the column and looked up at the ceilingless white void. "Did you hear that?"

Saffron smiled. "Whatever words the Fae Mother shares with you are for your ears alone."

She took a step forward. "The Fae Mother?"

"Yes. Danu. She is the goddess of Faerie Light. Those who worship her across all realms call her Mother. Though she possesses a fearsome streak, like all godly beings, she protects all that is natural and light, and she will speak to her children when we touch her."

"You mean the wall? I only touched the wall," Kennedi challenged. "And what do you mean by *all realms?*"

"There are many realms, and Fae rests between them all. In yours, those who practice Wicca pay homage to Danu. As for the wall, the stone is native to Faerie and therefore piece and part of our goddess, Danu," Saffron said, as if these things were the most normal notions ever.

"Aodh is her counterbalance, but let us hope you never have to meet the god of Faerie Dark and the entrance to Ifrinn."

Kennedi wanted to scream, *Myth, legend, fairy tale!* But then she laughed without humor. None of this spoke to the normalcy Saffron portrayed. Kennedi turned a hard look on the column, then glanced over at the mirror.

"I can explain the Fae Glass too, but walk with me so that I may do so in a safer place." His eyes darted to the window, then settled back on Kennedi.

"Safer? What's dangerous about this room?" She held her arms out, indicating the expansive bedroom and more. Within only four walls, it was bigger than her entire flat in Wickney, and it reminded her of rooms she'd seen in movies where an unsuspecting nobody of a girl suddenly found herself the object of some prince's affection. In truth, she'd half been expecting some servant to come in and tie her up in a corset. "Is it not your home? Why do you live here if there is danger?"

"Aye, it is my home. But it's within the Royal Palace, like all Noble homes. Amaryllis might arrive at any moment unannounced. As queen, she owns the palace domain and can sense where her subjects are at any time. Away, she'd need to seek other knowledge to find us. I'd prefer to be more at ease."

He still held his hand out in an offer or demand. Kennedi couldn't decide which. She stared at it until it went out of focus. The mention of Amaryllis flashed her back her frozen state. Why hadn't she been able to move then? *Amaryllis? Would she really intrude on her subjects' privacy thus?* The Fae queen had made no pretense toward kindness, and she clearly held a grudge against her own son. Raine. How had she sent him away? It had been obvious that she'd controlled his disappearance. *Saffron*

266

and Skye and Briar. Kennedi's head spun. *I need to go back to . . . Earth? The mortal realm? What the hell? I have a case I need to get back to. La Pointe . . . Quaid.* In her mind's eye, her captain at Wickney PD glared at and scolded her.

Aleks Quaid's booming voice echoed in her mind. *I gave you a week, Craine. That week is done. We're prosecuting.*

How long had she been away? But did her case or Quaid matter at all now when she stood only yards away from the person she'd spent half her life looking for?

"Kennedi-bee?" Saffron said.

She blinked several times, feeling a tug of desire. She wanted to follow him, to learn whatever he could share. "I'm no longer nine. You can drop the *bee.*" Her voice intoned her resignation as she stepped closer to him, her father. "I'll hear you out. But then, as you are the reason for Mother's present state, we will discuss how to pull her from the depths of her insanity." She held her hand above his open palm, half expecting something to happen between their hands. But nothing did. She waited for agreement.

When he nodded his acceptance, she lowered her hand until their palms touched. Kennedi kept her eyes on Saffron as the white void spun around them until they were seemingly the only beings in existence. Then the white faded and warmed to a golden summer's day in a countryside somewhere entirely new. In awe, she gasped. "Is this still Fae?"

"Aye, it is," Saffron answered.

Greenery spread before her. She rotated in a slow circle where they stood on a grass-covered hilltop at the edge of a verdant forest. Thick foliage rustled in a gentle breeze, yet the view of the forest was very different than the thick trunks and high canopies of the forest where she'd first entered Fae. Saffron released her hand. Kennedi narrowed her eyes to better see the dappling of small thatch-roofed huts across rolling hills. Above, the sky faded into the ever-present whiteness rather than blue. No sun or clouds, but nevertheless, the landscape painted a quaint, sun-kissed picture.

"Does this place have a name?" she breathed, feeling immediately warmer inside. If she had to be in this realm, she preferred this to the glittery palace.

Closing his eyes, Saffron breathed in.

Kennedi smelled the air too—clean, cut grass, and something lemony.

"She is called Nadarra," Saffron said and tilted his head to indicate a path along the tree line. "It's apart from the Royal Palace and Court, a place where politicking doesn't truly exist. At least the Fae who live here do not partake in such games." He tucked his chin, then looked across the hills with a small amused smile. "Faeries by nature are tricksters, but those who live here are a mite less so."

They walked for some time before Saffron spoke again. He seemed more at ease than he'd been, and his words came more freely. "We live a near immortal life, and given any luck, you, as a half-Fae, will live beyond the human expected lifespan as well. Though since your other half is mortal, I cannot say how long."

Kennedi's brow felt heavy at this, and she couldn't immediately decide which question to ask. He'd said the part about her being half-mortal as if it were poisonous. "Nearly immortal," she mused, then chose what she believed was a minimally invasive question. "How long have you lived?"

He pursed his lips, but didn't answer for a few more

strides. "That question truly has no answer."

"But your goddess said you're one of the oldest." Kennedi laughed, disbelieving she'd referenced his Danu. "And you look younger than me."

Saffron flitted a glance in her direction. "I went through my becoming at an earlier age than you. Skye and I spent our síobhra years in Ireland in the time of Brian Ború."

Without a clue who that person was, Kennedi raised her brows and waited for him to continue.

He reached over and pulled a bare branch from one of the bushes and played idly with it between his fingers. He seemed to consider or calculate some unknown notion as they walked, the landscape never changing around them. "I believe that would have been around the mortal year 1000 AD."

Kennedi choked on that, coughing and laughing. *Impossible!* When she recovered, she asked, "You're saying you're more than a thousand years old?"

"Not exactly. I may have lived less or more than that. Only Danu could be certain. My becoming arrived in my early twenties, at almost twenty-four. So, that is my mortal age, or at least how I appear. Skye came to Fae four human years later according to her recollection. So, though she is my twin, she is younger than me as far as Fae are concerned, and yet she has the appearance of a slightly older woman when unglamoured." He waved a hand dismissively in the air. "But time is a mortal construct, not something we track in Fae. Eons or their equivalent may pass in Fae while months pass on Earth. We only understand our age relative to other faeries."

"I don't follow."

"That, Daughter, is of little surprise. Understanding of these things will become clearer as you pass more time in Fae."

"Oh, no. I don't have eons to spend in Fae. I have things to attend to on Earth." Kennedi shook her head, then stopped, perplexed that they'd been walking, but seemed to have made no progress.

"As you will," said Saffron. He waved a hand again, dismissing the concept. "Regardless, you certainly have other questions before you go?"

Without thought, she asked, "Why couldn't I move while we were in the, ah, palace?"

"I had you in thrall," he answered. "As much for your own protection as for any other reason."

Kennedi stammered. "You're going to have to give me more than that. What the hell is *thrall*?"

"Ah, well, there are certain Fae abilities that you'll also learn with time. Thrall suspends another's voluntary actions. However, it is one of the more challenging Fae tricks to master. New faeries typically focus on intention first. That allows you to move between places in Faerie." He eyed Kennedi sideways. "Surely you've noticed that we step into the Light to move from place to place? You'll notice now that we do not make progress as we walk."

"How do I do that?" she begged. "And then how do I get back to where I entered—what was that place called?"

"The Wandering Wood." Saffron sighed. "Daughter, you will need to remain here for some time and practice the skills. If you intend to return to the mortal realm so soon, I'll see you back to the Wood. You can return when you are ready to learn more. Yet you should learn glamour immediately upon your return, else the humans may not welcome you as you would hope. That is one trick that is more easily mastered in the mortal realm than in Fae. Do you have someone who might help you with such things?"

Raine? Kennedi held her tongue on that one. With Amaryllis's ire against her son, she couldn't be certain how Saffron felt about him, or if he'd returned to Earth. She recalled Amaryllis's words: "Meanwhile, you, my son, will serve out the remainder of your exile in the mortal realm or Aodh's dungeon. Choose. Now." Aodh was Danu's counterpart, Saffron had said. Could Raine's mother have sent him into the Faerie equivalent of hell?

Saffron pulled apart the twig he'd been spinning between his fingers, and the snap and shearing sound pulled Ken from the memory. Not noticing her confusion, he said, "Let's get some more of your questions out of the way before I take you there."

Kennedi chewed the inside of her lip. What if Raine wasn't in Wickney? What would she do then? Wear sunglasses? She inhaled to clear her head and kept walking. What should she ask next? There were too many questions. She peered over at her father. As he glanced over the hills, his fondness for this place struck her oddly. "You seem so much more at ease here."

"As I mentioned before, we're almost immortal. And Fae are most typically fickle creatures. As such, mating isn't a life-long endeavor." Saffron tossed the twig he'd been fondling into the shrubbery. "A very long time before I met your mother, I mated with a faerie woman from Nadarra. Her name is Celestia, and she still lives there." He nodded toward one of the huts nestled in the hills. "And though we are no longer mates, we are still amicable toward one another. And I remain fond of that experience. She bore me a son who goes by Simmon."

CHAPTER 20

RAINE

W HEN HE AND DEWEY THORNE arrived back at Raine's flat on Aldgate, Raine tucked away the Rosie Thorne costume in his entryway closet. He pushed aside the juggling costume, clown getup, Musketeer outfit, and many more to make the elderly lady getup fit into the back corner. Hopefully he wouldn't need that one for a while, but it might come in handy to keep.

Dewey Thorne, the Fae Rosie had sprung from the iron-barred cell, had followed him to the apartment and blown through most of Raine's puzzles over the course of the afternoon. They'd been waiting for what seemed eons for the time when the Veil would open. Darkness had fallen hours ago thanks to the ending of the human notion of daylight-saving time, yet the evening just dragged. Dewey sat on a chair nearby, solving and unsolving Raine's V-Cube again and again. Raine glared at him for hogging his favorite fidget toy. He'd been stuck with one of those impossible metal puzzles. *Ha! Impossible, my arse!*

Finally, when Raine glanced up to the clock on the wall beside his desk and it clicked over to ten twenty-eight, he hopped up and tossed the puzzle onto his bed. "Let's go," he barked.

Dewey jumped, sending the V-Cube sailing across Raine's messy apartment and denting his new crime board before thudding to the floor.

"Would you be careful?" he growled to the clutzy faerie. He might keep his living area cluttered with puzzles and games, but he still took care of the things he brought into his home, and Thorne's carelessness combined with his utter boredom and the ceaseless waiting itched beneath his skin.

Dewey just shrugged, unconcerned as he slipped back into his glamour. His eyes settled, a fourth finger extended from the outsides of each hand, and the glisten on his skin muted. Raine did the same. After donning his parka, he pulled the door open and waited for Dewey to leave first. Hopefully, this would be the last time this particular Fae came to his flat. They'd sat there all afternoon and had absolutely nothing to converse over. Each time Raine had started a conversation, the other faerie simply mumbled and continued on with whatever puzzle occupied his mind at the time.

Their breaths fogged the Wickney night air as they walked west toward the square then turned north on High Street, bound for the Arboretum. Raine glanced up at one of the statues on the southwest corner and sniggered. The replica of Wickney's first mayor stood proudly looking toward the courthouse, wearing a 1920s gold flapper dress, cap with a feather, and a heavy smattering of makeup. The streetlights glimmered off the glitter in the eyeshadow. *Looks like Ludwig has been hard at work again.*

At the arboretum, Raine looked around, grasped the gate's new lock, and waited for its innards to fail. He chuckled to himself, musing over how many they must have replaced over the years. Beside him, Dewey Thorne twitched.

"Would you relax?"

Dewey shoved his hands into his coat pockets. "I should not be doing this."

"Well, if you want, I can walk you back up to WPD and turn you over to West." Raine quirked a brow.

Thorne pinched his face into a scowl and shook his head.

The mechanics inside the lock finally failed and it clicked in Raine's hand. He pulled it from the latch and examined it. These mechanisms seemed to take a little longer than the electronics to go wonky. Tossing it into the grass nearby, he swung open the gate. "It'll be over before you know it, and no one will be the wiser. There's really no connection between us, so you're *fiiiine.*" Raine didn't care if he were or not, or if the FVU picked him up as soon as he'd returned to the mortal realm from Fae. This faerie wore no marque and meant nothing to Raine. That he'd shown up just in time to satisfy Raine's purpose was enough. The only problem he had was that he'd made a Danu-forsaken vow to keep Amaryllis from punishing him. So he planned to get inside, then have Thorne return immediately. Easy-peasy. Done. But just in case, he warned, "If you don't follow my instructions to the letter, my vow is nullified."

Thorne nodded as they reached the faerie mound. They circled it once, twice, three times. The freezing grasses crunched under their feet. Around and around, again, and yet again, they strode.

Raine said, "Any idea how long?"

Dewey grunted.

"Tons of help. Thanks."

They kept pacing the circle, until finally they stepped through and onto the softer, non-frozen floor of the Wandering Wood. Their glamours slid away, and Raine reached for Dewey. The faerie faced him, silent questions written on his face.

"That's it. The end of your obligation," Raine started. "Now, turn around and cross back through to Wickney."

Thorne grinned widely, turned to his left away from the arched branches that surrounded the Veil in the Wandering Wood, took three steps, and disappeared.

Raine sighed. "At least I'm no longer beholden to that stupid vow." With no time to waste, he took a step and focused his intent on Saffron and Skye's Noble home. Since Saffron had Ken under his thrall, Ken had to be there by now.

He stepped into the white and out into the expansive gardens of the Noble house. Skye and Briar stood inside an alcove, talking, and turned to face Raine when he appeared.

Briar moved toward him, smiling and rolling her hips in that way that'd enticed him many times before. "My love, how ever did you get back into Fae?" Unfortunately for her, it only made him wince at the moment.

He brushed past her toward Skye. "Doesn't matter." Then he stopped. "Wait!" He turned, studying Briar. "Do you know a Dewey Thorne?"

The blank look on Briar's face told him all he needed

to know.

"Good," he said. *Now I only have to worry about Trevon.* But his brother wasn't present, thank Danu. "Noble Skye, where is Ken?"

Skye poised her lips to answer, but Briar cut her off. "You mean the *síobhra*?" She came to stand at Raine's side.

He groaned, "Yes, Briar." Then to Skye, he continued, "The last I saw of her, she was in Saffron's thrall on Mother's dais."

Skye remained silent, but Briar chuckled. "Well, the last I saw of her, she was in one of Uncle's rooms. The one overlooking the light, I believe."

"No, Daughter," Skye corrected, her voice firm but patient. She searched Raine's face for a moment, then added, "She's in Nadarra with my brother."

"Shite!" Raine yelled and paced around the alcove. He recalled Simmon's mention of his home apart from the palace and that Simmon wore Saffron's Noble marque. Nadarra had been a new and unfamiliar place to Raine then and still was, thus intention would not work for travel. He looked at Briar. *No, I don't want her there.* Then to Skye, he asked, "Can you show me? Take me there?"

Raine scanned the garden for signs of his mother or the guard. Danu-blessedly, nothing. He hated asking Skye for the help, because he'd be in her debt. But there wasn't another way.

"I'll take you," the Noble answered, her voice drawn like tight bow strings.

Briar clapped her hands together. "Oh, an excursion! I'll join you both in the country. It should be an exciting time, and a family reunion of sorts."

KENNEDI

AT THE MENTION OF SAFFRON'S son's name, Kennedi's feet turned to lead. "Wha-who did you say?"

"Simmon," he answered. "My son's, and I suppose your half-brother's, name is Simmon."

Kennedi's mind whirred, rewinding time to when she, Raine, Vic, and Harley went to see Maximus Linardi through the back entrance of the Local. She slid backward to that institutional hallway behind the club. A man in pure black had blocked the end of the hallway. Everything from his neck down had been covered, gloved hands even. His hair lay slicked away from his face, and he'd been too young and lithe to be Linardi. He'd spoken so familiarly to Raine. *When did you start keeping company with bobbies?* "Bobbies" had been another strange way to refer to the police, but Kennedi had brushed it off. *Simmon,* Raine had answered, *nice to see you again, too, and so formal.* And Simmon's response? *How is Briar these days?*

Briar!

Her eyes widened and she inhaled a long, slow, knowledge-filled breath as she searched Saffron's face. Rooted in place as details worked themselves out in her mind, Ken felt on the verge of being drunk. All the pieces came crashing into place. Shocking, yes, yet so strangely satisfying—satiating even—to finally have solved part of the puzzle around Raine Abarta. Since he'd known Simmon, that must be how he'd fingered Linardi.

A few steps ahead of her, Saffron waited. The tree line blurred behind him. He tilted his head and peaked his brows. "Kennedi-bee? Are you well?"

She opened her mouth to answer, a hesitant smile tugging at the corners. "I—"

A light glowed in her peripheral vision, distracting her from the answer, and Raine, the devil himself wearing his full Fae, ran onto grassy area a hundred or so paces away. She hardened and glared at him, at his longer and thinner face, glowing skin, strange hands and eyes. Kennedi balled her fists, willing her feet to move toward him. Whether he had intended it or not, he was responsible for all of this! But then, he'd come back for her. *He's here to save me.* Kennedi rolled her eyes and gritted her teeth at the absurd thought. He may indeed rescue her from this for now, but certainly saving her hadn't been his intent.

However, if by some miracle it was, she'd hug him after, and only after, she punched that perpetual smugness off his face. She took a step, two, then Skye and Briar stepped out of the white void at either of his sides.

Ken's inner rollercoaster flipped and turned, and she felt nauseous. Raine had come back for her, but he'd brought that bitter woman along—his planned mate.

Why?

Kennedi's legs grew roots once again, and she stared curiously at the trio.

"Mother, I told you this would be fun!" Briar's entire being radiated snide satisfaction as she waved a hand in Ken's direction. "Looksee at the little **síobhra** and her daddy."

Raine rounded on her. "Briar. By the Dark, would you leave? You know Amaryllis will sacrifice me to Aodh if she finds me here, and you may pass uncounted fertile periods before I return. I need to get Ken back to the mortal realm before that happens, or you'll never be able to bear the Danu-forsaken child you're so craving."

You tell her! Kennedi's gut tightened, and she felt a surge of warmth. He *had* returned for her. But what was that about a child?

Briar sucked in a breath, placed one hand over her chest and the other over her mouth. Her eyes frowned and glistened. She looked at Skye as if to ask: *Will you stand there and allow this to happen?*

Skye made no expression. From behind Kennedi, Saffron sighed aloud. Clearly, these theatrics were nothing new for the woman.

Then Briar looked at Raine as if asking: *Why would you say things that hurt me so?*

Briar started sobbing, but Kennedi felt more certain than ever the act was nothing but a show—just as audacious as Raine's mannerisms had always been. Then the woman spun away, took a few strides, and vanished into a white glow.

Raine sagged. "Let's hope she's not going to retrieve Mother," he muttered. Sure-footed, he marched over, looked inquiringly sideways at Saffron, and extended a hand to her. "Ken, let me take you back."

She looked at her father for . . . what? Permission? No, she wanted to know more about this place, about him, about herself. And she hadn't yet had the opportunity to find out how they might be able to help her mother. She shook her head in small jerks, but Saffron's eyes softened.

He nodded. "Daughter, you said you have matters to attend to. Raine of Lady Amaryllis, you'll watch over her when you're back?"

Raine chuckled and ran his hands through his hair. "Aye. Never thought I'd be watching a **síobhra** now."

Saffron ran a hand down Kennedi's arm. "Be careful

back there. Without control of Danu's magic, there's no telling what could happen." He cut his eyes over to Raine. "The prince there will help you. Come back after your business. With Danu's blessing I will be here to answer whatever questions you might have."

Kennedi looked from her father to Skye then finally at Raine, confused. "But Saffron said Queen Amaryllis won't bother us here in Nadarra?"

Raine pressed his lips into a tight line, then curled his fingers into the palm and withdrew his hand.

Instead of him, Skye responded, "Kennedi—yes?—of Noble Saffron, I love my daughter dearly, but if she has indeed gone to Amaryllis, we can no longer guarantee that."

Kennedi jerked and blinked several times at the title. *Ken, you must return to Wickney and settle the case.* And after a moment, she said to Saffron, "I will return, and when I do, you must undo whatever was done to my mother or tell me how."

Something ghosted across Saffron's eyes; she couldn't tell what. The only promise he made was: "I will do my best."

With a fleeting look at the gorgeous forest and landscape, she moved closer to Raine. "All right. You got me into this, and now you can get me out of this crazy world."

He smirked. "As you wish." He offered her an elbow, a gesture implying he'd gladly be her escort into whatever awaited.

She rolled her eyes.

Together, they walked into the void again, but instead of stepping out into the forest with the tall, thick-trunked trees, they stepped into another bedroom. This one had the bed dressed in velveteen red with a plush white rug at the bedside.

Kennedi extracted her hand from his arm and clenched her fists at her sides. "Damnit, Raine. Where are we now?"

"Doesn't matter," he snapped, looked around as if they might get caught, and grabbed her around the wrist.

She resisted when he pulled her toward the mirror. "Oh no you don't. I saw one of those creepy things in the prison they had me in before."

"Ken, stop. I need to show you something about the La Pointe case."

Oh yeah, the La Pointe case. She went with him cautiously. At the mirror, Raine lay his hand on the glass.

A scent of roses accosted Kennedi's nose. The same scent she'd smelled before . . . on Briar. She pulled away again. "You brought me to your bedmate's room?" she asked, heat suffusing every corner of her body.

He removed his hand from the glass before any images formed. Raine breathed in, then exhaled, puffing his cheeks. "Ken, Briar is not my bedmate. I can explain all of that, but not now. Look, or more specifically listen to this. Please." He narrowed his eyes.

She mimicked his expression, narrowing hers in return. But she moved closer—actually, was tugged closer.

"Would you not?" she demanded, but she then stood at his side.

Raine ignored her and replaced his hand on the glass. Images spun past in a flurry. The precinct materialized in the mirror, someone sat down behind a corner office desk with a phone to their ear. She and Raine watched through the viewer's eyes. The image panned down to the floor, and cowboy boots kicked into view. West! Kennedi sucked in a breath. She now recognized the office on the seventh floor of WPD, the FVU. Her heart thudded hard once.

She looked at Raine. "Did Raymond West discover you're Fae? Wha—"

"Watch, Ken," Raine demanded. "It's *your* case. Your puzzle."

Her ears buzzed at the word.

Raine narrowed his eyes.

She held up her hands. "Okay. None of that *nudging* shit."

The vision in the mirror continued. Over the line came a voice, a woman's voice: "Just keep it all quiet. As it stands right now, there's not enough evidence. We have the best lawyers, and they'll cast the necessary shadow of doubt."

She stared at the mirror, breathing through her open mouth to avoid the rose scent. Unfortunately, she tasted it still.

Raine pulled on her wrist to grab her attention. "Do you recognize that voice?" The images stopped.

It sounded familiar, but she couldn't quite place it. Kennedi shook her head. "Play it again."

Focusing back on the glass, Raine narrowed his eyes again. The images moved in reverse until the viewer backed toward the door; Raymond West stepped backward, reached for the knob, and pulled it closed. At that point, Raine's face relaxed as he watched West's point of view resume. The captain of the FVU circled to the backside of his desk and lifted the phone.

"Wait! Slow it down," Kennedi said. Despite this faerie shit, her training and practice scratched at her consciousness. She'd become a cop, an investigator, to ensure cases didn't go unsolved like the one that haunted her. But she was on the verge of solving her unsolved case. She couldn't worry over what Raymond West was doing back in Wickney. But damnit, Raine was right. That was her case too. Her vow to herself and those who couldn't speak for themselves pushed her onward. She couldn't let it go. Something this small—seeing something that begged for a reason—snapped like a rubber band against her nerves. "Get the number."

"It's not a DVR back on Earth, Ken," Raine snarked.

Kennedi slipped her hand from Raine's. *When had he started holding it that gently?* She shook her head. "Well, it clearly has a rewind. Why wouldn't it have a slow-mo?" She flipped her hand toward the mirror. "Look, now we missed it."

Raine rewound it again, and they both watched West dial the number.

Focusing only on the last digits, Kennedi said, "Six-eight-nine-four," then repeated it three times under her breath.

When the voice answered, West said, "I can't get Quaid to close the case, and Craine's acting like stink-on-shit to clear him."

The female voice replied with the same words Kennedi had heard before, a sweet and silky voice, and it reminded her of—

"My love, I'm so happy you've come home to my chambers, but should we dismiss the extra faeries so we can be alone?"

Kennedi and Raine, mirroring one another, turned slowly. Briar stood next to a . . . a what? A male? A faerie dude? A man faerie? Whatever, he was familiar from the thick-trunked woods.

Raine squared his shoulders. "Trevon," he said, his voice low and gritty.

The bitter woman faerie added, "I'm quite certain your brother will care for the **síobhra**."

"Say my name, bitch!" Ken snapped.

"Shite!" Raine hissed, snatched Kennedi's arm, and moved toward Briar and Trevon.

Without warning, the white void engulfed them, then faded into the forest with the heavy trunks Ken had seen when she'd fallen into this place.

"Run!" Raine shouted, looking over his shoulder.

Kennedi skipped into motion.

"There!" he shouted, pointing. Before them, an arch of entangled branches spread between two trees. As they neared it, Raine slowed and pulled her to a stop. "Listen, Ken." He moved closer to her, so close their breath mingled. She'd never seen this side of Raine before, but he seemed dead serious. "You have to do this part. We can travel within Fairie by only one Fae's intent. But to travel from Faerie, you must want it with every fiber in your croí."

"What's that?" She pinched her throat to imitate the cough-like sound: "Croí?"

"Heart." He squeezed the hand he still held, then waved his other hand hurriedly in the air. "Self. It's the Fae inner being. I'll explain when we're safely away. As we go through the arch, you need to forget everything, and I mean *everything*, around you and focus only on the hill at Wickney University Arboretum. The place where you followed me through the Veil."

Her brows felt heavy as she connected the name to the woods with the thick trunks and heavy canopy high above and the Veil. "The *Wandering* Wood," she mused, then an electric surge thrummed through her body, cold fear of reliving what had happened when she had entered Faerie. She widened her eyes, gripped his hand, stopped breathing, and jerked her head back and forth in quick motions. She'd rather stay in this God-forsaken place than go through that again.

Raine peered forcefully into her eyes, his a swirling silver-blue. He breathed slowly in and out several times until she started to match his rhythm. All the while, he held onto her hand with a strength she wouldn't have suspected. "Coming through the first time is the worst, I promise this time will be easier if you can clear your mind and focus."

A light flashed to her left, Raine's right, away from the arch. She started to look, but Raine reached up and held her chin gently. "Don't look," he said, his liquid silver eyes boring into her own and reinforcing that she clear other thoughts from her mind. When he seemed satisfied she was ready, he flourished his hand toward the arch.

Kennedi pressed her lips tightly together, focused on the rainy night, on the video she'd watched a thousand times before, and on the hill. She nodded.

Raine emphasized, "Only the Arboretum," and turned her away from their pursuers.

Hand in hand, they walked through the arch.

CHAPTER 21

KENNEDI

THE WANDERING WOOD DISSIPATED AROUND them, and Kennedi held onto Raine's hand for all she was worth. Instead of a white void, things turned gray, cloud-like, thunderhead-like. The vision around them reminded Kennedi of when she'd flown through storms in an airplane, so much so that she searched for lightning.

Then, she felt turbulence, weightlessness.

Focus, Ken. Focus. The Arboretum. Wickney.

The winds gathered, invisible or misty hands pushed at her back. Raine's grip slid from hers. A wind gusted, thrusting her forward. Her hair whipped in front of her face, further blocking sight. It didn't matter. There was nothing but gray and a gale moving her toward . . . what?

Oh yeah, Wickney.

The force remained at her back, but the air within the gray began to rotate.

Raine, where are you? You said it's better after the first time.

Kennedi felt weightless, lifted on a blast of air. Her body spun, stomach churned.

It's better, but not good!

The pushing stopped, and she spun. Dizzier and dizzier, she reached out to stop the revolutions.

I can't do this again. I don't believe I can go back. Mom, I'm so sorry!

Where was Raine? Where was she? What if she got stuck here in this gray void? White voids, gray voids . . . was there a black void too? The spinning waves of air lifted and lowered her, and thankfully she hadn't eaten. If she had, surely she would have lost whatever she'd consumed. The nothingness engulfed her. She lost all thoughts except for controlling her stomach.

"Raine," she called into the emptiness, but received no reply. "I can't find the way!"

She twisted, turned, but the cyclone kept spinning her in circles. Hope waned, and her breathing came in bursts until Raine's words from before returned: *You must want it with every fiber in your croí.* She did want it, didn't she? Raine was there, but not; a dream. *Forget everything around you and focus only on the hill at the Arboretum,* he had said in the Wandering Wood before they crossed.

But I can't.

You have no choice, Ken! Kennedi inhaled, clearing her mind. *I have to get back. I can't lose myself in this nothingness or tornado or cyclone or whatever it is. Think, Ken, and focus! The hill. The Arboretum. The rainy night. Mom. Wickney. Raine.*

The hands returned. This time, they latched onto her arms and pulled.

"Kennedi!" her name echoed on the wind. Raine's voice calling.

"Raine?" she yelled. "Where are you?"

The hands pulled harder.

Then she thudded onto dewy grass. Pain exploded in her shoulder and hip, and she grunted. As she rolled onto her back, bright light blinded her. The sun. There had been no sun in Faerie. She smiled, welcoming its warmth on her face again. Then a shadow blocked the light. Kennedi opened her eyes to a dark form standing over her, haloed by the sun.

RAINE

"**S**HITE!" RAINE YELLED AS KEN fell to the ground before him with a grunt.

She rolled over with a groan, disoriented. She squinted her eyes against the sudden light, smiling deliriously. He ran over to help, then skidded to a stop. Helping someone? Not in his nature. That was about the last thing he knew how to do. He'd already glamoured up, but Kennedi Craine, now Kennedi of Noble Saffron, lay on the wet grass before him. Peering up at the sun, Raine judged it early in the morning, and scanned the Arboretum. *Good. No one in sight.* He scratched his chin, looking at the unglamoured faerie on the ground.

She rolled from her side onto her back, groaning and holding her hip. He reached down to help her up.

Kennedi looked up at him with swirling amber eyes.

Her smile dissolved. She recoiled and slapped his hand away, scrambling backward.

Raine held both hands in the air. "I know this is confusing, Ken, but you need to let me help you."

"Ken?" she repeated. "Raine? Is that you?"

"Hey, there," he said as gently as possible, or as he knew how. "You're doing all right now, aren't you? I lost you when we crossed the Veil."

"The Veil?" she repeated again, but at least she finally accepted his hand and stood. "Ow," she complained and wiped at her hip as if she could swipe away the wetness that'd soaked into her jeans. "I'm never going back into . . . whatever that was."

"Aye, Ken, you will." Raine fidgeted a second, still battling with how to help her. In a rush, and speaking as much with his hands as his words, he started. "Trust me. The first time I went through, I thought it'd never end. All the thrashing, pushing, pulling, wind, whirling. I vomited first thing. At least you didn't do that. And I swear I was in there for hours, maybe eons. But then I made it to the other side and met my dear sweet old mum. Well, maybe she's not so dear, or sweet. Ifrinn, she's probably not the most motherly being you could imagine, but she's old. That she is. She's at least got that going for her. You'd think that would mean wisdom now, but eh . . . not so sure about that, either. Regardless, it was hard, but I practiced and now I can do it with my eyes closed. The time I spent in New Orleans in the 1920s with my sister Anemone, I used to go back and forth all the—"

"Raine!" Ken yelled. "Would you just shut the hell up?" She rolled her eyes.

He scratched his head. "Oh, yeah. Sorry."

Ken rolled her shoulder, then forward stroked like she was getting ready to go for a swim. Raine watched, mesmerized. Why was he so enthralled and acting the babbling idiot? Ken stretched from side to side, and he scanned the gardens for others while he waited for her to finish.

"Done?" he asked after what seemed like for-ev-er.

"Impatient?" She flashed her liquid amber eyes at him.

"Nah," he flipped a hand nonchalantly toward her. "Just worried some human's going to see you standing there with eyes swirling and skin glowing in the sunlight."

"Oh, shit." She flung her hands to her face, then peeked between her fingers. "That's still there? Not a dream? What am I supposed to do?" Her mouth stretched wide, then set into a grimace.

Raine stepped back and smirked. Maybe she had a little performer in her yet. "Well, I suppose I have to teach you to glamour. Easier now that we're in the mortal realm. Trying that little Fae trick while in Faerie is a real—"

"Geez, Raine." She dropped her hands and rolled her eyes. "Cut the bullshit. Why am I out here at the crack of dawn? I need to get to work." She blinked several times.

Had she already forgotten that she'd just admitted to being Fae? Or perhaps she just didn't believe. Shite. He had to stop her, and quick. "Ah, yeah, Ken, about work . . ."

Ken studied him then, narrowing her eyes.

"Heya, careful with that," Raine snapped, throwing his hands forward in a *please-don't* motion. "You don't know what you're doing yet."

She rolled her eyes. "Will you ever be less confusing?"

Raine puffed up his chest and shook his head. "Nope."

Kennedi grunted. "You know, you're a really big pain in the ass." She started walking toward the gate.

Raine skip-stepped and caught up to her. "Where ya headed?" he asked, pitching his voice coyly.

"WPD," she snipped as she slipped out of the gate.

He paused mid-step. That was about the worst idea he'd heard since . . . When he looked up, she'd already made it to the corner of the street. Danu, that girl could move. He marched up to catch her and stepped into her path just before she made it to the Local. They were beside a women's clothing shop that wouldn't open for hours. He grasped her by both wrists and turned her to face the window. "Look. You cannot walk into WPD looking like you just stepped out of a fairy tale."

"Ha ha, Raine," she snarked, still not looking at herself.

"I'm serious, Ken." He gave her chin a little push toward the window. "Look."

When she finally did, she went deadly still. No breathing, nothing. Raine pumped his knee, looking up and down the street, and hoping beyond hope that none of the FVU patrols were out this early. Surely they wouldn't be, because most faerie-human incidents happened at night. And most of the faeries still living in the mortal realm only went out with a glamour securely in place. Still, he couldn't risk her getting thrown behind iron bars or locked in a ring of salt. He sloughed off his coat and wrapped it around her.

She still stood there stiffly, looking at her near-transparent reflection. "I thought for sure this would all go away when I woke up from that crazy dream." She turned her eyes to him. "But it's not a dream. It's real? I'm . . ."

"Yeah, you are." He urged her forward. "Let's go to my flat. I'll work on teaching you how to navigate this realm and not tip your hand."

"Fine," she said, her voice thin, but wannabe stern. It seemed to take all the courage she could muster to continue. "You win. Do you ever not win, Raine Abarta?"

Raine squelched the surge of words that flooded into his mind. He didn't say, "Not if I can help it," or "only when I have something worth losing for," or, "yeah, I lost this one time . . ." Instead, he just kept walking, urging her along. At the corner of Wickney Square, he turned her to the left, and they strode past his favorite performing corner and toward Aldgate a few blocks up. The early people were starting to emerge for their morning routines. "Just keep your head down and let your hair shade your eyes. Don't look up or make contact with anyone."

She nodded and mumbled something unintelligible. Becoming was confusing enough, but she'd also had to deal with Briar's antics and slipping through the Veil. No wonder she was so out of her wits. Mentally, Raine patted himself on the back for how patient he was being, allowing her to work all this out in her head, becoming the little caregiver. Maybe he was cut out for this after all.

Suddenly, more clearly, she said. "Raine, you know what?"

"Mmmm?" He inclined his head.

"Not only are you a pain in my ass, you're—quite literally—a *royal* pain in my ass."

KENNEDI

SHE HAD BEEN TO RAINE'S apartment once before with the intent of arresting him. Now, as they arrived at his door, Kennedi's brain felt like the white void, full of nothing. Yet it also felt like the turmoil within the endless grayness. Standing behind him while he reached for the door, she rubbed her temples. He turned the knob and pushed inside without a key or other means of security.

"Don't you lock up your flat?" she asked, puzzled.

He stood to the side. "Nope. That's another thing you'll learn about me, and now you." He winked. "Mechanics and electronics are totally not Fae friendly. The lock's been broken since I moved in. The first time I touched the knob, it went all haywire." Inside, he moved to a small desk holding a laptop bag with said laptop sitting open inside. He picked up a pen with a rubber tip and twirled it in the air. "Any time you can stop by one of those tables where people want you to buy something and they're giving away junk with their company names on it, grab as many of the rubber tipped pens as you can. They'll come in handy." He squished the rubber tip. "These little things and speech-to-text are the only ways I can use these modern human widgets."

Kennedi gulped. "That's crap! You can't mean to say I won't be able to use a computer? Or my phone? Or the . . ." she trailed off as she noticed a huge whiteboard on casters in the corner of his studio-style flat. Pointing, she asked, "What's that?" then glimpsed her own hand. All four fingers were back. She held it in front of her face, wriggling the digits.

"Well, you've seen *CSI*, right?" he answered absently.

"Raine, look." She held out her hands.

He had slid back into his Fae form as soon as the door behind him had closed. Now, he reached for her hands with his own four-digit hands. He narrowed his eyes at her. "Are you learning to glamour without instruction? That's kind of amazing." He drew his brows together. "And a little disturbing." He grabbed onto her pinky finger and squeezed.

"Ouch!" She jerked her hand away.

Raine furrowed his brows, eyes swirling faster.

"I'm not learning or doing anything. And I presume *glamour* is some kind of super-secret Fae shit since I'd never heard of it until Saffron mentioned it in Nadarra." She extracted her other hand from his and tucked both of them into her armpits. Besides the pain from him squeezing her finger, the last thing she wanted to admit was that his touch sent a zing through her spine. "Maybe there's nothing Fae about me. Maybe I'm just turning back to plain old mortal Kennedi Craine. Where's a mirror?"

"Your eyes are still going to give you away. The only thing that confuses me is the finger. You didn't have that in Fae, right?"

Kennedi shook her head.

Raine sighed. "Give it a little time, Ken."

She huffed and jutted her chin back to the board. "Are you serious? *CSI*?"

Raine shrugged. "Or one of those other detective-y shows." He moved over to the sink, opened the lower cabinet. "Maybe *Castle*," he said, his voice muffled by the cabinet, then resurfaced. "Yeah, like Beckett and Castle, we're like—"

"We are not anything like TV cops, Raine."

"Castle's not—ah, never mind." He wagged his brows, holding a large, intricately carved box. "No." He cocked a half smile. "We are Raine and Craine, as I said that night at the Local."

Kennedi let out a plaintive sigh. "If anything it would be Craine and Raine, but it's absolutely not." She looked back and forth between him and the board. "If you're going to have a board, why don't you have anything on it?" She walked to the suspect board, rubbing her fingers over a huge dent in one corner. "What happened here?"

"Oh, that's a V-Cube mishap."

"A . . .? Forget it. I don't need to know."

Raine placed the box on his bed, he said, "Oh yeah, and as to why it's blank, well, I wasn't quite sure where to start. I know they always stared at the board when talking through a case. I have no clue why a board helps, but I didn't have anyone to talk it through with. So, you'll help me out with that bit later." He didn't look up and continued working a series of turns on the interlocking pieces.

"What?" She shook her head. How could he not infer how to use it from the shows? That's one thing they had pretty accurate. "How hard can it be? It's a suspect board. You put the, uh, suspects on it, along with any other information pertinent to the case."

He didn't answer, and soon, he pulled the box apart with a grin and an overly satisfied smile.

Weird.

"Come here." Raine waved her over.

She went, taking careful steps.

He'd clearly forgotten or hadn't heard her. Instead, he said, "You asked about locking up my flat. These are why

I don't need to. Anything of value is locked up by these babies."

He slid out some cash and counted it with a scowl on his face.

"Raine"—Kennedi raised both brows—"anyone could just pick that up and waltz out of your apartment."

"That's why there's a little charm to keep others from pilfering it." He tapped his index finger against his head as if he'd thought of every detail. "I paid the head mistress of the 3WC dearly for that little spell."

"Oh yeah, the 3WC. Because I know exactly"—she yawned—"what that is."

"Western Wickney Witches Coven. Three Ws and a C. Get it?" He closed up the box. "It's my little nickname for the coven."

"Witches? You're yankin' my chain." She wanted to slap her palm against her forehead.

He threw a hand over his chest, drawled, "Moi?" and shook his head. "Never." A smile flashed across his face. "But Isobel might have my head if she knows I'm telling you about that."

Kennedi stood there trying to keep her lower jaw from hitting the floor.

Raine patted the now-empty box. "I'll need to hit the street later today. Anyway, you won't let her know, right?" He slipped the puzzle box back under the sink. He stood and pocketed what cash he had, looking at her in a way that echoed his question.

Kennedi blinked several times, rubbed her forehead, and closed her eyes. Her body swayed enough that she had to open them immediately to prevent stumbling. She moved a foot forward to keep her balance. *Breathe, Ken.*

Witches weren't real, right? At the academy, she'd learned about the Fae Extirpation when most of the faeries had been eradicated from Europe and the Americas, and all the reasons the FVU had been formed. There had been too many instances in history where faeries and humans had clashed, and typically, the humans had ended up worse for the wear. But over many years the instances had dwindled, and the faeries who remained played by human rules. They were nothing to toil over in this day and age. Despite West's claims, Ken had believed the faerie population had either diminished to a point where the FVU was no longer necessary or had become better behaved.

But you're one now. West will want you behind iron bars. That much felt truer than true. The man had an ingrained hatred for Fae that Kennedi couldn't quite understand. She curled her fingers, feeling each one individually as she did. Still four. Why hadn't she had a clue as to the extent of Fae differences from normal human beings? And why were her hands behaving differently than Raine had expected? Yes, Fae were reality, more so than she'd imagined. And now Raine was telling her witches were real too? Or was she imagining that? Maybe it was just a name. The Salem Witch Trials had been nothing more than superstition. True? Or not?

"Ken? You won't say anything to Isobel, right?" Raine urged.

"Yeah. Sure. I won't." Besides the fact that she had no idea who Isobel was, she also had no reason to go out of her way for that. Hell, she didn't understand what the 'little charm' would do on the box. Her stomach roared. Placing her hands over the offensive sound, she asked, "Hey, didn't you say you were going to grab something to eat?"

The box. Kennedi readied herself to inspect it upon his departure. She needed to find out what that spell would do.

"I did." Raine rustled through a pile of game boxes and other trinkets piled on a side table. His eyes lit when he found what he'd clearly been searching for. "Here. This'll keep you busy while I'm out."

Kennedi held it up disbelievingly. "A Rubik's—" she started, but then it, the inanimate object in her hand, whispered to her. "What the—?" She narrowed her eyes at the thing, lowering herself to the bed. The apartment faded into the background, absent from her vision. The suspect board: forgotten. The witch thing: unimportant. The puzzle box: who cared? Everything zeroed in on the whispering toy in her hand. Tiny orange, red, blue, green, white, and yellow squares vibrated under her fingers. She saw arced lines like tiny shooting stars moving around the cube. What it whispered, she couldn't understand. *Die*-something, but it begged her to solve it. She twisted the cube along the brightest of the arcing lines, then another flared brighter.

"Goooood," Raine cooed. "I'll be back in a snap."

RAINE

RAINE SIDLED OVER TO THE door of his flat, headed downstairs to grab pastries from the bakery, and smiled smugly. That toy was the perfect distraction to keep the new faerie in his flat totally obsessed. The newest edition to his V-Cube collection, the nine-block, had turned out to be a wonderful tool for visitors. He glamoured up, opened the door, and took the steps by threes downward toward the street. Time, something that'd never mattered to him before, seemed to work against him at the moment. Set aside the fact that Ken wanted to get back to her mortal life. *Thank Danu she's got the puzzle-love.* Otherwise, she surely would have vacated his flat as soon as he stepped away. However, his bigger concern was the extent to which he'd depleted his cash stash. He needed to hit his favorite spot in Wickney Square and deliver a killer performance today. Money . . . that Ifrinn-awful thing that made the mortal realm spin.

At the door of Loaf at First Bite, the adjacent bakery, he pulled on the metal handle, opened the glass door, and paused. A woman in a business suit slipped in while he held the door, muttering, "Thanks!" and just then, a yearning sensation in the back corners of his mouth pulled at him. He wanted—no he *needed*—a mocha. Baked goods wouldn't do the same as the jolt of caffeine and sugar. He hooked a right, bound for the nearest Starbucks.

This time of the day, when all the mortals were heading to monotony in their nine-to-fivers, the line at the coffee house felt like purgatory. Raine took his place and waited, stepped forward, waited, stepped forward, tapped his toe impatiently, waited . . . All the humans stood there with their phones out and necks hunched over. *In another hundred years, they're going to return to the Neanderthal shape of their ancient ancestors,* Raine thought. Allowing his Fae sense to open ever-so-slightly, he watched the woman in front of him and her screen as she scrolled through Instagram. A little thread of lavender spread throughout her aura, and he salivated.

"Hey there, that's great advice!" he said over her shoulder, referencing to the motivational quote she'd stopped on. "You should take it. Follow what fills your soul," he added. "If you never take the leap, you'll never know."

The woman turned. At first, she seemed shocked that someone in line would dare break the unwritten and unspoken code by speaking to a fellow person jonesing for their morning coffee. But Raine dazzled her with a huge smile and *nudged* her just a wee bit. Her entire demeanor lifted, a sparkle shining in her eyes and a smile growing on her lips. "Thank you, sir." Then determination set in. "I think you're right."

Raine inhaled deeply and sighed. He had no idea what she meant by the last, if she'd quit her job or move to Paris or something else entirely. He didn't care. As he soared on her levity, the line moved. He held out a hand urging her forward.

"Heya, Raine!" a deep voice called from further back in the line.

He glanced backward to see Harley waving from the door. *Shite.* He hadn't considered having to deal with a bobby, especially one he'd been getting to know. However, being a little high and ever the actor, he put on a smile and motioned them over. "I've been waiting. Hope you don't mind I saved our spot in line."

Harley wove and sashayed through the line of annoyed coffee junkies. Raine's slight levity high dwindled. *How long were Ken and I gone? Ifrinn, Ken's been gone since that first time she followed me through.* That'd been before Rosie, so more than a day in mortal time. Raine glanced over to a table see if he could read the date on a sprawled copy of the Wickney Weekly—oddly named for a *daily* newspaper in the city. No luck, and it probably wouldn't help anyway.

What would Harley have to say about Ken's absence? Suddenly, it became more urgent to get her glamoured up than it had been before. But he couldn't say any of this to Harley. *Play it cool; play it cool.* As Harley arrived at his side, Raine asked, "How are things at the cop-shop? And with the murder? Everyone still convinced La Pointe did it? Maybe with the candlestick in the library?" He winked.

Harley chuckled. "Well, ya know . . ." They shrugged. "Other than the fact that boss lady's MIA, it's all just hunky-dory. Vic and I are swamped with her workload. We have to get in at the ass-crack of dawn to cover. Then finding time for coffee and lunch is hard. I haven't hit the weights in days. Feelin' a little puny."

Raine drew his brows together, painted shock on his face, and gasped. "Ken's missing? For how long?"

Harley looked up at the coffered ceiling, considering. "Well . . ."

Raine could almost see smoke coming from their ears.

"It's only been a couple days. Last we knew she was heading up to Minocqua to see her mom. She's stayed a few days before, so no big deal," they said. Just then, Harley lurched forward.

"Excuse me, sir," an elderly lady behind them said.

The woman reminded Raine of the persona he'd put on with Rosie. But he remembered how considerate Harley had been to her at the station.

Not acknowledging that she'd referred to them so, Harley reached a hand forward to steady the woman. "No worries. Are you all right, ma'am?" When she answered, "yes," Harley ushered her into the line ahead of them.

The line moved forward until Harley and Raine were next up to order. Harley looked at their watch.

"Hey, it looks like you're in a hurry," Raine said, holding out a hand toward the counter where a youngish boy with acne and bright-red hair punched in people's lattes. "You can order first."

Harley stepped up. *Thank Danu*, Raine thought, again rolling his eyes to the skies again. What would Harley think if Raine ordered two drinks in front of them? And one of the coffees black? Would it tip Raine's hand? Would Harley put together that he had Ken tucked away somewhere? He couldn't afford that while Ken didn't know how to control her eyes. The hands . . . okay. Somehow she'd figured out how to make them look human. The slight glow to her skin, that'd be fine too. She could pass that off as a fantastic night's sleep and new makeup. But the eyes. The shifting sands would be a dead giveaway.

The brusque bobby finished his order and stepped to the end of the counter. They'd ordered for both themself and Vic.

Raine stepped forward. "Venti triple five-pump mocha with extra whip and a venti Americano."

The kid gave the price, and Raine handed over one of the bills. Change in hand, he moved to the next waiting station at the end of the counter.

"Gold," the barista shouted, and Harley swiped the two cups as the barista placed them on the counter.

"Sorry to fly, Raine, but we're swamped."

"No concerns here. Catch ya later." Raine held his sigh of relief until Harley turned away. He'd ordered an Americano for Ken just so the barista had to prep it and he wouldn't be holding a black coffee. He'd been around enough for them to know Raine liked his coffee chocolatey and syrupy sweet.

As Harley stepped backward toward the door, they pointed at Raine with one finger lifted from the go cup. "You should come down around noon for a workout. Vic can't hang. And it'll get me away from work for an hour."

"Yeah, I've gotta hit the square for a while to make a little cash, but I'll try. Don't wait for me, though," Raine answered.

Harley pushed through the door just as Raine's two drinks came up. "Raine," the barista called, and he snatched the cups. At the door, he looked left in the direction of WPD to make sure Harley had moved far enough away before stepping onto the sidewalk and heading back toward his flat on Aldgate. Holding a coffee in each hand, he shuffled, two-stepped, and did a few spins as he walked, preparing himself for his performance later. But the conundrum of Ken's faeness scratched at the back of his mind. Today, or at least this morning, she needed to eat and sleep. Food would probably send her into a near-coma after all she'd been through. The earliest he could get her back to the station would be this afternoon, but that didn't leave him time to teach her to glamour. Those eyes. He couldn't risk her getting tossed behind a barrier of iron, and he didn't really want to have to repeat the Rosie Thorne scene so soon. *Hrmmm, how can we do this?* Raine stopped and looked across the street to the green-and-white sign over the glass storefront.

"That's perfect," he told himself aloud and skipped into the street. A horn blared, and he held up one of the cups of coffee. The cabbie yelled out the window. "Whad're ya doin? You're gonna cause a crash! Get yer ass out of the road!" Another horn blared as Raine skittered to the far sidewalk and scooted behind a man who'd just thrown the door wide, into the Pearle Vision.

BACK AT HIS FLAT WITH coffees in hand and a shopping

bag cutting into one wrist, Raine kicked at his door. "Ken?"

He waited.

Nothing.

He kicked again. "Ken, it's Raine. Open up."

No reply.

"Shite," he muttered. Had she left? That would be all he needed. Being a faerie wasn't against the law, but so many humans feared them. That's why faeries glamoured up all the time. She likely wouldn't get arrested unless she harmed a mortal, but the shifting irises would be a tell-tale sign. If she kept her gaze on the ground and didn't make eye contact with anyone, maybe she could make it to her destination uninterrupted. But she'd been all about that V-Cube, so her nature was definitely starting to come through. And, being a new faerie, she'd be out of control for sure. But this was *Ken*. She wasn't the affectionate type, so if she slipped out, she'd be all right. He hoped.

Why did I end up here? In this situation with a new faeling? Ifrinn, Ken being Fae is probably why I couldn't leave her or her case alone. He tucked one cup between his arm and chest and reached for the knob. Inside, Ken sat precisely where he'd left her, working the V-Cube 9. Raine closed and reopened his eyes. *Thank Danu!*

She didn't acknowledge when he entered.

"You gave me a little scare there. I thought you might have slipped out."

Staring at the tiny colored blocks, she kept spinning the cube. She almost had it solved, so he'd timed his return just right.

"Got it!" she shouted and leapt up from the bed, holding it out. She bounced on the balls of her feet like the little girls with pigtails in the square when he'd given them a huge colorful sucker during a performance.

She had become a child by Fae measure, confused, innocent, easily distracted, and not yet able to use the powers Danu gifted to all her children. Raine smiled and handed her the Americano. "Black, like you like it."

She looked at the paper cup then back at Raine. "You know how I take my coffee?"

"I tasted yours that day we first met. Remember?"

She huffed. "Oh yeah. How could I ever forget?" She lifted the cup to her mouth, sipped, and gagged hard. Pulling it away, she sputtered and coughed until her eyes watered. "That's disgusting!" What did you put in there?

"Just black. Or, well, it's an Americano, but I thought that wasn't much more than black coffee." He eyed her as he set the pastry bag on the counter.

"No flippin' way," she pulled off the lid and smelled, then wrinkled her nose again. "I've always taken my coffee black. The bitterer the better."

"Don't worry over it too much, Ken." Perhaps being Fae came with a sweet tooth. He couldn't recall. His becoming had been too long ago. "I think your change in taste might have something to do with becoming Fae. Here, try mine." Raine pulled the cup from her hands. "I think I have some creamer in the fridge. Maybe I can sweeten this one up to being palatable."

Kennedi took a big gulp, her eyes widening and the sands swirling faster. "What's in this? It's delightful!" The little girl was back. She took another drink, then another.

"It's a triple five-pump mocha. Like it?" Raine ducked into the refrigerator and pulled out one of the six bottles of coffee creamer—mocha latte flavored. "This isn't quite the same, but it'll have to do seeing how you've gulped down half of mine." He opened her Americano, poured a little of the bitter black liquid in the sink, and tipped in a hefty amount of the chocolaty creamer. He sipped.

Deeming it passable, he reached into the bag and spread the pastries out on the counter. "I have blueberry scones, blueberry bagels, blueberry muffins, and a number of other things. I told Charlotte to just fill it up like I was having a party. But she knows I like the blueberry ones best. The scones have a lemon icing that's to die for!" He grabbed one for himself.

Ken, vacillating between her prior snappy reactions and the tiny changes still taking place in her, didn't speak, only gaped at the spread.

"Eat," he urged her. "Your body needs it after all that." Raine bit into the scone and edged around her toward the closet, moving by feel and keeping one eye on her. "Doesn't matter if you don't think you're hungry, eat. After you fill the belly and get a nap, you'll feel like a brand-new Fae."

She scowled. "Not helping at all, Raine." She reached for the lemon-topped blueberry scone as if it might bite her.

He pulled out a button-down shirt from the closet and tossed it on the bed. She chewed more vigorously with every bite. Raine grinned. "Told ya that one's the best. But have two or three. Ifrinn, you can have five or six if you want. When you're done, there's something for you to slip into and take a nap."

"You said that before, but I'm not ready to sleep." She yawned.

"Whatever you say." The first bite of the scone hit her

stomach, and she sighed, her eyelids drifting shut. Once she finished, she'd be snoozing in minutes. He patted the shirt. "Trust me. You'll wanna sleep here in a few."

"What about you?" She looked from him to the only bed in the room.

Squeezing past her toward the entry way closet for his case, he said, "No worries about me creeping in there with you now. I'm heading out to the Square to work. Need to make a little money while you rest. When I get back, maybe we'll have a little time to play with your"— he flourished a hand toward the white board. "What'd you call it?"

"The suspect board?" Ken asked.

"Yeah, but not long, because we have to figure out how to get you to WPD. I, uh, might have told them you're back." He shrugged.

"Told who, exactly?"

"Don't worry about that now." He pulled out his rolling case with the juggling equipment inside and grabbed the costume he was using for this act.

She finished off the scone, licking the last bit of lemon icing from her fingers. "Where can I change?" She patted herself down. "If we're heading to the station, I'll need a fresh set of . . . oh shit!" Her eyes grew to the size of the muffins on the counter as she patted her side where she normally wore her harness. Her jaw set and face hardened. "Where's my gun?"

Raine had bent to clear a few games including the now completed V-Cube from his bed. Straightening, he waved his hand in the air. "Ah, you probably lost it in the in-between when you fell through the Veil. Faerie doesn't care much for such contraptions anyway, so if you didn't lose it in-between, Danu probably saw the thing destroyed."

Ken paced, her hands shoved into her hair. "Damnit, how am I going to explain that?"

"What's to explain?" Raine picked off a blueberry, popped it in his mouth, and chewed. "Once you learn to use Danu's magic, you can just give 'em a little *nudge* when you tell 'em you need a new one, now can't you?"

She spun on her heel, flinging her hands out to either side. "Just because I found out I'm a faerie doesn't make me any less of a cop. This may be a game to you, but . . . Wait, maybe you're on to . . . No. That's a lie." She deflated.

Raine chewed his scone. "Report it stolen or missing? That's not really a lie now, is it? Eh, you know what, who cares? Can't we just swing out to that gun shop in the Burgh? Tofers?"

"I can't go buy my own firearm. Against WPD policy. And for a personal buy, there's a three-day waiting period. I'll have to wear a jacket. She looked down at herself again.

Raine grabbed his costume and moved to the tiny bathroom. "I'll get changed, then you can either change in here or wait for me to leave." As he grabbed the door to close himself inside, he caught her worry. "Write down your address. I'll stop by your place while I'm out and grab you some clothes. Got a key or code?"

CHAPTER 23

KENNEDI

WHEN RAINE RETURNED THAT AFTERNOON and woke her from a dead sleep, he'd handed her a box of colored contacts.

Now, as she tried to insert one, the contact fell off her finger again. That must have been the eleventh time. "Why do I have to wear these?" she called out to the other room where Raine waited.

"We've been through this," he said, the eye-roll in his words more than apparent.

The contact still cupped upward on the tip of her finger, she looked at herself in the tiny mirror in the cramped bathroom. Why couldn't she just wear sunglasses? "Oh yeah, Ken," she said aloud but softly so he wouldn't hear. "If you wear them inside the station, people might think you just came off a bender." She laughed once without hilarity. *If only that were the case.* She tried to insert the little piece of plastic again, failed, and sputtered her lips. She rummaged through the box with the saline solution, found a blue-and-white contact case, and dropped the contact into the blue side with L on the lid. She stuck her head out the door, the same question on her face.

Raine pointed two of his three fingers at his eyes then to hers and said the obvious, "Swirly eye thing, remember?"

"I know that, smart ass." It was the evidence of her faeness she'd just seen for herself in the mirror. "But why can't you just teach me to do that glamour thing, or whatever it is?"

Reclined in the chair at his desk with both feet kicked up, he twisted his lips to one side, then the other. He glanced down at her hand resting on the door jamb. "Well, you did your hands now, didn't you? Just do the same thing with your eyes then."

"I didn't *do* anything with my hands."

He leaped up from the chair. "Put the contacts away and come here now." He straightened his denim jacket like he was preparing to perform.

Kennedi slid the package to the back of the sink board, staring at the array of contact crap. *Thank God I've never had to deal with failing eyesight.* In fact, her vision had always been better than 20/20. So having to put something in her eye clawed at her pride as much as it did her eyes. She flipped off the light by habit and joined Raine in the main room.

"All right. Come here," he said, motioning her over. "Stand there." He positioned her by the shoulders. His manner seemed silly, like he was about to size her up for a ball gown or something.

She groaned. "Daylight's wasting." *La Pointe, then my mom.,* she didn't say aloud.

"You have to stand a certain way?" Ken asked.

He sighed and rolled his eyes. "No, I suppose not." He looked out of his element.

"Have you ever done this before?" She squinted at him, skeptical that he had the slightest idea how to teach her something she clearly needed if she ever wanted to blend in with the humans. Ken lifted her arm, palm to her forehead, and pressed hard. *Great. Now I'm referring to other people as humans like I'm not one myself.*

"Done what? *Glamoured?* Of course. Every mortal day," he snipped, folding his arms over his chest.

Was he parroting her? *Keep it moving, Ken.* She narrowed her eyes. "No, not that."

"Whoa, I told you not to do that didn't I?" Raine held both hands forward, palms toward her, waving.

Kennedi flung her hands out to the sides and blew out a breath in exacerbation. "Seriously, I have no clue what you're talking about . . . *yet again.* What I meant was: you have no idea how to teach someone this glamour thing, do you?"

He smiled from one side of his mouth. "Well, you may have me on that one. Nope. I certainly have not. I'm not a dad, and I hope not to be one anytime soon." He nodded once, decidedly.

Kennedi muttered, "Thank God for the sake of all the kids you don't father."

"Hey, I *am* standing right here."

"Good. Glad you heard. Are we getting on with this mess or what?"

"Fine."

"Fine."

Raine seethed and so did she as they stared off. He finally broke into a smile and split the silence. "Well, there's this thing all Fae have. I've mentioned it before. We call it croí. It's the core of every faerie, and it's the source of our abilities."

"Yeah. Your magic. I get that."

"Noooo." He shook his head as if she'd just told him the sky had turned hot pink. "Our abilities are gifted from Danu herself, or Aodh in the case of the Dark Fae. But don't worry about that, 'cuz you're totally Light."

"Raine, would you stop babbling?" Kennedi started to cross her arms, but remembered his imitation of her and pressed her palms into her thighs instead.

"Oh, yeah." He scratched his chin. "So, the croí. You first have to find that within yourself, and that's the trickiest part. Mine feels like it's in the center of my back along my spine. Others say they feel it in their gut or behind their eyes. Yoga or Thai Chi or sometimes just meditation can help with figuring that out too, but if you want to get to WPD today, we probably don't have time for that." He laughed aloud. "Funny, I can't wear a watch, but here I am worried about time. Maybe it has something to do with seeing Harley at Starbucks."

Kennedi's mouth dropped open. "You saw Harley today? And you're just now telling me? What did they say?"

Raine flipped a nonchalant hand. "Something about your mom and Minocqua. Wait. Your mom? Minocqua? Why would your mom be . . ." His eyes grew to the size of a handcuff ring, irises swirling faster and faster. He lifted a hand and covered his gaping mouth. "Your mother is *human?*" Then he apparently changed his mind. "Nah, she must just be your **síobhra** mother."

"What? No." Kennedi shook her head. "No, she's definitely my birth mother."

"Yeah, okay. Wink, wink." Raine dismissed her and started to pace while talking softly to himself.

His constant muttering distracted her, and as she focused, she recognized his words as the foreign tongue from the other side of the Veil and the churning gray . . . the time when she'd been in thrall. Yet she couldn't understand him now, here, in the—*what had they called it?*—ah yes, the mortal realm. "Raine, snap out of it," she called, clapping her hands.

He stopped and stared at her, his face whiter than she'd ever seen it. And then, he slid into his glamour and donned his performer's mask. Why now? He stood before her appearing fully human again. Nicer hair, but fully human. Then it dawned on her. Glamour was more than a disguise. It was a faerie guard, a shield, some way to protect himself from . . . her?

Whatever, focus on the La Pointe case, then—shudder—*go back and find your father.* She rolled her shoulders back. "Okay, so you were saying I have to find my croí." The harsh letters and oddly blended vowels twisted her tongue, but she needed to try. "Down my spine. In my gut. Behind my eyes." She nodded, shifting her weight from foot to foot. "How will it feel? And what do I do when I find it?"

Raine still seemed skeptical when he began. "It should feel warm and bright, like when we moved through Danu's Light in Fae." He flourished his hands in the air when he spoke of Danu's Light. "Once you have that"—

his words started flowing faster, his volume rising—"you have to will your body to change. You'll need to envision something while pulling from your croí and believing you can make the change to your physical form."

"What?" She recoiled. "That sounds entirely off the wall. Imagine it and it will come true?"

Raine shrugged. "In a nutshell." He stood on the far side of the room now and waved both hands at her. "Go ahead. Try. Maybe closing your eyes will help."

Kennedi closed her eyes. *This is so not going to work.* "Okay. What now?"

"Can you feel it?" he asked.

"I don't feel shit. My spine is stiff. My gut's churning. Too many scones. But I don't have a headache." She kept her eyes pinched shut.

"Well, the headache was probably because you were resisting your Fae nature. You have to accept and embrace your croí for this to work."

She breathed in through her nose and out through her mouth, feeling every part of her body for something warm and light. She thought she felt something in the back of her neck, then she imagined her eyes still, as they had been for the entirety of her life. "I think I have it."

"Hold it tight, then slowly, open your eyes."

She didn't breathe as she lifted her lids, looking to Raine, who'd grabbed the V-Cube and worked it while still looking at her. Her irises had to be still now, right? *Please, please say they are.*

His face drooped.

Kennedi let out her breath, shoulders falling with the exhalation. She repositioned her feet and held her elbows at her side with hands relaxed like she was ready to sprint. "So, what else? I have to make this work," she rushed.

Raine quirked a brow. "You really, truly don't wanna wear those contacts, now do you?"

Of course I don't, fool. "Can we just focus? The sooner I get this down, the better." Not only did she not want to wear them, she couldn't figure out how to get them in her eyes.

He tossed the finished cube up in the air with one hand and caught it with the other. "Well, once you've found the Light, think about something that represents the change you want to see. Don't just think, 'I want my eyes to stop moving,' or 'I want my nose longer.' Instead, picture something that represents a longer nose." He snapped his fingers, ideas lighting his face. "Like that girl who sings the cups song. What's her name? You know the one, something about a ticket and a long way around. What is her name?"

Kennedi hadn't the foggiest clue what he was talking about.

Apparently, he recognized that and flipped a dismissive hand in her direction. "Not to worry. It'll come to me then. Just think of someone other than you who has the nose you want. Then imagine your own nose moving to look like that while feeding the idea with your croí's Light. But be careful. You're damn powerful as a faeling, and if you give it too much, you might end up looking like Pinocchio."

She glared at him, the reference not helping in the slightest. "It's not my nose I want to change."

"Well, then, think about your eyes. Or someone who has eyes you want. Although, it might be weird if you walk into the station sporting blue or green eyes after yours have always been that gorgeous butterscotch color." He shrugged.

Kennedi felt suddenly flushed. He'd compared her eyes to something? And gorgeous? *Ugh, stop it. Focus, Ken. No gushy feeling. Not. Allowed.* She closed her eyes again, imagining butterscotch candy—since that's the visual Raine had just implanted. *But they're not that yellow, right? Maybe he meant caramel? What? Focus, Ken!* She imagined a Werther's Original candy—her mom's favorite and what she took up to Minocqua when she visited. She took a deep breath and popped her eyes wide open.

Raine shook his head. "Thinking we should just go with the contacts."

She gritted her teeth. "Give me one more try. Just one more idea."

Still maintaining his distance, he tapped a finger on his chin thoughtfully. "Maybe if you imagine a calm lake. Something like glass in the morning. Maybe that'll stop the shifting sands."

She closed her eyes—the third and final time—and when she opened them . . .

"Still swirly." Raine lifted one shoulder then picked up another cylinder-like puzzle from his windowsill, this time looking down at the toy.

"Shit!" Kennedi stomped to the bathroom.

"Shite's the better term." Raine's voice followed her into the only private space in his apartment. It grated against her nerves like rock salt against ice.

She struggled with the contacts until they stayed in her eyes, but they burned and itched as if she'd been on a beach on the windiest of days. She had to figure out how to hide the oddity she'd developed and quick. She exited the bathroom. In the main room, she held out both arms, waiting for Raine to approve of the visual.

"Good." He moved for the door. "But don't blink so much. Looks like you have something in your eyes."

"I *do* have something in my eyes!" she yelled.

But he ignored her and kept walking. Kennedi followed and crashed into him when he stopped cold. He pivoted back to her, and she scooted backward to stay out of his accidental embrace. Raine grinned and peered around her. "But this is a tragedy. We don't get to use my, um, thingy." He pointed.

"The suspect board?"

"Yeah. The suspect board. On second thought, maybe we should stay here."

RAINE

KEN WALKED CONFIDENTLY AND AS fast as she possibly could out of the elevator, hooked a right, and pushed through the glass doors into the WPD fifth-floor investigations unit. Raine followed at a much more leisurely pace, watching her every move to check for any signs she'd give away their little secret. Vic sat at his desk and Harley looked over their shoulder at the computer, a blue hue casting both their faces in a sickly gray shade.

Vic caught sight of them first. "It's about time you came walking in here, Craine." Then softer, appearing more concerned, he asked, "How's your mom?"

Ken halted and tilted her head. Standing behind her, Raine couldn't see her expression, but it surely read confusion by her posture.

Harley stood, refreshing her memory. "Your note. It said you went to the hospital upstate. Is everything okay?"

She nodded then, but her confusion transferred to Raine.

He stepped up next to her. He'd known her mother was in Minocqua, but a hospital? Impossible. Faeries didn't go to hospitals. *Sounds human, Raine.* "Your mother's in a hospital? Is she sick? And why upstate? Are you from up north? I assumed you were from Wickney now." How could that be? Saffron and—who had he mated with? They would have had to travel so far from the Veil access to drop her off. He didn't think there was another Veil north of here in Wisconsin. Unless . . . *no way.* He pursed his mouth, but—

Ken brushed him off, asking Harley and Vic, "How's the case?"

She still blinked constantly, but Raine grinned. That was his Ken, always down to business.

The junior bobby twins stalled, Harley kicking at the toe of their boot and Vic tapping his fingers on the keys idly.

"Spill it," Ken snapped.

Harley took a deep breath. "Quaid canceled the investigation since, I quote, 'If Craine had time to go see her mom, there must be nothing to report.' And then you weren't here the next day either."

She rounded on Raine, eyes wide as if to ask: *How long?*

He shrugged. He'd have to explain the time slippage thing later.

Vic added, "Yeah, they've got the court date set for

day after tomorrow."

Ken put her hands on her hips. "Well shit."

"Shite," Raine corrected.

Harley snickered and put out a hand. "Good to see you again so soon, but surprising you showed up with Craine. You two getting close?"

Kennedi rolled her eyes then blinked several more times. "If that's the case, let's get to work. Forty-eight hours and counting. Where's Linardi's bank information?"

Harley picked up a spiral-bound booklet from the corner of their desk and handed it over to Ken. "Ya know, Craine, we've already pored over them. He bought tons of gifts for Michelle La Pointe . . . flowers, chocolates, lingerie"—they pronounced it linger-EE—"Nothing original at all." They rolled their eyes dramatically.

Raine considered asking Harley to perform on the street corner. They'd do a bang-up job.

Harley continued. "Man, if I were his girl, I'd be super disappointed with all that crap." They jutted a hip. "Couldn't the man think of anything more original?"

Ken snatched the spiral and asked, "What about Tofer's and the guns?"

Vic answered that one, tossing some more papers on her desk. "We've been through all that too. Signatures checked out. It all looks legit."

Kennedi pulled her chair out, dropped into it, and flipped through the printouts in her lap. "If you aren't on the La Pointe case anymore, what are you working on so intently?"

As they answered, Kennedi seemed to ignore them, blinking over and over as she stared at the bank statement.

Vic said, "While you were out, Captain Quaid dropped a missing persons case on your desk. Girl's from West Wickney. We were just reviewing her family and friends, and about to head out to chat up her schoolmates."

"Wanna ride along?" Harley asked.

"Hrmmm?" Ken asked, not entirely looking up. She absolutely hadn't heard a word either of her junior officers had said.

Harley looked over to Raine with a question on their mug.

Raine lifted one shoulder to his ear and said, "Why don't you both go ahead now? Let her get caught up." He assumed Ken was succumbing to her faediom.

After both her junior bobbies headed for the door, Ken finally acknowledged Raine. "You wanna see a *real* suspect board?" Her face glittered with excitement. She stood, her chair scooting out from under her. "C'mon." She moved away without waiting for his answer.

Inside the same conference room where they'd watched Vincent La Pointe's press conference, she strode over to a board that looked suspiciously like the one Raine had ordered for his apartment. "Is that—?"

"Yeppers." Ken went to the computer on the counter to one side of the room.

"Wait." Raine nearly ran over, but just as he did, the board he believed was not animated at all flickered to life. "How'd you do that?" he asked. She shouldn't have been able to use a computer that easily. Maybe she could because it was a separate keyboard from the laptop. Possibly? He'd have to try it out.

Ken furrowed her brow and blinked at him several times. "Do what?" She moved over to the board, folding her arms across her chest. When she stood at the center, she reached out for the little file folder picture in the center.

"Don't!" Raine called.

KENNEDI

SHE PAUSED. *WHY IS HE acting like such a fool? I mean more so than he normally does. This is a whole different kind of fool.* "Raine, this is what I do day in and day out."

"You mean this is what you *did*. Have you already forgotten my warning about electronics and mechanical devices? You're going to send that thing to the computer graveyard."

Kennedi took a deep breath and finished closing the distance to the screen, her eyelids fluttering furiously against the contacts. When the folder popped open and images of the persons of interest spread across the screen, she said, "See, no problems here."

Raine staggered backward, his mouth working wordlessly. When he finally found words, he said, "How'd you . . . ?" but couldn't finish the question.

She looked around the room as if someone might appear in one of the corners. Skeptical, she lowered her voice just in case the walls were thin enough for her voice to be heard. "I'm thinking all that faerie stuff doesn't apply to me. The fingers wore off, and I've got no issues with electronics. Now, if my eyes would settle down, that would be fantastic." She scanned the room again and looked through the glass. With no one in sight, she walked over to the window and pulled the blinds. Then, she reached into her eyes and extracted the annoying little plastic things.

"W–what are you doing?" Raine stammered.

"Don't worry about it. I brought the whole box." She looked up at him. "Still swirly?"

"Yeah. They are. And you didn't bring it in here, now did you?"

"Seriously, Raine, would you stop acting like my keeper and let me focus on the case? I'm almost out of time."

Raine flung his hands up, turned to look at the board, and pointed. "Why am *I* on there? I gave you my alibi. Didn't Candi check out?"

Kennedi flinched. Why did hearing or thinking about the cute little pink-haired girl from the Underground send a buzz through her? She shook her head, clearing the thought. "I had to. You kept poking around my case, and it would have looked bad if I didn't. Besides, you had more information about the case than was logically possible." She didn't say that her allowing the said poking around would have gotten her benched if she didn't address it.

The door opened, blinds clattering against the glass. Aleks Quaid stuck his head in. Kennedi tucked her chin and looked down at the floor.

Quaid said, "Hey, good to have you back, Craine. Your friend down at Wickney Weekly just called." He snapped his fingers three times. "What's her name?"

"Amy Jennings?"

"Yeah, that's her. Anyway, the La Pointes called another press conference regarding the case. Starts in an hour."

She kept her gaze downcast. "I'll head right over."

"Fantastic," said Quaid. "Seems like they're finally accepting that dear old Daddy isn't so dear. Anyway, I'm outta here. There's a charity golf thing that West and I are playing. You should catch up with Harley and Vic on the missing girl on the west end." He started to leave, then turned back. "Oh, and there's a squad setting up for the conference too, just in case. This ordeal can't be done soon enough." He pivoted toward his office. The door swooshed shut in his wake.

"C'mon, Raine. Let's go." She grabbed his arm and pulled him toward the door.

He raised both brows and stood firm. "All right. But not until you take care of hiding those eyes."

RAINE

KEN LEFT HIM IN THE room in a huff.

Raine went to the door to peek out the blinds after her. With her head down, she stopped by her desk for her bag and slung it over her shoulder as she moved toward the back of the office. Raine turned back to the electronic crime board and went to study the suspects sprawled across the screen. Kennedi called it a suspect board, but it seemed to contain anyone and everyone related to the case:

Michelle La Pointe, victim

William La Pointe, prime suspect

Vincent, son; Coralyn, daughter-in-law

Vanessa, daughter

The house staff, several people from the mayoral campaign underway

Joel Dixon, current mayor

Maximus Alan Linardi (MAL), lover

Elanna Bell, best friend

Sean MacCaibe, neighbor / shut-in / magazine writer

Alan Tofer from Tofer's Gunshop

And . . .

Raine Abarta, person of interest

Geez, something was still missing.

Raine twisted his mouth and bit the inside of his lip, considering all the puzzle pieces. Then his thoughts drifted back to Ken and her attempt to accept her Fae nature. She might not need to hide it all the time, but she definitely needed to learn. And with the prejudice in today's society, she needed to figure out if people were sympathizers like Linardi or faerie persecutors like West. She'd been so cute earlier that day as she'd tried to find her croí, but in the end, it would take much more time than they'd given it. Raine closed his eyes, remembering how her eyes shifted like liquid amber with rich golden flecks. Gorgeous. Much more enticing than Briar's depth-of-night brown with a lighter brown sand shifting inside.

Shut up, brain! Raine did a little 360-degree turn on one heel and a slide to the right, something physical to try to distract him from all that. He sighed and ran his hands through his hair, the numb extra digits catching. He looked down at his glamoured hands. How had she not been able to reach her croí, yet she could still disguise her hands?

Clenching his into fists, he turned away from the board, diving into the faediom himself. The memory walk, how William had been totally surprised, how MacCaibe had praised his service. No, William La Pointe

326

hadn't murdered his wife. Of that Raine felt certain. He wandered over to the window overlooking the parking lot out back. He leaned onto the cold metal windowsill, looking up to the sky as snow started to fall. He shivered at the thought of the upcoming endless cold, then scanned the scene outside WPD. Several pedestrians wandered toward the square. When he took note of a couple holding hands and laughing, his croí sank a little at not being there to perform for them. Certainly their levity would be delectable.

The statues in the square had been cleaned again, but apparently the investigations unit had nothing to do with it now since they had their culprit. They had moved on to more obscure cases. Raine wondered if one of the beat cops had gone back to arrest King Ludwig after the last incident. To his right, a line of panda cars was parked in the center row of the back lot. To one side sat the unmarked cars too. Then at the far end, putting golf bags into an SUV, Captain Quaid and Raymond West bantered back and forth. Once the bags were in the back and the hatch closed, they both slid into the front seat, West driving.

Raine turned back to the board, scanning until he found a little square with a plus sign inside. That phone conversation he'd heard half of . . . maybe he should add West. His hands hovered over the image. *Ken touched it. That means I should be able to, right?* Yet he hesitated. *All I need to do is open that puppy on the screen and put in West. How could we have forgotten this? The numbers Ken had mentioned when they watched West in the Faeglass. 'Six-eight-nine-four?' right? I think so . . .* He moved his finger closer and felt static electricity sizzle in the air between the board and his hand.

He backed off, rubbed his hands together, and glanced at the door again. *Paranoid much?*

Focus back onto the board, he held his breath and moved in. Sizzle, sizzle, POP. The screen went blank. He stomped around the room shaking the electric shock out of his hand. "Shite!" he said. *How in Ifrinn had Ken managed to touch that thing?* Raine shot furtive glances toward the window, the door, and the now-fried board. Hopefully he didn't have to come up with a reason for frying the crime board, but if so, *nudging* would be his friend. Well, he thought for a minute. There's definitely more than one way to solve this puppy. He pulled out his phone and pressed the side button—the one programmed to activate the voice input feature. He waited for the beep.

"Text Morgana."

CHAPTER 24

KENNEDI

BLINKING AGAIN AGAINST THE IRRITATING contacts, Kennedi moved through the crowd to a position closer to the front door of the larger townhome in Devereux Court. She and Raine stood a dozen paces away from the reporters and gawkers murmuring to one another as they waited. Appraising the scene, Ken noted they still had a good vantage point of the stage and the front door. The squad Quaid mentioned had set themselves up strategically to insulate the La Pointes from the crowd as they moved between the door and the stage.

Vincent La Pointe took the stage in the same manner he did at their last press conference. On his arm, his very-pregnant wife Coralyn held onto his arm, smiled, and waved at the crowd. The way they moved, Kennedi thought this mayoral race might just be a stepping stone to the White House. If they played their cards right, this family could eventually create a dynasty rivaling the Kennedys.

"Check that out. Same as last time. Their stage crew must have this setup nailed to a tee," Raine commented, and Kennedi fought the urge to snap back at him again.

The mayoral candidate tapped the microphone, and it wailed. Kennedi and Raine both winced. With his crowd-dazzling smile, he excused his wife to go stand beside his sister, stepped forward, and said, "My father goes into his arraignment the day after tomorrow."

As he said the first words, Kennedi glanced over to his sister, Vanessa, who welcomed Coralyn into the crook of her arm where they both stood, appearing to watch intently and without emotion. Vanessa sported a hot-pink business dress and, if Kennedi wasn't mistaken, the same stilettos she'd worn that day she'd walked into WPD insisting that her father was innocent.

Now, Vanessa seemed deflated, dabbing at her eyes with a lacy handkerchief. Coralyn had turned down the dazzling smile as well, and rested a hand on the top of her turquoise baby bump. Kennedi rolled her eyes. They certainly painted the image of a picture-perfect family.

Vincent continued, "I'd like to offer my family's most sincere thanks to the Wickney Police Department for being as patient as they have been in allowing time for our family to deal with this unfortunate situation. We understand they are simply doing their jobs and maintain faith that eventually, they will come to find the truth that our father is not guilty of murdering his beloved wife . . . and my mother. We miss Mom with everything we have, but we recognize that our family exists in the public eye. Therefore, as servants to the people of Wickney, we felt it was our duty to speak with you today."

Raine whispered, "Dead right, Vinnie. Daddy's abso not guilty."

Ken eyed him sideways, then leaned closer, lowering her voice too. "How do you know? Or how are you so utterly certain?"

"Ah, well, that's thanks to the memory walk, another ability I'll have to explain later. It could come in handy in your line of work, but you gotta be careful. Look at him. Does he look like he could murder anyone?" He tipped his head toward the stage and William La Pointe.

The La Pointe patriarch sat with his chin tucked and eyes cast toward the ground, doing his duty by being there with the family this one last time. How could Raine be so very certain he was innocent? Kennedi recalled the suspect board, running through everyone related to the case. Linardi acted more like a husband than William seemed to. Did William feel regret that his wife had died? She couldn't tell by watching him now. Then, behind the former senator, a woman stepped up, wearing a powder-blue pantsuit. Elanna Bell clearly didn't realize someone might be watching her as she placed both hands lovingly on William's shoulders and caressed them in a *we'll-all-be-all-right* manner. Kennedi inhaled sharply and narrowed her eyes at the woman, whose strawberry-blonde chignon gave her away.

The stage shook and the microphone wailed again. A rumble went up in the audience until Vincent La Pointe raised his arms to calm the crowd.

"Didn't I tell you not to narrow your eyes that way?" Raine said.

She turned to him, eyes widening. "The phone conversation with West. The one you showed me in the mirror. It was Elanna Bell!"

Raine tilted his head in response to that, questioning. Kennedi ignored him and searched her memory of the notes on file about the woman. "I never would have considered it, if it wasn't for the way she looked at him when she ran her hands over his shoulders. But that's the answer. *She* is the answer," she said, bouncing on the balls of her feet.

Raine grasped her arms and held her tight. When did he become the sensible one?

"What gives, Ken?" he asked. "You're looking like you . . . ah, yes, you are. Go ahead, enjoy that rush." He waved his hand in a *carry-on* motion.

She didn't care what he meant by that, but she felt like the world had just come alive. Everything seemed brighter, her heart started pounding faster, and the ends of her fingers and toes tingled. Then she babbled, "Don't you get it, Raine? It makes perfect sense. Elanna Bell must have been planning this since college. It's a perfect love—or jealousy—triangle. They were all three college friends. When William and Michelle moved to Wickney, Elanna Bell, Michelle's best friend and sorority sister, stayed behind to get her master's degree, then her doctorate in psychology. When she'd finished, she followed her, quote-unquote, best friend to Wickney. But was she following Michelle?" Kennedi paused, eyes stretched wide and a finger in the air. "I think not! All the while, she was following William La Pointe. And as Michelle's supposed best friend, she would have known about Linardi too. It's perfect."

She pulled out her phone, dialed the station, and waited.

Raine started, "Ken—"

She held up a hand, cutting him off when Quaid's

assistant answered. "Hey, Kimber," she said, then lowered her voice again. "Can you check the La Pointe case and pull Elanna Bell's bank account history and phone records for the time around Michelle's murder?"

"Sure thing, Detective Craine." The clackety-clack of her fingers flying across the keys came over the line.

"Thanks, Kimber." Ken ended the call, hit the speed dial again, and waited for an answer.

"Vic," Vic answered.

"Hey, it's me. I've just ordered some background information up on Elanna Bell. I'm at Devereux Court now. Another God-forsaken press conference. You two get back to the station pronto, grab that information, and meet me at the La Pointe townhouse."

Kennedi clicked end on the cell phone and turned it over in her now seemingly normal hand several times. What the hell had Raine been talking about with electronics freaking out at his touch? It certainly wasn't doing that for her. *Maybe because I'm only half Fae.* She pursed her lips. *I'll keep that one from him a bit longer.* She needed the upper hand in something with the bard.

Raine appraised her smugly. "We already know the La Pointes had an open relationship, now don't we? This doesn't mean Elanna would murder her best friend." He motioned his hand toward the conference still in progress.

But it no longer mattered what they were saying. Kennedi knew for certain this was the clue she'd been looking for. "You don't have to buy in. I'm sure I can prove this." She started toward the stage.

Raine grasped her by the elbow. "It doesn't fit, Ken. Someone that put-together wouldn't deign to destroy her tailored costume, manicured nails, or those fabulous heels." He pulled Ken closer. "You know how you felt solving that cube in my flat?"

Ken nodded, unable to see the correlation.

"Well, this case is just a stronger version of that draw. Finding a clue just tickles your Fae nature. I've known women crazy enough to murder, and they're never as composed as her."

She pressed her lips together, turned back toward the stage, and crossed her arms over her chest. He'd given her pause, so she'd wait until the press conference ended before going in. What did Raine Abarta know, anyway?

Fucking faerie.

RAINE

VINCENT FINISHED HIS SPEECH WITH, "Thank you all for coming and understanding our distress over this matter." He dipped his head, turned, and motioned to the family.

They all stood and started for the brownstone.

The reporters clamored forward with microphones held out and cameras aimed at the stage. Raine recognized the lawyer from before as he stepped forward.

"The La Pointe family will not be taking any questions today. Please," the lawyer said, "give the family their space to grieve over this. Thank you." He followed the family into the front door while the row of bobbies held the crowd away.

Kennedi made her way to the foot of the steps leading into the townhouse.

Raine followed.

She slipped past two of the cops guarding the house, asking, "All good, Callen?" to the one on her right.

"Right as rain," he answered.

Kennedi moved right through the line, but Callen, the one she'd spoken to, held up his baton, blocking Raine's path.

"Wait, Ken?" he called.

She turned around and lowered her chin so that she looked at him out of the tops of her eyes. With a smile— one only a faerie would wear—she finished climbing to the door. At the top of the steps, another bobby stood overseeing the others in the line. There were only about six, but this one seemed to take his job very seriously. Raine considered *nudging* Callen but thought better of it given how outnumbered he would be. Ken leaned over to the officer by the door and whispered something, then knocked on the door. As she waited, she shot back a devious smile.

"Really, Ken?" he pleaded with his words and every ounce of acting ability he'd developed over the years.

The door opened, and a servant standing to one side held out a white-gloved hand. Kennedi flashed her badge and walked inside.

The servant closed the door, blocking her inside and Raine on the street.

KENNEDI

BEFORE CLIMBING THE STEPS INTO La Pointe's Brownstone, she'd had an idea. Ken had approached Officer

Yarrow, who stood at the top overseeing those guarding the La Pointe residence. It thrilled her that she'd finally gotten the upper hand with Raine. Leaning nearer to the officer who normally led the WPD patrol department, she said, "Things must be slow on the streets to have this kind of team here."

"Too slow," Yarrow replied. "And your captain has his tail feathers in a bunch over this one with the election pending."

"Yeah, I sensed that. That one there"—Ken looked back at Raine—"Let him sweat it a bit. Hold him behind the line until Clark and Gold arrive."

Yarrow answered, "Sure thing, Detective Craine," then pressed his lips together as if holding something back.

"What is it?" Ken asked.

"Nothing, Detective."

"Yarrow, spill it."

"There've been some rumors about you and that street performer."

Kennedi rolled her eyes. "He's just an informant. My juniors will be here soon, and he can come in with them."

Raine called her name, frantic, but she just turned, smiled, and waved before she walked into the mansion. She passed the butler into a grand foyer with a curved marble staircase to one side, a long hallway before her, and a formal sitting room to her left. She waited while the butler closed the door and ushered her to the back and into William La Pointe's office, where the family had gathered.

"I'm sorry to interrupt your family time," she began.

Shocked silence fell over the family. Vincent sat behind the desk with Andrew Gorman, the senator's lawyer, standing at his side. Vanessa and Coralyn sat at a small, round table to the side with two leather wingback chairs. In front of the bay window, Senator William La Pointe sat casually on a chaise lounge facing the center of the room, his feet on the floor and one arm resting on the curved side. Elanna Bell stood beside the chaise. *Interesting positions.*

Andrew Gorman stepped forward. "Detective Craine, the family would like to spend their last few—"

Kennedi held up a hand. "My apologies, Mr. Gorman, but I believe we might have had a break in this case that's pertinent to my timing here."

Gorman tilted his head and cut his eyes over to the senator on the couch, clearly preparing to ask the senator what his wishes were in the matter.

Ken continued, "I'm quite sure we might be able to avoid the arraignment all together if you'll just hear me out."

Vincent La Pointe dropped a hand on the desk, calling everyone's attention to him. "It's all right, Andrew. Let's hear her out." He held out a hand for Kennedi to continue, clearly having taken over as the patriarch of the La Pointe family.

However, Gorman chimed in again. "I'm uncertain how that's possible at this stage of the proceedings. Captain Quaid and DA Mitchell were adamant that they'd begin proceedings."

"Well, I am waiting on some corroborating evidence." She glanced at the door over her shoulder. "My junior officers should be here with that soon. But we have a hot lead that I wanted to address immediately while you're all in one place. Well, at least the Senator and Dr. Elanna Bell."

The woman gasped and lifted her hand to her chest. Fondling her pearls, she acted confused. "I am uncertain why I would be of consequence, Detective."

"We will get to that part." Ken paused, wishing Vic and Harley would hurry.

Vanessa stood and rushed over to the chaise lounge, taking a seat at her father's side and grasping his hand. To Ken, she said, "I told you Daddy had nothing to do with Mother's death."

Fatherly as expected, William squeezed her hand and said to his daughter, "All will be well enough, sweetheart. Let's just listen to the rest of what Detective Craine has to say."

Elanna leaned over the arm of the couch and whispered something to William, her hand brushing his shoulder and trailing down his bicep. *Geez. Was she this overt about her affections before Michelle was murdered?* When the woman stood again, William La Pointe held out his hand, a mirror image of the way his son had done seconds before. Kennedi scanned back and forth between the two, noting how strongly Vincent appeared to be a darker-haired, less wrinkled version of his father. *Not important now, Ken.* She walked around the room, keeping one eye on the door at all times. She thought on potential ways to stall the conversation while they waited for Vic and Harley. "Senator La Pointe," she finally began, "do you truly wish me to begin this with your children in the room?"

The man had the gall to look indignant at her suggestion. "I have no secrets from my family." He said, dropping one brow in consternation.

Truly? Ken looked at Vincent, then Vanessa. Had he really shared that their mother had been having a long-running affair with someone in a high position in a crime family? Well, the crime part had never been proven, but it'd been long suspected that Max Linardi had his hands in the mob. At the very least, he ran a club that catered to the Fae. Kennedi winced. Being a faerie itself wasn't the illegal part. It was the result of Fae-human interaction. Thus, the result of her mother coupling with Saffron.

Not that now, Ken! She shook her head. "Very well. Let's trace things back to your time at Brown University, shall we?"

Senator La Pointe and Elanna Bell exchanged a confused look, which they both turned on Kennedi when they came up without an answer.

Kennedi continued, "Michelle moved into her dorm at Brown University from the tiny town of Westphalia, Indiana, not knowing anyone at the college. Naturally, she clung to the closest person to her—her roommate."

Elanna's expression went blank, a mask, likely the one she wore when one of her psychology patients told her an incredibly challenging tidbit of information. Kennedi narrowed her eyes at the woman. *What would seem incredibly challenging to you, Elanna? Murder? Adultery? I think not.* As Ken squinted and watched, Elanna started to fidget.

Her hands moved to her chest to play with the pearls again. One rose to her cheek, then her forehead. Then she fanned herself and chuckled uncomfortably as she fanned her face. "Does anyone else think it's hot in here?" she asked, worry taking over every feature on her face and creating lines Kennedi felt certain the woman wouldn't want anyone to see.

Kennedi continued, "Senator, you didn't meet Michelle until her sophomore year, is that accurate?"

William looked up at Elanna, then back to Ken. "That is true. Elanna introduced me to Michelle at a pep rally for one of the football games when Brown was getting jazzed up to play the Rhode Island Rams. Although I'm unclear what this train of thought has to do with getting out of my arraignment." As he spoke, he took on the demeanor of the politician he'd been for years and years.

Dr. Bell took a deep breath and settled herself again. Her eyes looked confused as whatever heatwave had overtaken her continued. Hardening her face again, she patted William on the shoulder. "It doesn't. That was almost forty years ago. It makes no sense that events four decades ago would have anything to do with Michelle's death this year." She tilted her head at Ken—a challenge.

Ken continued to pace. *C'mon Vic, Harley . . . get your asses here!* "Ms. Bell," Kennedi addressed her then.

Elanna Bell bristled. "Doctor Bell, if you please."

"Very well, doctor," Ken continued. "In our standard procedures, we run backgrounds on all family members, friends, and random acquaintances."

The woman went back to fiddling with her necklace, seeming a touch indignant that Kennedi would imply her ignorance over police proceedings. "I understand that much well enough, Detective. In my profession, we're well acquainted with investigation and legal proceedings, as I am very often referred clients by the court systems."

Ken pursed her lips and considered. Yes, she would have that knowledge. "I understand as much, Dr. Bell. If I am not mistaken, you have testified in some of my very own cases over the years. Do not read my comments as insult, at least in this regard."

The woman inclined her head, looking down her nose.

Kennedi continued, "However, in your background check, we could find no relationships outside of your friendship with Michelle La Pointe and her family. Michelle and William were married after Michelle's junior year, and they both moved to Wickney after she graduated. You continued on with your master's degree then your doctorate. However, we still cannot find any records of past friendships or relationships. Then you followed your college best friend here. I presume that was an effort to be closer to the La Pointes."

Ken strained her ears toward the front door. Damn, no footsteps yet.

Elanna swallowed, her throat visibly working. "I'm a very busy woman, Detective Craine. My work takes a lot of time. And is it so unusual that I'd desire to be close to my best friend?"

Good, Ken thought. She had her on the defensive. "Not at all." Ken feigned her own surprise. "But why wouldn't you return to Hudson to be near your parents? I believe your father was very sick at the time you attained your doctorate. It would have made the most sense for you to return home. Can you explain your thoughts at the time?"

Elanna looked down then. "It is a truly deep regret of mine that I didn't spend time with my father in his final days," she murmured, but then perked up almost as quickly as she'd turned sad. With a smile that made Ken believe she might grow fangs, her eyes bored angrily into Kennedi's as she spat, "Yet, I still fail to follow what this has to do with my best friend's murder."

"Oh, but I think you do, Doctor Bell. I don't have all my Ts crossed yet, but I believe you are in some way directly involved in your so-called best friend's murder."

Vanessa and Coralyn gasped in unison. The La Pointe men turned to Ken with identical scowls.

Ken, disregarding it all, continued, "What would cause such a well-composed woman with a promising career to turn on her supposed best friend?"

Vincent stood, dropping a hand on the desk. "That's outrageous! And quite enough of these empty accusations." If his words did not, his expression said *I'll be your superior in a matter of weeks. Do not cross this line.*

Ken appraised the likely future mayor. "Is it absurd, now, Vincent? Jealousy can be a powerful thing, not to mention a motive. Elanna has always been in your lives, has she not?"

His brow furrowed. "She has, and she has been a loyal friend and caregiver when Mother needed a break from managing this household. We've known her all our lives and cannot believe she's responsible for Mother's death any more than we believe Father is capable of such an act."

Noise sounded from outside the office, the front door opening and footsteps marching down the hall.

Finally, Ken thought with a sigh.

Every head in the office swiveled to the source of the noise, Kennedi's included. And the first person who stepped into sight was . . .

Raine Abarta, a file folder held high in the air. "You guys started the party without me?" He appeared energized, like he was just about to take his stage on the northeast corner of Wickney Square. "I have some fun, fun, fun goodies here!" He shook the folder.

Kennedi blinked several times, remembering the

contacts and blinking some more when they annoyed her again. Then she widened her eyes and bit down so hard her jaw ached. She marched over to Raine. "Seriously?" she hissed, snatching the folder from his hand.

Raine shrugged, waggled his brows, then danced into the room. Vic and Harley stepped through the door.

"Why do you allow that from him?" Ken hissed to her junior officers.

Harley giggled. "It's fun to watch him get your goat."

Through gritted teeth, she said, "I do not have a goat." Then she opened the folder and read. "That's it. Read her rights." Kennedi pointed the folder to Elanna Bell. "We can finish this at the station."

Dr. Bell's eyes and mouth fell wide open as Vic pulled out his cuffs and read her the Miranda.

Vincent turned to Andrew Gorman.

Andrew replied without a prompt. "I'll phone the office."

CHAPTER 25

KENNEDI

BEFORE HEADING BACK TO WPD, Kennedi had stopped by the Local to speak with Maximus Linardi. What he'd hinted at had been quite eye-opening. Now, inside and ready to run the official interrogation on Dr. Elanna Bell, she had tons of little gems in her back pocket. Vic and Harley took Raine into the observation room, and she headed for the door behind which Dr. Bell waited with her lawyer, Thomas Slagle. Inside, she dropped the folder on the table and took a seat across from the now-prime suspect.

"Go ahead, look inside." Ken blinked against the damned contacts. "I'm sure you'll find those details just as enlightening as I did."

Elanna reached hesitantly for the folder and scanned the documents inside before passing it to Mr. Slagle, the eldest of the partners at Slagle, Bernard, and Gorman. The man's double chin shook as he read through the file.

Elanna said, "So what? Those are my phone records."

"What frequent business do you have with WPD?" Kennedi asked.

"I told you that I consult on many cases here. Given my background and awards in the mental health field, I'm an expert on mental illness and behavioral science."

Kennedi chewed the inside of her lip and folded her arms across her chest. "That's interesting. We did a little further digging. You see, the phone records only show the main line at WPD, but we—my partners and I— thought we should understand who exactly you've been conversing with so much."

Elanna raised her brows.

"What business do you have with the FVU, Dr. Bell?" Kennedi pressed.

A shadow crossed Dr. Bell's face, but she recovered quickly, lifting both hands in a half-shrug. "The Fae are the most frequent cause of mental illness here in Wickney. Why wouldn't I be speaking with the Faerie Victims Unit on occasion?"

Ken glanced over at the one-way mirror and bit the inside of her lip. Not pertinent to the case, but . . . "Have you ever known someone to recover from the mental damage inflicted by the Fae?" Maybe she wouldn't have to go through that shitstorm again if she could find a way to help her mom here. She'd never asked to be a faerie, half-faerie, síobhra, or whatever else the Fae had wanted to call her. Saffron had been nice enough, and she *had* been curious. But hell, she'd be just fine if she never saw any of the others. Ever. Again.

"I . . ." Elanna started, glanced at her lawyer questioningly, then looked back to Ken. "Not that I can recall, but why?" She turned to Mr. Slagle.

The lawyer nodded and addressed Ken. "What Dr. Bell means to ask is, what does this line of questioning have to do with your case?"

Kennedi fluttered her eyelids yet again. "That's irrelevant." Damn, why'd she let herself get distracted like that? Time to turn up the heat. "Back to the phone records. More specifically, you've been in contact with Raymond West quite frequently." She tried to keep her voice steady. Her connection to Ray didn't matter here. If her mentor had been involved, he needed to come clean too. "If you were researching one of the FVU cases, wouldn't you have spoken with Jory or Jericho at some point? Yet I see no records of any conversations with a line other than West's." Kennedi grabbed the file Mr. Slagle had closed on the table and flipped through the pages toward the back. "It does seem you've only conversed with West. That's odd, if I do say so myself."

In a scraggly old voice, Slagle said, "You don't have to answer that, Dr. Bell."

Kennedi shot him a glance, despising the fact that he was absolutely right if—and only if—the answer would incriminate Dr. Bell. Ken dropped her eyes back to the paper. "It seems you've spoken directly with Captain West three . . . four . . . no, make that seven times since the day Michelle La Pointe was killed. And there were five phone calls in the month leading up to the murder. Do you have an explanation for those conversations?"

"Detective," Slagle started. "Dr. Bell will be exercising her right to remain silent in response to this line of questioning. Do you have charges you wish to file against her? If not, we will be on our way."

Elanna Bell rested her hand on the old man's arm. "It's all right, Tom." Then to Ken, she said, "They were all official cases. If you'll allow me to visit my office, I could provide you with the names. I'd be at liberty to do that given they are official police business."

Kennedi flipped through the pages again. "Hrmm." She tossed the folder onto the table, the papers inside slipping out as it slid across the metal surface. "Well, Dr. Bell, if you are not willing to speak about West, maybe you'll talk about Mal?"

Elanna blanched, her mouth falling open. Bingo. She looked at her lawyer, who, wearing a blank look, shook his head. Eventually, she said, "I–I am not familiar with a . . . Mal."

Kennedi narrowed her eyes. Then something flashed warm between her shoulder blades. Heat bloomed and filled her chest, and it felt light, like when she'd moved through the white void in Fae. She inhaled, widened her eyes, then narrowed them again at Elanna Bell. A current radiated from the space between her shoulders, filling her chest and tingling out to the ends of her fingers, the tips of her toes, and the roots in her scalp. She squinted further at the woman. With just a little *nudge*, Elanna Bell would spill absolutely everything.

RAINE

STANDING BETWEEN VIC AND HARLEY, Raine watched from the other side of the glass. When Ken narrowed her eyes, widened them, then pulled them back together, he stopped breathing.

Shite–shite–shite! Is she? Yes, she is!

He threw his elbow to the side, bumping into Harley. "Watch this. Elanna Bell is about to divulge her deepest and darkest secrets to your boss lady."

Vic barked a laugh. "Yeah, sure. No one's going to shake that woman's composure."

Harley said more skeptically, "How do you know?"

"Just listen." Raine tipped his head toward the show.

The lawyer said, "Elanna, as your lawyer, I advise you to remain silent."

Elanna uncrossed her legs and leaned forward. Her voice sounded muffled by the speaker system, but she waved off the lawyer and started talking in a daze, her voice deeper than it'd been so far and her words hard. "You cannot understand, Detective," she spat, then threw her perfectly straight posture up against the back of the chair. She'd clearly been holding this in for a long, long time. "First, my best friend Michelle stole William from me when we were in college. He and I grew up together in Hudson and were destined to be together. Then she had the children I'd always imagined I'd have with the one and only man I'd ever loved. Of course I stayed in their lives. They're mine, not hers."

The lawyer leaned closer to his client, but Elanna waved him off.

Raine watched the show in sheer awe. "I can't believe she found it, now of all times."

Vic looked over. "Found what?"

"Oh, sorry, er . . . her skill at this." He waved both hands toward the glass and Ken beyond. "Whaddaya call it?"

"Interrogation?" Harley offered.

Raine snapped and held up his pointer finger. "Yeah, that thing."

Harley furrowed their brows. "Craine's always been the best at interrogations. She learned from West, who is pretty darn good too. Together, they're the best at WPD."

Raine inclined his chin. "Oh, okay." Then he focused on the room where Elanna was beginning her diatribe again under Ken's *nudge.*

"It wasn't fair at all." The woman threw her hands up and let them fall. "Why would they both fall for her? What did she have that I did not? After years, I'd learned to deal without William, but she had to have Maximus too? When I found out about that, it was all over." Her voice remained distant as she kept right on spilling her entire motivation. "No, Michelle Bayer La Pointe was my curse in life, and I simply saw to it that the curse was removed."

The old lawyer's eyes grew wider than it seemed possible in the folds on his face, but Elanna only laughed.

She pushed the chair away from the table with a scraping sound, stood, and marched around the room, gesticulating as she continued, "My so-called friend finally got what she had coming. West, well, he was nothing more than a tool. So easy to convince him that I loved him. So easy to manipulate his need for money. That man doesn't manage his finances at all, so I simply slipped in and made him an offer he couldn't refuse. Oh, true, he hesitated at first, but pretty soon, I had him eating out of my proverbial palm." She laughed again and leaned onto the table toward Ken.

Ken held perfectly still with all her Danu-graced focus on Elanna.

The woman straightened her light-blue jacket, stood

straighter, and checked her hair. "I cannot tell you how easy it is to seduce someone who is already so goddamn full of himself. The only thing in this world he wouldn't have accepted was if I'd been Fae." Bell rolled her eyes.

Kennedi flinched, her eyes widening.

Hang in there now, Ken. You got this.

Elanna continued, "The man's obsessed with the, uh, Fae." She drew her brows together.

C'mon, Ken. Keep it going.

Finally, Kennedi recovered and narrowed her eyes again. Raine puffed up proudly. She had it. She'd finally found her Fae.

Elanna's face eased into a trance-like state again. She set her jaw again and folded her arms over her chest. "All it took was a tiny bribe and a little piece of ass. And after a month, I finally had a means to the end of my personal curse."

RAINE PLAYED WITH THE PUZZLES on Kennedi's desk for the next several hours while she, Vic, and Harley put in a background check as well as search warrant and arrest warrant requests for West's apartment. By the time they were finished, everyone else on the fifth floor had left. Kennedi excused Vic and Harley for the evening too. "We'll get him in the morning. Elanna's in lock-up, so no one's going to tip him off," she'd said with a yawn. "If by some chance the bureaucracy comes through tonight, I'll call."

Raine stood and walked them to the glass doors. He

shook hands with Vic, then Harley held up a fist.

"Catch ya tomorrow," Raine said, bumping their fist.

"Workout this time, man? Promise?" Harley glared at him sideways.

"You got it, dude," Raine answered. "I'll catch ya after the lunch crowd thins out. Promise I'll make it this time."

Vic tilted his head toward Ken. "Make sure she's all right, dealio?"

"You got it!"

Finally, alone with Ken, he wandered back to the desk with a swagger. "How we doin'?"

She sighed, glanced up at the clock, and rubbed the back of her neck. "It's been a long day. Or . . . more?" She released the hair binder and ran her hands through her hair.

Raine pulled over Vic's chair. "Well, you're not wrong about that, but how amazing is it that you found your croí at precisely that time?"

Ken smiled an entirely unconvincing smile.

He asked, "Aren't you happy about that? No more contacts."

"Oh, yeah. I'm happy about that part. It's just . . ."

Raine only waited a beat. "It's West?"

"Yeah, it's West. He taught me everything I know about being a cop and helped me become a detective. I wouldn't be who I am today without him, and I'm about to send him to prison. I'm just stunned that he'd do something like that, and I keep hoping we'll find evidence to the contrary. But I think that's just wishful thinking at this point." She looked around, then dropped her glamour, something else she'd figured out after Elanna Bell's interrogation. It probably helped that she only needed to disguise her eyes and mute her glow a little.

Raine sighed. "You probably wouldn't have been able to remain close to him anyway with his hatred for our kind."

"True. But I'm having trouble with where he'll be going. He won't last a week there amid all the criminals he sent up the river."

"Weeeelllll . . ." Raine started. "We *could* send him to a different prison, of sorts. It'd be against human law, but who'd ever know?"

Kennedi sat forward with a jolt. "What are you thinking?"

KENNEDI

THE NIGHT WAS CLEAR AND ice cold in the Arboretum. Breath fogging the air, Kennedi pulled out her phone. "Ten-forty. By the time he gets here, it'll be the right time to slip through, right?"

"How do you know so much of this?" asked Raine.

"I watched my father slip through at precisely 11:11 more than a thousand times on a snowy old video." She inhaled and exhaled slowly. She really should stay there, find Saffron, and figure out how to save her mom. Yet she also needed to be back in time for Elanna Bell's arraignment. As the officer who took down her statement, she'd certainly be called to the witness stand.

But if I'm in Faerie, who'd care? Kennedi shook her

head. *Later, Ken.* She scrolled through the contact list and found West. She still didn't have the same issues with electronics as Raine, and she'd save worrying over her mother and father for a later time. Right now, she had a show to put on. She pressed send.

After two rings, the answer came. "West."

"Heya, it's Craine."

"Craine!" Ray said.

The front legs of the chair thudding to the floor sounded over the line, and she imagined him sitting forward abruptly from one of his classic positions, reclined-on-two-legs.

"Heard you nabbed the perp in the La Pointe matter," he continued.

"Yeah. Arraignment's next week." She looked over at Raine, who gave her a *hurry-it-along* wave. Ken swallowed. "But that's not why I called. We have a faerie incident. Wanna meet me at the University?"

"Bet your ass!" he said in a manner where she could almost hear him leaping up from his chair. "What building?"

"Well," Kennedi searched Raine's face, then added, "it appears someone broke into the Arboretum."

"Great. Be there in twenty-five minutes." *Click.*

To Raine, she said, "He's on the way. You better hide."

"I'll be right around the Faerie mound." He skipped away.

When West arrived, Kennedi waved him over.

"What's going on?" he asked, arms held out as if to ask the obvious: *Why're you here alone?*

"This way. Walk with me," she answered in a rush.

He fell into stride at her side, and they walked around the mound. Kennedi looked at her phone to check the time. Almost there.

"Why are we circling this hill?"

"Ah, well, you see, I called you out here because—"

He stopped, looking at her sideways.

She grabbed his arm at the elbow. "Keep walking with me; I'll explain." She pulled to keep him moving. "There's this case I'm on."

"Thought you just wrapped your case. Q already assigned another one?"

Kennedi checked her watch and kept walking. "He had it lined up well before I wrapped the La Pointe case." She continued walking. Step, step, step, then . . . the Veil opened. West jerked, wriggled, and Ken latched on tighter. As they stepped into the gray maelstrom, Raine appeared at West's other side, grasping his free arm. She focused on what she could remember of the magical woods with the light sparkles showering all around her. They fell through the cyclone, tethered by the man between them. West lost his breath, then sucked in another, then screamed like a terrified child. Kennedi, recalling her similar first experience, grimaced.

When they stepped into the Wandering Wood, thanks to Raine's guiding them down, Kennedi felt the glamour she'd donned ripped away. West looked her in the eye and gasped, stumbling backward. "What the fuck, Kennedi?"

She moved slowly after him as Raine called, "Aimery! Come to us in the Wood."

West still hadn't caught his breath by the time the faerie Raine had called appeared. Aimery's white hair hung to his waist, and he peered at Raine with his head tilted and a confused look.

Raine clasped arms with Aimery and said, "Take this human to Mother. He could use a little convincing that the Fae are not evil."

"Do you not wish to deliver him yourself? Your mother might view it as amends." Aimery inclined his head.

Raine shook his head. "I don't think my mother can forgive just yet. You know better than most how tightly she holds her grudges. And I'm not keen on seeing my, ahem, betrothed, either."

"Understood." Aimery reached for Raymond West, who trembled, scared to silence and blubbering at being forced to face his worst fears.

"Let's go, Ken," Raine said, grabbing her arm and pulling her toward the arch of branches.

She pulled away. "No. I'm responsible for this." Kennedi stepped close to her former mentor. "Elanna Bell signed a sworn statement about who fired the bullet that took Michelle La Pointe's life."

West's face contorted, then released, when he clearly understood her meaning. West finally found his voice. "Ken, you're . . . No. You can't do—"

"I am. And I can. I won't ask you why. It doesn't matter anymore." She lowered her gaze, took a deep breath, and let a tear flow down her face before she looked back up. "It will be better here than in prison, Ray."

His lips quivered and eyes glistened.

Ken turned away, returning to Raine's side. Again, facing the Fae guard and her old mentor, she said, "Take him."

Aimery turned, took a step. Raymond West stumbled at his side, looking back, a plea in his eyes. Another step; another stumble. On Aimery's third step, they disappeared.

Kennedi slumped, hoping she'd made the right choice. Saffron and Raine had moved her through the white void when she'd been in Fae before. They'd planned to enter, drop West, and get out. But Ken couldn't leave just yet. She sighed as she looked at Raine.

He held out one arm toward the arch, wrapped the other around his waist, and bowed to her. "Shall we now?"

"Not yet." She scanned the Wandering Wood, held out a hand to catch a falling point of light, and took a deep breath. "Show me that intention thing."

EPILOGUE

KENNEDI

EACH TIME THE GAVEL DROPPED, Kennedi felt it mark the pulse in her throat. She'd been through criminal trials a time or two—well, ninety-three, but who was counting? Regardless, her heart always leaped into a sprint just before the verdict came down.

"Defendant stand," said Judge Daily, a scowl on his rotund face as he read the note from the head juror.

As one, the audience leaned forward and held a collective breath. The head juror accepted the slip of paper back from the bailiff. Judge Daily peered over to the juror, the *are-you-ready* question to her seemingly leaping through the air.

"Dr. Elanna Bell," the judge started, "The jury has arrived at a verdict." He held a meaty hand palm up toward the head juror.

A wisp of a woman seated nearest the judge stood pushed her spectacles higher on her hooked nose. With a deep breath, she opened the paper and read, "Elanna Bell. On the count of Solicitation of Murder for Hire, the jury finds you guilty as charged."

The people in the court room began to murmur. Behind the prosecution, headed up by none other than Kennedi's ex, DA Rhyse Mitchell, the La Pointes huddled together. They each seemed to deflate slightly, or perhaps they breathed a sigh of relief. Kennedi could only imagine how horrible it would feel to have a second mother figure betray them in such a terrible way. The investigative reporter from Wickney Weekly tapped her photographer on the shoulder and had him take a picture of the La Pointes as well as of Elanna Bell peering over at them longingly. Beside Ken, Vic, Harley, and Raine bantered, celebrating the win.

Just when Vic mentioned West's disappearance to Raine, Judge Daily picked up the gavel and slammed it down, calling the room back to order. "The minimum sentence is twenty years in prison. Given that this solicitation resulted in a death, the maximum is life in prison. Dr. Bell, you are fortunate you do not reside in Alabama, Tennessee, or Texas where the death penalty is still an option. A sentencing hearing will be held next Thursday." The gavel fell again, and Judge Daily stood and retreated to his chambers.

Commotion ensued, but a knot in Ken's stomach released as she sank back into the chair. Beside her, Harley and Vic stood, looking down at her expectantly. Raine had already left the room. When they walked through the door at the back of the courtroom, they saw Raine lurked near, leaning on the wall with his hands shoved into his pockets. He stepped up and joined them.

Ken shook his hand. He squeezed, seemingly a question about if her hands were really human or a part of their glamour. Based on their little dip into Fae and immediate return, she believed the extra finger on each of her hands was tied to which realm she was in. But she hadn't mentioned that to Raine. She'd keep him in the dark for a little longer. Everything she could think to say after the trial and what they'd done with West seemed worthless. *Thank you* was unnecessary. He'd either started acting in a more tolerable manner or Ken was beginning to enjoy his antics. She didn't know which. Raine pointed from her to himself and back again, the look itself echoing his suggestion of their partnership.

Craine and Raine? It did have a ring.

Then, after he'd shaken hands with Vic and fist-bumped with Harley, he gave her a final appraisal that seemed to echo, *Case solved. I'll see ya soon.* He turned and strode away.

"Admit it." Harley nudged her in the side with an elbow. "You're gonna miss that boy."

Ken smiled, watching him walk away. "Maybe a little, but it'll be nice to have things back to normal." But she didn't add the remainder of that thought: *Or as normal as they can be after all I've learned.*

Noisy silence lingered in the air amid all the people bustling from the courtrooms, but the three of them stood watching Raine Abarta weave between the others and dance his way out of the building.

Finally, Ken sighed. "Back to work." Then turned on her heel and marched toward the elevator bank.

RAINE

BACK IN HIS FLAT ON Aldgate, Raine leaned into his entry-way closet, tossing costume pieces over his shoulder as he considered what his next act should be. Winter was on Wickney's doorstep, and the good people of this mid-Wisconsin city wouldn't be walking about the square as frequently. He appraised a clown costume, twisted his lips, and tossed it aside. He smiled when he came across the Rosie Thorne outfit, but that had nothing to do with his livelihood. He set it gently to one side. He could dance, he thought as he came across a pair of tights. *Nah, boring.*

Maybe he'd have to come up with something entirely new. He could perform at the Local U on Wednesday nights through the winter. That'd get him partway there, but he still needed something more. Then, finally, his hand ran across something that might have promise. Maybe? Soft, fuzzy. The most magical time of the mortal year had arrived. He latched on and pulled. It snagged on something, so he reached further inside the closet to free it from the hanger. A moment later, he held up the red and white coat and pants with a huge black belt hanging through the sewn-in belt-loops.

He smirked, and his eyes drifted back to the tights he'd tossed into the pile of clothes. Green. He'd played Santa before, but he'd never done the Grinch.

KENNEDI

SAFFRON BROKE THE SILENCE IN the car with a long

"hrmm" sound.

"Thoughts?" Ken prompted.

"I'm curious what you've learned about your faerie abilities."

"Not much. It took me a long time to access my croí. And since then, there've been too many things happening to think on it." She turned north on the final stretch of road. Only a couple more miles.

"Did Raine tell you about Fae sight?" her father asked.

She shook her head.

"It's a glittering halo around the humans. It can let you know how a person is feeling. If they're happy, it's all yellow light. If they're angry, a deep orange. And—"

"Wait, you mean like an aura?" Ken glanced over to Saffron in the passenger seat.

"Exactly," he answered.

"Intriguing," Kennedi mused. Her migraines had always been a symptom then. "And?"

Saffron looked at her blankly from whatever'd grabbed his attention outside. "I'm afraid I don't follow."

"You listed yellow, orange, *and . . .*" She held out a hand in a palm-up *please-finish-your-damn-sentence* gesture.

"Ah, yes now," he said, his voice flat, not rising in the slightest. "There is a point on the spectrum of human emotion beyond happiness, when a lavender glow threads through the yellow halo." Saffron paused, ran a hand over his jawline, and faced her. "Have you experienced mortal levity?"

When she looked at him askance, he gave her a small

smile and turned back to the passing greenery. "You'll know when you do by the surge of energy rushing through you, but have great care with that. It can be dangerous."

"What are you saying? Is that what causes the withdrawals? But no, it's the humans who experience that, right? It's why—"

"It's both." His voice sounded haunted. "There was a time in human history when levity was considered a magnetic force similar to gravity. That's not far from the truth where faerie-human relationships are concerned. Levity holds a singular power that few Fae can resist."

Several silent moments passed.

Kennedi sifted through questions in her mind. "So if—"

Saffron shivered hard enough she could feel the movement.

That was enough of an answer to her brewing questions. "Is there a problem?"

"I'm, what would you call it? Not frightened, but . . ." He shook his head.

"Scared? Nervous?" Ken offered.

"Aye, I believe nervous is the right word." Saffron twisted his unglamoured fingers in his lap. "The notion of meeting—" He took a deep breath, shifting in the seat. "Well, that doesn't really matter now. What about *nudging*? Did Raine of Lady Amaryllis teach you that?"

Frustrated by the change in topic, Kennedi took a drink of the pop she'd grabbed at the last gas station and swallowed. "No." She let off the gas as they approached a stop sign. She didn't want Saffron to change his mind, so she'd let the other topic rest for a time. "That is, Raine didn't teach me, but he said I had the instinct, that I nudged Dr. Bell during the interrogation. The concept is perhaps useful." After a proper three-second stop, she accelerated through the four-way intersection. "Honestly, I don't know how I did it or if I can do it again at will. That doesn't have any weird mojo attached like the levity thing, does it?"

"Not that any faerie has discovered." Saffron leaned closer to the windshield. "Is that it?"

Kennedi let out a long breath. "It is. Maybe we can work on that *nudging* trick on the way back to Wickney." She pulled into the guest parking lot outside the gates, cut the engine, and eyed his four-digit hands. "Glamour up."

Stepping from the car, Kennedi reached for the Fae magic in her croí, dimming the glow of her skin and halting the movement in her irises. By the time Saffron joined her, he'd altered his appearance to that of a distinguished older gentleman, the same person depicted on his new Wisconsin state ID card. The hair at his temples was near white, steely-gray salted the rest of his pepper-black hair, and small lines demonstrating the effects of age spread like spiderwebs from the corners of his eyes. The paperwork they'd forged to reestablish Glenn Craine's identification still niggled at her, but some things were more important than human law. She took a deep breath as they walked to the gates together.

Kennedi's father grabbed her arm before she could ring the bell and waited for her to meet his eyes. They glistened when he asked, "You're certain about this? Putting together the pieces of Brenda's fractured mind may not be as easy as you imagine."

Detective Kennedi Craine of Noble Saffron looked at the huge stone building, at her father, then at the sign that read Minocqua Mental Health Center. "Whatever we can do . . . or whatever we *must* do—" She swallowed against the lump in her throat. "It's gotta be better than the life Mom's living now."

Thank you for reading

Raine of Fire

Also by Susan Stradiotto

Look for *Fight for Darkness*, a paranormal romance set in Wickney and a featured novel in the *Realm of Darkness* box set along with 40+ paranormal romance and romantic fantasy novels. Available on October 4, 2022.

Preorder at https://books2read.com/realmofdarknessset/

The Serpentine Throne

Call of the Storm Sorcerer

Call of the Ryū Dragon

Call of the Syrensea

Call of the Scorched Empire

Call of the Maelstrom

Into the Evernight

Anthologies & Short Stories

Once Upon a Name

Twice Upon a Name (2023)

The Muse of Wynter

Golden Eyes

ABOUT THE AUTHOR

SUSAN STRADIOTTO WRITES ADULT FANTASY and romance. She favors themes focusing on relationships of all kinds: family, coming of age, and finding oneself or one's destiny, or finding one's person.

She lives in Eden Prairie, Minnesota with her husband, two of her three children, and two fur children. She has worked in Technology for more years than she'd like to admit, but storytelling is her true passion. She has always been a voracious reader, lover of worlds, and a "werd nerd." Susan's infatuation with well-developed characters sometimes rivals her relationships with real people.

Susan fills her own soul by spending her free time writing, networking with other writers, and occasionally camping "up-north." If you're from Minnesota, you'll get the reference along with "hot dish" and "grey-duck." If you're not from Minnesota, you probably don't want to ask. Note that she's originally a Texan, and that also never leaves you.

CONNECT ON SOCIAL MEDIA

https://www.goodreads.com/susanstradiotto

https://www.instagram.com/susanstradiotto/

https://www.facebook.com/susanstradiottoauthor/

https://twitter.com/StradiottoS

https://www.bookbub.com/authors/susan-stradiotto

www.ingramcontent.com/pod-product-compliance
Lightning Source LLC
Chambersburg PA
CBHW070820190726
48292CB00006B/2067